For Frankie + Bev.
with much love,

Thomas R.

July 22/80

Come back + see us soon
and bring our darling Stephanie

D1566860

Lucien's Tombs

By Marion Rippon

Lucien's Tombs

MARION RIPPON

Marion Rippon [signature]

PUBLISHED FOR THE CRIME CLUB BY

DOUBLEDAY & COMPANY, INC.

GARDEN CITY, NEW YORK

1979

All of the characters in this book
are fictitious, and any resemblance
to actual persons, living or dead,
is purely coincidental.

Library of Congress Cataloging in Publication Data

Rippon, Marion.
  Lucien's tombs.

  I. Title.
PZ4.R594Lw [PR6068.I6]   813′.5′4
ISBN: 0-385-14429-6
Library of Congress Catalog Card Number 78-8217

for Thomas J. and Judy L.

Lucien's Tombs

Chapter One

The old lady was trying to dig a trench. The patch of garden where she worked hugged the back wall of a small two-story stone house which sat in the center of a place of encroaching wildness. She paused, closing her eyes, both stained hands grasping the handle of the shovel. The pounding in her ears was fading, but she was still feeling weak and frightened. "I must do it," she whispered to herself. "It is the only way, so I just won't think about it."

She lifted a hand to wipe at the beads of sweat that mushroomed on her upper lip and reached for the end of her scarf to mop at the moisture. She felt as gray and heavy as the mist that shrouded the garden, and chilled in spite of her heavy clothing. A thick dark skirt hung almost to the tops of her ankle-high rubber boots, a worn coat was buttoned closely to her throat, and above it all her neck and head were enclosed in a dark coif, topped with a large-brimmed hat of a once silky velour, now wilted and stained.

When the moment of panic had passed, she listened to the silence and opened her eyes to look around her. The garden had become a patch of strangling vines, of crawling moss, of dormant destruction. Once it had been formally beautiful, but now it was being suffocated by nature—almost like Amélie, she thought with a shudder. "I won't think about it," she repeated aloud, and she forced herself to remember when they had been children and the Couronne property had stretched as far as St. Denis and beyond the château. Now this was her world, this was all that was left, and she had to keep it—she would keep it!

She grasped the shovel again, awkwardly pressing one muddy boot on the metal edge and pushing as hard as she could into the rich earth. This section of the garden had been cultivated with care over the years, and last summer Amélie had decided it would be suitable for an asparagus bed, deep and layered with compost. "It will have to be deeper now, Amélie," she whispered. She had dug down less than half a meter, but already her bent shoulders and small arms ached, for the weeks of almost continuous September drizzle had made the soil heavy.

She dropped the shovel into the shallow excavation, leaned on it for support and eased herself down, pulling her skirt behind her. The ground had an unmoving dank small, and she thought about other smells and the sickness began to rise in her. She raised her head to take a breath and looked out beyond the garden area once more. The mist was moving off in great patches, and she could almost taste the rain in the small gusts of a rising wind that had started rustling the evergreens in the far grove and swirling the fallen beech leaves. She prayed it wouldn't rain too heavily; if it just held off, she might be able to finish the digging before nightfall.

The small bank of lumpy earth built up very gradually along the edge of the trench, and for a time the only sound was a dull thudding, and once a clang as metal scraped a fragment of stone. She didn't look up at the plane droning low overhead. She had become accustomed to the noise of progress over the years; what else could one do, living so close to Paris and Le Bourget, but for a moment the shovel was stilled as she remembered the war and the evacuation and the dive bombers on the highways. Then the roaring faded, seemingly in another gust of wind that caught the brim of her hat, so she lifted both hands to grasp at the crown and pull it down over her ears in a desperate attempt to deafen herself to the past and to the present.

She didn't hear the voices, for the figures of the two men were only just visible beyond the pathway through the opening in the overgrown lilac hedge, but from their movements she could tell that they were talking. The small figure was strange to her; he would probably be the estate agent from Joddard et Fils. The big man was Lucien, of course. His stance and his profile were as familiar to her as the top of the great oak etched in the sky. The short man pointed toward the house. Lucien tipped his beret. Were they coming to the house? They must not come now—not yet!

She left the shovel where it stood, propped crookedly against the edge of the trench, and scrambled out awkwardly, pulling herself up on her hands and knees. She stood and, without stopping to brush the mud from her skirt, stumbled toward the house, limping her way through rows of winter cabbage. Out of habit she slowed once to bend over and pick up a little pail of green tomatoes and again, in a grassy clearing, to reach for a basket of garlic, before she mounted to the open shed that framed the back door. She dropped the basket into the pail, pulled back the bolt with her free hand, and pushed the door open. Once inside she turned, fumbled with another bolt, then leaned against the locked door, trying to control the tightness in her throat. She made herself stare down through the dimness at the pail and its contents, trying to think rationally, but something happened to the strength in her fingers and the pail dropped with a clunk at her feet.

The stone larder where she stood was lined on two sides with shelves of assorted jams, preserves, pickles, and baskets of vegetables. She let her gaze follow the neat line of labels on glass containers and then lower to concentrate on a large oblong vegetable marrow—until she was forced to acknowledge the existence of another larger and more misshapen object. It lay near the center of the cold gray room on the bare concrete floor—a small human form rolled up in a gray-blue mohair blanket. The soles of white-stockinged feet were just visible at the open end of the bundle, close to her own muddy boots.

She pressed both hands against dry lips and her panicky words were audible only to herself. *"Mon Dieu . . .* I will have to tell Lucien . . . I cannot do it myself." Then somehow she forced herself to turn away and move to another door, open it, enter the big kitchen, still and chilled and unlit, and stumble to the open hearth, where she knelt down and held out trembling hands over crumbled gray ashes, in a vain search for warmth.

* * *

Lucien Anjou glanced down at the impatient figure at his side, then lifted his eyes to the tops of the gigantic evergreens that provided the boundary line on either side of the property, their tips swishing in the erratic wind. The form of the house that had been visible earlier, now appeared to have taken on the gray-green hues of its surroundings, and the stone chimney seemed to stick out of swirling hammocks of rain clouds that were ready to split open.

"It is as you see it, M. Chamillion," Lucien stated. "It is prime property, but I would feel it was hardly big enough for a good-sized parking area, to say nothing of the apartment buildings themselves. It would be suitable for a fine house, and then some of the shrubbery could be preserved." He pulled his beret more firmly over his thick gray hair and stuffed the ends of his muffler inside a rough jacket that covered heavy shoulders. His trousers flapped against long legs, and soggy leaves stuck to the toes of old fisherman's boots.

"Only a wealthy man would build such a house, Corporal Anjou," M. Chamillion commented rudely, "and aristocrats no longer choose to live in this district, as I am sure you are aware. Leave such decisions to the professionals, monsieur." His smile was condescending. "You would not make a good salesman, but of course . . ."

"I do not pretend to be," Lucien interrupted bluntly. "I am here only as requested by the Couronne sisters. As I explained earlier, Mlle. Amélie is not well and Mlle. Ghislaine did not wish to become involved in business matters." He bent down, and with one large stained hand he pulled a blackened mustard weed from beside what remained of a stone footpath, and rubbed the thick soil between his fingers, then tossed the weed onto a mound of overgrown iris roots.

"I am aware of the situation of the Couronne family, Corporal." The agent straightened his glasses over the bridge of his nose and pulled at the brim of his wilted gray hat. "But contrary to your opinion, monsieur, there is adequate space here and I have a client who is interested . . . most interested. His plans call for underground parking beneath the apartment complex. Are you sure the dear ladies will not consider selling the remaining land? I have heard rumors of their financial problems and I . . ."

Once more Lucien interrupted, his voice almost a rumble. "The loge de garde and the bit of land beyond the hedge is not for sale."

"As you say . . . as you say. Still, the dear ladies are no longer young, and the last of their line. It will be interesting to learn who will fall heir to the property when the time comes. It is valuable land, so close to Paris."

"That does not concern me."

"No . . . no, certainly not." M. Chamillion shrugged, then proffered a gloved hand. "Well, I must not keep you longer on such an unpleasant day. You have been obliging, and I thank you and can promise you the sale is imminent. The Couronne sisters are most fortunate to have you to serve them so well. Family loyalty is admirable."

Lucien's heavy chin tightened and he ignored the outstretched hand. "I am the servant of no man, and my one loyalty is to my country which I served well through war and peace."

"No offense meant, Corporal Anjou, I assure you. My apology." The agent withdrew his hand and pulled once more at the brim of his hat, making his adieus in a confusion of movements. "It was only that I understood that your family were in the employ of the Couronne estate for generations and one can take pride in family history. My father also served our country, as you know, and gave his life for it. I remember he spoke well of you, although I was only a boy. Didn't your father tend these gardens at one time?"

"I tend my own garden and mind my own business, monsieur."

"Certainly . . . certainly. I shall be in touch soon and shall contact my client at once. I am sure there will be no problems for a quick sale. Please extend my felicitations to the ladies and express my wishes for their good health. *À bientôt,* Corporal."

The agent turned away and Lucien watched the wind whip at the shabby raincoat until it disappeared along the path to the upper level of a dismal arch of spikes and leaves and rotted wood of what had once been an arbor of roses. What a stupid creature, Lucien thought, then turned his mind to other things and started back in the opposite direction along the leaf-choked path that skirted the grove of oleander.

The skies were darkening, the wind had stilled and a dirty mist hung from the branches of the evergreens almost obliterating the passage ahead, but Lucien moved along without slowing his pace, taking note of familiar landmarks that did not need to be seen with his eyes. How ironic, he told himself, that this place that had survived the violence and destruction of wars would soon succumb to what was considered the progress of peace. Progress? Concrete—parking lots—another unsightly building oozing faceless people without souls. But it was necessary, and why should he care; he'd never wanted any part of this tainted Couronne land. Still that arrogant little agent had stirred memories; it was true, generations of Anjous had cultivated this soil, and Lucien's own father had planted these beech trees and trained the yellow roses to cling lovingly to the arbor back there and tended the beds of aromatic carnations around the decaying birdbath just ahead. He remembered himself as a boy, standing on tiptoe to reach over the rim of the bath and dangle his muddy fingers in the water. But it was always all theirs—never his—not the water that cooled his hands, or even the birds that were attracted as he'd been to the little pool, and thinking of it now, the old corporal once again began to feel the rise of bitterness and resentment. From the beginning he had been determined to escape the Couronne suffocation, but then as now, he had been cursed with involvement until it became a thing he could not discard, and it had started here, in this very place.

That day, a lifetime ago—an autumn day, as now, although not gray and aching as now—bright—the smell of warm soil—

The old man straightened, as if once more feeling the heat across his shoulders, and he reached for the recollection so long put away.

The lilac hedge is new now; my father is pruning it. I must be almost six because my shoulders are above the level of the green marble rim. I was always tall for my age.

Yes, a warm day—and bright—and the chaffinch standing in the shallow water of the birdbath, dipping, bobbing. Then suddenly, unexpectedly, the splash, and a confusion of movements as I pull back, almost tripping, while the bird swiftly sweeps upward and outward . . . unharmed, *le bon Dieu,* unharmed! Still, there is a small boy's anger at such an intrusion, and I cry out, but before more words can be voiced, once more the unexpected . . . another voice . . . another child's voice . . . a girl. "It was only a bird."

The tiny girl stands to one side of the oak tree, her face shadowed by a straw hat, the brim bent on either side by a tie fastened beneath her chin. Her dress is a shapeless blue. On her feet she wears boys' black boots. Beside her, grasping one hand, stands an older girl, much taller, pale faced, pale eyed, also in shapeless blue.

It is the little girl who has spoken, for she goes on timidly, as if reading his thoughts. "She didn't want to splash you. She just likes throwing stones." But the tall girl jerks at the small arm, tightening the grasp, and her words are not timid. "It is my garden, and my bird, and my water! I can do as I want. You don't belong here."

". . . what I want. It is my land, and I shall do as I see fit. You will get your fee as an agent. Now go, you don't belong here!" The same words, only spoken last night, and now Lucien almost shouted aloud, but he had learned the uselessness of anger. This is here, he told himself, and this is now. They are old . . . I am old . . . the mist is cold upon my shoulders, and my father's gravestone leans into the moss in the churchyard. But what was it my father said that day, his hand on my shoulder to stifle my angry retort? Ah, yes: *"Bonjour, jeunes demoiselles . . . bonjour.* Come along, my son. The work is done here for today, and we shall leave God's creatures in the hands of the saints." And later as they walked past the huge decaying château where its only occupant was soon to perish, Lucien had inquired about the oddity of the little girl wearing boys' boots:

"Ah, that is Mam'selle Ghislaine. She was born with a crooked foot, poor little one, and is not treated kindly. The older sister, Mam'selle Amélie . . . her disability is not so visible. She was born of mildewed seed and has no compassion for the weak. They are the children of the old Conte de Couronne, so we do not discuss it. Later when you are older you will understand."

"Understand! *Nom de Dieu,*" the old corporal whispered into the mist. "I came to understand, but that makes it no easier."

The lilac hedge, now nearly twice his height and wild and thick, loomed ahead. The gate had long disappeared, leaving an opening, and he ducked his head to avoid the overgrowth as he passed through. He paused by the old elm to pull his tightened fists from his pockets, raise the collar of his coat, and stare at the small house which appeared as if in an uneven circular frame of broken cloud. The blank windows of the upstairs dormer seemed suspended from the sharp triangle formed by the roof of the house and the sagging shingles of the back shed. The windows on either side of the shed were securely shuttered and there was no light anywhere, just heavy dusk, and silence. Then as he straightened his beret the rain started, and at first the soggy overgrowth muffled the downpour, but suddenly the deluge on the tiled rooftops was deafening. Lucien broke into a trot, cutting through the middle of the garden, noticing nothing, not even the fresh mound of earth at the side of the trench. Beneath the protection of the stoop he wiped at his wet face with his wrist, then rapped at the door.

Again he tightened his knuckles, pounded and waited. Where were they? Possibly the noise of the storm was muffling the sound. He would have to try the front door with the metal knocker.

Once more he lowered his head, hunched his shoulders and, keeping to the leeward side of the house, hurried around the corner. He almost slipped on the stone-slab steps in his haste to mount to the railed veranda along the front. He was wet now, and cold, and impatient to have done with this business, and he lifted the heavy brass knocker with both hands and pounded at the weather-bleached door as hard as he could.

As the echo faded, he picked up a new sound: the latch was being loosened and a key turned in the lock. "It is I, Lucien." He spoke to reassure, then as the door swung open he nodded briefly, *"Bonsoir."* He was able to see little but a profile of her draped figure framed briefly in a light from the far end of the passageway. She moved aside and he entered, latching the door behind him before he followed her down the hall into the big kitchen. Her appearance and her awkward gait were as familiar to him as the rest of the scenario and he took no notice.

"I think it is arranged," he began. "The agent has a client. They will pay the price but they want to build apartments." He spoke without enthusiasm.

She did not answer. Instead she stood apart from him, small and remote in her dark garb, gripping the straight back of a spool chair. He sensed a tension and for the first time tried to search her face, but she kept her coif-covered head turned into the shadows.

He began to feel an unease and a chill in the room. A small flame licked aimlessly at smoke spirals in the big open hearth, but nearby, the iron cookstove gave out no warmth, and no steam simmered from the copper kettle to condense on the chrome warming oven above. "It is a chill night. Why is there no fire?" It was as if he were asking himself the question. "Are you not well?"

"It is Amélie." It was a whisper.

"Is she worse? Has the doctor been?"

"She is dead, Lucien . . . she's dead."

He didn't grasp the words at first. They had been spoken with no emotion. He looked quickly around the room as if to reassure himself with something normal: the bare scrubbed oblong table in the middle of the room; the dimly lit lamp with the elaborate glass shade, sitting on top of the old treadle sewing machine near the fireplace; the sideboard along the far wall, its upper open shelves holding an assortment of jugs and blue-rimmed dinner plates; the brass-bottomed pots and an enormous frying pan as discolored as the mantelpiece from which they hung; in the corner a long, pale, shallow stone sink, quite empty. The cot was empty too—the cot which he had moved from the bedroom last year when Amélie had become too ill to climb the stairs. It stood neatly made, with the blankets tucked beneath the mattress, pushed against the worn brown velvet curtains that covered the window, and for some unknown reason Lucien remembered how ludicrous he'd thought such curtains looked in a kitchen, but they had been part of the kind of life that Amélie had demanded, just like the faded satin-covered chaise longue that sat adjacent to the fireplace.

The little velvet wing chair was pushed close to the hearth also. Lucien moved toward it, hesitated and turned, standing with his thick legs nearly screening the grate in front of the struggling fire. He reached up slowly to remove his beret and loosen his muffler, and with his curly gray hair exposed above his weathered face, he looked almost youthful for his years.

"When?" he asked at last.

"I'm not sure." She put her hand to the side of her cheek then lowered her fingers to her lips, a habit he recognized. "It must have been in the night."

"Nom de Dieu, why didn't you send word? Where is she?"

"You don't understand, Lucien."

"Understand what? Where is she?"

Ghislaine nodded in the direction of the door that led to the larder, explaining in one phrase, "It's cold in there."

"The larder!" Lucien was incredulous.

Ghislaine nodded again. "I didn't know what to do, so I rolled her in the blanket and . . . and I dragged her in there this morning. I want to bury her in the garden, but I keep having this pain in my chest that takes my breath away. Oh, Lucien . . . Lucien, please help me."

The old corporal's face, usually so stoic, was now showing disbelief. "Bury her in the garden? Have you really lost your mind?"

She fumbled her fingers across the chair back and moved at a shuffle until she almost fell onto the seat. She tried to gesture but her trembling was too obvious, so she dropped her head into her hands and her words came out muffled in dry sobs like a frightened child. "Please don't be cross with me, Lucien. You don't understand. They mustn't know she's dead . . . nobody must know. They'll take me away . . . they'll take my house away." She was shaking and Lucien almost went to her, but held back as he'd always held back.

"Now why would you be taken away?" He lowered his voice, trying to be soothing, to lessen what he felt must be her state of shock and, at the same time, clear the mounting confusions in his own mind. "Amélie was sick with the tumor . . . she was dying . . . we knew she was dying. It was just a matter of time. And now everything is yours."

She lifted her face, pale and unmoving. "That's what you don't understand. Nothing is mine. It is something in the will, Lucien . . . our father's will. All the land . . . the little bit of money each year . . . it was only for Amélie. Now it will all go to the church."

He stared at her. She sounded stunned. It was useless to argue, to suggest that she didn't understand these things, that she had never been able to learn to read more than the simplest of words. And this was too much too fast; there were too many implications. He needed a moment to put his own thoughts in order, so he turned to the fire and, taking the last log from the box by the hearth, he concentrated on stirring up the flames. When he stood up once more he said simply, "I want to see the paper . . . the will. Where is it?"

"I don't remember, Lucien." The hand went to the check again. "It's been so hard . . . so mixed up. Amélie always told me where to put things, but she's not here anymore."

The little-girl voice again, thought Lucien desperately. Always the grasping for what no longer existed, the retreat to the past to avoid reality, to avoid punishment. He kept his voice low and patient. "Didn't Amélie keep most of the accounts and papers in the sideboard? Why don't we look there?"

"Yes, yes . . . of course, in the sideboard." She was still sounding stunned and stood up with difficulty, but he left her to do it in her own time. Don't push her, he told himself, don't hurry her. She limped the few steps across the room where she opened the top drawer. She pulled out a handful of papers and long envelopes. He met her and took them from her, and then without thought he placed his big arm beneath hers and helped her to the chaise by the brightening fire. It was the first time he had touched her in half a lifetime and it stirred no memories.

"Your coat is damp, Lucien," was all she said, so he shrugged it from his shoulders and hung it over the back of the spool chair.

For a time the only sound was the faint crackle of heavy paper, then he moved the chair nearer to the lamp and seated himself, turning pages, flipping them over, until at last he went back to the first page and began to read the precise script half aloud in a slow monotone: "To my daughter, Ghislaine Lucrèce Monet de Couronne I give the sum of one franc, which is more than I received in value from her mother when she deserted me."

The room was deadly still until Lucien rattled his cigarette package, flicking a match with the edge of his thumbnail. He made no comment but read on silently until once again a few words, a few phrases, became audible, as if in actually hearing them he could believe that they were really what his eyes revealed. He coughed, clearing his throat from time to time, and some of the words seemed to come forth in jerks surrounded by puffs of smoke.

"The remainder of my estate, movable and immovable, where-soever the same may situate . . . including all property over which I may have power of appointment . . . disposal to my trustees in trust." He stumbled over some of the unfamiliar words, then went on. ". . . to pay all my just debts and expenses of my funeral. The remainder of my property, movable and immovable, I bequeath to my daughter, Amélie Bernadine Monet de Couronne, until her death, the usufruct of all remaining property for her disposal as she wishes, and on her death to her children. In the event that she dies childless, I bequeath the ownership of what remains of my property to the Église de . . ."

Lucien stopped and sat in silence for a moment, then muttered to himself, "There will be another copy, of course." He shuffled papers. "The firm of advocates, Matieu et Dalmas in Paris . . . they send the annuity."

He got up, dropping the papers disdainfully on the table, and made his way to the fireplace where he tossed his cigarette into the flames. "So, even from the grave, more turmoil," he whispered before he turned to Ghislaine.

"Can you remember what happened last night, Ghislaine? I know you must be very tired and confused and frightened, but try to think and remember."

He waited for her to begin, knowing her difficulty in putting her thoughts into words if she was pressured.

She appeared to be calm now, staring into the fire, her hands back in her lap. "It's better when you are here," she began, and paused for a minute. "You heard her before, lots of times. She promised she would take care of me . . . we would take care of each other, she used to say before she got sick, even though sometimes she said I was sinful and told lies. But I had to tell lies sometimes, Lucien. You know that . . . so she wouldn't shout at me so much . . . and I tried . . . and I went to confession, and . . ."

"I know. It's all right, I know. And so last night what happened?"

"After you went away last night, for a time she was fine because there would be more money when the land was sold, but she got cross with me because I couldn't find her pills, and you know how she got when she wanted her pills, and she said I hid them and I was lying again, and she said she wouldn't give me any money from the land." She was sounding matter-of-fact, her tone not quite adult but not childish.

"But you found the pills?"

"Oh, yes. She had lost them herself. They were underneath her pillow, so she took some and I fixed her hot milk. She said I was a good nurse. She took some more later too."

Lucien watched carefully, but her face was as expressionless as a ventriloquist's dummy. Only her lips moved. He had to keep her from getting upset again, to use his questions to guide her reasoning. He would try to keep off the subject of the pills until another time. "And after that she wasn't cross anymore?" he asked.

"No, she was nice . . . but she started explaining about the will again. She'd talked about it before, ever since we were little . . . oh, often before, but she'd made me promise I wouldn't tell . . . not even you. But it was hard to understand. And I wouldn't tell . . . why would I? They'd take me away from my house and put me in a home. I've been good, Lucien, and tended the garden and looked after her while she was sick, and cooked. And I went to church as often as I could when my foot didn't hurt, and I always pray for forgiveness and do penance for my sins, and always keep covered like a nun the way she said . . . and I didn't even talk to you, even after you'd been gone all those years and you came back to fix things here for us."

It was like listening to the girl again, and Lucien began to ache inside and he wanted to shout out, 'No more. No more! I know!', but he simply lowered himself into the wing chair and let her go on.

"But do you know, Lucien, last night after she was better from the pills, she said she would look after me, but if something happened to her, that you would look after me. She never said that before. . . . She used to hate you . . . not all the time though. She didn't hate you in the war when you took us away to the mountains to escape from the Boche." Her voice had lowered gradually, and she had dropped her head back, and now she closed her eyes. "It was nice in the mountians. Yes, it was lovely there . . . so warm. Remember, Lucien, how warm it was, even in the water?"

Enough of this . . . enough, Lucien decided suddenly. "Yes, it was warm, but it is cold in this room. You are tired now. You've talked enough. Rest a little, while I fix the fires."

He stood up and went to the stove and lifted the lid. "Have you eaten today?" he inquired, but there was no reply and he was glad she was no longer listening. He busied himself with kindling and

coke and matches, finally moving the kettle and the pot of soup to
the top of the warming lids.

Then he went quietly to the back door that opened into the larder
and closed the door behind him. He wasn't gone long, but long
enough, and when he returned he carried an armful of logs. He
placed two logs on the open fire and put the others, one by one, into
the box on the hearth.

She seemed to be sleeping, breathing lightly, curled up like a
brown blot on the once-pink chaise longue. He pulled the quilt from
the cot to cover her. "Ghislaine," he said, touching her shoulder.
"Ghislaine . . . I have to plan and I have things to do, but I will be
back. I will take the back door key . . . the key to the shed, and let
myself in and return in a little while."

She stirred. "Will you look after me, Lucien?"

"I have never refused."

"Once."

"That was beyond my control." He put on his coat, took his beret
from the pocket and placed it firmly on his head, then twisted his
scarf around his throat.

"Where are you going?" Her eyes were wide open, staring, afraid.
"What about Amélie? She's in there. We can't leave her in there."

"I am coming back soon. I have to see to the child. Go back to
sleep."

"She is no longer a child, Lucien. I saw her in church in the summer and she is not a child anymore."

No, Lucien admitted to himself, but you are still . . . clinging
. . . frightened . . . and unpredictable.

Chapter Two

Old gendarme Maurice Ygrec stretched his long legs out toward the
fire and felt the warmth on his slippered feet and closed his eyes. He
was happy—almost indecently happy, he admitted to himself. He had
longed for this holiday in St. Denis and was determined that not even
the miserable weather would be allowed to interfere with his content-
ment. This evening he had purposely chosen the big wing chair with
its back to the curtained french doors so he could ignore the drench-
ing darkness outside, and he concentrated on listening to the crackling of the freshly lit logs in the hearth.

He was looking unusually tidy—at least he hoped that he was, because he had gone to a great deal of trouble to attempt to flatten his unruly gray hair with a dampened brush, had shaved carefully after his afternoon rest, and had even tried to smooth out the white wiry hairs of his eyebrows. He was wearing his best tweed trousers, the ones without the knee patches, and he had put on a clean shirt and the new blue sweater that Vanessa had sent him for his birthday last May. She had written on the enclosed note that the color of the sweater matched his eyes, but he'd been a little sad that day, admitting to himself that his ailing lungs and tired heart were making him feel even older than his advancing years, so he'd left the sweater folded neatly in the box in which it had arrived, not daring to hope that he would be able to wear it on such a night as this. He had felt that he was past believing in miracles and that he'd never see the lights of Paris again.

But here he was, here within a few kilometers of his beloved Paris —here in this pleasant apartment with his dearest friend, Inspector Paul Michelin, and best of all near Paul's wife, Vanessa. Old Ygrec smiled just thinking of Vanessa—how her copper hair swished across her shoulders when she was angry—how she swirled around the room in her bare feet and long skirts when she was happy—her amusing chatter, often directed at no particular audience—and the touch of her fingers on his cheek when she was concerned about him.

It had been her concern that had been partly responsible for this visit. Since his retirement, the old gendarme had remained in the village of Moulins in the Moselle Valley where his comforts had been more than adequately attended to by his devoted, if exhausting concierge, Mme. Lachance. He had been reasonably content, but the physical limitations demanded by the good Madame and her ally, Dr. de Grace, and the desires of Ygrec's active mind, had been a source of constant conflict. It hadn't been so difficult at first when young Michelin, then a sergeant, had been working in the nearby gendarmerie, but after Michelin's promotion and transfer to Paris, the village had become almost a prison. Each time Ygrec had suggested a short holiday such as a trip to Paris, Dr. de Grace would stare through his thick glasses as if Ygrec were a wayward child, throw up his hands, and make his usual speech. "Go . . . go ahead . . . the polluted air is exactly what your emphysema needs. Go . . . you may get as far as Verdun, and then be shipped back in a coffin!" So Ygrec would dutifully take the medicines administered by Madame and sleep away the long lonely days, and because there was no one else, he'd talk to his great hulking dog, Mademoiselle Larme, and word went around the village that old Ygrec was getting senile. Michelin and Vanessa visited when they could and only then did the old man seem to come to life.

Then the miracle came to pass. Mme. Lachance was called to the bedside of her only sister who'd had a stroke, and Ygrec, who was really a very compassionate person and didn't wish such a disaster on anyone, was jubilant. There were hurried phone calls and consultations, then suddenly one bright sunny morning Vanessa was there in Madame's proper little parlor, pulling Mademoiselle Larme's ears, kissing Ygrec on his pale forehead, packing his belongings, and stuffing his pills and medications into her purse. Ygrec almost chuckled aloud thinking of the sight they must have presented to the startled villagers that day as they drove through rue Moulins: a yellow Lambretti stuffed with battered suitcases, a large excited rusty dog, a beautiful redheaded girl, and an old man wearing a faded kepi (the only hat that Ygrec owned and Dr. de Grace had insisted that he wear a hat). The trip had been glorious—except that the dog had been car sick twice.

Ygrec opened his eyes just a fraction. He could hear Mademoiselle Larme padding across the tiled foyer floor on her way to the kitchen. He knew that Pippa, the little *femme de ménage,* who was preparing the vegetables for the evening meal, was fond of the dog, and as it was forbidden to keep animals in the apartments, Ygrec felt that it was a good idea to encourage the relationship between the two, for he had discovered that Pippa was quite the gossip if she was given the chance, but also that she enjoyed secrets. As she didn't like the dour concierge who managed the building, she was only too pleased to be in on the conspiracy.

Pippa came to work at noon on the week days when Vanessa worked in Paris at the fashion studio, and although Ygrec had been here less than a week, it had rained almost continually, confining him indoors, so he found the girl entertaining, and he felt that already he was beginning to learn a great deal about some of the inhabitants of St. Denis, if even half her stories could be believed. She was an odd, almost gypsylike little thing who often wore long skirts beneath her shapeless smocks and was given to moods of preoccupation, then sudden outbursts of chattering. She was pretty, with short, dark undisciplined hair, and when she became involved in the relating of one of her tales, her eyes became radiant like pools of sherry in her sun-browned face. Perhaps she did belong on stage in front of an audience, as she had suggested to Ygrec. At any rate, she brightened the long gray afternoons for him.

"I'm not just an ordinary femme de ménage, you understand, M. Ygrec," she had informed him, earlier on in the afternoon. "I've already finished school at the convent. I finished in June with excellent grades and I'm going away to the *Académie* in Toulons, perhaps next year when my gran'papa has saved a little more money. It is very expensive at the Académie, you realize, but Mother Superior told my gran'papa that it would be a sin to waste my talents."

"Oh, most definitely that would be a sin," agreed Ygrec. "And what will you be studying at the Académie, little mademoiselle?"

"Oh, I expect I will have to become a professor of languages. I would rather study the arts, of course, especially poetry and drama, but my gran'papa frowns on the idea, even though I do have the gift. Sister Manette said I had a very unusual way with words, and last spring I even wrote a poem that Jean-Louis put to music, and he said I have a true insight into the 'passion of words.' Isn't that a lovely expression, M. Ygrec . . . 'passion of words'? Jean-Louis knows about these things because he's almost nineteen and a talented musician. He plays the guitar and has his own band . . . not a big band, you understand, as there are just three of them at the moment, but soon he'll get recognition. He's on tour right now and was playing for a time in a club at Dramont near St. Tropez, and he sent me a postcard from there in July. I would love to go to St. Tropez. Have you ever been there, monsieur?"

She'd paused for a small breath but didn't wait for a reply. "Jean-Louis plays so beautifully it would just take your breath away, but his parents don't take his art seriously either. They live down the lane from us near the Bistro Céleste where that weird Armand works for his aunt. I'm glad that Jean-Louis stopped being friends with Armand as he was a bad influence on Jean-Louis and doesn't appreciate the finer things in life. Armand has been helping clean up at the mortuary next door over the summer . . . imagine doing that kind of work; it makes me feel quite shivery. He will get as queer as that M. Fouschie, the mortician who I told you about yesterday, just wait and see! So you can understand, monsieur, that there isn't much culture in our neighborhood. It is so difficult for poor Jean-Louis, having a father who is a pastry cook with no soul, and Mme. Hugo, his mother, is even more unfeeling because she thinks Jean-Louis should stay at home and learn about the business, and then they could all move closer to Paris and open a bigger shop. Can you imagine, M. Ygrec, what a sin it would be to waste one's musical talents just driving a pastry truck around St. Denis!" She'd sighed morosely. Most of her sentences were punctuated with dramatic sighs.

Ygrec had made sympathetic noises and managed to keep the amusement from showing on his face until she returned to her chores. Yes, she certainly was entertaining. Yesterday it had been the alcoholic mortician who spent most of his time sitting in the Bistro Céleste insulting all the customers, and today it was a "weird" waiter from the bistro and a pastry cook with no soul. Who knew what tomorrow would bring!

But the old gendarme had not that long to wait. Once more the staccato of the dog's claws on the tiles interrupted his reverie, then Pippa's bright voice.

"Do you want me to stir up the fireplace before I go, M. Ygrec? I filled up the dog's water bowl and everything else is done. Mme. Michelin said I was to take good care of you and Mademoiselle Larme."

Ygrec smiled. "And an admirable job you do, little mademoiselle. I assure you I am very warm and comfortable, so you'd best be on your way before it gets too dark. Your grandpère will be anticipating your return, I'm sure."

"Oh yes, he waits the evening meal for me. Tonight I think we are going to have rabbit pie. He is a very good cook, monsieur, and he is teaching me. But he will worry if I arrive late; he wanted to come and meet me each evening, but I am grown up now, and it isn't far . . . just back of the old gardens on rue Lutétia is where we live. It used to be a part of the Couronne estate, you understand." She stood in the doorway buttoning up her convent-blue coat, and in Ygrec's eyes she still looked like a schoolchild. "I didn't want to work here at first, but my gran'papa has respect for Inspector Michelin, and of course Mme. Michelin is a true lady and rich besides. Gran'papa made inquiries, of course."

"Of course." As usual, Ygrec hid his amusement.

"But I really don't like it around here, even in the daytime. This château is cursed, you understand. Do you know about the curse of St. Denis, monsieur?"

"I know of the legend of St. Denis, the first bishop of Lutétia, and how after being beheaded at Montmartre, he walked away carrying his severed head in his hands, but I can't say I've heard of any curse."

"Oh, yes, that's all true, but before they arrested St. Denis"—she paused to cross herself with a hand clutching a striped head scarf— "he was sheltered here in this very château by the original Conte de Couronne, and when they found out, they arrested the Conte too, and they tortured him and buried him alive . . . right here beneath this very room in the vaults, and his lady with him . . . and she was expecting a baby. Then all the lands and buildings and the title and even the name were given to the traitor who told on the Conte. The traitor's name was Monet, so after that he called himself le Conte Monet de Couronne. My gran'papa knows all about it, even though it happened hundreds and hundreds of years ago."

"Indeed . . . . your grandpère must be a very remarkable man."

"Oh, he is!" Pippa's enthusiasm increased, as always, in direct proportion to Ygrec's nodding interest. "He was a hero in the army and the Maquis too, and he has lots of ribbons on his uniform, even though he only puts it on once a year now, on Bastille Day. And he knows about history and all about the Couronne family curse because, you see, the Anjous . . . my gran'papa's name is Lucien Phillipe Anjou . . . they worked on the estate for years and years, even at the time of Joan of Arc. That was before the lands were divided up and sold, of course. And Gran'papa, when he was a little boy, used to see the last old Conte de Couronne, who was *dérangé,* just like all the Couronne aristocrats."

The girl's eyes were wide now and she was holding her twisted kerchief between her small hands close to her chest, enjoying herself thoroughly. "That's the curse . . . they're all dérangé, or at least very queer. But the last old Conte didn't have a son, just two daughters who were both queer, of course, even if they did have different mothers. They still live near here in the loge de garde that used to be the gatehouse for the estate. It's back of the château parking lot hidden behind the jungle gardens. Mlle. Amélie hasn't spoken to anyone for years and years and they say she makes soup out of awful things —strange herbs and even dead dogs, they're very poor now, you understand." Pippa shuddered and suddenly bent down to caress Mademoiselle Larme who had flopped on the rug at her feet.

"And the other sister?" Ygrec quickly inquired to divert Pippa's attention to a less morbid subject.

"Oh, Mlle. Ghislaine has a crooked foot that they tried to fix a long time ago, and wears awful old clothes and talks to herself and prays all the time, they say. She keeps her head covered up like a nun, and probably because she is so ugly. It is really very sad, you know, because the old Conte made them live in the loge de garde even when they were little. Mme. Fouschie, the mortician's old aunt, was their nursemaid, but she used to drink too much wine, just like M. Fouschie does, so she wasn't much use. As Mme. Hugo says, it must have been a disastrous situation." Pippa shrugged, and Ygrec had to bend down and pretend to pat the dog to keep from laughing aloud. It sounded like a plot for a third-rate motion picture.

"I presume, then," Ygrec went on, "that the two sisters never married."

"Oh, no! They were much too ugly, which was just as well because now the curse will go away. Jean-Louis says there's no such thing as curses, but his mother says you never know. What do you think, M. Ygrec?"

Ygrec evaded the question. "What does your grandpère say about it?"

Pippa, still crouched by the dog, stood up thoughtfully, straightened the kerchief and placed it over her untidy hair. "Well, sometimes he goes to the loge to help out the old ladies because they are so poor. . . . He digs their garden in the spring and fixes things because he has a kind heart, but he doesn't talk about them at all. Once when I asked, he just said to stay away from the loge and leave people to live their own lives." She paused again, slowly tying the scarf beneath her chin. "But Mme. Hugo says she heard that this whole apartment . . . \right here where I'm standing now, was once the ballroom of the château and it was right outside those doors"—she waved one arm in a sweeping motion toward the curtained french doors—"they found the old Conte de Couronne's body after he had been pushed off the roof balcony by the curse, and my gran'papa's father was with them when they found the body, all broken and bloody, and so was Gran'papa, even though he was just a very small boy. That's what Mme. Hugo told me, so I expect that's why I'm discouraged from discussing it . . . do you think so, monsieur?"

"Without a doubt, mademoiselle."

Pippa seemed to stir back to reality. "It's been a great pleasure talking to you, M. Ygrec, but now I really will have to hurry or my gran'papa will be coming out in the rain to look for me, and I don't want him catching cold. He's quite old, you understand, over sixty, although even Mme. Hugo says he acts young for his age."

This time Ygrec couldn't help from smiling broadly. "And it's always a pleasure talking to you too. I apologize for keeping you. *Bonsoir, mademoiselle . . . à demain.*"

After the door had closed firmly, the old gendarme did laugh aloud. It was wonderful to be young, he thought, but far more comfortable to be old. He wished for nothing more than he had at the moment—warmth and the company of his dog and his friends. He leaned over to rub the dog beneath her chin. "I regret nothing," he said aloud, and then he placed his hands on the arms of the chair and stood up slowly. His legs were a little stiff from sitting so long, but he stood erect and walked to the record player to switch on his favorite record that he had been listening to earlier in the afternoon. There was a little click, then the vibrant voice of Piaf filled the room, *"Je ne regrette rien."*

Vanessa would be home soon and they would probably have a small apéritif and a game of backgammon while they waited for Michelin to return from duty. Ygrec pushed aside the drapes and peered outside. The rain had diminished to a soft drizzle, and he knew that not far beyond the diffused spotty lights of St. Denis, Paris would be gleaming. Long uneven beams from endless cars would be circling the Arc de Triomphe and streaming down the avenue toward the Quais, and as he remembered the city, gradually he became taller and straighter, as if he were back striding down the greasy black uneven streets around the Quai des Orfèvres in his gendarme's cap and kepi. The ache left his legs and his arms stretched out to lift the latch and open the doors just a fraction. The air wasn't as cold as he'd expected and his chest seemed to fill and expand. He would see Paris again . . . he knew he would.

Chapter Three

Valin Chamillion was studying a travel brochure of the Spanish Riviera. As soon as the evening meal had been cleared from the table he had moved the floor lamp as far as the cord would stretch, adjusting the lamp shade so that the light would shine over his left shoulder.

He had been tired and chilled when he'd arrived home, but first the Pernod and then the wine with his meal had warmed him, and now he was feeling almost elated, and in his imagination he had spent and respent the commission he would receive from the sale of the Couronne property.

Valin was not a good salesman, for what he felt was his public air of confidence manifested itself in an attitude of nervous arrogance, but he had managed to keep this fact from his employer, M. Joddard, for almost two months, and even from himself most of the time. He hadn't been a good schoolmaster either, but had lasted in the profession for almost ten years until circumstances had released him from the necessity of tolerating the domineering pity of his colleagues and the utter confusion of endless streams of small boys bent on exposing him to the world as a bespectacled joke. He had kept the fact of his hatred and humiliation hidden by erasing the cruel childish caricatures from the schoolroom blackboards with steady strokes of a chalky brush, and had kept his hand steady by calming his nerves at regular intervals from the contents of a flask kept close at hand in his attaché case.

His precise penmanship, his skill with figures, his respectable family background, and his intimate knowledge of St. Denis and its environs had persuaded the officious director of Joddard et Fils of his possible value to the firm. However, over the summer, Valin's sales had been minimal and recently M. Joddard had been watching him and haunting him with the only too familiar look of doubt. Then old Corporal Anjou had come to the office and had asked for an agent to handle the sale of the Couronne property, and Valin had been given the assignment. Now he would be respected; now he would be on equal footing with the other agents; and now perhaps Gabrielle would see him in a new light and once more treat him as a man, as a husband.

If Valin had been listening, he would have heard the sounds in the kitchen where his sister Estelle was finishing the evening chores, but he had become inured to his surroundings. He had been born in this house and had spent over half his life under its domination. At one time, the dining room where he was seated had been formally austere, but since maman's illness, the salon had been converted into her bedroom and now he was surrounded by walls lined with furnishings of shabby leather, threadbare brocade, and dusty oak, all piled with books, old clothing, and boxes of knickknacks that had been waiting over a year for Estelle to sort out. He was also surrounded by an infusion of smells: the acrid mixture of strong soap and garlic from the kitchen; the stale traces of sickness from behind the drawn curtains to the salon; a heavy oil of wintergreen and camphor stench that had become embedded in his sister's woollen clothing; and now, as too frequently lately when Gabrielle returned from work, a lingering, and to Valin, a nauseating heavy perfume. But at the moment his conscious world was circled by lamplight, so he was smelling only the freshness of salt water and sand and warm winds.

He'd had the Spanish travel folder for some years; it was but one of many he had collected and it was almost worn through on the creases from frequent folding and unfolding. It was spread out in front of him, and his shoulders were hunched in concentration as he moved his finger along a small insert map.

"Estelle . . . 'Stelle!" The thin voice of his mother called weakly from behind the curtain, and Valin looked up as Estelle emerged from the kitchen wiping her reddened hands on the front of her apron, complaining as she passed him. "Mamam has been demanding all day. The dampness swells her joints and I have to rub them with the liniment." She pulled the tasseled curtains aside and hurried through the shadowy folds still muttering, and Valin was left with a growing feeling of desperation. Would he never be rid of this house of whining old women? Little wonder that Gabrielle, humiliating as it was to him, had taken the job in the cafe. He reached for the glass of milky Pernod beside him, draining it in one gulp.

Estelle must have turned on the radio for maman—he could hear faint music, so he didn't hear Gabrielle, but he felt her presence behind him, and smelled her heavy perfume. She had come in after their meal was finished, going straight upstairs to change from the tight skirt and thin frilly blouse she wore to work, covering her small body with dark shapelessness before confronting him—as she always did these days. He tried not to think about her body, concentrating instead on the curves and indentations of the Spanish coast.

"Valencia," he said, trying to sound confident. "I don't think many tourists go that far south this time of year. . . . They usually stay near Barcelona. Yes, a month there, then on to Majorca."

"Valin!" Gabrielle's voice was barely audible but the anger was there, so he ignored her.

"I think I'll go tomorrow to the travel agent on avenue St. Joseph," he went on quickly, "to obtain more information before we decide. Majorca can be cold and damp in the winter . . . as bad as Paris. It would be best—"

"Valin!"

This time he looked up from his monologue and turned in his chair. She was standing in the doorway to the hall as he'd imagined, framed in the watery light, and when she moved into the cramped shadows he could see her arms tightly held by her sides and her hands shoved into the pockets of her sweater. She hadn't removed the heavy eye makeup or the pale shiny lipstick.

"No more, Valin," she went on tensely. "No more . . . not again . . . not ever again."

His index finger that had been pinpointing the island on the paper collapsed gradually until his hand spread, covering the whole of the map. He tried to speak with confidence but his words came out with a pleading whine, almost like that of the invalid hidden by the curtain. "Now don't be like that, Gabrielle. This time it's true . . . it's only a matter of a few more weeks. The Couronne property . . . you've heard of the Couronne property and how valuable it is . . . I told Estelle during supper . . . if only you'd been here on time. It's a big sale so the commission will come to at least—"

Her disgust became a shrillness. "No more. I say it for the last time. When we were first married it was to be the cruise through the Greek Islands, then later it was Cannes and Nice and luxury hotels . . . and instead we lost the house on rue Pasqualle while you looked for another job. And what came after that? Oh, yes . . . it was Corsica . . . or was it the villa in Algiers and the pilgrimage to your father's grave . . . only I had to find work while you got over your 'nervous collapse'!"

Her eyes were wide open now as she approached the table with tightened fists. "Do you want me to go on, or do you remember? Nervous collapse . . . mon Dieu . . . you were drowning in anisette! And now this—this stinking museum!" She tossed her head in a derisive circle and Valin was forced to the reality of his surroundings. He couldn't look at her face anymore, so he concentrated on a collapsed fly whisk protruding from the mouth of a grotesque vase that stood surrounded by medicine bottles on the buffet.

"And this!" she repeated, picking up the bottle of Pernod from the table then slamming it down on top of the brochure. As she went on, her words rose above the music from the sick room. "You stink of licorice and live in a world of drink and travel folders. For four years I have put up with promises. 'Just give me a chance,' you say.

'It's not my fault,' you say. It's always the fault of someone else. Maman is sick. You're sick. Well, I'm sick of waiting!"

"Gabrielle! How could you!" Estelle had thrust aside the curtain and materialized behind the table. There was disgust and horror in her voice, while behind her a wail was rising and falling above the staccato of a violin. "She heard you . . . listen to her. You're sinful and cruel. I spend all day easing her pain and soothing her and now you have her in hysterics again."

Gabrielle went on as if she'd never been interrupted. "Well, Estelle! And what about our Estelle . . . gray and wizened and lumpy like a sack of winter potatoes. If you don't get out of this place, you'll be as crazy as your brother, or is it too late already? And what will you do when your precious maman dies? Valin will sell what's left of the house and sit crying into his Pernod and you'll be out on the street."

"Someone has to do the work . . . someone has to sacrifice! Listen to her, Valin . . . she's evil and sinful . . . I told you before. . . ." Estelle's voice quivered; then she broke into harsh sobs that were muffled by her raised apron as he rushed into the kitchen. ". . . hateful . . . sinful . . ."

Valin shoved his chair back and started to rise, but Gabrielle's voice above the crescendo of music from one direction and crying from the other direction brought him to a standstill.

"Let her enjoy herself, Valin. She likes to be miserable, so let her suffer in peace."

"But maman! Can't you hear she's upset?"

"Yes, and maman enjoys being upset. It gives her all the attention she can't get any other way. She's old and she's poor. . . . Because of her own stupidity, she's poor, and she's turned you into a failure and Estelle into an ugly old spinster and I'm not going to stay and get old and ugly and poor too." She swept by Valin and down the hallway to the stairs.

He had slipped back into his seat during her tirade and now sat grasping the scuffed arms of the chair. She couldn't leave—she wouldn't. She'd always stayed before. Besides, where could she go on a night like this in the pouring rain? She had no family—they'd all died during the war. She'd told him all about it, all her pitiful story, the first night he'd met her in the cafe in Norbonne, and afterward when he'd taken her to that nice little place for dinner. They'd talked over their wine for hours and she'd been impressed because he was older and reliable and well educated. She'd needed someone to look after her, to love her.

Valin, remembering the details of that time, covered his face with his hands. If only she'd be patient a little longer. Maman couldn't live forever and then they'd have the house all to themselves and he'd fix it up for her, and with Estelle to do all the cooking and cleaning, Gabrielle could stay home and rest. She was just tired, that was all. That cafe was a common place and he shouldn't have let her go to work there. Well, he'd just tell her, tell her he didn't want his wife working. What she needed was a holiday—a month, at least a month, in Valencia. They would lie on the beach in the sun, and later they would lie in a wide bed with a soft wind blowing at the curtains through the open window. Her shoulder would be cool and he'd gently pull the sheet to cover her, and her head would be on his bare shoulder. His touch would be welcome too—she wouldn't lie there stiffly, her back to him, her face turned away. Never again would he feel the insult of rejection.

Valin hadn't realized he was sitting in silence, a horrible silence of anticipation, until he heard the firm closing of the front door, and then Estelle's sniffing voice that seemed to answer the question he'd been asking himself all along, but which he didn't want answered.

"She's gone to one of the other men. She was just looking for an excuse to go, and this time she won't be back. That's a good thing. Now it will be like it used to be." Estelle put her hand on his shoulder and sniffed again.

He could still smell the wintergreen and it sickened him and he wanted to smash at the hand and scream something obscene, but maman was whimpering once more, so he shrugged her hand away. "Go see to maman."

He smoothed out the folder in front of him and peered down at it. He would see Valencia. He would . . . and Gabrielle would go with him, and perhaps to Madrid, and then on down to Algiers . . .

He reached for the glass, forgetting that it was empty, but that was all right—there was still some in the bottle and more upstairs in his bedroom.

Chapter Four

Over the years, the small district around rue Lutétia, back of the Château Couronne had developed into a kind of little village all on its own. There were a few small business establishments: an untidy greengrocer's adjoining a meat shop where rabbits hung stiffly over the counter; the spotless Pâtisserie Hugo noted for its pastries and fancy rolls; a salon coiffure where the overwhelming Mme. Hugo had a regular Friday morning appointment; a photographer's shop that displayed dusty cardboard-framed altar boys and white-veiled small girls, all with identically stunned eyes, and over the road, set back slightly from its neighboring gray-stone buildings, M. Fouschie's peaceful mortuary, next door to the usually peaceful Bistro Céleste. Most of the shopkeepers lived above or behind their premises.

During the day, small trucks sometimes bumped to a standstill to drop off supplies, and hand-pulled barrows loaded with milk cans or vegetables rattled by, but there was seldom a distraction to cause the housewives in their aprons and dark skirts to bother looking up from their daily scrubbing of the smooth stone doorsteps.

At night only two streetlights shone on the deserted cobblestones; one at the far end where rue Lutétia intersected the wider avenue Côte and eventually joined boulevard des Anges; the other in front of Pâtisserie Hugo and the turnoff to Anjou's Lane.

The lane was tree-lined and in the summer bright with color from the grass and wild flowers that flourished on either side. Once it had been wide enough for a farm wagon to pass through to the patchwork of market gardens and to the canal that could be seen in the distance, and it had been beaten to a near-concrete hardness by generations of tramping hoofs and boots. Now it was little but a pathway which came to an abrupt stop in front of Lucien Anjou's sprawling cottage.

Mme. Hugo's dining-room window, at the back of the shop. looked out directly on Anjou's Lane.

"It's stopped raining and Lucien is on the prowl again," Mme. Hugo announced to her husband. "That's two nights in a row he's gone out after nine o'clock." She let the lace curtains drop back in place, straightened them, then reached for the cord to lower the shutters.

Pépi Hugo didn't bother to answer. He was half asleep in the depths of his scruffy armchair, an empty wine glass cradled between his plump little hands. The tiny dining room opened onto the immaculate darkened baker's kitchen beyond, and Pépi was half dreaming of what kind of tarts to make tomorrow.

"Are you listening, Pépi?"

The small man stirred. "Perhaps he's gone to the Cafe Khedive to look for a friendly girl."

"Pépi! Be serious!"

"Ah, but *ma chérie,* weren't you the one who used to call him a womanizer?"

"He's too old for that now."

There was a chuckle from the chair. "Then he'll be going to the Bistro Céleste. There's nothing tempting there. Now turn off the lights, Marie-Thérèse and come to bed. Morning arrives too early these days." He stirred and handed her his empty glass.

But Madame seated herself in her usual place by the window and picked up the last custard tart from the plate that sat on a doily in the center of the round polished table. "I don't think Lucien was going out to be sociable. He was carrying something, some kind of a bundle, and what would he be taking to the bistro in a bundle? And besides it's only Thursday and he doesn't go drinking these days except sometimes for an hour or so on a Saturday."

"He could have run into one of his old compatriots from the army and he's taken some of his souvenirs, or else the medals he got. You know how he gets sometimes, as if thirty years haven't passed, and he sits and drinks to the war and the Boche he killed."

"Not so much since he brought Pippa here, he hasn't. You have said it yourself, how he's changed, settled down, these past few years, hardly drinking at all and staying home all the time to keep his eye on that girl. He babies her if you ask me." Madame wiped her sticky mouth with the tips of her dimpled fingers and brushed at the crumbs that had settled on the chains and sparkly stones of the assorted necklaces that dangled down her high bosom. She then reached across the table for a glass and the wine bottle. "Coddles that girl, he does. Why when I was little more than her age, I had you off in the war and a child on the way, and I walked south with the refugees and slept on the side of the road. I'm just surprised that Lucien has allowed her to work at the château, although by the sound of things she's not doing much work, and I don't think that Mme. Michelin is a good influence on her, encouraging her to traipse around in those long skirts and put on airs. I mentioned it to Lucien, but he didn't even listen to me."

"She's a handsome woman, Mme. Michelin is. Her picture was in a magazine last month." Pépi reached for his wine glass that his wife had filled again, then added quickly, "She's too skinny for my tastes, of course."

"She has nice hair and a pretty face, but as you say, she looks like she hasn't had a decent meal in months." Madame smoothed her hands across the floral rose dress that covered her well-corseted abdomen. "Well, one thing for certain, Pippa will never end up like Mme. Michelin, being a photographer's model, not with her thick hair and swarthy skin. I wonder where she gets her queer looks. Say what you want, the Anjous all had good features, and Jacques was a nice-looking boy from what I remember . . . tall, like Lucien too. It must be from the mother's side . . . they say she was a Basque. Strange how Lucien never mentions Pippa's mother at all . . . or her grandmother. He's never even mentioned his own wife's name . . . imagine that, Pépi. But one of these days I'm going to ask Pippa. Surely the girl would know something about her own relatives, even if they are all dead. Lucien is quite beyond me. You'd think he'd want to confide in his friends sometimes, wouldn't you?"

Pépi had finished his wine while he listened to his wife's singsong voice, then he peered up at the clock on the wall, grunted, and raised his small pudgy body very slowly. The rooms were warm and heavy with smells of yeast and fruity preserves. He started toward the stairway. "Fresh peach tarts tomorrow, before the fruit gets too soft," he mumbled absently. "I wish Jean-Louis was here to help with the deliveries."

"He'll be along soon, now that the tourist season is over." Madame popped the cork back into the wine bottle. "It was good for him to be away this summer and meet new people. He'll be ready to settle down when he gets back. I didn't like the way he was starting to hang around Anjou's cottage this spring. He's going to be something in life . . . he's got ambitions, and they don't include the granddaughter of Lucien Anjou. I made that clear to him before I gave him the money for the motorcycle, and I felt like mentioning it to Lucien too, when he told me I was foolish to let Jean-Louis have the machine. Just because his Jacques had to drive like a maniac and kill himself doesn't mean that my Jean-Louis is careless."

Madame's voice droned on, while Pépi, only the fat rear of his shiny blue trousers visible, waddled and wheezed up the stairs. Finally she rose, straightened the doily on the table, carried the plate and wine glasses to the kitchen, turned out the light and followed. Pépi was right; morning did come too early these days.

* * *

Lucien bent over the sleeping Pippa, touched her hair with his thick fingers, pulled the blankets over her shoulders and left the room, closing the door softly behind him.

He hadn't turned on the light when he came home. His eyes, accustomed to reacting with an instinct in the dark, had guided him around the kitchen table to hang his damp coat near the warmth of the stove, and then to the sink where he washed his hands in the water that was left in the basin, before going to check on Pippa. Now he passed through the kitchen once more and stepped outside onto the little piazza. The rain clouds had cleared and he could sense a change in the darkness, a kind of shifting in the shading that was like a breath of sound, and he knew it was the beginning of dawn. It was the time of day he liked best, when he could scan the sky above the darkly etched spires of the church until the brilliant green of the copper roofs began to reflect the rising sun.

He could see little at the moment except the shadows of the garden around the cottage and the stone path widening into the lane, and the trees, and he felt as he had only a few hours before, when he'd walked through the Couronne gardens in the dusk, and now as then, he allowed the past to come to life in his mind. Near the corner of the cottage on his right was the spreading ash tree, and hanging from a sturdy branch was the swing he had put up for Pippa. It had a wide, smoothly sanded board seat, wide enough to take a man, and supported by thick ropes, for when Pippa first came to the cottage she'd been afraid of the strangeness and the newness and had clung to him for security. He had built the swing to take his own size and weight and had held her on his knee at first, the two of them swinging high, brushing the branches of the other trees, and soon she had learned to love the freedom and excitement of the world as seen from her tall moving perch.

How brown her thin arms were that first summer; how confidently her tiny hands clasped the ropes; how delighted her laughter. And, praise be, how different was that child, Pippa, from the other child, Ghislaine, even before the accident.

"Was it I who brought about the little Ghislaine's injuries? Out of kindness did I bring on the weakness in her brain?" Lucien's father had gone to his grave with the question unanswered, leaving Lucien the heritage of guilt.

It was about a year after the first encounter at that birdbath. Lucien had climbed a big oak at the rear of the loge de garde, to hold the ropes for his father who had built a kind of small wooden chair seat with a back and sides to support the fragile little Ghislaine, but when it was finished and Amélie had placed her in the swinging seat, Ghislaine had clung desperately with both hands to one rope and begged to be taken down. "Don't be a baby. You must get used to it. Mlle. Fouschie says you need fresh air," Amélie had stolidly insisted, then began pushing the swing back and forth, higher and higher. Lucien, seeing glimpses of the small, drained face, at times blinded by whipped strands of long dark hair, a face petrified with fear, had wanted to rush forward and stop the agonizing performance. But his father had restrained him with a whisper. "Amélie Couronne is like her father. Try to stop her and she will defy you by going farther." So Lucien had watched from behind heavy foliage, doubting the severity of his father's wisdom.

It was the last time he needed to doubt. For the next few days he went, at his father's bidding, to hide behind the hedge and watch and report the unfeeling stubbornness of the older girl, Amélie, and the tortured panic of the small sister. And then one night, the night after Ghislaine fell from the swing and was left in a crumpled heap with a telltale red oozing from her head, Lucien went again. He went with his father, and armed with his father's knife, he climbed the tree in the moonlight and severed the ropes from the great branch.

Lucien considered the wisdom of his father again, as daylight touched the basilica spires, and he weighed a justice that, as he'd matured, he'd come to see, to truly believe, was a kind of right—the right to protect, by any means, what was yours and what was loved, or what was weak and deserved protection.

Tonight he had done what had to be done. Ghislaine was weak; for whatever cause or reason was of no consequence now, for the past was the past. Right or wrong in the eyes of the law, it was done. Love? If there ever had been a kind of love, it had been too confused with pity to be of any depth.

And what of love, or for that matter, of any depth of emotion for his son, Pippa's father? From the first, even after the bitterness had come and gone, Lucien had been forced to admit to himself that he never had been able to feel anything for the boy—he'd hardly known him. He had sent money for support as the child grew, and when he'd visited from time to time, it had been as a stranger, just a soldier on leave to whom the child was taught to politely proffer a hand and call, "Papa." The Basque family who had reared Jacques were good people and it was the only way, for Lucien was a career soldier and went where he was ordered.

Jacques had come to St. Denis only that once, running away from life and its hurts. Did he have a weakness or simply a lack of strength? Whatever it was, Lucien had felt no pride in this nineteen-year-old, so unlike the Anjous, who never turned away from trouble. The young man was polite to his strange father's ways and whims, but he kept to himself and remained unknown, untouchable. He'd been pining for the runaway girl, his unfaithful child-wife, whom Lucien never did meet. When Jacques heard where she was, he'd left without thanks, without warning but with Lucien's money, riding off on that devil's machine like a fiend. Lucien had not known him, so felt nothing when they told him his son had died in a ditch on the side of the road.

No, that was not quite true, he told himself now. He had been relieved when the young man was no longer a burden of guilt: the ties with the Couronne blood were severed forever. He'd celebrated eventually by going back to the Pyrenees to bury his ghosts and his guilt, but he'd discovered another guilt was there and would not be buried. He'd left, and returned, and left again, until one day he felt old and he wanted a past before he had to face an empty future and real death, so he'd brought Pippa back with him and built her a swing in front of his father's cottage.

She was his life and his immortality. If she were ever threatened, he would not hesitate to use his father's ropes.

Chapter Five

The dog, its lean rusty body blending with the golds and scarlets of layered leaves underfoot, paused in a shaft of sunshine, raised its head slightly, and listened. The succession of steady, shuffling footsteps that had been trailing the dog's gentle padding had ceased, so now the animal turned its head to search back along the path.

Ygrec was standing in shadows beneath a sagging arbor that appeared to be held together by little more than wild rose vines. His long arms reached up without effort toward a cluster of faded yellow roses, and when he touched them, he watched the petals drop into his palm. He smiled and lifted his hand, and with a little puff, he blew until the soft avalanche of color floated and dipped to settle at his feet. When his shuffling footsteps commenced once more, the dog moved too, trotting on ahead, its floppy ears brushing the leaves as it nosed a path around a mound of iris roots, through a patch of couche grass, and finally out of the sunshine into a small grove of oleander and beech.

Ygrec followed the dog's trail, but more slowly, for Mademoiselle Larme was young and he didn't try to fool himself that he could keep up with her. The sun that he had longed for all week had appeared with the dawn, its heat increasing with the progress of the day. He could feel the warmth on his shaggy head and across his back through his old jacket. His alert eyes followed the progress of the dog as it circled tree trunks, disappearing and reappearing in the distance.

This morning he had walked the dog along boulevard des Anges in front of the château, but it led to the noisy, smelly highway and the fumes had started Ygrec's cough, and the dog had had to be kept at heel on a lead. After his light noon meal and a little rest, Ygrec had been determined to find a place where the air was clean and the dog could run free, and Pippa had directed him to what she continually referred to as the jungle gardens of the old Couronne estate.

Pippa had been in a quiet mood, mostly preoccupied with her appearance, and Ygrec, as usual, had been amused. She had worn a short skirt for a change, with a yellow scarf tied around her throat, and had stopped frequently to adjust the knot and smooth the ends just so, and, at one stage, had even tied it around the waist of her smock. He'd also seen her standing in front of the big mirror in the hall, lowering her eyelids and pulling bits of her wavy hair, first in front and then behind her ears, and when she'd noticed him watching, she asked without self-consciousness if he thought she should let her hair grow long like Mme. Michelin, and if he felt she looked more "elegant" when she wore long skirts; and he replied that long hair and long skirts looked very elegant indeed, but that she was very attractive just the way she was.

"She gave me this scarf . . . Mme. Michelin did . . . and two

skirts that she didn't need that I made over for myself, and she's
going to teach me to walk properly . . . like a model, you know.
Jean-Louis will be very surprised when he comes home and sees how
elegant I am, don't you agree, M. Ygrec?"

Ygrec had agreed and smiled knowingly to himself, and tried to
remember what it was like to be sixteen and in love for the first time,
and came to the conclusion that at any age it was a kind of blissful
agony.

When he had inquired about the Couronne gardens, mentioning
that he didn't want to venture into private property, Pippa had assured him that the land was up for sale, so lots of people might be
wandering around looking at it.

"If you see anyone near the loge de garde, don't pay any attention
. . . it will just be old Mlle. Ghislaine. Like I told you yesterday, the
other sister is sick and never goes out anymore. Mme. Hugo says she
has a dread disease. They've lived there forever, you understand, except for a while during the wars when they went away to escape from
the Germans, and a couple of times when Mlle. Ghislaine went to a
clinic to get her club foot fixed."

"Didn't they ever live here in the château?"

"Oh, for a time, ages and ages ago. Mlle. Amélie lived here when
she was a little girl, so they say, but then her mother, the first countess, died. I expect that was because the count was cruel to her and
beat her; he was mean and crazy, of course. After that the little girl
was sent to live in the loge with old Mme. Fouschie, although I don't
suppose the nursemaid was all that old then, and the count went
away and traveled. Then after a while, when he was getting old,
about forty, maybe, he married a very young girl, really beautiful she
was, so Mme. Hugo said. M. Hugo's father used to see her sometimes because he helped the cook. She used to walk in the gardens,
the poor young wife, looking very sad and lonely."

Pippa was "acting" the part of the character as usual, her eyes
sad, her hands clutched together, and Ygrec felt that the child indeed
had a talent for the dramatic.

"Well, then, monsieur, the beautiful new wife had a baby, because, you see, the count had to have a son to carry on the name
. . . at least he thought he should. So she had this baby, only it was
another girl and it had a crooked foot and the count was in a terrible
rage and he sent the baby to the loge too so he wouldn't have to look
at it, and then the young countess ran off with another man, and I

don't blame her, do you? And the count really went crazy and made the gardeners plant all those trees and bushes around the loge so he couldn't see the little house. Then, of course, he fell off the balcony, and after a while Mme. Fouschie died, so the sisters just looked after themselves and it was very difficult because they were poor. Their father had spent nearly all the money, so they had to sell off most of the estate, and now they are getting very old and have to sell what's left, all except the little house. I really feel very sad whenever I think about it."

* * *

Mademoiselle Larme had disappeared now, and Ygrec, who was beginning to feel a little winded, decided to wait where he was for her return. Pippa had been right, he began to think. It was a sad place and wild like a jungle, with a feeling of derangement about it. But if you took the time and care to look, he observed, there were still a few indications that the hand of man had held back nature for a time and produced formality and conformity. Over there in the center of a large, almost square patch of brown spiky grass was a circular marble birdbath with a carved rim, now nearly hidden by vines and moss, and beyond was a long straight line of enormous lilac bushes that must have been a neat hedge at some time. Right beneath his feet, beside a few spindly bronze chrysanthemums, he could see bits of ornate pastel stonework that formed a path going nowhere. He had been enjoying the peace and warmth and delighting in the autumn colors, and yet an impression of desolation had begun to touch him, another kind of "fey" feeling. Had nature attempted to bury the errors of man? He thought of Pippa's tales, exaggerated no doubt, but probably based on some truth, and he wondered about the children who had been banished to this place. Was that what nature had frowned upon?

He'd been standing and waiting some time now and was feeling tired and longed to sit down because his feet were beginning to ache in spite of the fact he had worn his most comfortable old gendarme boots. He felt a little chilly too and wished he'd put on a sweater beneath his jacket. He must not arrive home in an exhausted state or Vanessa would forbid him to walk alone again. Mademoiselle Larme had had a fine run and now it was time to turn back.

Ahead of him was the tree line where the dog had disappeared. He walked the short distance, hurrying a little, then whistled and waited.

Finally he called her name, but there was little power in his voice and the effort made him cough. He supposed he had walked too far after a week of inactivity; his chest was beginning to tighten. He stepped farther into the shaded area to try and call the dog's name again, but it was mushy underfoot and his feet sank into the dank compost of leaves, and the air was heavy with decay and all he could do was cough more. His medicine, which he had been warned to keep with him at all times, was back in the apartment on his bedside table, and he cursed himself for his carelessness as the coughing increased and the familiar gasping for air began.

He must not panic; he had learned that much—that apprehension really aggravated the problem of his breathing. The thing to do was get out of this musty area and into clean moving air once again. He tried to take small breaths and moved forward one step at a time, but it was almost like plowing through wet snow, and he felt the leaves that touched his ankles weighing heavily around his feet.

He stumbled once, then once more, until one hand reached out blindly for support. He found something and for a long moment he didn't realize what he was grasping until he felt a sharp stab of pain in the palm of his hand, and he looked and discovered it was a splintering picket fence almost hidden by creepers near an opening in a hedge. He pulled his hand back, closing his eyes, trying to control the dizziness and the coughing.

The voice that penetrated his confusion was soft and sounded young, but with an old-fashioned accent. "Monsieur . . . monsieur, are you all right?"

He opened his eyes and saw the woman. She was small and had something dark swathed around her head. If there were distinctive features they were indistinguishable to Ygrec right then.

"Come this way, monsieur. That's right . . . to the opening," she instructed him, and as he moved, he suddenly felt the dog nudging his thigh and he was filled with a great relief. He lowered his hand to return the reassuring nudge and he felt a stickiness in his palm and another little pain, but it didn't seem to matter now.

His coughing eased a little as he followed the woman through sunlight, but the details of the next few minutes never did become really clear in his mind. He remembered being seated in a chair in the warmth, his long legs stretched out, his feet on a grassy area, the dog's head against his knees, and finally icy-cold water brought to him by the woman. When he realized he was breathing more normally, he moved and managed a smile.

"That is the most delicious water I have ever tasted," he murmured.

"It comes from our own well," she replied. "A little more?"

"No, madame, thank you . . . and I am grateful for your assistance. These wretched lungs of mine . . ." He pressed his chest with long, veined fingers. "I am most grateful and trust I have not inconvenienced you."

"No, monsieur. Your dog liked our water too. It had some from my bucket, then it began to whine and led me to the fence."

"Then I should introduce the two of us." Ygrec patted the dog's head. "Allow me to present Mademoiselle Larme, and I am her devoted servant, M. Maurice Ygrec." He lifted his hand.

The woman barely touched his fingers, then raised her hand to rub at her cheek in an odd manner, almost covering her lips as she replied, "Mlle. Ghislaine Couronne."

He looked up into very pale gray eyes and felt a stirring of curiosity. Her head was covered with a coif, like the wartime Balaclava helmets, only of a finer black material, revealing the kind of face often seen in paintings of the children of ancient royalty, almost expressionless. There were lines and wrinkles of age, yet an innocence, an absence of awareness generally seen in the retarded, but in no way did she act abnormal. Her appearance was odd, he had to admit, yet he had seen the young on the streets of the city in no stranger outfits. She had on an old stained sweater on top of a long shabby skirt, and rubber boots on her feet.

There was a short silence, so to break the bit of tension, Ygrec indicated the garden he was facing. "You obviously have a great love for growing things. This place would be a gratifying sight in midsummer . . . those vines must have been heavy with tomatoes for the stalks are tall and strong." The soil was heavy from the rains, but his eyes admired the straight rows of cultivation, then came to a stop at a long pile of freshly turned earth heaped as if on a fresh grave.

She had been following his gaze. "A new asparagus bed ready for spring," she stated, glancing back at him, and once more he felt the blankness about her. He had raised his hand to illustrate his admiration of her garden, and now she suddenly noticed the coagulating blood on his palm. "Oh, monsieur, you have hurt your hand. It is bleeding."

With that she turned without waiting for him to reply and made her way slowly between rows of winter cabbage toward the house. One foot seemed to favor the inside of the ankle as she limped. So, thought Ygrec, at least one small detail of Pippa's wild tales was correct, the deformed foot.

He was feeling better. He took a deep breath, rubbed his head on the back of the old wicker chair, and glanced around. He was seated in a tiny square of trimmed grass surrounded on three sides by the garden and on the fourth by one wall of a two-story stone house. The whole area was hemmed in by huge trees, mostly evergreens, all meshed together by tangled scrub and the overgrown hedge. The woman had disappeared into a lean-to shed that covered the back door, and near the shed, yellow and bronze dahlias drooped heavily against the corner of gray stone, giving the one touch of color to the otherwise drab atmosphere of the place.

Ghislaine Couronne returned as slowly as she'd left, and once more Ygrec watched her with an unusual curiosity. She brought a clean, but unironed, *serviette,* handing it to him politely but keeping her distance.

While he spread out the cloth, folding it diagonally, and awkwardly wrapped it around the oozing palm, he tried to question her without being too direct. "You have assistance with the heavy garden work, mademoiselle?"

"At times, monsieur."

"And you live here alone?"

"With . . . with my sister. She is an invalid. We have always lived here. Now, monsieur, when you get home you must wash your hand well. Amélie . . . she's my sister, and she always says that one must keep a wound very clean."

Feeling that he had become a nuisance, Ygrec stirred and was anxious to be gone. "Yes, I will attend to it. I thank you and must be on my way. I am visiting friends who live in the château apartments and they will be getting concerned if I am late in returning. They know I am a stranger to the area, and I would feel like a silly schoolboy if they thought I was lost and sent out the gendarmes to look for me." He smiled, hoping for a return of the smile. Instead he was startled by her reaction.

"The gendarmes!" The quick retort and the unmistakable fear in her voice was reflected in her eyes, and once more she pressed her cheek and covered her mouth with a stained hand.

"Oh, that's just my own little joke, mademoiselle. You see the friend I am visiting is Inspector Michelin of the Special Branch in Paris. He was once my pupil, and at one time I was a gendarme in Paris myself, but I have been retired. I am inclined to make little jokes about my confreres."

Ygrec stood up slowly and held out his good hand to make his adieu and was once more surprised by the chill he felt in the fingers she proffered so stiffly. "Again, my deep gratitude," he went on cheerfully, "and I shall return your serviette, if you will permit me to stop by when next I am out walking my dog."

"That will not be necessary, monsieur. It is just old . . . nothing but an old rag. Bonjour, monsieur."

Ygrec, still puzzled by the abrupt dismissal, but wise enough not to press the matter, nodded politely, turned, and, followed closely by Mademoiselle Larme, made his way through the opening in the hedge and did not look back.

He would walk home very slowly, he decided, and would not mention his weak spell to Vanessa or Paul. The little scratch on his hand could be easily explained: that old rose arbor, when he was trying to pick a flower for Vanessa—yes, that would do nicely as a reason. But he also decided that he would, at an opportune time, return the serviette. He was very curious about the enigma of Mlle. Ghislaine Couronne; something had frightened her and he wanted to find out the cause. She had been kind, he owed her a debt of kindness in return, but more than that, she had aroused a peculiar feeling in him.

Chapter Six

Valin had little opportunity to take notice of the warmth or brightness of that Friday. From the time he'd pulled his clothes on in the cold silent bedroom and gone downstairs, the worries and frustrations began to build around him, and by evening he was too impaired to care.

He had slept eventually last night, after finishing off the Pernod—a drunken stupor, Gabrielle would have called it, but Gabrielle hadn't been there to berate him last night, nor in the morning to ignore him.

He had eaten nothing for breakfast, simply standing in the dirty dining room, more depressing than ever in the bright morning light, thinking of last night and gulping down a cup of bitter coffee he had grabbed from Estelle's hand before she'd had the chance to stir in the sugar for him. He'd gone out the back door followed by Estelle's rasping accusation ". . . but maman will cry all morning if you don't kiss her good-by . . . Valin . . . Valin!"

The Peugeot had coughed and started only after three attempts, and when he'd parked it in the lane adjoining the offices of Joddard et Fils, he slammed the brake with his foot, holding the pedal to the floor long after the motor had stopped and until his ankle ached with the strain, and he sat there exhausted, wondering how he would get through the day. He'd felt a burning in his stomach and the beginning of a headache and, with it, the beginning of an anger at the injustice of it all. It wasn't fair that he should have to shoulder all the responsibilities alone—maman, Estelle, and now Gabrielle too. She was his wife, and it was her duty to help him when he was worried and not well. Where was she? Where could she have gone? She didn't have any money; wasn't she always at him for money like the others? Well, he wouldn't think of it anymore. He'd get busy with the papers for the Couronne property, and when she came home, which of course she would after she was over the little temper tantrum, he'd present her with the accomplished fact of his success.

Valin usually spent the mornings in the back room doing the accounts for M. Joddard. If the two other agents were absent from the establishment, he was expected to attend the front office as well, and generally he looked forward to the change from piles of papers and percentages. Today, however, M. Joddard himself was present, busy on the phone in the semiprivacy of the glassed-in cubicle that housed his big desk and leather chair, so Valin remained out of sight in the windowless rear office, and when he was sure he wasn't being observed, he would pull the bottle from his drawer and moisten his lips and dry throat and relieve the gnawing in his stomach.

The morning dragged, and Valin tried to concentrate, his head bent over the ledgers, frequently adjusting his glasses over the bridge of his nose and checking his wrist watch, wondering if it would ever be noon. Gabrielle might be home by then, and also he'd need a refill for his bottle. But M. Dubois, the son-in-law of M. Joddard, who arrived about midmorning, left with a client shortly afterward, and M. Costello, the energetic young agent, had not come in at all, and promptly at twelve o'clock M. Joddard, who never failed to take a full two hours for his midday meal, summoned Valin to his office.

"I have a business luncheon, M. Chamillion, so you will, of

course, remain here until M. Costello returns," he stated as he settled
a new pearl-gray hat on his bony forehead and smoothed his precisely trimmed sideburns. "He is out showing some property near Le
Bourget to M. Roget Matieu."

Valin was stunned. "But I understood that M. Matieu had decided
to consider the Couronne property. I have started to draw up the
papers. I don't understand . . ." The words tumbled out in a near
stutter.

M. Joddard fastened the buttons of his gray coat and brushed absently at a speck of lint on the immaculate lapel. "Oh, I'm sure
someone will be interested in the Couronne land sooner or later, but
I felt it was not suitable for the development that M. Matieu had in
mind."

"But I was given assurance that . . ."

"Not now, M. Chamillion. I do not wish to be late for my luncheon." With that, M. Joddard turned and Valin was left with the feeling that he was as insignificant as the spot of lint on the collar of the
coat.

A nausea welled up in Valin. He returned to the back room and
sat staring blindly at the clutter of papers on the desk, and when he
heard the telephone, he didn't bother to move.

The next hour was a kind of unmoving agony, but the second time
the phone rang he managed to pick it up and mumble, "Joddard et
Fils." It was M. Dubois, who announced that he would be in by six
o'clock to lock up, as M. Joddard was involved in important business
and would not be returning to the office for the rest of the day.

The Épicerie Minette was just around the corner from where Valin's car was parked. He didn't bother putting on his coat or latching
the office door. He demanded a bottle of Pernod and a slice of
Münster cheese from the startled old proprietor, ordered him to be
quick about it, grabbed his change, and stalked out.

He didn't know what time it was when the jubilant M. Costello returned, but the sun had dropped behind the buildings across the
street and the Pernod bottle was almost empty. M. Matieu had been
pleased with Le Bourget property and had made out a check for
the initial payment. Valin had a blinding headache. He lifted his
wrinkled raincoat from the peg on the wall, and muttering something
about feeling ill, hurried to his car, leaving the open liquor bottle sitting on his desk. M. Costello watched the staggering departure,

picked up the bottle, shook it gently then shook his head and carried the bottle into M. Joddard's office.

Valin found that he was grasping the steering wheel of the car with a tension that was whitening his knuckles. He was almost sobbing with anger. He was exhausted, thirsty, his head was pounding, and he was caught up in the heavy noisy boulevard traffic. He couldn't stand much more.

He turned right at the first opportunity, driving at a near crawl along a narrow cobbled road that ran between old stone tenement buildings like a tunnel; he wasn't sure where he was and he didn't care. He wanted to stop to wipe his glasses because he wasn't seeing very well but kept bumping along until he emerged into twilight once more and he finally realized he was at the back of the market square. It was quiet and empty, although the few little shops and grubby houses were not yet shuttered for the night. The towers of the basilica were straight ahead, silhouetted in a blinding pink sky, and beyond the edifice were the great trees that guarded the ancient cemetery.

He stopped the car against the curb at the far corner beneath a half-stripped tree and dropped his head back on the seat. Finally he managed to open the door to slide out and make his way in the direction of the church. The town square was as familiar to him as his own street; ahead around the corner was the Hôtel de Ville with its arched entrances and clock tower, but he didn't bother glancing up for the time. He cut across the square, past a triangular bed of dilapidated flowers that formed a traffic divider, until he approached the Cafe Khedive on the corner opposite the clock tower. The door stood open, he entered, and sat down at the first empty table. Only then did he remove his glasses to wipe them and brush the moisture from his forehead.

The waiter, wearing a soiled pink shirt and a once-white apron, was a bearded young man with Arabic features. Valin ordered an arak. The front of the cafe near the cash register where cigarettes and magazines were stacked was still in dim light, but the rest of the long room was in deepening shadows. There were only a few other customers; near the door was an Algerian rug peddler in a filthy striped burnoose and wearing thickly lensed glasses, his wares rolled up at his feet, and in the far corner were a couple deeply engrossed in each other. The rest appeared to be local workmen.

Valin settled forward in his chair, his elbows on the bare table top, his forehead resting loosely on clasped fists. He heard the glass being placed on the table in front of him, and a woman's voice and her laugh and he stirred. Where was Gabrielle? She might be home. He gulped down the milky drink, and just as he was about to make the effort to move he heard another voice, a familiar one.

"Bonjour, M. Chamillion. How fortunate to find you here."

Valin looked up trying to clear his vision, and out of his confusion that was quickly becoming apprehension, he managed only an inane reply, "Ah, Corporal Anjou, and what are you doing here at this hour?"

"I came for cigarettes, monsieur. I stopped by Joddard et Fils earlier, to be told you had left for home due to an illness. I trust you are feeling better now?" The big man pulled out a chair, sat down, removed his beret and motioned to the waiter. "A small drink, M. Chamillion? Perhaps an arak? I shall have a brandy, having just finished my meal. There's nothing like a quiet drink to cure an illness, wouldn't you agree?"

*   *   *

Ygrec held his glass up to Vanessa. "A small refill of that excellent Rémy Martin, if you please, chérie. It has been known . . . since early times, that cognac has remarkable healing powers, and you do want this hand of mine to heal quickly, don't you!" He smiled, glancing over at Michelin.

"Don't look to me for sympathy, old man." Michelin, looking not in the least like a detective, in scruffy pants and a turtleneck sweater, was lecturing Ygrec at the dining-room table. "You should know better than to wander around trying to pick roses in that jungle garden . . . if that's what you were doing."

Ygrec smiled again and shrugged. He was enjoying himself. His right hand, having been cleansed, disinfected, and tenderly bandaged by Vanessa, now rested on the bright tablecloth, while his left hand toyed with the bowl of a brandy snifter. There were yellow candles glowing in front of him and a centerpiece of autumn flowers, but best of all there was Vanessa in a white, long-sleeved dress leaning across from him, trying to look disapproving but instead looking altogether beautiful.

"Will you stop treating me like a murder suspect, *garçon,* and leave me to digest my meal in peace," retorted Ygrec, in mock testiness. "You're out of uniform, so stop trying to act like a *'flic.'* Besides, I believe you're just jealous because I thought of bringing your wife flowers and you didn't. You could say I was sorely wounded while performing an act of gallantry."

"Would you just listen to him!" Michelin raised his eyebrows to his wife, then turned back to Ygrec. "You were up to something this afternoon and you're more senile than you realize if you think you can fool me . . . after all, you taught me all the tricks. Vanessa removed a long, dirty splinter of wood from your hand. Now, since when did rosebushes produce wood splinters instead of thorns?"

"Oh, *pic, pic, pic!*" Ygrec peered into his glass rather sadly. "Why they ever promoted you to Inspector, I'll never know."

Vanessa began to laugh as she reached for the decanter and splashed a little brandy into Ygrec's glass. "You two! The first time all week we've all been able to sit down to a civilized meal and it ends up in an interrogation."

Michelin was laughing too. His appearance was in complete contrast to the untidy Ygrec; not quite as tall as the old gendarme, he was heavier, with clean-cut features and neat dark hair. He reached over, covering Vanessa's hand with his own. "Very well, we'll put an end to the interrogation after one last question: Mme. Michelin, did you or did you not remove a big ugly splinter of ancient wood from the right hand of the accused . . . whose credibility has long been in doubt?"

Ygrec spoke up before Vanessa could answer. "Very well yourself, garçon, I will save the beautiful witness the necessity of perjuring herself. She did. Now shall we get on with this gala dinner. I, for one, would like a little of that Brie, or perhaps a small taste of Camembert." He reached for the cheese.

"You're evading the issue. You admit covering something up."

"I admit nothing. I went for a walk with Mademoiselle Larme. We had a most enjoyable time. I communed with nature and I met a most unusual lady called Mlle. Ghislaine Couronne, whom you already have admitted is well known in these parts. I was a little late returning because it was such a delightful day. Now that is all. . . ." Ygrec lifted his glass, savored it, took a small sip, raised his wiry eyebrows, and bowed formally to Michelin. Then absently he lifted his bandaged hand to rub at the hairline of his neck. As he winced, he stopped, realizing what he had done, and when he caught Michelin's glance he shrugged, grinning guiltily.

"So that is all?" Michelin repeated. "Then why are you rubbing your neck? You only do that when you're puzzled and have one of your funny feelings."

"Oh no!" Vanessa groaned dramatically. "I've heard about your funny 'fey' feelings, you wicked old man. It's silly to believe in such nonsense, but all the same I think I'll take the phone off the hook. Paul has three days off and I intend to enjoy every minute of this weekend, and I don't want him being called away by some crisis or other."

It was Ygrec's turn to touch her hand reassuringly. "I shouldn't worry, chérie. I admit I have been a little preoccupied, but I expect it's just because of all the exaggerated tales about this château and the Couronne family that Pippa has been stuffing into my head all week . . . bodies lying on the terrace and probably ghosts in the vaults below." He began to chuckle again. "What a perfect excuse for reaching for the cognac . . . the ghosts are moving my arm!"

There was general laughter before Ygrec went on. "Seriously, I believe that Pippa has enjoyed a captive audience in me while we've been alone here is the afternoons, but I must say that my curiosity has been aroused. What exactly did happen around here in the dim and distant past, so to speak. And what about the two old ladies in the loge de garde?"

"I can't help you, old man," Michelin replied. "I deal with facts and the present, and, at the moment, drug traffickers and their associated crimes are keeping me busy. This was the old Couronne family château at one time and that's all I can tell you. Sorry about your ghosts, old man. Now you will have to look for another excuse to empty the brandy bottle."

"Oh, I'll think of something." Ygrec's eyes twinkled as he raised his glass again.

Vanessa stood up. "Well, I'm still going to take the phone off the hook, and I'll make more coffee. The last was a bit bitter, wasn't it? I keep forgetting and it boils. It really is humiliating that Pippa can make better coffee than I can! Isn't she the oddest little thing you've ever met? So dramatic . . . but remarkably bright." Vanessa kept talking as she disappeared from the room. "I do hope her grandfather can manage to send her off somewhere for more education. He's ambitious for her, I know. He's quite a remarkable man himself . . . really respected in the town. He was decorated by de Gaulle in person. Oh . . . there you are, Mademoiselle Larme! You know you shouldn't be here in the kitchen. Very well, then, just a small bit of ham. . . ." Her voice finally faded.

The old man and the young man grinned at each other across the table.

"She's incredible," commented Ygrec. "You don't deserve her."

"I keep telling myself that," laughed Michelin, pushing back his chair. "I'll go keep an eye on that coffee, otherwise it probably won't be fit to drink . . . and you'd better whistle for that dog, old man, before Vanessa stuffs her full of ham."

"If you say so, Inspector." Ygrec bowed in mock humility, then pursed his lips, but at the same moment the whistle was magnified by the shrill ringing of the telephone.

Vanessa, followed by the dog, materialized in the doorway. "Don't answer it," she pleaded, but Michelin was already moving down the hall. She dropped to her knees to hug the dog, muttering, "There goes our evening."

"I won't be long," Michelin tried to explain when he returned, buttoning up his coat. "I'll be back in less than an hour. I don't have to go into Paris. Something has happened in a nearby cafe where we have one of our men undercover, and I have to talk to him, that's all."

Vanessa didn't move. She just hid her face in the dog's neck and murmured, "I knew it . . . I just knew it! Why didn't I marry that dull lawyer my mother liked so much . . . why didn't I stay single . . . why don't I move out and have a wild affair with Jules Matieu at the office in Paris!"

The door closed, and after a moment she lifted her head and peered at Ygrec.

"Would you like me to help you pack your bags, chérie?" the old gendarme asked.

Her lips began to twitch, "Oh, dear old man, what would I do without you?" She smoothed back her hair and held up one white-draped arm and he helped her up. "Will you stay here forever, you and Mademoiselle Larme?"

"Ah, don't tempt me. But for now, don't you think we should do something about that coffee? I think I smell it boiling over."

"Well, let's just throw it out, pot and all, and have a little more cognac." She tossed her head and started to laugh, and he joined her.

"I knew I'd find another reason for a drink," he said. "Who needs the Couronne ghosts!"

Chapter Seven

There were varied versions of the fight that took place in the Cafe Khedive that Friday evening, but because it was only a minor incident, the details didn't seem to matter. The local gendarmerie had not been notified, which was understandable—after all, what was unusual about a jealous husband and a wayward wife? Besides, the proprietor of the cafe not only did not welcome the presence of the law but, on occasion, had gone to expensive lengths to smooth over more serious problems which took place on the premises from time to time.

By midmorning Saturday the St. Denis market was bright and buzzing with jostling shoppers, who, if they had heard about the trouble the night before in the nearby cafe, were too busy or too preoccupied to give it any thought.

Michelin, who enjoyed the anonymity of market-place crowds, was content to follow Vanessa past the open stalls of smelly fish and cheeses, vegetables and poultry, and tables covered with potted plants and fresh flowers, but Ygrec was finding the confusion tiring. Vanessa had noticed his fatigue, so suggested tactfully that it would be a good idea for him to visit the basilica. "It's time you soaked up some culture, old man. It's just around the corner and you can rest your feet while I finish stuffing my basket with things I don't need."

"An excellent idea," Ygrec decided. "Perhaps we could meet somewhere for a little apéritif. I noticed a place opposite the Hôtel de Ville called the Cafe Khedive. It doesn't look exactly like Maxim's, but it should do nicely."

"No!" Michelin's unexpected reply was quick and positive, and Ygrec looked over at him rather curiously.

Then the two men's eyes met, and Ygrec, knowing his friend and recognizing a seriousness, went on lightly. "What's the matter, garçon, are you afraid it might be frequented by *les filles de joie,* and I might be tempted . . . even though it's only noon?"

"Sounds interesting," Vanessa laughed, shoving her sunglasses up over her bright hair and twirling her shopping basket. "I might get propositioned too. Let's go!"

Michelin, back to normal and smiling again, shook his head. "No fear . . . you're too ugly. Now behave yourself." Then he turned to

Ygrec. "Go along, old man, and light a candle in the nave for me, to give me strength to keep my wife under control."

"That will take two candles at least," Ygrec quipped. "Very well, I'll see you back at the car in about an hour." He turned and threaded his way slowly past the booths, stopping long enough to buy a fat apple from a fat vendor, then headed down a narrow, cobbled side street.

He took his time, savoring the sunshine, the clear air, and the juicy apple. When he reached the corner intersected by the square, he paused to wipe his mouth with his hand and it was then he heard the young voice.

"Oh, M. Ygrec . . . monsieur!" Pippa was crossing diagonally from the direction of the Église and had broken into a gentle trot. Her dark hair bounced over her forehead, and her small young body, beneath a striped blouse and rather wrinkled long red skirt, bounced too, and the old gendarme smiled and waved. She had the yellow scarf tied around her throat, he noticed, and was carrying an empty string bag in one hand and a straw purse in the other, and she returned his wave with both outstretched arms and beamed at him.

"Bonjour, mademoiselle. You are looking elegant today. Are you going to the market?"

"Oh, yes, monsieur. Gran'papa is going to help me to make soupe au pisto. You take bean stock and add leeks and garlic and tomatoes and cheese and lots of other things, and it is delicious. Did I tell you that my gran'papa is a gourmet cook? If you wish, I'll make you some on Monday."

She was quite breathless, but before Ygrec could reply she went on. "Gran'papa usually likes to come to the market too, but he had a traumatic experience last night so is going to spend a quiet day. He didn't mention it to me, you understand, in case I might worry, I expect, but he could have been injured! Still he's very big and strong and knows how to protect himself . . . and other people too. Did you hear about the fight in the Cafe Khedive, M. Ygrec . . . that cafe . . . right over there. . . ." She waved her string bag and looked over the road.

"No," Ygrec replied, not having to pretend interest. He was aware that he always welcomed any little excitement, especially these days.

"I thought you might have heard, Inspector Michelin being a gendarme, you know, although Mme. Hugo said they didn't have to call the gendarmes because Gran'papa just walked over and stopped the fight and picked up that foolish M. Chamillion like a sack of grain and carried him to safety . . . and there were broken bottles flying everywhere, and tables knocked over . . . and one man, a poor old Algerian rug vendor, even got hit in the face by a bottle and was bleeding. Wasn't it fortunate that Gran'papa didn't get hit?"

"Indeed . . . yes indeed." Ygrec was becoming especially interested in Pippa's recitation now, as he remembered the brief conversation he'd had with Michelin last night. "It was nothing important," Michelin had stated briefly when he'd got home. "One of our officers happened to be in a cafe when a fight started and our man was in the line of fire from a flying bottle. That's all."

"That's all? Then why were you called out?" Ygrec had inquired, but Vanessa had come into the room just then, so Michelin had changed the subject.

Ygrec's attention returned to Pippa. "Nobody else was hurt . . . only the Algerian, you say?"

"That's what Mme. Hugo told me. She wasn't there, of course, but M. Hugo heard it from M. Fouschie, the mortician. He always knows about these things . . . Mme. Hugo says he's just hoping for business . . . but he drinks too, you understand."

Ygrec started to chuckle.

"It could have been serious though," Pippa went on, the dramatic tone and gestures becoming more pronounced. "M. Chamillion tried to strangle his wife because she came into the cafe with another man, and if he hadn't been so drunk he might have succeeded. That's why the other man hit M. Chamillion and then smashed a bottle and there was pushing and shoving and that's how the fight started. Mme. Hugo thinks it's a pity in a way that Gran'papa stopped the fight because the wife, Gabrielle Chamillion . . . that's her name, Gabrielle . . . isn't that a pretty name for a bad woman? Well, anyway, she's just a *'braie poule'* and it's been very hard on M. Chamillion's poor old sick mother having a braie poule under her roof. The family used to be very respectable. It's quite a tragedy, don't you think, M. Ygrec?"

Ygrec realized his feet were getting very tired. It was all very well listening to Pippa's detailed monologues while he sat comfortably in a chair in the apartment, but standing here on the street was another matter. "Well, it is best to look on the bright side. At least nobody ended up in M. Fouschie's mortuary. Now, don't you think you should get on to the market before all the fresh vegetables are picked over? Your grandpère will need some good nourishing soup, particularly after having survived such a 'traumatic experience.' And I must be on my way too. I am going to visit the basilica to absorb some culture."

"Oh, you're quite right, monsieur." Pippa sighed happily. "It's always such a pleasure talking to you. You are a very interesting person. I've told Mme. Hugo all about you and she feels you must be very cultured already."

"Why thank you, mademoiselle, and au revoir."

She beamed up at him once more, then was gone as suddenly as she'd appeared.

Ygrec breathed a sigh of relief, resolved that he would have a little fun with Michelin and the story of the cafe brawl, and proceeded gently on his way.

*   *   *

The curious young woman came to see Ghislaine about midmorning. She said she was interested in the garden property, but Ghislaine was more interested in the pretty clothes the stranger was wearing, so that was all she mentioned to Lucien about the visit.

Ghislaine had wakened early. The cot in the kitchen was narrow and the mattress sagged, and her shoulders ached when she moved. At first she couldn't decide what day it was—somehow it felt like Sunday—but Lucien had promised to bring her a fresh chicken from the market, so it must be Saturday. She'd lain quietly for a time trying to remember other things as well. Finally after she'd rubbed at the stiffness in her fingers she got up in the chilly dimness, pulled the top quilt off the bed and, wrapping it around her shoulders to cover the skimpy gray flannel nightdress, limped to the near window.

The shutters opened easily. The sun had not quite risen over the hedge, so the garden was in shadow. The asparagus bed was a long smooth mound; Lucien had raked it. She stood, a little stooping gray figure, her tangled hair the color of her nightdress, thinking of little except the sight of the freshly turned soil, then the sight of the soil in summer when the sun baked it. She wasn't sure when she realized once again that Amélie wasn't here anymore, nor would she be here at planting time in the spring, but she said half aloud, as if experimenting, "It's nice that Lucien raked the asparagus bed, isn't it?"
. . . then louder, "It's better since Lucien came home and oiled the hinges and fixed the shutters, isn't it? And he's going to patch the

roof too." There was no reply—no interruptions, no sermons, no banishment. Amélie really was gone and with her, the guilt; yet the relief was something Ghislaine could not quite accept without experimenting.

The floor was icy beneath her bare feet, but she smiled mischievously as if she had an audience. "My feet are cold," she announced to the silence, "and I think I shall go back to bed." She forgot her aching shoulders and dragged the quilt behind her, feeling like a queen carrying a train, then she curled up with her knees close against her chest, her feet tucked beneath the nightgown, and for a time she was not old anymore.

Later she had her tea and bread in the garden, sitting in Amélie's chair. Out of habit she wore the same heavy shapeless skirt, matted sweater, and coat, the stained brimmed hat in place over her coif. After a time when the garden lay in full sunlight, she took off the hat and was loosening her coat when the woman emerged from the hedge path.

At first Ghislaine was so taken by the visitor's appearance that she forgot her fear and shyness. She was a small woman and looked very young until she drew nearer, then the sun revealed lines fanning out from the sides of her red mouth and beneath her shadowed eyes. Still, she was youthful enough to make Ghislaine envious. Shiny dark hair was tied back with a pink splashed scarf, her dress was a darker pink, and she carried a fluffy woollen shawl. Her arms were bare and brown, and a black purse hung by a wide strap from one shoulder.

"Bonjour, Mlle. Couronne," she said. "I hope I am not disturbing you. I have been looking at the garden property, which I understand is for sale . . . not for myself, of course, but for an acquaintance."

"Of course," Ghislaine repeated in surprise. "But we are not selling the house . . . this house or this garden. We would never sell our house. Did M. Joddard send you?"

"One of M. Joddard's agents."

Ghislaine was staring at the woman's shoes. They were of a woven straw fabric with built-up soles and high heels. "You will ruin your pretty shoes and tear your stockings, walking in the old gardens," she pointed out seriously. "You had better go back by the old road."

"You are Mlle. Couronne, are you not?" the woman went on, obviously observing the rubber boots, the old clothes, and the coif.

Ghislaine began to feel uncomfortable. She lifted her hat, settling it in place on top of the coif to shade her features, then slid her fingers down against one cheek. "Oh, yes, I am Mlle. Ghislaine Couronne. My sister is sick. If you want to know about the property, you should see Corporal Anjou in the cottage near the basilica. He looks after everything for us." She was looking at the dress again. "How many buttons are on your dress?" she went on after a little pause, her voice rather wistful.

The woman was staring at her curiously, then she smiled oddly, almost without humor. "I don't know. I have never bothered to count. I expect your property is worth a great deal of money, mademoiselle. Has anyone else come to look at it?"

"Oh, yes . . . yes. I think it has been sold, but you will have to talk to Corporal Anjou. My sister is an invalid. We don't think about business. If you go along that pathway by the side of the house, you will come to the old road. It isn't far." She was getting a worried feeling that she had talked too much. She wanted the woman to go.

"Merci, mademoiselle. Bonjour." The visitor nodded politely, but not heeding the advice about ruining her shoes, turned, and balancing herself gracefully on the high heels, disappeared through the hedge opening.

Ghislaine wondered if she had dreamed it all, but even with her eyes closed, she could see the pink dress and the dark hair. She removed her hat again, to lean back on the chair and let the sun warm the small oval of her exposed aged skin. She didn't hear Lucien until he was beside her, then she opened her eyes, squinting against the dazzling brightness.

"You are well today, Ghislaine?"

"Of course I am well, Lucien. I had a lady here to look at the property . . . not exactly a lady, but she had a pretty pink dress and blue shawl and lovely shoes made of straw."

Lucien didn't seem surprised. "Did she tell you her name?"

"I forgot to ask her, but it doesn't really matter because you told me that the land was sold anyway. She had nice dark hair too, with not a sign of gray in it. I can hardly remember when my hair was dark."

"There may be a small delay in the sale, Ghislaine, but I will see to it." He was watching her without being obvious and tried to keep his tone unconcerned.

"That's good, because earlier while I was sitting here I was thinking about things and I have decided I will not plant any vegetables in the spring. Flowers would be nicer to look at, so I shall put in all kinds of flowers everywhere, even in the asparagus bed, and I shall buy my vegetables from the market. When the land is sold, there will be plenty of money. I never did like weeding vegetables. . . . It made my fingers ache . . . but I won't mind weeding flowers." She gestured with her hands, the joints enlarged, the fingernails split and stubby.

"Flowers should grow well here," was all he said. "In the spring I can bring you seeds and young plants from the market. I am going there now. Do you need anything more than the chicken?"

"Yes, sugar . . . I think. I couldn't find any sugar for my tea this morning . . . nor yesterday either. I thought there was some, but I forgot where I put it. I might have used it all up when I preserved the plums, but it's so hard to remember all these things. I hope I did the jam right this year . . . Amélie always told me what to do, but this time she kept taking pills and falling asleep. I don't suppose it's important though. If the jam goes bad, I will just throw it all out and I will buy what I need from the town. Would you like a cup of tea, Lucien, and some plum preserves?"

He shook his head. "I must go. I will come back later with your food."

"Did you see the woman in the pink dress, Lucien? She left just before you came and went back through the gardens."

He didn't seem to hear her as he had already turned to leave. He never stays, she thought. Amélie isn't here to say mean things, but still he never stays. She wondered why he had been looking at her so strangely. She smoothed the hat where it lay in her lap, then for the first time in a very long while she noticed her hands, resting on her lap in the sunshine. The visitor in pink had had soft white hands with rose-tipped fingernails. She noticed her ugly green skirt, as well, and finally the black boots on her feet, and suddenly she made up her mind.

The few remaining souvenirs of her disordered life were shut up inside stacked trunks and boxes in one of the small upstairs rooms. She'd been too young, she'd often been told, to remember Mme. Fouschie packing the boxes and taking her and Amélie into a besieged Paris during the first war, although she remembered being taken to the château to see her father in his coffin a few months before the evacuation. Still, those years were mostly blanks in her mind, and as the enemy soldiers had not reached St. Denis or Paris, afterward life had gone on as usual. There had been a few periods in the convents, but Ghislaine, unable or unwilling to learn from prescribed books, had come back with little but some black dresses with stiff white collars and the ability to pray for forgiveness for sins she did not understand or realize that she had committed.

The second time the Germans had invaded, it had been Lucien who had come to take them to safety, and they had not been given time to pack more than they could carry. Ghislaine remembered those days because it had meant an excitement and a freedom she had never known before. Amélie's anger and fears, and even tears the night they had left, had been little more than puzzling to Ghislaine, to whom a spoon was useful simply for eating, and the fact that it was one of a set of crested silver spoons and should be carried with other such valuables to safety was, she felt, rather silly. Of course, as Amélie frequently pointed out, Ghislaine's mother had left her daughter a heritage of little but disgrace and a crooked foot—certainly no family heirlooms.

When the war ended, they returned to the loge alone, and it had been Ghislaine's period of tears and fear, and of desperation, and the memories of the following years were allowed to overlap into a jumble of confusions, so they would never need to be acknowledged; and her mind, like the boxes and trunks, remained closed.

Her own bedroom at the top of the landing was as austere as a nun's cell—in actuality it had purposely been set up as such in an attempt to teach her to avoid the worldly temptations of the flesh. She hated the room because it contained her anger. She walked past it now and into Amélie's bedroom that looked out onto the back garden. It was a horrid room too, she decided, and she would never sleep in it. She drew back the curtains and opened the windows so that some of the freshness of the bright day entered, although the roof overhang provided a continuous shade.

She took off her coat and draped it on the carved post of the stripped bed, then slowly opened the doors of the wardrobe. The hangers were layered with what remained of Amélie's clothing, all from another era, but the five best dresses hung singly at the far end. Ghislaine considered the soft blue wool with long pleats. She touched it, then let her fingers brush the skirt of the gray silk and the black crepe de chine next to it. She hesitated. No—the wine velvet had always been the favorite. She slid it from the hanger.

As she undressed, she moved almost dreamily, dropping her old clothing on the cedar chest at the foot of the bed. Her cotton petticoat on top of her soiled bodice was mended beneath the arms and frayed along the bottom, but she took little notice of the undergarments, instead frowning at the ugly boots on her feet. She would have to change them later because her one pair of hand-made shoes were in her hateful room and she didn't want to spoil the day by going in there.

She pulled off the coif, lifting it over the top of her head as she did each night in the darkness, then she struggled into the dress, stepping into it from the bottom then pulling it up until her arms and shoulders were covered. It opened from the high lace-edged neck to well below the waist and the task of pushing the tiny covered buttons through the loops was painstaking. "Seven . . . eight . . ." She counted the buttons aloud until she reached the waistline, when she stopped to sink on the edge of the bed and rest her fingers before continuing the fastening. When she reached the neckline, she found she had two loops too few, and she had a moment when she wanted to cry, but she brushed at her eyes and straightened her tired back, then concentrated on the pale lace-frilled cuffs, smoothing them and noticing with pleasure that they partially covered her worn hands.

She stood again. Once the rich fabric had fitted snugly over other fleshy breasts and rounded hips; now it hung loosely from her thin shoulders, but again she didn't care. The skirt was long and full and felt soothing to touch.

Amélie's dressing table had three mirrors, the two small ones winged at an angle on either side of the oval center, so that when Ghislaine turned, she couldn't escape the multiple reflections staring back at her. She had never been allowed the vanity of a mirror in her own room since she was a girl. She knew her hair was long and gray—she'd seen that much each time she'd washed it—but she had long ago taken no notice of it. She stared; the three strangers stared back, then all three moved as she examined the sides of her faded neck and the thin layered wrinkles like parchment covering her cheeks. Her hair was pure white at the temples, darkening to a tangled gray mass flattened on top of her head. She pulled out the two big hairpins and some of the strands drooped over her high forehead.

She knew her eyes were gray but now they seemed colorless and were underlined with pockets, but when she pushed her hair back and looped it over her temples, her eyes looked darker, and the rich color of the dress gave a tint to her cheeks.

She picked up Amélie's silver-handled brush and started stroking it down over the crown of her head, then back to the nape of her neck. Even when her arm began to ache she kept brushing until all the strands were smooth.

"I'm not ugly," she whispered at last to the three women in front of her. "Amélie was prettier at first, but she wasn't when she was dead. I'm alive, and I'm not ugly."

She put down the brush and, parting her hair down the middle with her fingers, divided one side in three sections and began to braid it. "Over . . . and . . . under . . . and over . . ." she said aloud, until the voice interrupted her in her mind. "If you can't tie your boot laces, at least try to learn to braid your hair!"

"Go away," Ghislaine retorted. "I don't need you, Amélie. I might even cut my hair if I want to and I'll be pretty and Lucien will notice me and come and stay to look after me." But some unease in the eyes of the three mirror faces made her stop and glance away, while her hand moved, as if on its own volition, to make the sign of the cross.

Chapter Eight

The huge doorways to the basilica were a greenish-bronze, and Ygrec gazed up at the representation of the Last Judgment on the spandrel of the arch, then opened the center door and went inside. He had never been one to attend religious services, but he automatically crossed himself, feeling not so much a spiritual relief as a physical one; he was thankful to find a peaceful place to sit down for a few minutes because he was warm and weary. As he passed the rack of stubby, flickering candles, he grinned to himself and wondered irreverently if he should really light one for Michelin, but thought better of it. He peered at a little bronze plaque noting that Joan of Arc, wounded before Paris, came to the church to offer her arms to St. Denis, and he wondered, again irreverently, if her feet had been as tired as his were now, and then decided that as she usually rode a horse, it was probably another part of her anatomy that was tired, and he grinned again as he settled in a back pew.

Gradually he felt as if he were in another world. The magnificent church was bright and quite deserted. Ahead, the long aisles were lined with funereal statues, and the stained-glass windows were beautiful, especially a lower one ahead, a blue field covered with gold fleur de lis. He was reminded of his wartime years when the symbol meant so much to him and to all his compatriots. He closed his eyes against the radiance, dreaming a little, and realized that if he let himself he could easily doze off. He would really feel foolish if he was late meeting Michelin and Vanessa with the excuse that he had fallen asleep in church, so after a while he forced himself to move, stand up, and turn round.

He wasn't surprsied to see the center door opening, for this was, after all, a tourist attraction as well as a place of worship, yet he was somewhat surprised at the size of the man who entered. Just as the door closed, a slice of daylight followed by instant shadows of the nave caught the man's profile, and Ygrec, not quite out of his dreams of the past, was stirred by a recollection.

The only other person Ygrec had ever seen to compare with this heavy dark figure, had been known as *le Loup Noir,* a member of the wartime resistance movement, who for a time, had traveled back and forth across the Pyrenees helping patriots and escapees over the border into Spain and sometimes indirectly to North Africa where the Free French were active. Ygrec had met the man only once, and that for a period between one night and a new dawn. He had sat with the group—le Loup Noir, two guides, and two couriers, if he remembered correctly—around a small open fire, high on a pass near Andorra. It had been a warm night, the stars very low, and, in spite of thick black hair and a heavy beard, the profile of their leader had stood out clearly. Because of his leathery features, Ygrec had placed him as a Basque.

Now the stranger turned toward the candles, pulling off his beret before lifting his hand to genuflect. His hair was steely gray, he was wearing dark pants and a heavy cotton jacket with huge pockets, and looked like an ordinary laborer, but the feelings were so certain in Ygrec's mind that the words seemed to be uttered without his bidding. "Le Loup Noir," he breathed.

The thick shoulders tensed, then the body turned. The tanned face was freshly shaven, but the nose and narrow face were the same, with surprisingly few added lines. He must be about my age, Ygrec reasoned quickly, and yet he looks as if time has passed him by.

The big man was staring at Ygrec, no sign of recognition on his face, and yet his body had taken on a guarded stance.

Ygrec, his voice soft, repeated the name. "Le Loup Noir. It was July, was it not . . . the fourteenth? We celebrated with wine,

Macon, I believe . . . or was it Volnay? It was an unusually good
wine to be found in the caves of the Pyrenees."

"Macon . . . always for a celebration," the man answered,
wariness changing to curiosity.

"Mont Louis?" Ygrec prompted.

There was a moment's thoughtful hesitation, followed by a dawn-
ing movement of a smile. "Yes . . . yes, of course. Bastille Day in
the mountains. The guides were François and Xavier. I remember
now, for it was the last trip Xavier ever made. He was one of the
faithful who gave his life. But you, monsieur . . . I can see your face
in the firelight, yet your name has slipped my memory."

"Ygrec, simply Ygrec. I never remained in one place long enough
to need another name."

They stepped toward each other, and as the memories grew, both
right hands were proffered, and the big man, noticing the bandage on
Ygrec's palm, touched it gently with his own fingers. "Ygrec," he
said. "The name does sound familiar."

They had been speaking in undertones and now that the recognition was complete, they seemed to realize where they were and the
fact that the setting was too confining for the pleasure that had flared
up between them, so of one mind they pushed the great door open
and stepped out, blinking into the sun.

Ygrec threw back his shaggy head and smiled. "You did not remember my name, but I never did know yours, not your true name."

"Anjou . . . Lucien Anjou, known to the populace hereabout as
the Old Corporal."

"Then you must be . . . you are, Pippa's gran'papa!"

"And you must be the famous gendarme with the dog who she has
been telling me about. You are visiting Inspector Michelin?"

"Indeed, indeed." Ygrec's pleasure was building as he accompanied the corporal down the steps and along to the pillared gates.

"Such a long time ago, and yet the memories return as vividly as if
it were last week," Lucien commented. "It is always this way when
one has been through the war, I expect. I am often accused of living
in the past."

"You are not alone, Corporal," Ygrec replied. "These days I keep
losing my shoes and my hairbrush and I often forget what day of the
week it is; yet I can recall intimate details of events thirty years ago,
and so sometimes I am accused of being senile." He shrugged and
laughed a little, then went on. "But we must arrange to meet, you

and I, at an early opportunity and share some memories. Unfortunately at the moment I am on my way to meet the Inspector and his wife, but perhaps one day next week you could spare an hour or so."

"More than an hour, monsieur . . . hopefully many hours while you are visiting here. I have no telephone, but I know that Pippa will be delighted to act as a messenger. I too am on my way to attend to some business and am disappointed we cannot talk longer. Still, I shall look forward to our next meeting. We will find a quiet spot and drink to you, my old friend, and then to Xavier and the others whose bones rest on the mountain, and after that to le Loup Noir who should also be laid to rest. Au revoir, monsieur."

"Au revoir." Ygrec nodded as Lucien Anjou turned and crossed the street, but the old corporal's last words had jarred him a bit, and he felt a sadness for the past and a touch of unease, and wondered why. It was a lovely day, he was happy—there was no reason to feel uneasy, and yet he found he was anxious to get back to the château. Probably a bit of food and a glass of wine was all he needed, he reasoned with himself. Mademoiselle Larme would be getting impatient for his return too—she was unhappy being left alone. He'd give her some cheese for a special treat.

But when they arrived home, the dog was nowhere to be found.

*   *   *

Gabrielle Chamillion arrived home about noon that day. She came to pack her belongings. She also came prepared for a scene with Valin and she wasn't disappointed.

Valin heard the front door open and close and took for granted it was Estelle and didn't move from his chair by the window. He felt dreadful. His jaw ached, the bruise on his shoulder was stiffening his arm, and he hadn't been able to keep anything on his stomach, not even the aspirin he had washed down with the last of his diluted Pernod.

There were blank periods in what he had tried to recall about the events of last night, although some of them had been filled in by Estelle when she'd come up with a tray of coffee and bread for him. "The disgrace!" Her voice, like chalk squealing across a blackboard, had made him grit his teeth. "It's God's blessing that maman is too ill to know the disgrace. A corporal from your own dead father's regiment, having to put you to bed like a baby! You . . . the son of an aristocratic father to be seen in public like that. Still, you should

get down on your hands and knees and give praise that Corporal Anjou was there to save you from worse disgrace? Just wait until
M. Joddard hears about it."

He'd wanted to throw the coffee in her face, but he'd felt too ill
and had simply turned his back on her and covered his head with the
blankets. Later he did get down on his knees—to look for his glasses,
and then he'd been sick again. He'd ended up huddled in the chair,
still wearing the ripped shirt and dirty trousers he'd had on last night.

He couldn't believe it was actually Gabrielle standing in the doorway, and he peered across the room trying to focus his eyes. She
looked fine—she looked wonderful! Her hair was parted in the middle
and tied back with a bright scarf at her neck; her eyes were darkly
shaded and her lips were bright pink. She had a frothy blue woollen
shawl draped over her shoulders.

She was back—everything would be find now. She must have understood why he had acted a little roughly—just to protect her honor
and bring her home where she belonged. Women liked men who
acted masculine once in a while—he had heard M. Costello say so,
that hot-blooded men were exciting to women.

He started to stand up, even though the movement pained his
shoulder.

Her first words shocked him out of his fantasy. "Don't come near
me. I only came for my things. I can't go on borrowing from my
friends forever." She sauntered past him, pulled a chair beside the
wardrobe, stood on it, and lifted down a large leather suitcase with
buckled straps.

All he could do was stare at her legs. He wanted to put his hands
on them, to feel the smoothness against her ankles, her thighs, but he
just looked, and tasted the raw bitterness in his throat.

She jerked the untidy blankets across the bed, placed the case on
the foot and undid the buckles and opened the lid with a deliberate
nonchalance.

"But you can't, you can't go now, Gabrielle." The words once
started, poured out over one another almost choking him. "I didn't
mean it about last night . . . I love you . . . You don't know how
much I love you . . . I wouldn't hurt you. I only wanted to bring
you home. I'm not well; I've been sick ever since you left. You
shouldn't have been there, with all those men looking at you. I
wouldn't hurt you. I'd just had a little too much to drink . . . some

wine. It was that Corporal Anjou's fault. . . . He's a client, you know, and he insisted that I have some wine with him."

Her back was to him. The drawer in the bureau beside her was open and she was lifting out her underwear and putting it carefully in one corner of the suitcase.

"Oh, please, Gabrielle." This time he managed to stand, although he was dizzy, and the moisture in his eyes made him squint.

She swung around. She took the shawl from her shoulders and slowly folded it, placing it beside the case. She looked at him, then suddenly she started to laugh in odd little jerks. "I was going to show you the bruise on my neck, but you're as blind as a mole without your glasses. If you're looking for them, why don't you search in the trash bin behind the Cafe Khedive? Have you any idea how stunned you look without your glasses, Valin? Stunned and stupid like a little washed-out mole." The tight laughter rose. "It's the funniest thing I've seen since last night. You should have seen yourself staggering around and sliding across the table top like a clown . . . after you let go of my throat, of course."

"Don't be afraid . . . I promise . . ."

The staccato giggles went on. "Afraid! Oh, get out of my way, Valin, before you fall down at my feet. I have a car waiting downstairs and I don't want you blocking the door." She flung open the wardrobe door and began pulling dresses off their hangers, folding them quickly and flattening them into the case.

"You've no place to go, Gabrielle. Where will you go?"

She turned to him again and her contempt was clear. "Who knows . . . who cares? Out there the world is beautiful . . . if you know where to buy rose-colored glasses." Then she began to sing "La vie en rose," in a soft controlled voice. She kept humming as she shoved a sweater on top of the dresses, closed the lid of the case, and snapped it shut.

Valin heard the humming as if from a great distance, and even later, much later, the tune stayed with him until he wanted to tear it from his brain.

*   *   *

It had been obvious how the dog had escaped—the doors to the terrace were ajar. There had been a short discussion about who had closed the doors, and then Ygrec, trying to pretend nonchalance, had shrugged and said, "I expect she got lonely and pushed at the latch.

She's got a devious brain from living with gendarmes. She never goes far. She'll be back soon, after she's had a little run. I'll go whistle for her." He'd tried to hide his concern by bending over to change his shoes but started out the back door in his sock feet, and Michelin had to call him back.

Eventually Vanessa had driven all along the boulevard, then circled the adjoining roads, while Ygrec whistled and called out back as far as the Couronne gardens, to no avail.

Just after six o'clock Michelin finally phoned the St. Denis gendarmerie, asking them, as a special favor, to keep a lookout for the dog. Ygrec was exhausted and upset and beginning to wheeze badly. Vanessa, almost in tears herself, finally persuaded the old man to lie down, promising to let him know the minute they heard anything.

"Mademoiselle must be hurt or she would have come back long ago," she whispered to Michelin, a catch in her voice. "It will be dark soon. You don't suppose she was stolen, do you? A lot of people with sick minds hate gendarmes and might do awful things to . . ."

"Now, chérie," Michelin interrupted, "you're being foolish." He kissed her quickly. "I'm going back on foot through the old Couronne gardens to the back road. She might have been hit by a car and could have crawled into a ditch or shrubbery."

Michelin had never been near the loge de garde and all he knew about the place was the brief description given by Ygrec. The garden was tidier than he'd expected and the house smaller, and in the twilight it looked forlorn and deserted. As far as he knew, this was the only place Ygrec had taken the dog, so it seemed possible it might be the one place she would seek out.

He came in along the old front driveway, circled the house once to look for any sign of movement in the surrounding overgrowth, then mounted the steps to the front door and lifted the knocker.

He wondered later if Ghislaine Couronne had either heard his approach or expected somebody else because the door was opened promptly. Again he had only Ygrec's description by which to judge the odd little woman and again he was surprised. She did look, in a way, as if she'd stepped out of an antique painting, but not the same picture that Ygrec had seen. She seemed at first like a little girl, dressed up for a costume party, until he saw the lines and pockets of tissue wrinkles on her face. She wore some kind of rubber shoes that showed below a long elaborate skirt of a rather beautiful Burgundy velvet dress trimmed with lace. Her hair was really peculiar. It was

cut in a white fringe that had been plastered down across her forehead and crowned with circular gray braids tied on top with a blue
ribbon bow. Her smile was continuous, her voice monotonously
sweet. At times, one hand moved in a kind of flutter across her
cheek, muffling her words, but she was anxious to help.

After his introduction she proffered her hand quickly. Oh yes, she
remembered the inspector's friend, the nice gentleman with the nice
dog; a dear dog, so funny and friendly, the way it retrieved rocks and
sticks. She was so sorry the dog was lost, but she hadn't seen it today
at all, just that once last week. She had to stay with her bedridden
sister, so she'd never left the house. She seldom could go anywhere
anymore, not even to attend mass, but she would pray that they
found the nice dog. And she hoped the inspector's friend was feeling
better now. When he'd had that bad attack in her garden, she had
been quite frightened at first, his breathing had got so bad—and his
poor hand, was it all right now? Oh, that was good that it healed well.

The meandering words were interrupted then by a sound from the
interior of the house, a kind of cough, Michelin thought, and the
conversation came to a sudden end. The pleased smile became anxious and she nodded without shaking hands and closed the door.

A real weird one, Michelin decided as he retraced his steps. Then
he put the woman out of his mind and wished he'd thought to bring
his flashlight because it was getting too dark to see anything in the
thick shrubbery.

Chapter Nine

Lucien Anjou watched the inspector's tall figure disappear into the
dusk, then he let out a small breath of relief and turned back to
Ghislaine.

"I did fine, didn't I, Lucien?" she said brightly as she hovered over
the table, straightening the settings of knives and forks and spoons.
"Isn't the table pretty? I had to look way down into the bottom of
the cedar chest upstairs for the linen tablecloth. The serviettes were
down here, of course. Amélie always liked linen, even when I served
her on a tray. The candleholders need to be polished, but I never
liked polishing things. Amélie used to make me do it and my hands
got all black, but I don't have to do it anymore."

The kitchen was bright in lamplight and candles; the hearth crackled; a pleasant spicy aroma came from the bubbling pot on the glowing stove, and Lucien looked at it all, and at Ghislaine, in growing desperation.

"I did fine, didn't I?" she repeated.

"You talked too much," Lucien said quietly, "but you did very well. Try to remember if anyone comes to simply answer their questions politely and quietly, and nothing more."

"But nobody comes anymore, so there's nothing to be bothered about, Lucien . . . and I have practiced and practiced and I can write Amélie's name as well as she could herself, so when they come for the papers to be signed to sell the land, we won't have to be bothered about that either. This last while, almost ever since spring, Amélie's writing was just like little wiggles anyway, and when I took the annuity check to the Caisse Populaire the last time, they didn't say anything because they knew she was sick and weak. Everything is just lovely now, Lucien."

She reached over and picked up a wine glass from the table. "We could open the wine now. The glasses look pretty, don't they, with the candlelight shining on them? They're real crystal. They belonged to Amélie's mother. We have only four left."

"Ghislaine, I have told you I cannot stay to eat with you tonight. I only came to bring the chicken and the sugar and to tell you about the agent, M. Chamillion. There are rumors that he may not be kept on at Joddard et Fils, and that worries me. Whatever happens, it is going to be longer than you expected before the land can be sold."

"Of course you can stay." She kept admiring the crystal in her hand, moving it slowly as it caught and reflected rainbow colors in the light. "Isn't this a nice dress? I knew you'd be surprised to see me in a dress; it's been such a long time, hasn't it? I'm nearly the same size as Amélie was when I made it for her so many years ago. Amélie said I was good at sewing. It took me a very long time to sew all these buttons down the front. There are thirty-two buttons. . . . Amélie made me count them over and over. For a while I had trouble after twenty, but I learned and I've never forgotten."

Lucien was still standing by the window, his coat on, his beret in his hand. He pulled the curtains together almost violently. "Ghislaine, you are not listening to me!"

"I am too listening. If M. Chamillion is a silly man who drinks too much wine as you told me before, then M. Joddard can sell the land."

"Perhaps, but M. Joddard is not silly or stupid, and he might insist on coming here to witness Amélie's signature on the papers. We need M. Chamillion. He is so anxious to make a sale, to make some money, that he will do whatever I suggest. Why do you think I wasted a whole evening last night sitting in that cafe listening to him whining out his troubles about his family and then carrying him home? We need him, Ghislaine, and now I have to go and try to get him on his feet by Monday."

"You have to eat something first."

"I am expected at home."

"It gets lonely here. It's nice when you come." Now there was petulance in her voice.

"I will come as often as I can, to make sure that you are well and have what you need, but I can't stay tonight."

"I got all dressed up and set the table with the best things and made the chicken for you. I do nice things for you all the time . . . things you don't even know about." The hand was fluttering around her cheek now and rubbing under her eyes. "You could stay if you wanted to. It's different now. Amélie's gone."

She would pretend to cry; he knew the signs. He put on his beret. "I will bring in more wood for you before I leave. I may not be able to come tomorrow." His words were firm.

She spoke quickly, suddenly. "I have enough wood."

"Not enough to last until Monday." There had been an odd change in her attitude and he frowned a little, then started for the back door.

"I don't need any wood! This is my house now, and my wood, and I can get it myself!" Instantly it was almost Amélie talking. The manipulating child had vanished in one sentence; she was acting out another role, which she usually did when she wanted to divert attention from something she'd done wrong.

"What have you done, Ghislaine? What is it this time?"

"You're not being nice anymore. I want you to go home right now, and you are to use the front door, the way you came in."

He had thought little of the fact that the shed door had been wide open this morning and bolted this afternoon on his return. He felt it just another of her changing moods. She started across the room, trying to hurry, dragging her foot and almost tripping on her long skirt, but he had opened the door to the larder, so she stopped, standing very still.

He stopped too, peering down at the floor, then caught his breath. "*Dieu vivant* . . . it's a dog! It must be the dog that Inspector Michelin was looking for . . . and it's dead!" He turned on her, his anger flaring out of control. "How did it get here?" He stepped into the chill little room and dropped to his knees.

As he examined the animal—eyes, mouth, neck, running his hands slowly over its limbs, its body, he could hear her in the background, no longer acting, but being her usual pathetic, wheedling self, probably telling half lies, but it would be the truth as she saw it.

"It was digging at the asparagus bed and I had to stop it, Lucien . . . I had to stop it for your sake. I tried to send it away. I went outside and ordered it to leave my garden and I threw rocks at it, but it just picked up the rocks in its mouth and tried to bring them back to me, and then it barked and raced around and I was afraid someone might hear and come, and it went right back to its digging and it was making a big hole. What if it had dug up Amélie? You'd have been in awful trouble and they would have said you killed her. They would have sent you to jail, Lucien."

He could see her in the doorway, her hands crossed and pressed against the lace at her throat, the ridiculous bow at the top of her head.

She spoke seriously now. "It had such strong paws and it was flinging the earth in all directions and I shouted and threw more rocks and even hit it with a stick, but it just stopped for a minute and stared at me with mean eyes and I was afraid it would bite me, and I even got that pain in my chest I was so afraid. So I came inside and thought.

"I got a good idea, Lucien, a very good idea and I got a piece of boiled mutton I had left over from before Amélie died. She was very fond of boiled mutton with carrots. So I got the meat and held it out and the dog followed me right inside the larder here, as friendly as could be and I closed the doors and left it here. But I couldn't let it out again, could I, or it would dig up Amélie. So I got another piece of meat and jabbed big holes in it with the knife and I got Amélie's pills that were left in the bottle . . . the strong ones for her pain, like they gave me when they were trying to fix my foot. I jabbed and jabbed and pushed the pills into the holes until there were no more pills left. And the dog ate it all, just gobbled it down. It was very hungry, Lucien . . . I don't think they had been feeding it properly at all. Then afterward I washed my hands really well. I never liked the smell of mutton."

Lucien stared up at her, the anger turned to a kind of futility he couldn't express.

"It's only a dog, Lucien. You can dig a hole somewhere in the woods and bury it and nobody will know the difference. I was going to ask you to do it after we'd had supper."

*   *   *

Pippa's day that had begun so happily hadn't gone well, and she ate supper alone. Gran'papa hadn't come back to help her with the special soup, but she had gone ahead as best she could, and when it was ready and simmering, she had waited and waited. Finally at dusk she had eaten with little appetite, and now she stood in the doorway of the cottage feeling resentful and more than a little restless.

It was a nice evening, almost velvety like some summer nights, but with a coolness in the air. The trees that lined the lane were so still that she felt they were holding their breath for fear they might disturb their fading fragile leaves and have to admit summer was gone. She felt that way too. She stood very still, not wanting to move, while at the same time wishing that something would happen.

She was glad that her school days were over—it was the first time she could remember not having lessons to do on weekends, yet there was a kind of lost feeling inside her. It was fine going to the château in the afternoons; the work was easy and everyone was kind, but it was just filling in time. She was waiting for something, a change, but because it was an unknown thing, she was restless. She wished it was spring; she longed for a newness, and excitement. There was nothing in St. Denis, no music or bustling along the streets, no happy crowds even on Saturday night. Everyone around here was old, she decided morosely, and acted like the saints in the basilica tombs.

Earlier while she had been waiting for Gran'papa she had changed her clothes for something to do. She had put on the long plaid skirt she had made over from the one Mme. Michelin had given her, but she only had the same old blue sweater to wear with it. She'd tried the yellow scarf, then the flowered one, but they looked anything but elegant, and the whole effect had been very discouraging.

The reflection in her little wall mirror was discouraging too. She decided that no matter what anyone else said, she was going to let her hair grow long and she was going to buy green eye shadow, and next summer she would wear a hat the whole time so her skin wouldn't turn so brown and muddy-looking. She sighed, then recalling what M. Ygrec had said about her looking elegant this morning, she'd changed her clothes again, putting on the red skirt with the striped blouse on top of the blue sweater, the way Mme. Michelin often did. Then she'd gone back to wait for Gran'papa, watching until the sunset faded to a warm purple, and gradually darkness settled on the garden.

When she finally heard the footsteps coming up the lane, crunching in the fallen leaves, she took for granted it was Gran'papa at last. She supposed he would tell her to read a book until it was time for bed, time to get her rest before early mass tomorrow, although he never went to church himself anymore. She loved him dearly, but she wished he would stop treating her like a little girl. She didn't want to go to bed on such a nice night, with the stars beginning to hang so low that they looked almost within touching distance of the treetops, and now a bright half moon had appeared. She didn't want to go to early mass either and have to put on the sensible black shoes and the blue school coat with the horrid round-brimmed hat. Again she wished she had something new to wear—a black velvet skirt like Mme. Michelin's, or even better, velvet pants with a loose blouse that had a low neck and puffy sleeves, worn with strings of gold necklaces. She'd seen the outfit on a model in the window of a boutique in Paris when she'd gone to the museum in June with her classmates from the convent.

The voice broke into her dreaming and she peered down the lane.

"Bonsoir, Mlle. Anjou. Are you alone?" The whispered greeting was formal but she could hear the teasing in the words.

"Jean-Louis," Pippa sighed. "Oh, yes, I'm alone . . . all alone."

She stepped down onto the piazza, and he stepped up, stopping close to her. He was bigger than she remembered, and different. He had on a light shirt with a scarf looped into the open neck. Then she noticed. "You've grown a beard," she exclaimed in delight. "That's why you look different!"

"I thought you'd like it." He smiled, pulling at the dark growth on his chin. "You look just the same."

"I know." She pulled back into the darkened doorway.

"Now, Pippa, don't be shy with me. After just one summer have I suddenly become a stranger?"

"No."

"Well, what's the matter?"

"You're different, and I'm not."

He laughed. "Now why would anyone want you to change? You're perfect the way you are. Come out where I can see you . . . there's a moon, you know . . . come on." He touched her arm and she moved. "That's better. Don't you remember what I said before I went away?"

"Yes . . . you said you'd be back in the autumn."

"And what else?"

". . . and that you'd sing to me . . . and you'd bring me a present."

"And so I have." He pulled the scarf from his neck, wrapped it around hers, and holding the ends, pulled her closer to him and bent down to kiss her forehead.

She touched the silk, then his hand that held it, and she couldn't say a word because she was so happy. Finally she laughed a little and asked, "What color is it? I can only feel it."

"Shades of blue and green, because when I looked at the sea at St. Tropez I was thinking about you." He lifted her chin and kissed her properly this time. "Now come along and we'll go somewhere and I'll tell you all about my summer and how much I missed you. You'd like a ride on my motorcycle, wouldn't you? I'll push it down the back road until we get away from here so we won't alert the whole neighborhood."

"Oh, Jean-Louis, I can't go, especially on your bike. Gran'papa will be home any minute and you know how he was even before you went away. He says I'm too young to go anywhere alone with a boy, especially you. He doesn't like the way you dress, or your friends, and he says you're unreliable . . . and now you've grown a beard . . . and he hates motorcycles more than anything . . . I just can't. . . ." He was brushing her cheek with his beard and her protestations came to a gradual standstill.

"Where is he?"

"I don't know. . . . He's been gone all day . . . but he'll be back soon, I'm sure."

"It's Saturday night, Pippa, so he'll probably be in the bistro. Papa mentioned that he'd seen him around noon outside the basilica shaking hands with someone who looked like an old friend from his army days. They'll be talking over old times and he won't be back until late. We won't go far and I'll bring you back long before he gets home."

If it had been any other night she might have hesitated, but she didn't want to wait any longer for something exciting to happen. Besides, she felt it had already happened, whatever it was. She kept her hand in his and let him lead her down the lane, and when he put his arm around her to pull her close she decided that this was what she had been waiting for all her life.

At the end of the lane they slipped behind some trees to peek over at the brightly lit window in the rear of the Hugo establishment. The formidable form of Jean-Louis' mother was nowhere to be seen, so they hurried to the back of the pâtisserie where the motorcycle was parked behind the small bakery van.

"Where are we going?" Pippa whispered, not really caring.

"Where there's music," Jean-Louis answered softly, and he began to whistle "La vie en rose."

*   *   *

"Do you think if I put on some music, it might cheer him up?" Vanessa wondered aloud to her husband. "He wouldn't eat any supper, just a few sips of consommé. I've never seen him like this before and it scares me a little."

"You can try," Michelin replied without enthusiasm. "I've done everything I can think of. I've scoured the whole area and stopped into most of the cafes and bistros to ask people to keep an eye out for the dog, and Sergeant Corvette at the gendarmerie here is being very helpful. Now it's simply a matter of waiting."

Michelin had built up the fire in the salon and crouched, poking absently at the logs. He was still in his heavy sweater and old pants. Vanessa, also in an old sweater and slacks, was sitting on the footstool, her chin cupped in her hands, her hair tied back in a scarf.

"Well, if anything . . . anything awful has happened to Mademoiselle, we could always get him another dog," she said, trying to cheer herself up as much as anything else.

"It wouldn't be the same . . . you know that. Mademoiselle was very special. Maurice has never had anything that was really his own before . . . no wife . . . no family, no home. His work was all he seemed to want for years. There was a girl once, when he was younger, during the war. I think you've heard him mention her . . . her name was Vanessa too, but you don't know the whole story. She was married and sounded like a bit of a vampire to me and he was probably better off without her, but you could never tell him that. When he gives his love, he gives it totally. . . . He pours it all out, and it's forever. That's his greatest weakness, I think. It's been like that with the dog . . . complete devotion."

Vanessa stirred, hugging herself as if she were cold, although the room was warm. "We have to do something, Paul. He's just lying there on his bed pretending to be asleep, but I can tell he's not, and his chest is bad. I could hear him breathing, almost like he had a cold, even when I was standing in the doorway."

"Put on a record then. He likes Piaf, he was playing one of her albums yesterday. I'll get him up and pour a large cognac into him, maybe even two. At least that will be a start and get him moving." Michelin stood up, then swung around in surprise as he saw Ygrec come slowly through the doorway.

"Pour the cognac by all means, garçon, and put on the music, but save your sympathy. This foolish old man has had his time of self-pity and has been a nuisance to you long enough." As he spoke he coughed a little but walked the length of the room and sat down in the armchair near the french doors. "I was thinking, as I lay in there, why I called her Mademoiselle Larme. Remember, garçon? You should remember, for it was the night after you brought her to me as a small gangling puppy that you met Vanessa. Mademoiselle Larme . . . out of a teardrop should come laughter . . . that's what I said." The old gendarme forced a smile. "It looks like quite a nice night outside. I hope Mademoiselle is warm . . . wherever she is."

Chapter Ten

Mme. Hugo should have been perfectly happy. Jean-Louis was home at last, and she was going to have poulet sauté à la Bordelaise for their noon meal tomorrow. Although Pépi had the precise touch with pastries and rolls, Madame's gourmet dinners were equally as memorable, and she loved to cook, yet tonight she seemed to be just going through the motions of preparation.

She finished wiping the chicken for the second time, wrapped it in waxed paper, and put it into the icebox. The artichokes and shallots had been washed and set aside too. All was in order. She rinsed her hands, being careful not to splash the sleeves of her green taffeta dress, removed her apron, hung it behind the door, inspected the kitchen again in one critical glance, then switched off the light.

The small dining room was as spotless as the kitchen, but she adjusted the fringed shade of the floor lamp and rearranged the figures of Ste. Thérèse and St. Denis that prayed on the gleaming sideboard, blowing imaginary dust particles from their garishly solemn faces. The window was slightly ajar, but not a movement disturbed the stiff lace curtains. She peered outside. It was a pleasant night, and she understood why Jean-Louis had wanted to go for a walk and stretch his legs after the long ride; he'd driven all the way from Provence, he'd told them at supper. But he should have been back hours ago. Just a short walk, he'd said, then they would sit and visit and he'd tell them all about his travels over the summer.

He'd always been a good boy, a loving boy, easier to manage than his sisters, and he really hadn't changed, she told herself. Hadn't he hugged her like he always did when he'd got home, telling her how young she looked? He just looked different, that was all, with the fancy shirt and tight pants—and that beard. He was thinner too. Well, she'd soon put that to rights; a few months of her meals and he'd be plump and healthy again. As for the beard, she supposed that Pépi was right—it was a stage, like the stage that Madeleine had gone through until she'd finally come to her senses and settled down to marry Pierre with his own fish shop, instead of that vagabond who wanted to reform the world. And Françette too, that time she'd gone on some kind of a silly diet trying to look like a film star. Now that Jean-Louis was home, the wanderlust out of his system, he would settle down and learn the business. Madame could just see the new sign in front of the pâtisserie—"HUGO ET FILS." He would have more common sense now, too, and choose steady friends, young men with ambition, an aim in life, and when the time came, when he had put down some roots, he would marry a nice girl, perhaps even someone like M. Joddard's granddaughter, from a good family with a business background.

The opening of the back door interrupted Madame's dreams. "Jean-Louis?" she called hopefully, but it was her husband's voice that replied.

"He's taken his motorcycle," Pépi announced with cheerful puzzlement. "I thought he was going for a walk."

"What do you mean? He couldn't have taken it. I didn't hear the motor start up. Look again, Pépi. Look behind the van!" Madame's unease made her voice shrill.

Pépi's little round belly seemed to precede him into the room. He always wore a vest and tie when he went out in the evenings, and on Saturdays, if he went to the Bistro Céleste, he wore a white shirt. Tonight as usual, the tie hung like a noose beneath his numerous chins, and a chubby expanse of white shirt oozed from between the vest above and his belt below. "I have looked all around the van . . . twice." Pépi was in a mellow mood. "It's gone."

"Well, take off your cap when you come into the house. You are getting very careless these days, Pépi."

She was upset; Pépi knew the signs. When she was cross at the world she always picked on him. He removed his cap, smoothed his thinning hair in place on top of his shiny forehead, and proceeded to smooth his wife's mood as well. "You are looking particularly attractive tonight, chérie. I always liked pearls with that dress . . . they make your skin glow. As I sat in the bistro, I said to myself, Pépi, what are you doing here with all these dull noisy people when you could be home enjoying the company of your own Marie-Thérèse . . . so here I am." He stood on his toes to plant a kiss on her perfumed cheek. "Now, chérie, shall we sit comfortably and enjoy a glass of something special together?" He beamed up at her.

Madame was momentarily pacified. She opened the buffet and took out two small glasses and a bottle of apricot brandy. He managed to fill both glasses without spilling any, handing one glass to her in a rather grand manner before sliding back into his armchair.

She took up her vigil on the chair by the window. "I don't understand how Jean-Louis could have . . ."

Pépi interrupted softly from the confines of his chair, pretending to have misunderstood. "I don't understand how some people can drink so much and stay alive. M. Valin Chamillion was in the bistro for a time. He had three large Pernods while I was there and only the saints know how many beforehand. It can make a man demented, all that drink. During the war I knew a man . . ."

This time Madame interrupted. "Never mind that spongy Valin Chamillion! What about our Jean-Louis? Where has he gone, on his first night home . . . and how did he start that motor without me hearing him? Perhaps Lucien Anjou was right for the first time in his life, and I shouldn't have allowed Jean-Louis to buy that machine

. . . but don't you dare let Lucien know I even thought such a thing."

"Jean-Louis is young, chérie. No doubt he's gone where there are some people his own age, looking for a little music. You know how he loves music."

"And looking for girls," Madame added prophetically.

"That's possible."

"But he's only a boy!"

"Not a boy . . . a young man, and a young man with a beard."

"You said it was just a stage."

"It is . . . that's all it is. There's no harm looking at pretty girls." Pépi chuckled a little.

Madame wasn't smiling. "He said he was going for a walk. He wouldn't lie to me, would he?"

"Of course not, so he's walking beside his motorcycle to get exercise, and he'll ride it home. I expect that's it."

"But it's getting late." She stood up, parted the curtains and stared down the dimly lit lane.

Pépi tried again. "That Inspector Michelin, the one Pippa is working for, he came into the bistro earlier tonight. He was looking for a dog . . . that big red dog that Pippa keeps talking about. It belongs to the other gendarme who is visiting. The dog is lost."

"You'd think an officer from the Special Branch would have more to do than go looking for a dog, especially in a bistro," Madame mumbled without moving. Then she turned suddenly. "You don't think that Jean-Louis has gone anywhere with that Pippa, do you?"

"What foolishness. She's only a child, and I told you so last spring when you said he was seeing too much of her. She's like a little sister to him, that's all. He used to push her in the swing and let her talk to him because he has a kind heart. Besides, did you see her come down the lane tonight? Of course you didn't. She'll be sound asleep in bed this time of night as always. You know how strict Lucien is with her."

"Well, there's no light in the cottage, so maybe you're right."

"Of course I'm right. Now drink up and you can pour me a little more. It's been a long day . . . market day always is." He reached out from the shadows of his chair holding his glass aloft. He was getting sleepy, but he knew he wouldn't get upstairs tonight until she had calmed down, so he kept on talking. "That Inspector Michelin is a very polite man. I liked him. He wasn't in uniform, of course. Céleste thought he was quite handsome."

"Was Armand helping Céleste tonight?"

"Yes, he was there, quiet as always. He doesn't look well."

Madame sipped at her liqueur. "I thought he was working in the mortuary."

"That's what they say, but only sometimes."

"No wonder poor Céleste has gray hair. It's too much responsibility for her, and I told her so when she first took him. You can never tell about an orphan, even if it is your own blood." She paused again, staring out the window. "Pépi, you don't think that Jean-Louis still . . . ?"

Pépi sighed. "Armand was never a friend of Jean-Louis, Marie-Thérèse. He just hung around the other boys, trying to be grown-up like they were and Jean-Louis was kind to him . . . until the trouble. There are times when it doesn't pay to be kind, I suppose. But speaking of friends, you'll never guess who I passed just as I was leaving the bistro on my way home . . . Gabrielle Chamillion, with a man, a young man. It was a good thing that her husband had been tossed out earlier, or there might have been another fight like at the Khedive last night. I didn't like the looks of the man she was with . . . he reminded me of a prison guard we once had in Germany, only with long hair."

Usually Madame would have brightened at such a choice bit of gossip, but although she seated herself once more, all she said was, "Did Lucien come in while you were there?"

"No, but as you said the other night, he doesn't go out to public places very often these days."

"Well, I wonder what he's doing. He's not like himself at all lately. Do you know I haven't seen a sign of him since noon, and when he passed me on my way back from the market he hardly nodded, like I was a stranger. Who did you say you saw him with outside the basilica?"

"A tall thin man with untidy gray hair and worn clothing . . . patches on the elbows of his coat. He carried himself well, though. I expect it was some old soldier who Lucien knew in the war." Pépi stood up, stretched, and proceeded to amble out of the room. "Come along, Marie-Thérèse. Jean-Louis looked after himself just fine all summer and there's no reason to start worrying about him now. He'll be home soon."

For once Madame seemed to agree, and switched off the light without bothering to collect the dirty glasses.

* * *

The fires in the kitchen of the loge burned brightly. Lucien pressed his fingers firmly on either side of the dog's neck and relaxed a little. The faint pulse had become stronger. The room was very warm and still. Ghislaine had been sleeping on the cot for some time, and Lucien hoped she would stay asleep.

Earlier, after the discovery of the animal in the larder, the words had been sharp and bitter. "It's not just a dog," Lucien had shouted. "It belongs to a good man, a friend of mine . . . gendarme Ygrec. You knew that . . . you told the Inspector that M. Ygrec had been here with the dog."

"You don't know him . . . he's just visiting! You're making a fuss to punish me. I hate it when you shout!"

Lucien had ignored her and picked up the dog as gently as he could, carrying it into the kitchen.

"What are you doing? Get it out of my kitchen . . . out of my house. I hate dead things." She'd started to whimper.

"Move out of my way, Ghislaine." He'd placed the dog on the carpet in front of the hearth. "It might still be alive. It's not cold or stiff. Now keep out of my way."

She'd found a chair, whimpering louder. "You can't tell on me, Lucien. They would want to know what happened. I was only protecting you. If they find out about Amélie, you know what they'll do, and we won't be able to sell the land and you won't get your share of the money for Pippa. You know what Amélie said before, that you could have some money for getting the land sold so you could send the girl away, and I was going to give it to you too, just like she said, but I won't if you tell, and then what will happen to your precious Pippa! She's all you ever cared about . . . you never cared about us. You left us to face the pain and shame all alone. Amélie was right. I should have listened to her. You are nothing but a peasant!"

He'd looked up from his massaging of the dog's limbs. "Ghislaine, if you don't shut up your mouth, I will have to punish you the way that Amélie did! Now listen to me. How many tablets were left in that bottle? You can count up to thirty-two! How many tablets did you shove into that meat?"

She wasn't listening, but at least she had stopped ranting. She'd dropped her head and folded her hands, muttering some unintelligible prayer, then finally crawled onto the cot, covering her head with the quilt.

Lucien had gone back to trying to revive the dog, trying to lift it to its feet, cursing, and half praying to himself from time to time.

Now he tried again, lifting the animal under its forefront, then when the rubbery legs collapsed, lifting once more, but this time he noticed an involuntary movement of one front leg. If he could keep the animal moving, bring it to enough consciousness to swallow something, some stimulent, it should be all right.

The cot squeaked. He could see Ghislaine rise slowly to a sitting position, smoothing the front of her dress with her hands. She really did look demented now, he decided. The foolish bow had fallen off the top of her head and her hair hung in two skinny braids on either side of her white fringed face. Le bon Dieu, he thought, what is to become of her?

"The candles have burned away," she remarked absently after a few minutes, "and the chicken will have fallen off the bones. It's getting late, Lucien. Look, it's dark outside. I must have fallen asleep . . . although I was just thinking of being back in the mountains . . . not dreaming, thinking. You must be hungry now, so I think I'll serve the supper on the plates. Be sure and wash your hands before you come to the table." She reached up into the warming oven muttering to herself again.

He knew he couldn't stay longer; he might lose control. The dog was alive and when it recovered it shouldn't have any ill effects; it would simply be stunned for a time like a human who came out of a drugged sleep. It must be kept warm, though, and given nourishment.

Ghislaine took his silence for assent and stood by the stove, plate in hand. "I must be careful not to spill gravy on my dress. You can't wash velvet, you know, because it goes all flat and horrible. That time I washed the green velvet hat, Amélie couldn't wear it to church anymore."

The dog's two front legs moved spastically. Lucien stood up, reached for his coat, put it on, then placed his beret on his head.

"Where are you going, Lucien?" The panic began again. "You can't leave me here alone with that dead thing . . . you can't. You promised to help me always. You promised, in the mountains."

He would try for the last time, try to talk to her like a rational human being. "Ghislaine, that was almost thirty-five years ago. There was a war on and I was living from day to day. I was young, and a soldier . . . we were all young, possibly not so much in years but in facing life. We had a period of foolishness, and I am still paying for it. I will not see you suffer . . . but that is all."

"You're being mean again. You're cross because I told what Amélie said about you. Well, I didn't mean it, Lucien, and I'll say I'm sorry. That makes it all right, doesn't it? I'm sorry. There now."

"You have spent your life being sorry and then doing something worse."

"But I forget . . ."

"You don't forget as much as you pretend to forget." He bent over the dog.

"Are you going to bury it in the woods and come back for your chicken?"

"The dog isn't dead, Ghislaine. I told you before, and I tell you again, the dog is alive."

"You could make it dead. If you buried it now, it wouldn't know the difference and it would smother."

"Is that what happened to Amélie? Is it?" The words were out, and it was too late to swallow them.

The plate was poised in Ghislaine's hand, then suddenly it came flying across the room and shattered against the stone of the hearth, splashing gravy in all directions.

Lucien stiffened momentarily, but without flinching went straight to the back door, threw it open, passed through the larder, undid the lock, and pushed at the outside door with his foot. He didn't look at her when he returned. He braced himself, picked up the dog, cradling it in his big arms, and strode out into the night, leaving her with the echo of her accusing words, "You've made me splash gravy . . . you've ruined my dress!"

* * *

It was the fourth straight game of backgammon that Ygrec had lost to Michelin. They were seated opposite each other, the old gendarme in the armchair, the young one on the big stool, the board covered with black and white discs on a small table between them. The logs were little but warm embers in the grate, the lights at the far end of the room were dimmed with just one bright lamp to shine over the two bent heads.

"I thought you were the expert at this ancient and noble game of '*trictrac*,' old man," Michelin said. "You even told me once that you had invented the game, although it seems to me that I read that Marie Antoinette used to play it . . . while she ate cake."

"Oh, pic, pic, pic. You are very funny tonight. You can't believe everything you read, and besides, it's the roll of the dice," replied Ygrec.

"When you win you say it's skill . . . when you lose you say it's the dice."

"Are you implying my mind is not on my game, garçon?"

Michelin was beginning to wish he hadn't said anything at all. He'd been trying all evening to keep Ygrec from worrying about the dog, but it seemed that his teasing had backfired. "Perhaps it is the dice. I have been throwing a lot of doubles."

Ygrec straightened in his chair. "Stop being so painfully kind and stop feeling sorry for me. My mind isn't on the game, and you know it. You're trying to be tactful, which isn't natural for you . . . never has been. And Vanessa is in the kitchen, the one room in the house that she dislikes, preparing some kind of fancy chicken for me tomorrow. Your efforts are noticed and appreciated, but let's get back to normal and stop pretending and start a new game."

Michelin smiled to himself. The old man was testy, which was a good sign that he hadn't given up, either on the game or the dog.

They began again. The only sound was the dull rattle of dice in the felt-lined box. The french doors were ajar, at an earlier request of Ygrec—"in case she may find her way home before morning. . . ."

"A double at last, and about time too," Ygrec muttered.

They heard the sound at the same time, looked the length of the room, and as they rose to their feet simultaneously, the table wobbled over and the game slid to the carpet.

The sight of the great dark man holding the big rusty dog was one that Ygrec would never forget. Lucien Anjou had pushed the doors open with his bulk. "Bonsoir, M. Ygrec," he said quietly, "I believe I have found your dog."

There was no excitement that accompanied Lucien and his burden inside, rather a great rush of blessed relief followed by murmurs of concern.

Lucien went on talking quietly, volunteering information that he knew was about to be asked. "She seems to be coming around. It doesn't appear to me that she has been poisoned, nor that she has any broken bones, but it is hard to say. I found her while I was taking a short cut home near rue Feu Follet." He placed the dog gently on the carpet at Ygrec's feet. "I should stir up the fire, Inspector, if I were you . . . and perhaps an old blanket if you have one . . . ?"

"Of course." Michelin started out of the room as Vanessa entered and they stopped momentarily to touch each other and watch the scene of the two old men on their knees beside the animal.

Ygrec looked up once. "Corporal, what can I say, except that I am in your debt forever."

Chapter Eleven

The Chamillion house, Maison Feu Follet, had been named after the street. The house wasn't large but had been artistically designed and, when it had been cared for, had stood proudly with an air of enduring gentility. Sometimes even now when its neglect was cloaked by a smoky dawn, it still held an attractiveness, and this Sunday as the basilica spires began to take on the blue-green hues of the skies above and the trees below, so Maison Feu Follet began to take shape.

First the shadows slid down the gray chimney stacks, then a gleam and another and another appeared in succession from tiny, leaded panes of oblong upstairs windows. The dark criss-crossed beams of the upper outside walls looked freshly painted and the stonework below, a polished pearl gray. When the daylight reached the domed glass roof of the little conservatory, a sudden flash of diamond coloring reflected unevenly across the garden to collect on the dewy curves of wrought-iron fencing. There was one enormous weeping willow tree growing in the center of the courtyard and beyond it, to the right of the front porticos, stood a statue of a sallow-cheeked Virgin Mary, her eyes raised to the level of the treetop, her blue-draped arms held out in supplication.

Valin stood unmoving in front of the leaded windows of his bedroom. Last night when he had stumbled in after his tour of the local bars and bistros, he had tried to undress but had ended up lying on top of his unmade bed wearing all his clothes except his jacket and shoes.

He knew he must have slept because when he wakened he'd recognized the beginning of daylight, but he'd had strange dreams and he felt as exhausted as if he had been up all night. He'd lain stiffly, his eyes alternately tightly closed, then wide open, his mind as mixed up as the shapes that took form in front of his eyes. Once when the first distorted light from the windows formed an unmistakable Greek cross on the wall beside him, he'd wondered if it was a sign that he should take his holiday in Cyprus but the light had changed the symbol to a sacrificial cross, then to a blot, and had finally disappeared entirely. He remembered then that he would not be going anywhere, and he felt desperately ill. He'd got up and sneaked downstairs to the kitchen, returning with a bottle of vin ordinaire.

The first few mouthfuls made him shudder, but he'd begun to feel as if his mind was clearing. Then the church bells began to chime and the echoes became the taunting song that Gabrielle had hummed. He sat on the edge of the bed and drained the bottle.

After a while the front door opened and closed. It would be Estelle scurrying to mass, so this would be a logical time to search the back rooms downstairs. Estelle sometimes hid the wine these days; once it was behind a washtub in the scullery. He was shivering with cold and with desperation when he returned from the search. He'd found nothing; even the remains of the coffee on top of the cold stove looked unfit to drink. He put on a sweater and stood in front of the window until he heard the sounds of Estelle's return. Then he scrubbed at one dirty window pane with his fist, forgetting that the latch was broken, allowing the pressure to push the window open.

He leaned out. The years of weathering had bleached the cross beams of the house to a streaked gray and pitted grime into the stone and stucco below. The glass sections of the conservatory roof were cracked and many fragments were missing. Inside, where once had been carefully cultivated color and greenery, there was now a rubble of broken pottery and dried stubs sitting in tubs of cementlike earth. He couldn't see clearly through his haze, but he knew that, behind the tangle of hedge, the railings were undermined with rust, and the sign on the half-closed driveway gate hung crazily by one screw.

He leaned out farther to look down at the stone courtyard below. The weeping willow grieved; the Virgin statue accused with blank eyes and pointed at him with amputated hands, and Valin wondered: If he fell, would he land at the foot of the statue?

*   *   *

A miserable and chastised Pippa, wearing her hated coat, brimmed hat, and sensible shoes, had also attended early mass. Afterward she prepared breakfast silently and just as silently sat across the spotless kitchen table from her grandfather, picking at her ham and watching him pick at his. Sunbeams wavered on the braided rug in front of the open back door, but, for all Pippa cared, it might as well have been pouring with rain because she knew she was imprisoned indoors today and probably, she decided desperately, for the rest of her life.

"Midnight!" Lucien said at last, and for at least the tenth time since last night, Pippa noted with an inward sigh. "Out with that Bohemian until almost midnight. Tearing around on that devil's machine too, and down by the canal. You could have been killed, and it doesn't matter what your reasoning was . . . even big cars have missed the turn in that road and gone off into the canal. Be that as it may, I don't blame you entirely. You are too young to know about a lot of things and are easily influenced . . . but I will see that it never happens again. I have thought about it, Pippa, and it is time you went off to the Académie to further your education. I should not have been so lax in making my decision. I will see the Mother Superior tomorrow. If I remember correctly, the first semester doesn't start for about another week. It was wise that they prepared all the forms at the convent at the end of your school year."

"But I would need some new clothes, Gran'papa," Pippa whispered morosely.

"I will discuss those matters when I go to the convent in the morning."

"But the money . . . you said we didn't . . ."

"Such things are of no concern to you. You tend to your studies and I will look after the rest. Today, as you know, you are to remain here, inside the house. You can read, to prepare yourself for your new school. . . . You know more about that than I do . . . what to read, I mean. . . ." Lucien was finding it very difficult to be severe with the girl, especially as she was looking so forlorn, but it had to be done. "Read those poems you seem to like so much, if you wish . . . anything you like. But you are not to go outside the door."

"Yes, Gran'papa." She took his plate and fork, piling them on her own.

"And don't go putting on any of those long skirts and foolish clothes you have been traipsing around in, nor that blue scarf. For once in her life Mme. Hugo was possibly right, although I'll be damned if I'll tell her so when I go over to see them later. But you are to keep on what you are wearing." He tried not to notice her full young body pushing against the straight gray dress, and he didn't look directly at her face. What will I do if she starts to cry? he asked himself. I've always wanted her to grow up to be free and natural . . . but I must be hard this time; it is the only way to protect her. "When you are older you will be glad I made this decision for you." He snatched his beret from the hook on the door and started outside, muttering, "It's because I love you."

Later he told her that he had also decided it would not be necessary for her to go to work at the château any more, and that he himself would tell Inspector Michelin not to expect her tomorrow, and Pippa did cry. It was the first time she could remember when he had said out loud that he loved her, and then to go ahead and do what he was doing—it was too cruel to understand. It wasn't the way she thought about love at all. She loved Jean-Louis and wouldn't dream of doing anything that would upset him, let alone ruin his life.

She couldn't read any more because her tears just kept dribbling onto the pages, so she opened the bottom drawer of her little bureau and took out the precious blue silk scarf and put it almost defiantly around her neck, but tucked it carefully beneath the white collar of her gray dress. If she was to make plans about going off with Jean-Louis, she wouldn't be able to carry anything without being suspected, but she didn't mind anyway. She hated all her belongings, except the poetry book, and the scarf.

*　　*　　*

The interview Lucien held at the Hugo household was less than successful. Deep in his heart Lucien had hoped to discover that Jean-Louis was home only for the weekend, and it would not be necessary to send Pippa away so soon. It wasn't just the shortage of money and the problems it was forcing him to face. He admitted that to himself many times—that the lack of money hadn't kept him from making a decision about Pippa's future—and it wasn't just that she was so young to be thrust out into the world on her own. He simply didn't want to face the fact that one day he must part with her. Another year, he had promised himself over the summer, just one more year before the loneliness and silence would fill the cottage once she had gone.

Lucien didn't see Jean-Louis at all. Mme. Hugo met him at the rear door, asked him in with forced politeness, then Pépi appeared. They were both attired in their Sunday best, although Madame's royal purple dress was covered with a large blue apron. She held her head stiffly, her black hair pinned in precise elaborate sausagelike rolls on the top of her head, glittering earrings dangling steadily on either side of her well-powdered neck. Pépi was in starched white and shiny navy blue.

Lucien, wearing his usual rumpled workman's pants and big jacket, set the tone by standing just inside the doorway of the steamy kitchen without removing his beret. He came directly to the point, demanding to speak to Jean-Louis and was told that the young man was "busy elsewhere." From that point the three-way conversation developed into a useless argument, Lucien stating his case that their son had kept Pippa out half the night, thus blemishing her reputation and the Anjou honor and therefore should be made accountable for his actions. Madame denied the accusations, stating that Jean-Louis had, out of the kindness of his heart, gone with Pippa at her insistence to help look for a lost dog, which that foolish Pippa was afraid the Couronne sisters might find and turn into soup!

At first Pépi tried to keep the peace. However, when Lucien announced that from this day forward, Jean-Louis Hugo was never to set foot on Anjou property, and if he did, Lucien would have him arrested, Pépi crossed his arms stubbornly, causing his gold cufflinks to strain across his muscular wrists, and said that Lucien was acting like a clucking mother hen, making something out of nothing. Lucien, in turn, replied that Pépi was strutting around like a Bantam rooster and deafening himself to reason with his own voice.

The dialogue then disintegrated into a series of petty insults about each other, their respective blood lines and their respective offspring, and eventually Mme. Hugo disintegrated into tears. Pépi finally ordered Lucien out of his house and off his property. Much later when Ygrec heard about the incident, he told Michelin he thought he might write his own version of Romeo and Juliet.

Lucien, more discouraged than angered by the quarrel, knew then that he must go ahead with his plans to send Pippa away. He went back to the cottage, spoke to Pippa briefly, took a bottle from the cupboard by the sink and put it into his pocket and left, this time closing the door firmly behind him.

Ordinarily he would have enjoyed a Sunday stroll in the sunshine, and although when he took the short cut from rue Lutétia to rue Feu Follet, he did stop at the edge of the cemetery and sit for a time beneath the great trees, it was not to contemplate the colorful last fling of summer. He had to take time to put his thoughts in order, make plans, and decide on his approach to the problem of M. Valin Chamillion. The very idea of having to go near the disgusting little man again was repulsive to Lucien, but in his lifetime he had been forced to play many roles, and this one would not be too difficult if he could keep his antipathy and impatience under disguise.

Estelle Chamillion stepped back from the front door, clutching a matted sweater to her neck. Lucien, who had seen her from time to time over the years, was struck by her distraught appearance. She looked twice her age, with pouchy eyes and graying wisps of hair sticking to the sides of her pudgy face.

"My brother has been ill since Friday, M. Anjou. I regret it is impossible for him to have visitors," she whispered. "Also maman . . . the doctor has examined her only an hour ago . . . she has dropsy, monsieur."

"My sympathies, mademoiselle, my deepest sympathies." Lucien eased himself past the threshold. "But it is a matter of some importance . . . a business matter that will please your brother . . . cheer him."

Little of the bright warm air followed Lucien into the dingy foyer. This was a day when doors should be thrown wide open, when bedding should be hung over the sills of upstairs windows so the healing freshness could blow through and replace the stale sickness he smelled on every side, but he felt certain that the house had been sealed against healthiness for so long that the disease of depression had penetrated even the woodwork.

Lucien went on politely. "Shall I close the doors, mademoiselle? We cannot have you catching a chill, can we? You need all of your strength to care for your family." He pulled off his beret and quietly pushed the door to. "You look exhausted, and I hesitate to trouble you, but my visit will not take long. Your brother need not tire himself by coming downstairs. He is in his room?"

"Well, monsieur, if you can cheer him . . ." She glanced apprehensively up the dusty carpeted staircase, then hearing a whimpering, much like that of a petulant baby, she started toward the double doors on her left, darting her eyes from the stairs, to the doors, to the big man. "I must see to maman, monsieur. If you really think . . . I know Valin has a problem, but he does not come out of his room. . . . If you . . ." Her whispers struck Lucien like the squeaks of a cornered mouse.

"I understand, I quite understand. Do not trouble yourself. Go tend to your mother and I will speak to you again on my way out. Perhaps I can be of some help." He smiled reassurance, and as she scuttled out of sight he mounted the stairs. The sour smells struck him again, hanging, clinging like a pollution. On the landing all the doors were closed except the one which was ajar at the end of the hall.

On Friday night Lucien had taken no notice of the bedroom, simply dumping his half-conscious human burden on the bed and leaving. Now in the daylight, the large dark pieces of elaborately carved furniture stood out against walls that were papered with gold and black roses, and gave Lucien the ridiculous impression of a once grand hotel that had deteriorated into use as a brothel. The curtains were gold too, and quite new. No doubt Gabrielle Chamillion's hand had been responsible for the redecoration that had taken place.

In the midst of a disorder of open drawers strewn with articles of clothing, piles of books, stacks of slithering magazines and brochures, and an open empty valise on a chair, Valin Chamillion lay curled up on the bed. Beside him on a table was a tray holding a bowl of coagulated green soup and a crust of baguette. The bureau was littered with square anisette and green Pernod bottles, all empty. On the floor near the bed was a vin ordinaire bottle, also empty.

Valin turned, blinking, trying to adjust his eyes. His pale hair was matted and bent up on one side and his cheeks were patchy with a growth of beard. He patted aimlessly at the bedclothes with one hand. "My glasses . . . they must be somewhere here," he muttered. "It's all very tiring, this packing . . . deciding what to take . . ." He patted the bed once more and finally raised himself on one elbow.

"Sit up, M. Chamillion!" Lucien's words were gentle, but the hand that pulled Valin from the bed to an unsteady sitting position was not.

Valin's first reaction was stunned, but the pallid face brightened. "M. Anjou? Oh, bonjour, M. Anjou." The words began to pour out in an unsteady stream. "You must excuse my confusion . . . it is so hard to decide what to take . . . so many books and of course the brochures. If I go to Spain I won't need the Greek ones, but on the other hand . . ." He squirmed. "Thank you for helping me, monsieur, but you are hurting my shoulder. You know I have a bruised shoulder from a little accident."

Lucien released his grip. "When were you planning on leaving, monsieur?"

Valin was now having trouble forming words and he was beginning to tremble. "Ah, well now . . . it will take some time to get packed, but Gabrielle will help, of course. Yes . . . Gabrielle . . . I have been waiting for her . . . she had to go . . ." Suddenly he raised his eyes and Lucien saw the void, then the tears as Valin began to cry softly, hopelessly, but the hysteria was there ready to burst forth.

Le bon Dieu, Lucien thought, what a day! First tears from Pippa, then Mme. Hugo, and now this.

"You've been under a great strain, M. Chamillion. What you need is a small stimulant and then we can talk." Lucien lifted the flap of his big pocket and pulled out the bottle. The sobs began to change into swallowed jerks as Valin held out two unsteady hands.

"We must be civilized, monsieur. A gentleman does not drink from the mouth of a bottle. Ah, I see a glass over there." Lucien bypassed the rubble on the floor and picked up a licorice-smelling glass from the bureau, but kept watching Valin out of the corner of his eye, for he was being purposefully slow in providing the drink. "There is no need to pretend with me. You should know that. After Friday night I have a complete understanding of your problems. Now, monsieur, I think we can solve them, if you do exactly what I tell you to do. . . . One step at a time, we can find solutions to your great worries . . . but only one at a time. Do you understand me?"

Valin, his trembling hands still outstretched, began nodding foolishly.

"First we must throw open your window so you can breathe fresh air, then you must have a bath, and put on fresh clothing . . . and shave, of course. Later we shall sit and discuss your position with Joddard et Fils." Lucien was pouring the liquor into the glass, very carefully. "I shall give you one drink before you proceed to cleanse yourself. When you are tidy in your appearance, your mind will also begin to put things in order. After that we shall have another drink. Do I make myself clear?"

Valin nodded dumbly, scrubbing under his eyes with a fist like a small boy. "Sacré bleu—children!" Lucien cursed to himself. "It is as if the whole world has suddenly been populated with children, like Ghislaine and this creature." He handed over the glass.

Valin almost choked on the first gulp and some of the liquid ran down his chin. He gulped again and wiped his lips, then muttered almost sensibly, "If M. Joddard hears about Friday, I won't have a job . . . that's what Estelle says."

"Your sister is worried, that's all. I think we can handle M. Joddard, if you can handle yourself. I have an idea, and I have friends, but, monsieur, I repeat, you must do exactly as I tell you, or I will walk away and leave you to your fate."

"It will be as you say, M. Anjou. Whatever you say . . . just tell me. . . ." Valin, both hands still clutched around the empty glass, extended his arms, less shakily but still not steady.

"Very well. First we tend to the body. Soak yourself well in a bath to get the poison out of your system. I will have your sister prepare a little nourishment for you too. By tomorrow morning you will appear at your office on time, looking alert and healthy. Now stand up and get started. I will stay until you begin to feel better, then I must go on another errand, but I will return, and when I do, I want to find a new man waiting for me."

"You will leave the . . . the bottle . . . you will leave it with me? It is Sunday, M. Anjou," Valin pleaded.

"I will take the bottle, but I will be back, and I will keep you supplied for the next while with enough of your stimulant to steady your nerves. Look on me as your doctor, monsieur. Carry out my instructions and your ailments will be kept under control and your troubles cured." Lucien managed to force a half smile, but added, "You are not taking any trips to Greece or to Spain today, so you might as well accept the fact and put the valise away."

"Yes, monsieur." Valin stood up rather unsteadily, looking like a bag of rags. "But one more thing . . . my glasses, I lost my glasses . . . somewhere, on Friday."

"Yes, on Friday night." Lucien's patience was wearing thin. "Have you not a spare pair?"

"I used to . . . I don't know where . . . Estelle, Estelle might know. . . ." The tremors had started once more.

Lucien took note, sloshed some more of the cloudy liquid from the bottle into the glass, and this time helped guide it to the chattering teeth. "Now pull yourself together and stop wasting time. There is much to be done before tomorrow. I will go down and talk to your sister."

"Why are you being so kind to me?" Valin's eyes were brimming with tears again.

"M. Chamillion," Lucien lied convincingly, "I knew your father. He was a young officer in my regiment and he died bravely for his country. I do this for his son, who can yet be as fine a man as his father. Hold up your head, monsieur! Remember, tomorrow you begin a new time in your life with the help of your friend, Corporal Anjou."

* * *

"Ah, my good friend, Corporal Anjou. How thoughtful of you to come." Ygrec proceeded to stand, but Lucien noticing the tired face waved him back into his seat on the patio.

"Don't get up, M. Ygrec." Lucien bent over, shook hands, then looked around for the dog. "She is all right, your Mademoiselle Larme?" he asked, although he knew the answer by the smile on the face of the old gendarme.

"Indeed, she was quite hungry this morning. The inspector and Mme. Michelin have taken her for a little walk. They should be back shortly. Come and sit, Corporal. I am pleased to have company. I'm afraid I slept poorly last night . . . the excitement seemed to stimulate me." He wheezed as he laughed. "So I was ordered to stay here and rest in the sunshine, an instruction easy to follow on such a fine day. I need not tell you, I'm sure, that your great kindness of last night has made the day quite perfect for me."

"My pleasure, monsieur. I am pleased the dog is well." Lucien loosened his coat and sat down in a slatted chair opposite Ygrec, and there were a few moments of silence as both men appeared to admire the hedge-enclosed patch of neat lawn with borders of marigold that surrounded the smooth stone patio.

"I have come about Pippa," the corporal said at last. "I regret the inconvenience to Mme. Michelin, but Pippa will no longer be able to come here to the château." Then he related the events of the night before, aired his reasons for his mistrust of Jean-Louis Hugo, and finally announced his decision to send Pippa away from St. Denis.

Ygrec listened with quiet attention. He smiled to himself when he heard of the quarrel with the Hugos this morning, and frowned at the facts that Lucien presented to support his suspicions of the young man's stability. He felt that Lucien was possibly overreacting on a few matters such as the driving of the motorcycle, but agreed that experimenting with drugs, which Jean-Louis had done last spring, was indeed stupid and possibly dangerous.

"I was a career soldier, M. Ygrec. I lied about my age to fight at the end of the First World War, and I spent over thirty-five years of my life in uniform. I did not lead a sheltered life. Once I was a sergeant until I was demoted. I know young men, their strengths and their weaknesses. I, myself experimented with hashish when I served in North Africa, and drank absinthe, which as you know contains the drug wormwood that can drive a man to madness, but I learned my lessons. It is possible that Jean-Louis Hugo will grow up to some responsibility, but I do not intend to have Pippa exposed to unnecessary risks. What he feels about her at the moment I do not know. I haven't even seen him since his return home yesterday. But Pippa thinks she's in love with him . . . she's sixteen years old, and she thinks she knows about love. I refuse to believe that I am acting like an overprotective mother hen!" Lucien's anger was apparent.

Nothing serious had happened last night, Lucien replied to Ygrec's inquiry. He had not pushed Pippa for facts, but she had never lied to him in her life. Most of the time had been spent looking for the dog, after Jean-Louis, stopping at a cafe for cigarettes, had heard the dog was missing. He'd joked about an inspector who had so little to do that he was tracing an animal. Pippa had realized what was taking place and had become upset, insisting that they cruise St. Denis to try and find "M. Ygrec's beautiful dog."

"But that is beside the point," Lucien had insisted. "She did not say so in so many words, but she is ready to hop on the back of that devil's machine and go off with him if he says the word . . . I know . . . I know! She thinks they were "made for each other"! Until she is away from this place and safely in the hands of the sisters at the Académie in Toulon, I will not have a moment's peace, and even then . . ."

Ygrec saw, for the first time, a dark side of the old corporal's character, for there was something, a warning, in his eyes and the set of his jaw. "I have known Pippa only a short time," he said quietly, "but it has been long enough to observe that she is not just an ordinary very bright young girl. She has a great touch for the dramatic, and deep feelings. I can believe that she would become irrationally involved in what she believes is true love. I have often said that love can be a form of temporary insanity, and not just in the very young. So, Corporal, you have my complete understanding of your concern. On the other hand, don't you think it would be wise to allow her to come here as usual in the afternoons, until the arrangements have been made for her to leave St. Denis? It would give her something to do, and she might talk to me or Mme. Michelin. We in turn could possibly reason with her. She can't run into any temptation here with me and Mademoiselle Larme."

Lucien considered, then nodded slowly. "I believe you are right. She will be most happy when I tell her. She was crying when I left her this morning, and I came away with a heavy heart . . . now I can brighten her day, and mine as well. I am most grateful to you, my friend."

"I have done nothing but listen."

"Often that is all a friend need do to lighten another's burdens." Lucien stood up. "I shall bring her here at noon and fetch her in the evenings. It will be no problem as this week I am going to the loge de garde to help the Couronne sisters . . . some repairs to the old house before the winter winds loosen more tiles from the roof and tear the shutters."

"Pippa has told me of your kindness to the Couronne ladies. It is very thoughtful of you, Corporal. These days one is inclined to put the aged out of mind as a nuisance."

Lucien shrugged. "They have no one anymore. My father was fond of them as children and now they are old and not well. Their small annuity can no longer cover more than the bare necessities . . . as you know, the franc buys less and less these days. If only they could sell off that garden property, they would be able to have a few comforts and be free from worry."

"I would have thought such prime land would be easy to sell."

"One would think so. I have done what I could at their request. I saw the agent last week, and a M. Matieu was thought to be interested and was about to make the purchase, but something changed his mind. The ladies were quite upset. Their situation is very sad. They are proud, of course . . . too proud, but that is the old way. On Saturday I discovered there had been no sugar in the house for some time."

Ygrec was touched by the corporal's concern, and he too remembered the kindness of the strange little Mlle. Ghislaine. "I wonder . . . the M. Matieu you mentioned, would he be a relative of Jules Matieu, the fashion photographer in Paris? Mme. Michelin works with him, as you may know."

"I do believe that Pippa mentioned the fact. About the Matieu family, I don't know, except that the agent from Joddard et Fils said they were a large firm . . . three or four brothers, I believe."

"I wonder . . ." Ygrec said. "I think I will speak to Mme. Michelin when she returns. It could be the same family, and they may not realize the advantages of the Couronne property."

"That is possible. The agent I spoke to has been ill and another agent took over the client. But do not put yourself out, my friend. In time the land will sell."

"It is no trouble, Corporal, and sometimes when one is old each day can be like a lifetime."

"True, M. Ygrec, so true. That is what I dread about sending Pippa away, if the truth be known . . . the loneliness. I have enjoyed this afternoon more than you realize, but I must be getting back to Pippa with my good news. Au revoir, until tomorrow."

Chapter Twelve

The new week began well.

"It hasn't been like Monday at all," Vanessa announced happily when she arrived home early in the afternoon. "Jules Matieu says it's the influence of the new moon on the psychic rays of the planets, or some such thing. I expect that's why Maurice's chest cleared up overnight, just like magic. Everything went right at the studio too . . . no temper tantrums, no problems with the lighting or cameras . . . just 'clickety click,' so here I am!" She'd kicked off her shoes and taken the pins out of her hair and was kneeling on the patio hugging Mademoiselle Larme.

"Well I hope it lasts," muttered Michelin. He'd also finished work early and was sitting shirtless in the sun, leaning back, eyes closed. "In my case it may be just a brilliant mind, good organization, and hard work . . . but I'd have to agree that the full moon often brings out all the psychos in the city. Jules Matieu has always been a bit of a psycho himself if you ask me, what with his tarot cards and health foods and weird friends."

"And séances," Vanessa laughed with a laugh. "He wanted me to stay and attend a séance this evening, at his apartment, of course."

Michelin opened his eyes just a fraction. "A séance! That's a new one. . . . I must admit he's original. What happened to the old approach: 'Come up and view my new etchings'?"

Vanessa just laughed again. "Aha, I thought that would open your eyes! But he's a smart businessman too, and when I told him about the Couronne gardens, he actually stopped fluttering around and said that his brother Roget was an idiot not to have bought the land, but that he was always retarded anyway . . . Roget is the construction engineer. There's a family feud been going on for years and Roget doesn't speak to Jules, but Damon, the advocate does, so Jules phoned him right away and now they're going to pick up something or other . . . an option, I think. Does that sound right?"

It was Michelin's turn to be amused. "You are a born genius when it comes to explanations, chérie. Now stop hugging that dog and come here. We may as well take advantage of the peace and quiet while the old man is off on his walk."

"Out here in front of Mademoiselle? The moon is affecting your senses! However, if you insist . . ." She stretched out her hand to his.

*   *   *

Whatever the reason, Ygrec's chest had cleared, and when Lucien stopped by just as Vanessa had arrived home, they had said there was no need for Pippa to stay longer and Ygrec proposed that he'd walk part way home with them.

Pippa hadn't appeared happy, although she hadn't mentioned Jean-Louis or any of her problems during the short time she'd been alone with Ygrec. But he'd understood her preoccupation and noticed that she'd been pleased to leave early. She was young, Ygrec decided, and her subdued mood would be short-lived. Her grandfather had certainly been in an expansive frame of mind.

Lucien was indeed optimistic in spite of an unusually tiring day.

Mother Superior at the convent was only too pleased about Corporal Anjou's sensible decision regarding his granddaughter's further education. The new semester would begin in ten days, but there would be time to make the arrangements if she wrote to the Académie immediately. Pippa's high grades should guarantee the acceptance.

M. Joddard, who had spent the weekend in the country, was in a benevolent mood, too, and quite understood why the dear Couronne sisters insisted that M. Chamillion handle their property exclusively. Older ladies were inclined to peculiarities, and when they took a liking to someone, well, that was that. M. Chamillion was new at the business, but in time might prove his worth—he certainly had a head for mathematics—as long as he could keep a clear head. M. Joddard had laughed at his own little joke; Lucien had managed a tight smile.

Valin himself, scrubbed, brushed, polished and pressed—and sadly sober—had peered hopefully through the glass from the back room, and Lucien, more from wisdom than pity, arranged to take him out at noon for a "business luncheon." Upon their return, M. Joddard had called Valin into his office to inform him that Maître Damon Matieu had phoned and was prepared to view the Couronne property and possibly take an option to buy. M. Chamillion was to meet with him tomorrow morning at precisely nine o'clock, so papers should be ready in anticipation. Valin, his nervous system slightly stimulated because of Lucien Anjou's generosity, had actually managed to look almost cheerful.

Even Ghislaine Couronne had a pleasant day. Since Amélie's death she had not bothered with morning devotions nor evening prayers and nothing but good had come to her—apart from a few small unpleasant incidents which were easily forgotten, so she decided to divest herself of her nun's role forever. She would never cover her head again, and she would buy a whole closetful of bright new dresses the minute the land was sold. Until then she would do what she could to fix herself up, the way she used to in the mountains before the trouble.

She washed her hair with rain water heated on the big stove, while the revived chicken, now a kind of soup stew, simmered on a back burner. Lucien had dropped in early, had noticed the new style of her hair, which was a loose bun perched on top of her head with the white fringe she had cut curled across her forehead, and told her that the property sale was imminent. He couldn't stay to share the chicken because he was to see the agent but promised he would come at noon tomorrow and stay longer.

After that she'd picked two bronze dahlias and sat in the garden in the sun for a long while, deciding which of Amélie's dresses she would wear tomorrow. She sat so long that the flowers wilted, but she put them in a squat jam jar in the center of the table anyway. When they doubled over with the weight of the blooms, she got out the butcher knife and cut the stems off bit by bit, experimenting, until they were merely stubs and the petals floated on top of the water. Then they looked dead, so she took them outside and stuck them on top of the asparagus bed. By then she was quite tired, so she had a little sleep, curled up on the unmade cot.

When she awoke it was cool, and the chicken had boiled dry even though the fire in the stove was little but ash. She picked up the pot, carried it outside, lid and all, made her way quite happily to the hedge, and tossed the whole thing into the shrubbery on the other side of the pathway into the old gardens. She'd never liked cleaning pots. When she got the money from the land she would buy new pots all the time—she would never get her fingernails dirty again, ever. It was then that she noticed the curious woman in pink again, standing in the distance near the old rose arbor. Her back was to Ghislaine and she looked as if she were waiting for someone, probably the person who was buying the land. Ghislaine didn't want to see anyone, so she hurried inside and bolted the doors.

She had half a jar of strawberry preserves for supper, then wandered down the hall in the dusk and opened the door to the parlor. It had been so long since she had even looked inside the room, she really didn't know what to expect. It smelled heavy, dead. She didn't put on the light. The spinette stood in its place by the shuttered window, the loveseat by the fireplace, her unfinished tapestry still in its frame in front of the high-backed chair that belonged to Amélie's mother. She'd get Lucien to bring the tapestry out tomorrow, and she might even rescue some of the cobwebby statuettes and figurines from the mantelpiece. A few were quite pretty; others reminded her of bad times and made her unhappy, so she'd get Lucien to throw them away.

*   *   *

Pépi Hugo should have been just a little bit unhappy and subdued. He was a peaceful man and he'd aways admired Lucien Anjou. During the war when tales of the brave exploits of le Loup Noir and other Maquis had trickled into the prison camp where Pépi had spent most of the years of conflict, he had been proud to boast that he personally knew someone in the underground movement. At the end of the war he had been even more proud and boastful. But even in the prison camp, Pépi had managed to stay reasonably cheerful, cooking for the Boche officers, and today, out of habit, he immersed himself in walnut tarts and a new recipe for Swedish roll, the name of which made him angry, so he was able to transfer his frustrations to the dough. He pounded and tossed the sticky mixture on the big table, swearing behind a cloud of flour. "Sacré bleu . . . Swedish indeed!

My own father, rest his soul, prepared this very recipe, only better, with more cinnamon and just a touch of almond in the icing."

Jean-Louis had to go to Paris to get parts for his motorcycle but assured his mother that tomorrow he would help with the deliveries. As there was no reason not to take the boy at his word, Madame was content. As she washed his shirts and hung them to dry on the line that stretched across the alleyway from the upstairs balcony, she admitted loudly to Pépi—who couldn't possibly have heard as he was downstairs talking to himself—that the fabrics used in the clothing nowadays, even in men's clothing, were certainly much easier to get clean and probably would take less ironing, and if the colors of Jean-Louis' shirts were brighter than his father's, well, wasn't the male peacock the brightly colored one of the species, so who were they to argue with nature?

She hummed loudly as she shook the parlor rugs and felt almost sorry for that silly little Pippa who was shut up in the cottage on such a nice day. Still, Lucien had learned his lesson about discipline and the girl. It was as well that Madame was in the kitchen ironing when Lucien escorted Pippa down the lane on the way to the château, and that she was having a little siesta in the afternoon when the two returned, otherwise her self-satisfied humming might have ceased.

Estelle Chamillion had been to the pâtisserie for bread and ". . . one lemon tart for maman . . . she's feeling much better today," Pépi reported later. M. Fouschie had been in too, for his usual two-day-old croissants at half price. He'd been stinking of stale wine and looking almost cheerful until Pépi had informed him of the improved health of Mme. Chamillion. Both Pépi and Madame had enjoyed a good chuckle over the mortician's obvious discomfiture, and when Jean-Louis arrived home for supper he was relieved to find his parents in such a good mood. The parts for his machine had been quite expensive, he told them . . . and also the new shoes with built-up soles had cost a lot but had been too good a bargain to pass up.

He had praised maman's good supper with a warm kiss on her cheek, then had got out his guitar and entertained her with a song and had gone on practicing some new songs until nearly dark, when with his mother's blessing and little joke, "Don't go looking for any lost dogs tonight, *mon cher,*" he went for a walk to clear his head.

*   *   *

"The moon's psychic rays have changed for the worse in one hell of a hurry," Michelin grumbled to Ygrec early Tuesday morning. He'd just phoned Jules Matieu's secretary to say that Vanessa wasn't feeling well and wouldn't be in today. "She thinks she's coming down with the flu or the black plague. She's gone back to bed."

"Probably the plague. I have a feeling it's going to be one of those days," wheezed Ygrec. "Perhaps if I go back to bed too and start the day all over again, things will improve."

"I hope you're right. I'd better get out of here before that phone goes again."

Michelin had received three phone calls before breakfast. Then they had discovered that Mademoiselle had chewed through her lead and was gone again. She returned before long in answer to Ygrec's insistent calling, was duly chastised, and spent the rest of the morning on the rug beside Vanessa's bed. The worry and exertion had tired Ygrec, but by noon things did begin to improve and both he and Vanessa had a light lunch outside on the terrace.

Michelin had stopped in at the cottage to tell the corporal that as Mme. Michelin was staying home today, Pippa wouldn't be needed. Pippa was relieved, although she pretended to be disappointed. Gran'papa was going to fix the roof at the loge de garde and wouldn't be home all day, and she felt sure that Jean-Louis would manage to sneak around and see her. She simply had to talk to him.

Lucien dropped into Joddard et Fils on his way to the loge, to be told that M. Chamillion was out showing the Couronne property to a client. Lucien didn't see them in the old gardens, but presumed all was well. He hammered his impatience out on the roof of the loge. As he wanted to keep Ghislaine in a receptive mood, he complimented her on the rubbery omelette that stuck in his throat, but he managed to wash it down with some rather good wine he found in a cupboard in the larder, then returned to his work on the roof.

He saw the woman from his perch on the gable over Amélie's bedroom. She was wearing a less elaborate dress of dark green that almost blended in with the hedge. She was standing just inside the opening staring up at him, one hand holding the strap of her shoulder bag, swinging it gently. It was the movement that had first attracted him.

He stood up slowly, staring back, then moving like a steeplejack along the slant of the roof, he made his way to the ladder where it rested on the far side away from the road and climbed to the ground.

He peered in the kitchen window. Ghislaine was playing with an old radio she'd found in the parlor, twisting the dial from one whiny station to another. The woman in green had disappeared from view. He strode quickly across the garden and disappeared as well.

"Where have you been, Lucien?" Ghislaine called from the back door as he returned.

"Talking to the agent. I have to meet him at the office. I will let you know about the sale as soon as I hear anything."

He lowered the ladder carefully, placing it along the side of the house. She waved happily from the shed as he left, then smoothed the long pleats of Amélie's blue dress and went inside to finish off the wine.

* * *

Maître Damon Matieu took one look at the location of the Couronne property, which adjoined the Château de Couronne apartments that his brother's Roget's company owned, managed to keep his delight to himself in case the puny little agent raised the price, and promptly suggested that they return to the Joddard offices to talk business. Damon Matieu was already making plans; he would begin building at once, the most elaborate house his architect could design, and then he would move himself and Marguerite, the black-haired, creamy-skinned, almost-divorced wife of his brother Roget, into the edifice. His brother Jules would, this very night, receive one of Damon's precious vintage bottles of champagne. Later Jules could have Marguerite as well, should his tastes demand her, and should her skin remain creamy. Property increased in value with age; women deteriorated, particularly those with expensive addictions.

Valin Chamillion was nearly beside himself with the intoxication of success. By two o'clock the papers for the sale of the Couronne land were signed by Maître Damon Matieu, the check was placed on M. Joddard's desk, and Valin took off in his Peugeot to find Corporal Anjou, once more dreaming of the Mercedes he would buy, and back to his indecision of where to go first, Spain or Cyprus. There was still the problem of Gabrielle, but his good friend the corporal would help find her and make her see reason. One thing at a time, he had said.

Lucien was not at home. His granddaughter reported shyly that he was at the loge de garde. What an oddly attractive child she was, with those big appealing eyes that reminded Valin of Gabrielle when they'd first met. The girl seemed anxious to have him leave, looking over her shoulder as if she were expecting someone, and on his way down the lane he noticed a darkly bearded young man watching him from the back of the Pâtisserie Hugo. It would be young Jean-Louis Hugo—Valin had heard Estelle say the boy was home and sporting a beard. The Hugo boy and the corporal's granddaughter—what a waste!

He needed a drink, he told himself, just one cool drink; he deserved it too; he had every reason in the world to celebrate. Surely Lucien Anjou would not care if he bought himself one small Pernod. Lucien's words of Sunday night jabbed at him. "I will keep you supplied with as much as is good for you . . . but if you so much as take one drink without my permission . . ." Valin blotted the words from his mind by adding figures and doing percentages and computing his commission. He wouldn't be able to buy a Mercedes at once, but now M. Joddard would give him more sales to handle, and by the winter he would be well off.

Lucien might never have got his hands on the papers that day, but the Peugeot began to cough suddenly, until finally it came to a stuttering halt at the intersection of rue Lutétia and avenue Côte, and within viewing distance of the Côte Impériale garage.

"You're out of gas, monsieur." The fuzzy-haired young attendant, whom Valin had fetched, peered through the car window at the instrument panel. Valin felt frantically in his pocket. If he had to buy gas, he would have little money left for his celebration.

Then another voice brought him to attention. "No doubt both you and your car are suffering from thirst," Lucien commented dryly. "I understand from M. Joddard that you have some papers for me. Shall we leave the car in the hands of Henri, here, and put ourselves in the capable hands of Mme. Céleste at the bistro around the corner?"

Some time later Lucien shook hands with a lighthearted and somewhat lightheaded Valin at the intersection and watched him cross over to the garage. Then the old corporal proceeded back down the street and home.

*   *   *

"It's been a good day," Lucien said to Pippa when he entered the warm kitchen. "Look at the red sunset like a halo on the clouds . . . and see how the light makes the geraniums glow in the window boxes. Would you like to walk over to the pâtisserie with me to buy a few tarts for our supper?"

"Oh, yes." Pippa took off her apron and smoothed her old school skirt and straightened her blouse, wishing she could change into something pretty, but being grateful for small mercies.

"Good. And when we get back I will push you in the swing, way up in the air, the way we used to when you were a little girl. You're not too old for a swing, are you?"

"Oh no, Gran'papa. I'll never be too old for that." She hugged him around his thick waist.

He touched her soft hair with roughened fingers. "Come along then. I have to go out on a short errand after supper but I won't be long. When I come back, you might like to read some of your poetry to me. I was never much good with words myself . . . never understood most poems, but I'm sure if you explain them to me I would like them."

She sensed something different as they walked down the lane together, and she put her hand in his as she'd done as a child. Yesterday as she'd been leaving the château she'd overheard Mme. Michelin talking about magic and the moon. She shivered a little.

"Gran'papa, does the moon really make things change, make people different?" she asked softly.

"That's what they say. My father would plant certain crops only in the dark of the moon and anyone who has lived with nature believes it affects animals. Wolves stay near their caves during a new moon, and, if it's the season, the cubs that are born then are strong, as long as they are kept from the moonlight. At half moon, packs become more daring and roam, attacking even large animals, although they follow their leader, obedient and alert. But when the moon is full they become restless, taking chances, and some wander away alone searching for stray lambs, often never returning."

"When are they the happiest?"

"When there is a mist on the moon, so it is said. When they look for a mate."

They had reached the end of the lane, and Pippa's heart sank. Jean-Louis' motorcycle was nowhere to be seen, either at the side or the back of the pâtisserie. The old delivery van stood alone, brilliantly clear in the sunset, but there might be a mist on the moon tonight, she decided hopefully.

Chapter Thirteen

Gabrielle Chamillion's body was found Tuesday, just before midnight, and her husband was taken into custody for questioning shortly afterward.

Michelin had been home only about half an hour when he was notified of the situation. He took the call on the telephone in the hall so he wouldn't disturb Vanessa. Ygrec heard him talking and was instantly alert.

"That's stupid," he was saying. "If he's that paralyzed from drink he couldn't have strangled a kitten. . . . Well, where were you, Benoit? Then let me speak to Sergeant Corvette . . . very well, I'll come."

Ygrec was standing in the doorway looking disheveled, but his blue eyes were bright. "Are you going to the St. Denis gendarmerie, garçon? It would only take me a minute to put on a coat and . . ."

"No, old man, you cannot come with me tonight . . . not even for the ride. It's almost one o'clock in the morning and there's a cold wind rising." Then noticing the bleak look on Ygrec's face, Michelin tried to compromise. "I'll tell you what, wait up for me if you wish, I shouldn't be long, as really this investigation has little to do with me. A woman we have been watching as a possible drug dealer has been killed, that's all. You heat up some milk and toss in a little brandy and I'll join you when I get back, then I'll fill you in on all the details.

"If you insist," Ygrec said rather testily.

"I insist. I may want to pick your brains later, unless of course the husband did do it, which I doubt."

"Whose husband?"

"Wait until I get back." Michelin picked up his coat and Ygrec wandered morosely into the kitchen muttering, "Hot milk indeed!"

*   *   *

The Hugo household had been asleep for some time.

"Pépi . . . wake up, Pépi! Something is going on downstairs. Listen!" Madame sat straight up in bed, reached out to the bedside lamp, shoved her feet into scuffed slippers, and covered her voluminous nightgown with a bright quilted kimono.

She was downstairs with the back door open, before Pépi, in a striped nightshirt, appeared. He peered around Madame, looking quite dazed.

Estelle Chamillion was leaning against the doorway, obviously on the verge of collapse. She was dressed in an assortment of sweaters and a heavy skirt, but was wearing carpet slippers on her feet. "I didn't know where else to turn to. They've arrested Valin . . . dragged him out of his bed . . . two gendarmes , . . right out of his bed!" She began to sob hysterically so that the rest of her words were unintelligible.

Madame half carried her into the kitchen and propped her on a chair close to the table. "Pour a drink, Pépi . . . some of that cooking brandy will do. Now, Pépi, don't just stand there gaping . . . and where is your robe? You shouldn't be down here without your robe . . . it's not decent, and you'll catch cold." She turned back to Estelle, pushing the wet face away from her kimono and brushing the wild strands of gray hair out of the woman's eyes. "Just calm down a little, Estelle, so we can understand you. What do you mean they arrested Valin? Why was he arrested? Was he in another fight?"

Estelle's swollen eyes were wide with terror now. "They said . . . they say . . . but . . . he couldn't have . . ."

"Couldn't have what?"

"Killed Gabrielle . . . they said he . . ."

Madame caught Estelle before she could fall, looked over at her husband who was standing expressionless like a little draped sculpture, and said quickly, "Pour two drinks, Pépi . . . and get the good brandy from the dining room."

"Could you make that three, Papa?" It was Jean-Louis at the bottom of the stairs in pajamas, looking rather wide awake but pale.

Pépi slowly took four glasses from the big kitchen cupboard, put them on a tray as if he was about to serve guests at a party, and padded quietly into the dining room in his bare feet.

*   *   *

Ygrec was asleep in the salon, his bare feet stretched out on the stool. Michelin was tired and would have preferred to leave the old man snoring softly in the big chair, but it had to be now, or in the morning, and besides Ygrec couldn't stay there all night.

"You've been a long time," the old gendarme said, moving his legs stiffly and rubbing his feet together. "Complications?"

"No, just confusion. It will be better when Sergeant Corvette comes in. . . . He's been called back from vacation."

"Well tell me, but make it brief. You look tired."

Michelin squatted on the stool. "We're on to some cocaine distributors . . . it's getting quite popular with the élite these days . . . but we don't want the small dealers, we're after the source, so we've had one of our men, a Sergeant Benoit, undercover in St. Denis. He is the Algerian who got hit in the face with a bottle during that fight in the Cafe Khedive on Friday night. He was just an unlucky bystander. Anyway, he's been tailing a known trafficker, a *cochon* by the name of Raoul Tusette, who has had contacts in Marseilles. We've been hoping Tusette would lead us to his source there, but he hasn't been out of this area in over two months, yet he's getting his supplies somehow. . . . Do you have the picture?"

Ygrec nodded.

"Recently Tusette made contact with a local woman, Gabrielle Chamillion, who Benoit says is new to the game. She's got a past but has been respectably married for about four years and came to St. Denis only this summer, so she's not just a tart, or a user. Benoit felt she was being primed for bigger things, possibly a courier. It seems she's hungry for money, and she must be getting some from somewhere. . . . She just moved into a rather decent apartment near La Porte de Chapelle on the weekend."

"This last weekend?"

"Yes. Now she simply may have been starting an affair with Tusette . . . his tastes run above the common street girls. Benoit has been watching the situation, and on Sunday night she met Tusette here in a little bistro on rue Lutétia and he passed her some money. . . . Benoit said it seemed to be a large amount of money. Now why would they meet here? Why not in the apartment in the city? Was someone in a hurry?"

"Isn't rue Lutétia where Pippa lives?"

"Near there. It's a quiet district, nothing much happens . . . mostly respectable shopkeepers and market gardeners. The bad area is on the other side of the basilica. That's what's so odd. Gabrielle Chamillion's body was found back of a garage near the intersection of rue Lutétia and avenue Côte. Her husband was seen staggering around near the garage about ten o'clock by the attendant, and since he also was reported to have tried to strangle his wife in the Khedive on Friday, because she had gone off and left him, the local gendarmes picked him up tonight for questioning."

Ygrec yawned. "I must be too tired. Somehow I can't stir up much enthusiasm about the affair so far. Besides my feet are cold." He stood up stiffly from the chair. "Did the husband do it?"

"I find the possibility doubtful. He's an alcoholic . . . on anisette, it is reported, and you know what that does to the brain. He's a weak, stunned little creature; at least he was when I saw him. But, of course, one never knows."

"How did the woman die?"

"Strangled, with a scarf she was wearing."

"Where was your man, Benoit?"

"Watching Tusette, who was in the Cafe Khedive most of the evening. Tusette is friendly with the proprietor there, who isn't any better than he should be. But Benoit said he's sure Tusette was waiting for someone . . . possibly the woman."

"So that's it?"

"Until morning when more complete reports can be compiled." Michelin followed Ygrec out of the room, speaking softly.

"Well, one thing for certain, it wasn't this Tusette, was it?"

"No . . . too bad . . . a nice, clean drug-related death means at least one less open file. But it could have been one of his cohorts."

*   *   *

Lucien didn't hear about the arrest of Valin Chamillion until early Wednesday morning. The fool, Lucien said to himself. The idiot!

The papers concerning the sale of the land, properly signed with Amélie Couronne's name in pale uncertain scratches, lay in an open file on M. Joddard's desk, and Lucien made the effort to return to the business at hand.

". . . so, M. Chamillion will be unable to retain his position with our firm," M. Joddard continued coolly, as if he'd been relating a weather report, and not the arrest of one of his employees. "However, my son-in-law, M. Dubois, will be at your service and that of the Couronne sisters, should you wish to consult him. It is a blessing that the negotiations for the dear ladies' property were completed so satisfactorily yesterday." He tapped the file with a manicured finger. "Everything appears to be in order and the initial check covering the purchase will be deposited in the Caisse Populaire, as agreed, this very afternoon. Maître Damon Matieu was as eager to be done with the dull paper work as I'm sure we all are. I trust the dear ladies are satisfied and that they remain in good health. Bonjour to you, M. Anjou."

Lucien was very thankful to be dismissed so quickly. He stood on the street outside the office, uncertain, for the first time in many days, which way to turn. It was early, just after nine o'clock and the morning had turned blustery, with a smell of rain in the air. He should be feeling elated, for Pippa was safe, her future assured, but instead he felt old and very tired. Everything was an effort; nothing was simple.

He had better go home first, he decided. He was worried about Pippa as she wasn't well. He must try to talk to her; she had been really distressed this morning, crying and taking to her room without touching her breakfast. He knew she had waited up for him last night because he had found her asleep with her notebook of poems at her side, her head propped on her pillow, facing her open bedroom door as if she had been listening for his return. He felt truly sorry he had not been able to keep his word about last night, and he'd told her so this morning, but there was no way he could explain what had kept him.

Lucien didn't think that Ghislaine even understood the meaning of the word blackmail, but it was becoming obvious that she was using the method to its fullest extent to try and get her own way, and her demands were becoming ridiculous.

She had barely glanced at the papers when he'd placed them on the table last night, but first of all demanded what had kept him, and then preened herself like a silly bird. She'd looked pathetic, her hair lying in long skinny strands over her shoulders, the white fringe plastered across her forehead. She had obviously been searching through the trunks upstairs, for she had found a half-bald, old brown fur cape that she had draped on top of a wrinkled, brassy lace dress. He realized then what she was doing, what had been going on ever since the discipline of Amélie had been removed from her life. She was clutching at yesterdays that had never really existed for her and most certainly would never return.

He'd done his best with shallow compliments, had accepted a glass of wine, then had carried the dusty tapestry in its frame, from the forgotten parlor that should have remained forgotten, bringing it into the kitchen, placing it by the little chair and the hearth. But she had insisted, before she would sign the papers, that he go back with her into the dank dusty room, where she proceeded to point out objects and pieces of furnishings, remembering aloud with painful accuracy the source of many.

"Mme. Fouschie brought that shepherdess figurine from the château when I was very small. She said our father gave it to her, but she stole it, I know she did. She was always stealing things from the big house. I used to help her." Ghislaine giggled. "A lot of things she kept for herself, but I didn't care, although Amélie used to get upset. I hated the big house."

She had then fingered a fringed silk shawl that lay in rotting splendor across the top of the spinette, its inlaid-pearl edges warped. "Mme. Fouschie took this shawl too. It's strange I should remember, but I do. She just picked it up, as bold as could be, and draped it over her shoulders, the day she took us to look at our father's body in the big hall. He was pushed off the roof, you know, Lucien. . . . He didn't fall. Amélie told me, not long ago she told me. Do you know, Lucien, I think she knew she was going to die soon. After she'd taken her pills sometimes, she used to talk to me, just the last few weeks, she did, but she talked to me more than ever before. Sometimes she'd forget that she had taken her pills, and I'd pretend she hadn't taken them and bring her more, with hot milk, of course. She did enjoy her hot milk."

Lucien had been torn by the whole performance. She had dragged him back to the past with her meandering recital, which didn't appear to affect her that much, but which left him exhausted with guilt and pity . . . and resentment, but he could do nothing until at last she began to tire as well. He had done what he could to repair the old radio by reconnecting worn wiring. He'd promised to move the furniture the way she wanted it and get rid of the things she didn't like "because they belonged to Amélie's mother." Oh yes, he'd promised and promised, until finally she'd signed the papers, sitting at the table, the blues and yellows from the glass lampshade making her skin look unhealthy and transparent. She'd concentrated as if she were creating a piece of art, then looked up at him slyly, giggling when she had finished. It had been a night of slyness and hollow laughter, and once more he had done what had to be done for Pippa's sake. If he could just last out until the child was away from this place where innocents were damned—but he would keep going no matter what the cost.

He was glad it was turning cold; the warmth of the past few days had been too soothing. He needed the challenge of the elements to

keep him alert. He would make some thick hot soup for Pippa. As he
turned down the lane he noticed the motorcycle at the back of the
pâtisserie. The boy wouldn't last long in the suffocation of his family
and St. Denis, but whether he stayed or not was of no consequence
anymore. The land was sold and Pippa would be safe.

*   *   *

Valin Chamillion had somehow lasted out the night in custody
but, after his release, had collapsed in the front hall at home.

Mme. Hugo, out of desperation to get the hysterical Estelle home,
rather than out of true compassion, had stayed the night at the Maison Feu Follet, and by the time she arrived back to her own well-or-
ganized kitchen, she was too exhausted to berate Pépi for being late
in getting his sponges started, and she didn't even inquire about Jean-
Louis.

Pépi had pushed his own old chair to the doorway of the dining
room so that his wife could see him, while sitting back in comfort, as
she related each detail of her "night of agony."

"Valin fell right at my feet," Madame went on. "You should have
seen him . . . filthy like the whole house, of course, and looking like
death. I expect the doctor will be there by now. But Valin would
have had to stay right there where he had fallen on the floor if it
hadn't been for Inspector Michelin, who had kindly driven him home
from the gendarmerie. He's a decent man, that Inspector . . . very
neat in his clothes, and strong too. He just lifted Valin to his feet and
steered him up the stairs. Estelle was useless. I've never seen anything like her . . . runs around in circles clutching her sweater to her
neck as if someone was about to tear it off her shoulders."

"Small chance," commented Pépi, as he stirred a steaming cara-
mel sauce gently with a huge wooden spoon. "You couldn't hire a
man to touch that one."

"Do be serious, Pépi. You know very well I wasn't implying . . ."

"I know, chérie . . . go on."

"You shouldn't treat these matters lightly. After all, a woman is
dead, even though she won't be missed. I'm just surprised she didn't
die of some dread disease before now. That kitchen! You would
never believe the filth of the room. I had to insist on making my own
tea and Estelle's as well, while I was at it, so I could scrub the cups
before I used them. There were mouse droppings everywhere, and
Estelle admitted there were rats in the larder. I didn't sleep a wink,

Pépi. I just covered myself with my coat and sat on a chair in the dining room. I had to clean the chair off first, piled high as it was with dirty clothes and rubbish. Now you can understand why I hung my coat straightaway out on the clothesline to air. I hope it doesn't rain. Look outside, Pépi, and see if it's raining."

The little man stood on his tiptoes to stare over the top of the chair where she was sitting. "No, it's just gray and blowing. Oh, there goes Lucien back to the cottage. I wonder where he's been this time in the morning."

But for once Madame was not interested in Lucien Anjou. "Is that coffee ready yet, Pépi? I couldn't make myself drink that foul stuff that Estelle served her mother this morning."

"Any minute now." He peered over at the espresso pot. "How is old Mme. Chamillion? How has she taken the news?"

"She's better than she thinks! She never did like Gabrielle, and we just told her the woman had died, not the sordid details. She certainly enjoyed the tarts you sent over with me. She keeps that radio of hers on so loud most of the time that she wouldn't hear the end of the world. I have the feeling that if someone would push her out of bed and hand her a scrub brush, her circulation would improve, and so would her arthritis."

There was a thoughtful silence while Pépi poured two cups of the fragrant coffee, handing one to his wife and sipping at the other himself as he went on stirring.

Mme. Hugo swallowed and sighed, "Ahh, now I shall live through the day. I must stir myself. It's a blessing the shop hasn't been busy so far this morning."

"Couldn't Jean-Louis tend to the shop today so you could get some rest?" Pépi suggested quietly.

"Where is he?"

"Still in bed."

"Well, it's best not to disturb him so early. He had such a dreadful night, with Estelle waking him with her hysterics."

"I don't think he was asleep," Pépi said. "He'd only just got in before she arrived."

"He was in hours before that! I heard him before I fell asleep and I'd been asleep a long time before Estelle came." Madame clunked her coffee cup onto the saucer. "Aren't you overcooking that filling just a bit, Pépi? And it smells to me like the pain-de-mie is done.

You'd better look in the oven. You've been getting very absent-minded these days." She stood up.

Pépi just went on stirring, but he was wondering why Inspector Michelin of the Special Branch had been called in on a simple murder in St. Denis.

Chapter Fourteen

Wednesday Pippa still wasn't well and stayed home. Lucien had come to the château with the message and left, not stopping for even a word with Ygrec, and Vanessa was ready to leave for the city.

"She may have picked up your black plague, chérie," Ygrec suggested lightly. "I expect she'll be better tomorrow. The corporal worries too much about her."

"Are you sure you'll be all right?" Vanessa asked for the second time. "Don't do anything foolish like walking in the rain. I don't know when Paul will get back, but I should be home early. I'm still not feeling too energetic myself."

"I hate walking in the rain," Ygrec replied. "I have skin that mildews easily." He watched her button up her sleek white raincoat and tuck her hair unceremoniously beneath her hood, then he returned to the salon where he stood watching the rain spit at the windows. He'd turned into a dull old weather watcher, he decided.

He was restless. He wished Michelin's drug case was more interesting. He needed something to exercise his brain, and he thought about the facts that Michelin had related to him last night, but somehow he couldn't work up any enthusiasm. The dead woman, Gabrielle, seemed to him cast from the same mold as innumerable unfortunate women he had run into during his own career—foolish, shallow, wanting too much too fast—to be pitied, of course, but no more interesting than the cardboard files that contained their statistics.

When Michelin did drop in for a few minutes for a quick cup of coffee on his way to another investigation, the rest of the details that he enumerated to Ygrec were of even less interest. The thirty-four-year-old woman had been dead between one and two hours when her body was found. They had no idea when she had last eaten, or where, so there were just rigor mortis signs for the coroner to go on and the detailed written report was not yet available. She had been strangled and there were no other obvious injuries to the body. She had not been sexually molested and she wasn't pregnant—although there were indications she had once borne a child.

The husband, Valin Chamillion, a one-time schoolmaster had recently been employed by a local estate agent and had been handling the sale of the Couronne garden property, which was Corporal Anjou's connection with the man. His father had been killed in North Africa during the war. There was a bedridden mother and a neurotic spinster sister and no love was lost between his family and the deceased wife. He had left his car at the garage yesterday afternoon because he'd run out of gas; and he had spent the rest of the afternoon drinking in a few local bars and, by evening, wasn't capable of driving anything. He had attempted to collect his car about half-past nine but had been discouraged by the garage attendant, so went staggering off into the darkness. His sister heard him falling up the stairs about ten o'clock, she thought, but she didn't see him; she was used to his "strange ways." And so it had gone on, Michelin's brief explanation and Ygrec's obvious disinterest, and Michelin had left shaking his head. The old man was really getting old.

* * *

The rest of the week brought no new developments and a kind of depressing lethargy settled on everyone involved.

Lucien was antisocial and withdrawn, worried because Pippa remained unwell. When he suggested calling a doctor, she protested, assuring him she was much better, and went to work halfheartedly cleaning the cottage, even the bleak little parlor that they never used, but she still only picked at her food and didn't even suggest going to the château in the afternoons. Lucien did accompany Ghislaine, by taxi, to the Caisse Populaire, where she behaved well, saying little, and withdrew an amount that Lucien felt was reasonable enough not to attract the attention of the bank officials. She was silent on the way back, preoccupied, fingering the money in her bag. He left her at her door, not mentioning his share of the commission, simply explaining that Pippa was not well and that he would return later. But a weariness of spirit seemed to settle on him and he put off the encounter until Friday.

There wasn't a sign of life from the Chamillion household. Estelle didn't even go out for bread, so Mme. Hugo took it upon herself to deliver two baguettes and some croissants on Friday afternoon.

"That Estelle! She sniffled all over the fresh loaves. I didn't go in
. . . I've had enough of her moaning and groaning!" Madame told
Pépi. Madame was particularly preoccupied because Jean-Louis was
disinterested in his meals and spent most of his time replacing parts
of his motorcycle, that as far as she could see, were already in perfectly good order. Pépi, for his part, sifted and stirred and stared out
the window a great deal.

Vanessa was unusually sleepy and somewhat irritable. She even
told Ygrec that she was "headachy" and she would rather he didn't
play the Piaf records so often. "This place is too small," she complained to Michelin. "We need a music room, like I had at home,
and a library too." Michelin was getting tired of hearing what she'd
had at home and was also getting tired of Ygrec's hopeful "Any new
developments?" every time Michelin came home.

Things came to a climax on Friday night, and later Vanessa wept
bitterly, blaming herself for what followed.

She was sitting in an old dressing gown on the stool near Ygrec,
the dog's head in her lap. "Do you know, Maurice, I never thought
my work at the agency would ever bore me, but it does. I'm getting
awfully tired of being dressed and undressed in outlandish outfits and
getting a stiff neck and aching back from posing under those hot
lights. I'd like to stay home and be a disorganized housewife for a
while."

"You'd be bored to tears here in a week," Michelin commented
from behind a newspaper. "You're not the domestic type."

"I wasn't talking to you. Go back to your reading about world dis-
asters," Vanessa said coldly, then turned to Ygrec again. "Every time
I bring up the subject of any of my plans, 'The Inspector' gets impossible. I'd like to buy a house and raise roses . . . and, well, dogs and
cats, and you could stay with us forever, Maurice. We could have a
big fenced-in garden for Mademoiselle. It would be quite, quite perfect, wouldn't it?"

"When do you intend to apply for a divorce?" Michelin commented again.

"Divorce!" echoed Ygrec.

"If she wants what I think she wants, she'll have to marry someone like one of the esteemed Matieu brothers who are rolling in
wealth."

"I could use the money my grandfather left me, and my father has
been begging me to . . ."

"Vanessa!" Michelin stared over the top of his paper.

"You could always start accepting bribes, garçon," Ygrec offered, in an attempt to ease the tension he could feel in the air.

"Excellent idea." The paper rattled as a page was turned.

Ygrec tried again. "What you two need is to get away from everything for a little while. Why don't you go out to dinner to some intimate little place in Paris and drink wine and listen to romantic music?"

"Well, I'm going to bed." Vanessa stood up, flipping her hair across her shoulders. "And next week I'm going to be sick again, and stay home!" She flounced out of the room, Mademoiselle Larme at her heels.

Ygrec raised his eyebrows. "It appears that the females of this family have taken a united front against us, but why they're annoyed at me is beyond my understanding."

"You didn't take her side in that foolish business of buying a mansion. She's just not practical, but let's forget it. Take out the backgammon board. . . . I'm in a vicious mood tonight and will take you in three games straight."

"Blessed are the peacemakers, for they shall throw double sixes with the dice," muttered Ygrec as he reached over for the game and spread it out on the table.

Ygrec threw a two and a one the first time, and then the phone rang.

"Developments at last," Michelin said as he put down the receiver. "That was Sergeant Benoit. Tusette is up to something."

*   *   *

Ghislaine Couronne sat in the little armchair by the hearth, picking viciously at the tapestry with a needle. Her hair was back in the skinny braided coronet and she was wearing the brassy lace dress.

Lucien, determined to ignore the outburst he knew was about to take place, looked around the room. It was warm and clean; nothing shone, but it was neat and tidy. She was obviously quite able to manage on her own.

"You are making up excuses," Ghislaine began, the pitch of her voice already high. "Pippa is pretending. She's not sick at all! I believed you Tuesday, that she was sick, and I was good yesterday at the bank, the way you told me to be, even covering up my hair again and wearing the old clothes so nobody would think I was different.

And I was quiet, too, and lied about Amélie being a little better. I did everything right. You said so." The needle was shoved through the mesh and the thread pulled through to the other side.

"You were fine, Ghislaine, but it was for your good, not mine." Lucien had decided to sit down. The tirade was beginning, so he might as well be comfortable and get it over with. He lit a cigarette, very methodically.

"I don't like you smoking. It smells up the rooms. I spent all day cleaning."

"I seldom smoke these days, but it is one of the few pleasures I am able to enjoy."

"Well, after the girl is gone and you come to live here, you will have to give it up. I suppose you want the money for the school now."

It's out in the open at last, thought Lucien. He made no reply.

"I'll count it out later. I really don't understand the way they count money nowadays, but you said . . ."

"It will be enough to pay the first year, with what I have saved."

"Then she can go next week, and you can come here and take care of me the way Amélie said you would."

He watched her pushing the needle in and out of the tapestry and even from a distance he could tell the stitches were erratic. He pushed his chair back and the noise sounded unusually loud. She looked up crossly, but he strode past her and bent down to drop his cigarette into the fire, staring as it glowed momentarily then disappeared into the bigger flames. "I am not moving from my cottage, Ghislaine. It is a pity that you got the idea that I would move, because I don't want to upset you."

The stitching became jerky and she pulled impatiently at the thread. "Of course you are, Lucien. You can bring your own furniture if it suits you. We'll put it in the parlor after you get rid of those things that belonged to Amélie's mother." She was chattering now, the words coming faster and faster. "All except the shepherdess figurine and a few other things . . . I always liked that figurine. And you can smoke once in a while, too, on nice days when we can keep the windows open. I won't wear any of Amélie's dresses anymore, either. I'll go Monday . . . I'll take a taxi . . . I have the money, you know . . . and I'll buy new dresses, and one very special dress, of course, to be married in. I've been thinking about that, about my wedding. It's not like we were young anymore, Lucien, so we will go quietly to the small chapel . . ."

He let her go on for a time, waiting for a pause. Then he could wait no longer. "I must go now, Ghislaine. When I came, I told you it would only be for a short visit. I must get back to Pippa."

"I haven't finished talking to you yet." She was using the Amélie voice now.

"I promised Pippa I would be home early. She is going to read some poetry to me." He was calm as he started toward the back door.

"Poetry! What do you know about poetry!" The needle was held in mid-air. "If you go, if you don't keep your promises, I will tell the gendarmes about Amélie, and they will come and dig her up, and I will tell them how you killed her. I will, Lucien . . . yes I will!" She jerked violently and the thread broke, dangling and waving as she pointed, half shouting, half crying. "They will believe me. They will believe that you forced me to sign those papers and give you money. I was afraid for my life . . . I was afraid you would lock me up like Amélie did before and make me kneel all day on the bare floor . . ."

"Ghislaine!"

". . . and give me only cold soup and bread for days and days, and slap me . . . hit me . . ."

"Ghislaine, I have never hit a woman in my life," he was shouting now, too, "but if you don't listen to me now, I will have to slap you to bring you to your senses."

Then there was the change in her, the instantaneous change, that he had seen so many times before—the heaving shoulders, the pitiful sobs. "You made me break my thread, and now I have pricked my hand with the needle."

"Hear me," Lucien said, his tone lowered, "for this is the end. I will always remain in my father's house. I will see to it that you do not suffer hunger or thirst or cold . . . out of duty I will see to that. As for the rest, Amélie is not buried in the asparagus bed. Do you think that I am that much of a fool!"

The door slammed behind him.

Chapter Fifteen

Mme. Hugo was in a fine mood, in spite of the fact that she had just returned from Gabrielle Chamillion's funeral. Jean-Louis had appeared at breakfast without his beard! He looked just like her "own dear boy at last," she told him as she'd smoothed his freshly shaven cheek with loving fingers, not noticing the expression of resentment that crossed his face. Afterward she'd whispered to Pépi, "A week . . . just a week at home, and he's come to his senses already. You were right, Pépi, it was just a silly stage."

Pépi had been pleased too, but more so because Jean-Louis had apparently run out of excuses and had actually taken the van out to make the Saturday deliveries. He'd also mentioned that he had decided to sell his motorcycle and had been looking at cars.

Madame had gone off to the funeral directly after breakfast. It was her duty to support Estelle, poor useless creature that she was. Afterward, Madame dismissed the ceremony as "Dreadful . . . hardly anyone there. A ridiculous time for a funeral anyway, on market morning, but what can one do when the authorities wouldn't release the body until the last minute. We left old Mme. Chamillion eating tarts and listening to the symphony on her radio and said we were going shopping. As for that Valin, do you know, Pépi, he wouldn't come with us to the church, and I wasn't sure he would even appear. But he did . . . half drunk and all alone. He sat in the back pew . . . the very back . . . then left before we even started down the aisle and didn't go to the cemetery! Still, the sun shone. I do dislike standing by graves in the rain. Well, I won't have to change to go to the market, will I?" She smoothed the mouton cuffs of her new black coat. "There's always a bright side to everything. I'm going to buy a nice piece of ham to go with the veal. Jean-Louis deserves a very special meal tonight."

*　*　*

Pippa was trying to eat. Gran'papa had threatened to call the doctor again, but more than that, it pained her to see how disturbed he was about her. All week he'd been so attentive and thoughtful, trying to show his concern and affection in any number of little ways and, in doing so, making her feel even worse. She had cried a little when she'd read the poems aloud last night, telling him it was the beauty of the words that made her emotional, but all the time feeling sick with guilt. She'd never deceived him before, never lied to him. That's what she kept telling Jean-Louis each time they'd had their secret talks, whispering through the parlor window at the back, holding hands . . . he'd even kissed her hand. Once she'd thought secrets were fun —exciting. Now she just felt more and more guilty, and more and more torn with indecision. Perhaps she should have gone to the château yesterday and talked to M. Ygrec or Mme. Michelin, but what could she have said . . . she'd promised Jean-Louis, promised on her sacred honor.

But she couldn't go on this way. Jean-Louis had driven off in the van this morning. She'd been watching the lane and seen him go, at least she was sure it was him and not his father. Somehow she would have to talk to him tonight—if only Gran'papa would decide to go out somewhere. She'd been so happy last week—how could life get so mixed up in such a short time?

She pushed her plate to one side, hoping it wouldn't be noticed that the food had just been played with. If Lucien did notice he made no comment on the fact. "Would you like to come with me to the market?" he asked hopefully.

Pippa only shook her head and carried the dishes over to the sink.

"Leave those . . . I'll help you wash them later," he told her.

"It's all right, Gran'papa. I really am feeling better. While you're shopping I think I'll sit on my swing in the sunshine."

When he returned from the market he brought her back a present —a surprise—without explanation. She held up the skirt, long and elegant, of a soft rose wool with embroidery on the waistband. "I met Mme. Michelin," he said. "She helped me pick it out. She says it will be a little too long but that, as you sew very well, you can fix it up in no time."

Pippa managed to keep her tears under control until he'd gone again, to have a little visit with M. Ygrec, he explained. Then she hugged the skirt to her face and wept into it.

* * *

The two old men sat inside that afternoon, playing backgammon near the open french doors. They looked comfortable together, Vanessa decided, so alike and yet so different; Ygrec with his unmanageable gray hair brushing the back of his neck, Corporal Anjou, his black tight waves only streaked with gray and cut closely to his scalp. Both of them wore faded blue shirts but Ygrec, as always, had on one of his sweaters, with mended elbows and cuffs, buttoned crookedly on top. Vanessa smiled. She kept buying new sweaters for Ygrec, which he appeared to honestly like, but wore only once or twice. The roomy bottom drawer of his bureau was stuffed with new sweaters, while the old man went around looking like a charity case.

"Did Pippa like her new skirt?" Vanessa asked after a while, as she picked up the empty glasses from the table beside them.

Lucien looked up. "She appeared to, Mme. Michelin. She smiled and held it up and even danced a little for the first time in days. I left her with a needle and thread busily sewing in the sunshine on the steps. I hope she has an appetite for supper. I think I will make her favorite crêpes with asparagus. I am quite a good cook." He smiled a little.

Vanessa smiled back. "Would you like to give me a few lessons, Corporal?"

"Did I hear someone mention crêpes? We'll have some tonight, chérie." It was Michelin, and Ygrec was pleased to notice the tension of last night was gone. Michelin had come in the back way and Vanessa raised her face to be kissed.

"Ah, garçon, any news?" Ygrec asked.

"Nothing significant." Michelin changed the subject smoothly. "It is good to see you again, Corporal. I trust you are teaching Ygrec a few things about the game. I trounced him three times in succession last night."

"There is little I can teach him, because he has the luck, so he tells me, and although I do not believe in such nonsense, the dice have been favoring him, so I think it is a good time for me to take my leave."

"Would you like to come back again this evening, Corporal? Perhaps his luck will change," Vanessa suggested, "and you can prove your skill. My husband has promised to take me out for dinner. It is the only way he can escape the telephone . . . and my cooking. You can keep Maurice company."

"Excellent idea," the old gendarme agreed.

Lucien seemed to hesitate.

"If you are still worried about Pippa, you shouldn't be," Vanessa went on. "You say she is better and I think she's probably been going through a period of 'growing pains' that are common to young girls. When you go home, tell her she can always feel free to come and talk to me. It hasn't been all that long since I was her age."

"Merci, Mme. Michelin, I will tell her." Lucien made his adieus and went on his way.

"It must be hard on them both in a house without a woman," Ygrec commented. "Still he appears to handle things very well. He is a good man." Then he looked over at Michelin. "Well, now that we are alone, what has happened to your M. Tusette? You sneaked out on me this morning without a word."

Michelin shook his head. "It looks as if the whole investigation has blown up in our faces. One of the St. Denis gendarmes stopped Tusette about five o'clock this morning, on a speeding charge, of all things, and just when we were sure he was going to make a contact with someone. Then the officer discovered that Tusette had a plastic bag containing what they think is cocaine or heroin in the car . . . the lab in Paris is confirming it now, but in the meantime, Tusette is sitting in the cells and Sergeant Benoit is furious and I'm not happy either. We've just had months of hard work wiped out because Tusette was in a hurry to get somewhere. He's not talking, of course, except to say he's innocent. Same old story!"

"Well, why did the officer search the car? They don't usually do that, do they?" Vanessa asked.

"He said he had a funny feeling that there was something odd about the way Tusette fumbled at the glove compartment when he was getting out the registration papers."

"Well, I can't imagine anyone feeling anything but tired at five o'clock in the morning," retorted Vanessa.

"You wouldn't! All you want to do is sleep these days," Michelin said. "But ask Ygrec about peculiar feelings . . . he's the authority. Which reminds me, old man, you haven't had any of your fey attacks lately have you?"

"Unfortunately no, except when I play trictrac with Corporal Anjou. He may give you the impression he's not a skilled player, but he is, and yet once in a while I can predict some of his moves. That's when I 'talk' to the dice."

"Do you really believe in luck?"

"Half yes, half no." Ygrec grinned knowingly.

*   *   *

"You play a wicked game," Lucien remarked later that night as he gathered up his black discs from the backgammon board.

"I come by it naturally." Ygrec smiled. "Do you know I first played this game during the war in the cellar of an old fisherman's cottage in

Brest. We used to play hours on end, waiting for messages that all was clear. Then we'd move our human cargo to the boats for England. The loser of the game would stay behind on guard."

Lucien nodded. "I would say that you made many trips by boat, my friend."

"Many."

"I worked alone. It was easier that way, crossing the mountains."

"And you preferred it also?"

"Like my father, I am solitary by nature, and I enjoyed the challenge of scaling the peaks."

"Have you ever considered going back to the Pyrenees to live?"

"I have considered it. I still have my climbing equipment . . . my ropes and my piton hammer. Perhaps after Pippa has grown up. . . ." Lucien folded the board. "I must be on my way. I have already stayed much later than I'd planned, but time goes quickly when I am in your company. I thank you for a pleasant evening."

"It has been my pleasure." Ygrec rose and walked to the french doors with the corporal and they both looked out at the clear night and the full moon.

"In the mountains the wolves will be howling tonight," Lucien said.

"By the sea, the waves will be lapping, and the fog horns silent."

The two men shook hands.

*   *   *

"They're all on the loose tonight, all the weird ones," young gendarme Lamarshe sighed, as he handed in his night report, "even that drunken Chamillion they had in here for questioning on Tuesday. He's been at the licorice again. Henri, at the Côte Impériale garage, found him staggering around at the back, talking to himself, looking for his wife."

"You should have steered him into the cemetery. They buried her this morning," the desk sergeant said with a jaded smile.

"I had Henri steer him in the direction of rue Lutétia, where he lives. I had enough to do with another motorcycle accident to straighten out."

*   *   *

She was gone! At first Lucien thought he must be mistaken and he pulled back the covers from her neatly made bed. Then he called her name aloud, as he jerked open each door in the cottage, switching on

lights. "Pippa?"—the minute bathroom that contained no bathtub—
"Pippa?"—the austere parlor, smelling of furniture oil—"Pippa?"—his
own bedroom with the bare floorboards and the bed in which he had
been born.

He stood once more in the center of the kitchen, just stood. He
thought of ridiculous places he hadn't looked—the dugout cellar no
longer in use, the attic that could be reached only by the ladder stairway in his bedroom—but he regained his reason. He knew where she
must be, where she had gone, and there was nothing to do but wait.
Eventually he retraced his tour of panic, switching off the lights that
dangled dimly from the centers of the ceilings, except in Pippa's own
room, where he had run an extension to a lamp beside her bed; he
left that one burning.

He never thought of checking the time. It had been after ten o'clock
when he had left the château—that was all he could recall later.

The disbelief that she would deceive him, the anger that she had
done so, the fear for her well-being, the despair that he had lost her
confidence—all these emotions criss-crossed as he sat by the kitchen
table, lighting one cigarette after the other. Again the emotions
welled up—guilt that he had left her alone tonight; fury directed at
Jean-Louis Hugo; helplessness because there was nothing he could
do, but wait—and wait—and wait.

He took out the bottle of wine from the cupboard and put it on
the table, then changed his mind and went through the ceremony of
rekindling and lighting the fire, waiting for the kettle to boil, making
the coffee, prolonging the process purposely.

When the coffee cup was empty he began to pace the room. Finally he walked stolidly down the lane to the Hugo establishment.
The van stood alone in the shadows back of the building, the motorcycle gone, as he knew it would be. The shutters upstairs and downstairs were lowered in place, not a light to be seen, not a sound to be
heard. He suffered through another moment of fury when he wanted
to pound on the doors and windows, then he stalked back down the
lane to his own silent cottage and his vigil.

Flashes from his boyhood had been brought to the surface during
his swift initial search of the rooms, and because he didn't want to
face tomorrow just yet and add to his welling feelings of helplessness,
he allowed himself to indulge in the past. When his mother had died,
he'd refused to believe even his father, and had climbed the ladder to

the cold airless attic, lying face down on the dusty floorboards, hiding for hours. When he finally admitted his loss he was too sick with anger over her desertion of him, to shed any tears. His father had been proud of him—Anjous didn't cry, even when they were seven years old. She and the stillborn child she had borne were both buried in the same grave, and Lucien stood beside his father, watching the lowering of the coffin, the tossing of the soil, the whole chanting, agonizing ritual, without a sign of emotion. Not long afterward, when the old Conte Couronne's shattered body had been discovered on the elaborate stonework at the foot of the roof tower, Lucien's father had muttered, "Justice has been done," and neither of them had attended the rituals for the man, whom Lucien understood, without explanation, had been responsible for his mother's death. She, like his father had worked for the Couronne estate. She, like Ghislaine's mother, had been pretty. His father, Lucien realized as he grew in understanding, had taken him to the château that morning for a purpose, knowing full well what the boy would see, knowing that the "discovery" of a "suicide" would be made. "The wages of sin are death," his father had told him simply as he'd waited in the doorway of what was now Pippa's room for a sleepy-eyed Lucien to dress.

Why was he dwelling on death? Lucien stirred himself and got up to pour the last of the coffee into his cup. Pippa had simply disobeyed his orders and carried out a rendezvous with a young man who was unacceptable in the eyes of her grandfather. My excursions into the past have been too frequent of late, he berated himself. I must concentrate on matters at hand, matters over which I still have some control.

He checked his watch for the first time then, and the first seed of consternation began to germinate in his mind. It was after one o'clock in the morning. Surely she hadn't really taken leave of her senses and run off with the boy!

He hurried down the lane once more, this time making a thorough check of the Pâtisserie Hugo and the adjoining buildings at the back —still no motorcycle. He returned, and noticing the swing silhouetted in the moonlight, began to push it, flinging his strength against the empty seat until it lost any rhythm of momentum and twisted on its ropes crazily. He turned his back, kicking foolishly at the long damp grass. What should he do? Wake up the Hugos and roar at them, "Your useless son has gone off with my Pippa?" Go to the gendarmerie and say like a doddering old grandfather, "I think my granddaughter may have run away with an idiot on a motorcycle . . . go after them!" They would laugh behind his back.

He returned to his vigil once again, only this time because his anger and fear were draining him, he sat back in the big chair near the stove. When he woke from one nightmare to another, it was daylight.

"I tell you he's in his bed, Lucien," Pépi Hugo stuttered. "He had an accident with his motorcycle. He only grazed his arm and his forehead, but the machine is at the garage . . . the front wheel . . . he was alone. Go and see for yourself, then. Ask him yourself. He's in his bed!"

So Lucien, taking two steps at a time, leaving Pépi puffing behind, and ignoring a tight-mouthed Madame in the hallway, stormed into the small bedroom.

"Pippa?" Jean-Louis was too sleepily startled to attempt to escape Lucien's iron grip on his shoulder. "I haven't seen Pippa! How would I know where she is? I haven't seen her for a week!"

Chapter Sixteen

The marble birdbath in the deserted Couronne gardens had been abandoned even by the birds years before. The carved lettering, praising the compassion of St. Francis of Assisi, which had decorated its circular rim, was obliterated by brown hairy moss, and its floral decorated base was wound round with twisted, thickened ivy vines, all surrounded by tangled weeds and spears of yellowed glass.

It was Ygrec's dog, Mademoiselle Larme, who discovered the body, nearly hidden from sight, in the overgrowth at the foot of the birdbath. Ygrec wasn't with the dog, much to the relief of most everyone except the old man himself. He was distraught—not that he would have been less horrified at the discovery, but rather that he was more programmed to the sight of violence and death and wouldn't have reacted as badly as Vanessa did.

"It was the face . . . the color of the face . . . all blotchy and . . . oh, Paul, it was hideous! I didn't even recognize her at first . . . it was the skirt." Vanessa sobbed hoarsely after the initial hysteria had abated.

Ygrec sat helplessly by, cursing himself and his age and the infirmities that compounded his uselessness and his grief.

* * *

He had wakened early Sunday morning, for no reason except that he had done with sleeping and he was restless, turning his pillow, jerking at the covers. He didn't think of Mademoiselle immediately; sometimes the dog slept beside his bed but more often than not, lately, near Vanessa. He pulled on his robe, drew the drapes, admired the new day, then saw to his morning duties in the bathroom, taking his time, searching for his hairbrush, nicking his chin with his razor.

He plodded down the hall silently, not wishing to disturb Michelin and Vanessa. Although they hadn't been late last night, he'd purposely stayed in his bedroom after their return as they had been arguing again, and he'd felt a little sad and wanted to keep out of the way. He'd try to leave them alone today too, he decided, and give them some time to settle their differences, which weren't serious . . . but still . . . it might be a good idea to accept the corporal's invitation and visit him at the cottage this afternoon.

He was careful and quiet getting out the bread and cheese and had decided not to bother with a hot drink just yet, when Michelin appeared, dressed for the day in old clothes.

"Going to a formal luncheon?" quipped Ygrec.

"I'm going to have a look at my car. It was acting up last night. Vanessa, of course, thinks I should buy a new one," Michelin replied, and Ygrec knew from his tone that he wasn't in the mood for jokes.

"Well, why didn't you take hers last night? It's newer and any Mercedes is more comfortable than that Renault of yours."

"When I take my wife out, I use my car," Michelin stated stubbornly.

Ygrec didn't bother to reply, concentrating instead on breaking off a bit of cheese. Usually Mademoiselle could smell cheese from any distance and would be at his elbow. "Is the dog in with Vanessa?" he inquired at last.

"I don't think so . . . I didn't see her, but the curtains are still drawn." Then he looked at Ygrec. "I'll just make sure."

Vanessa followed Michelin back to the kitchen. "She's gone again?" It was more a statement than a question.

"I give up!" Michelin's mood wasn't improving. "As I'm the only one dressed, I suppose I'll have to be the one to go trailing through the woods again."

"Never mind . . . I'll go," Vanessa snapped back at him. "It will only take a second to pull on some clothes."

Ygrec stood up. "I'll go. Have your breakfast. She won't be far . . . in the old gardens, I expect."

"Oh, sit down, old man," Michelin ordered more gently. "I don't mind, you know I don't. I must have had a little too much wine last night and I have a bit of a headache, that's all. The fresh air will do me good."

"I told you, Paul, I will go after the dog!" Vanessa disappeared.

Michelin shrugged and turned on the burner beneath the kettle, and Ygrec, wishing he was anywhere but where he was, opened the back door and began to whistle halfheartedly.

"I thought that patio door was locked last night, but I didn't check. You're right, old man, I'm a stupid detective," Michelin commented, trying to break the strain. "As you said before, she's a smart dog, but we may have to buy her a chain."

"I shouldn't bother. I expect I will be going back to Moulins very soon. I had a letter from Mme. Lachance on Friday and her sister is improving."

Vanessa slipped by both men without saying a word and leaving the door open behind her.

"Come on and eat your breakfast," Michelin went on, ignoring Ygrec's last remark. "And don't mind Vanessa. Our night out wasn't very memorable, and she's just in one of her moods."

"She's had a lot of moods, as you call them, since I've come, I'm afraid. She's right, you know, garçon. This is an apartment for two, no more . . . and certainly no place for a dog."

"She loves the dog! You know that. It isn't you, old man. It's partly me and my work with the unpredictable hours . . . and then there's this recent obsession of hers about wanting to buy a house, which I simply cannot afford . . . at least not the kind of a place she'd be happy in."

"If Mademoiselle and I were out of the way . . ."

"You're not in the way, I tell you. You're company for her, and she'd been complaining about this apartment long before you came. . . . She was brought up in luxury, and I think she's tired of 'playing house' here; it's the only reason I can come up with for her being so irritable lately. . . ."

"I'm not so sure." Ygrec played with the piece of cheese on his plate. "With the dog being such a bother, it doesn't help. I think I'll just go along and get dressed."

"Have some tea first," Michelin picked up a cup . . . then both men stopped talking and listened.

Ygrec dropped his cheese, rose to his feet, and followed Michelin to the open door.

They couldn't hear Vanessa's words, but the panic was evident in her shouting. She was racing across the parking lot, the dog at her heels. Michelin dropped the cup with a clatter and ran to meet her.

Later the autopsy report stated that Phillippa Christine Anjou had died between the hours of 11 P.M., Saturday, September 21, and 1 A.M., Sunday, September 22. Death was caused by strangulation.

*   *   *

The gentle days came to an end with the murder of Pippa. In the town square, the idle conversation was muted; young women were not allowed out unaccompanied, and even older women hurried about their business and then only in the daylight hours. Yet there had been violence and death in St. Denis since its inception, for it was a place created by death. The basilica, dedicated to the glory of God and a promise of an afterlife, was a temple to an act of anguish. Even St. Joan herself, who had prayed there in a vain attempt to prolong life, had been only a girl. Why then the shock and horror over just another relatively unknown girl?

Ygrec asked himself all these questions and found no answers, until finally as his mind began to adjust to the reality, he began to ask himself, "Why?" and "Who?"

The events of the rest of that Sunday, that awful Sunday, remained a blur of shock and remorse and guilt to those they touched.

"If I hadn't been so selfish and insisted that Paul take me out for dinner, and asked the corporal to come here, he'd have been at home with Pippa and it wouldn't have happened," Vanessa wept and, because she couldn't stop crying, Michelin called the doctor.

"If only we hadn't been so unreasonable and let Jean-Louis take her somewhere nice for the evening, she'd have been safe. She was only a child," Pépi Hugo mourned.

"Damn!" said Sergeant Corvette at the gendarmerie. "If only we'd got some kind of a lead on that Gabrielle Chamillion case, this might have been prevented. I'm sure it's the same man who is responsible . . . and it must be a man." Michelin could only agree.

The old corporal said nothing, not even to Ygrec and Michelin when they went to the cottage to notify him of the tragedy, only to learn he'd been at the gendarmerie when Michelin's call about the discovery of the body had come in. Lucien had barely acknowledged Ygrec's presence; he hadn't moved from his position by the kitchen window where he sat staring out at a swing hanging from an old tree.

"If only we'd come sooner, before they'd had him go out there to identify the body," Michelin muttered on the way home.

"If . . . if . . . we will get nowhere with 'ifs.' It has happened," Ygrec growled.

* * *

Monday was as gray as Ygrec's mood. Vanessa kept to her room. He paced, too preoccupied to even light the fireplace, preferring for a time to add to his mood by staring outside at the erratic winds that tortured the exhausted leaves in the garden. It didn't rain. "Even the clouds are all cried out," the old man mumbled to the dog.

He felt frustrated, being tied to the confines of the apartment. He had always been able to pick up "feelings" by observing the setting of a crime, and even more by conducting interrogations and interviews, or even by sitting back quietly and listening to such interviews. But since that was impossible, he must do what he could, beginning here and now.

What could he have learned, he wondered, had he been as healthy and young as Michelin and able to take an active role in the investigation? Very little regarding the scene of the tragedy. He remembered the lonely birdbath in the abandoned garden. He could see it plainly in his mind, and from Vanessa's only too vivid description, he could see the small body as clearly as he would ever want to see it, lying on its side in the wild dead grass, clothed in a blue sweater and a new pink skirt that covered the legs modestly, the blue-green scarf that was responsible for the discolored face twisted around the neck.

Ygrec nodded to himself; he might do as well here where he was, imprisoned with his thoughts, not distracted by discomforts of the flesh, as he put it to Michelin that afternoon. His feet were warm and comfortable in his old felt slippers, his chest protected by his heavy sweater, and his ailments were pushed aside by the counterirritant of his anger and his determination.

Michelin had promised to relay any reports from Sergeant Corvette at the local gendarmerie to Ygrec, and it was the medical report that the old gendarme was most concerned about at the moment. The word "rape" had hung unspoken in the air like a pall since yesterday. Vanessa, trying to mask the possibility and the associated horror of it from her mind, wouldn't look directly at either of them, but kept repeating, "Her skirt was just twisted a little, and it was right down over her legs," and added, as if it were terribly important, "Her shoes weren't muddy."

When Michelin finally arrived in the afternoon with the news, Ygrec knew the verdict immediately.

"Mon Dieu, talk about cold out there! I wouldn't be surprised to see snow and it's not even the end of September," Michelin said cheerfully. "Why haven't you put a match to the fire, you useless old man, I got it all ready for you to light, at the crack of dawn this morning." He rubbed his hands together, unbuttoned his coat, then bent down to strike a match.

When he stood up, he went on, "Pippa was not molested . . . in any way. She was stunned by a crack on the head, in all probability, as there was a concussion and a small abrasion on the side of her skull. The lab men are checking the edge of the birdbath. Then she was strangled. Now they're beginning to question a few people, including the young man, Jean-Louis Hugo, who it seems gave her the scarf for a present, and who, it has now been reported, was seen with her earlier Saturday evening. He's the one with the motorcycle, who the old corporal was so set against. You know the one."

Ygrec nodded. "But what motive would he have for killing her? From what I understood, he was very fond of her and now since the coroner discounts any possibility of . . ."

Vanessa's voice came from the doorway. She was standing in a nightgown with a robe tossed over her shoulders, looking distracted and pale. "I heard what you said, Paul. I'm so relieved. . . ." She started to cry again. "I couldn't have stood it if . . ."

Michelin hurried forward. "Back to bed with you, now. The doctor said a long rest in bed is what you need."

They disappeared into the bedroom and when Michelin reappeared, he said quietly to Ygrec, "I have talked to her father. He is coming this evening to take her home for a week or so. The doctor thought it would be best to get her right away from here for the time being. You and I can manage, I'm sure."

"No problem, no problem at all. I make an excellent salad, so we

won't come down with scurvy." Ygrec managed to keep his surprise
to himself.

"I'm trying to get someone to come in for a few hours each day.
Sergeant Corvette is getting his wife to ask around for a woman to
help out. He knows the local people and I don't."

Things were happening too quickly, and Ygrec frowned a little
and wondered if there was anything more seriously wrong with
Vanessa, but decided that at the moment it was best to keep his curiosity hidden. Michelin was being unusually efficient about domestic
problems and unnaturally cheerful, which made Ygrec uncomfortable, so he decided to change the subject and get back to the investigation.

But Michelin had gleaned no more details from St. Denis. "It's not
my jurisdiction, you realize, old man. Sergeant Corvette is keeping
me informed only as a favor, so I can't keep pushing him."

Ygrec understood but was determined not to let official formalities
keep him from doing some investigating on his own. If only he had a
contact in the town—anyone, but particularly someone who liked to
gossip. He hadn't realized how much he missed his birdlike little concierge, Mme. Lachance in Moulins. Her constant chattering had got
on his nerves many times in the past, but she had a way of bringing
the village life right into her immaculate kitchen with her, and he
could hear her now, calling out to him as she beat her soufflé with
the big wire whisk, "You'd never believe who I met today, M. Ygrec,
looking quite ghastly . . ." If only there was someone like her here
in St. Denis, he might get a feeling and know where to begin with at
least the "Why," which might lead to the "Who."

Then that evening Ygrec met Pépi Hugo.

Chapter Seventeen

Ygrec took a liking to the little pastry cook immediately, for although Pépi was overly apologetic and nervous, there was nothing
servile about the man.

He stood just inside Michelin's back door, holding his cap tightly
in both hands, nodding, bowing slightly, insisting that he would not
keep them a minute and could not possibly step beyond the threshold, but allowing that the door should be closed behind him as it was
a particularly nasty evening outside.

Both Ygrec and Michelin were puzzled by his visit, even after he had introduced himself, but they welcomed his interruption—for which he kept apologizing. An unnaturally subdued Vanessa had driven off with her worried father in his Mercedes about an hour before, and Michelin had been rattling around the apartment doing useless things like unfolding and folding an unread paper and closing and opening drapes at the windows.

Pépi addressed Michelin first. "My deepest regrets, M. Inspector, for invading your privacy, but my wife . . . I believe you met my wife at the Chamillion house last week, briefly, of course, the morning after that unfortunate problem . . . well, my wife is so upset . . . I didn't stop to consider . . ."

Michelin nodded. "Yes, M. Hugo, I remember your wife well. She was a great help at the time, very calm and reassuring to Mlle. Chamillion."

"That's it, Inspector, that's why I came. My Marie-Thérèse, all her life has been the calm one, the one to make the decisions, always so sensible and under control. Now she just sits, and she could not even cook supper. I have tried everything, to no avail. Ever since Jean-Louis went off with the gendarme, she has fallen to pieces." Pépi twisted his cap and looked altogether mournful.

"Has your son been arrested?" Michelin asked.

"No . . . no, they said they just wanted to ask him some questions, but they had already been this morning and talked to him for quite a long time . . . only because he was a friend of Pippa Anjou, you understand. And Jean-Louis answered their questions . . . I heard him myself. He answered everything, so we thought that was the end, but they came back again later and took him with them . . . and my wife has dissolved into tears ever since. I didn't know where else to turn, Inspector. You see, Pippa used to talk to my wife all the time, having no mother of her own, as you know, and the girl mentioned M. Ygrec often"—now Pépi's sad eyes were turned to the old gendarme—"and so Marie-Thérèse . . . I mean Mme. Hugo, she said, 'Pépi, if you could only talk to Pippa's friend, M. Ygrec, who was once a very famous detective . . .' Well, you understand, monsieur . . ." Pépi in his earnestness attempted to hold out his hands, dropping his cap to the floor. "Excuse me, monsieur." He bent slowly to pick it up, and they expected to see tears in his eyes. Instead when he stood once more, his round shoulders were erect beneath his tight overcoat, his pudgy face, below thin, mussed hair, serious but controlled.

Ygrec watched with admiration. The little man was obviously upset, but beneath the foolish, fat outward appearance there was character. He also obviously had made an effort to dress for this visit, for an uncomfortably starched white collar and a shiny crooked tie were propping up the flesh of his numerous chins.

Ygrec took over the situation. "I am only too pleased to talk to a friend of Pippa's. We are all devastated by the crime, M. Hugo. Now, I do think we could talk more comfortably if we were seated." He pulled out one of the bright yellow kitchen chairs and motioned Pépi to sit, then also settled himself at the small table with its cheerful flowered cloth. "Don't you think a small glass of wine would go down well, Inspector?"

Michelin agreed and went about the business of producing a bottle and glasses while Ygrec carried on with his subtle method of putting Pépi at his ease.

"I should loosen your coat, M. Hugo . . . that's it." Ygrec smiled. "I am very glad you have come. During a time of crisis, people of one mind are brought closely together, united in a cause, as we were in wartime. I'm sure you will agree."

Pépi agreed, and the strain began to leave his face.

"Now, if you will permit me, I shall sum up your present situation and then we shall decide how to be of help. I understand your son was a very good friend of Pippa, that he had known her since they were children?"

Again Pépi nodded, placing his hat on the table and picking up his wine with a murmured thanks.

"Very good. I know a little of the situation, as Pippa mentioned this friendship to me herself, so I shall go on and you can correct me if I make errors. Your son, who has been away for the summer touring with a musical group, returned home last Saturday. He brought a present for Pippa, a scarf. I believe . . . the scarf that was, shall I say, found on her body?"

"Yes, monsieur, but . . ."

Ygrec held up one hand. "There is no reason for alarm, M. Hugo. I am not accusing or even implying; I simply want to clarify the reason the gendarmes felt it necessary to question Jean-Louis. How did they know where Pippa got the scarf?"

"Lucien Anjou told them. It was no secret, although Lucien was very angry. He didn't want Pippa to have anything to do with my son, or any other young man, for that matter."

"I am aware of Corporal Anjou's protective feelings about his granddaughter." Ygrec smiled sympathetically. "So, the gendarmes came earlier today, Jean-Louis admitted he'd given the scarf to Pippa . . . as you said it was no secret, and I expect they had also learned of Lucien Anjou's attitude toward your son, and they probably asked if Jean-Louis had been with Pippa on the night of her death. Is that correct?"

"Yes, monsieur." Then Pépi looked away for a moment, and finally back to Ygrec, his face once more strained. "That's the trouble. At first Jean-Louis told them he hadn't seen Pippa at all for a week . . . not since the night he arrived home when he'd given her the scarf. When the gendarmes came back, they said that a neighbor, M. Fouschie, and also someone else had seen Jean-Louis and Pippa walking at the back of the basilica this last Saturday . . . the night she died. He'd lied to them the first time, M. Ygrec . . . but he'd lied because he was afraid of what Lucien Anjou would do if he found out, and because his mother would be angry too. He told the gendarmes that, but he had to go with them anyway, and now his mother is beside herself with worry. He wouldn't harm Pippa, monsieur. He's always been fond of her and good to her. When she was just a little thing, she was shy, but she would follow him around, and he taught her to sing songs, and pushed her on her swing, and even fixed her bicycle once when it was broken. Lucien didn't mind then . . . Jean-Louis was like a brother . . . none of us minded."

"But you began to worry, monsieur, when they were no longer children, and he began to bring her presents?"

"The others did," Pépi said sadly. "Her grandfather mostly . . . and my wife too, I admit, but I felt it was a fuss over nothing." He looked steadily at Ygrec. "Jean-Louis is young and may have done foolish things, but he never hurt Pippa. You must believe me, monsieur."

"But your problem at the moment is to convince the local gendarmes of the fact?"

"Only Jean-Louis can do that," Pépi replied with remarkable insight, Ygrec felt, "but his mother"—he raised his hands again in despair—"if there was any way you could find out why they are keeping Jean-Louis so long. Are they arresting him? It's not knowing, and

I can do nothing. It is so much like a pain in me because I can do nothing."

Michelin, who had been sipping quietly at his drink, spoke up. "M. Hugo, I have no direct connection with the gendarmerie here. Sergeant Corvette is in charge of the investigation."

"Oh, Inspector," Pépi hurried to explain, "I would not think to take advantage of your position. It was M. Ygrec we thought might be able to think of something, if he could help to find out who really did . . . did hurt Pippa . . . but, of course, now I think of it, what can any of us do? I was wrong to bother you, monsieur." He stood up very slowly.

"You were right to come," Ygrec assured him, "if for no other reason than that it helps to talk to someone at a time like this. I'm sure that your Jean-Louis will convince them of the truth. I understand that he had an accident with his motorcycle later on Saturday night?"

"Yes. He was only walking with Pippa a little while and then he went off for a ride to look at a new car. He was thinking of buying a car, you understand."

"So, his movements are accounted for during the latter part of the evening. In that case, I shouldn't worry, but to put your mind at rest, I'm sure that the Inspector wouldn't mind making a short phone call to find out if they are making any progress in the investigation of the case. They know at the gendarmerie that we are personally interested as we were also friends of Pippa." Ygrec looked over at Michelin and raised his eyebrows, and Michelin returned the glance with a resigned look.

"You are most kind, monsieur, most kind."

While he waited, Pépi sat clutching his hat once more, refusing Ygrec's offer of more wine with a polite shaking of his round head, until Michelin returned from the hallway with a smile on his face. "They are holding no suspects," he said briefly. "I expect by the time you get home, Jean-Louis will be there and your wife will have dried her tears."

After repeated, effusive thanks, Pépi Hugo left, his relief evident in his smile.

Michelin sat playing with his wine glass. "You don't look too convinced about this whole situation, old man, in spite of your assurance to M. Hugo," he said.

"I have lived too long to accept innocence blindly," Ygrec replied.

"There are a few questions I would like to put to a few people myself, but I shall have patience. In the meantime, you have no idea
how pleased I am to have a place to begin. I shall tenderly cultivate
this chubby new acquaintance of ours. He is a likable man, but more
than that, from what Pippa told me, I gather that his wife is a well of
information, and one never knows what small pieces of gossip can be
pieced together to produce ideas and 'odd feelings.' "

"Oh, I knew what was going through your mind! I've never known
you to sit and drink wine of an evening . . . it's always cognac."

"I didn't want to overwhelm our guest on his first visit . . . and,
besides, Pippa once mentioned that Mme. Hugo and her husband
relax most evenings with a glass of wine, while Madame peers out a
window to watch the world go by . . . and check up on her neighbors." Ygrec grinned. "But as you have been kind enough to suggest
it, garçon, I do believe I'll have a small cognac. It has been well
known since early times that a little stimulation helps senile old
brains to begin to function when they have become lazy from lack of
practice!"

*   *   *

Ghislaine was beginning to discover the pleasant effects of wine.
Amélie had only allowed her a small glass on very special occasions,
so the "wine cellar," which in reality was a locked cupboard at the
far end of the larder, was still almost full. On nights like tonight with
the shutters rattling and the wind gusting down the chimney, sometimes making the flames quiver, it could be unpleasant, she told herself, but after a glass or two of the Burgundy, she was able to relax
and not notice. Her mind seemed to work better too, and the colors
of her tapestry threads were brighter. The tapestry was really coming
along nicely and she might even finish it by spring. She'd always
liked doing needlework, which was why Amélie had punished her by
putting it away in the parlor and allowing her just to look at it when
she went into the room to clean; then they had stopped bothering to
clean the unused rooms and Ghislaine had almost forgotten about it.
She quite liked the design, which was a picture of the basilica and the
tombs before the revolution, so it had lots of dark blues and grays
and blacks, and it didn't matter if she got the threads mixed up and
some of the colors in the wrong places.

She was wearing her old thick sweater and soiled woollen skirt because they were easier to put on than the dresses, but she had the lit-

tle fur cape around her shoulders and every once in a while she would rub her chin against the softness of it. She sat on a straight chair near the good light on the table, and also near the wine bottle. Finally, she pushed the tapestry aside, poured a bit more wine, then reached over to turn the knob of the old radio. It was a blessing that Lucien had been able to fix the radio for her, and although sometimes the music and voices faded and other times it crackled noisily, it was a great comfort to have the silence of the room filled with something soothing, and the last two days had been a great trial to her.

She had been very upset when the gendarme came to question her yesterday but had done what Lucien had told her to do if anyone came. She'd just stood inside the doorway and answered the questions in a whisper, so she wouldn't waken Amélie, she'd explained to the young officer.

She had managed to keep her real thoughts to herself. No, she hadn't heard anything unusual on Saturday night. She slept downstairs to be near her invalid sister and they had not been disturbed by anything, and she'd heard no cars or motorcycles use the old road.

After the officer was gone she'd felt almost ill, so she'd had a glass of wine and spent a long time refueling the fires because it was turning so cold outside, and all the while reminding herself how pleasant it would be this winter with Lucien to keep the fires going. Now that he had no more ties with his old cottage, he would change his mind more quickly about coming to take care of her.

When he'd arrived to dig her garden this afternoon, she had been very surprised. She'd been wise though; he hadn't come near the house, so she had just watched him from time to time through the window, the cold wind slapping his coat and pant legs against his bent body as he slashed at lumps of sod with the sharp shovel. She supposed they'd have the funeral soon, and when that was over with he would be back to stay. She considered the funeral, then blanked it out of her mind.

The music was nice tonight, the sound clear with no annoying crackling. She'd never danced in her life, but she had watched them in the Basque village in the mountains, when they'd had their festivals, how they stepped forward and backward, and turned. She had never even been allowed to try because of Amélie, and her foot made her awkward, but she decided to try now. There was no one around to see if she did trip a little, and if she practiced she might be able to surprise Lucien when next he came.

She stood and picked up the side of her skirt as she'd seen the village women do, wishing she'd worn one of Amélie's long dresses with a fuller skirt. She took one small step but was a little off balance, so she paused and stood where she was, waving the skirt back and forth and bowing now and then to the strains of the music. When the loose bun on the top of her head tumbled down, she simply pushed the hair out of her eyes. She tried to hum to the music too, although she had never heard the tune before, but suddenly the sounds began sticking in her throat so that they came out in painful shallow sobs. She was crying; she couldn't be crying—there was no reason— things had worked out just fine. But still the sobs came, growing deeper and deeper until she could no longer control them.

She reached for the chair, her shoulders heaving, and she raised her face letting the tears come until she could taste the dribbles along the sides of her mouth. She wept for the childhood she had never had, for warmth and love she had never known, for losses she could no longer remember, until at last she realized she was weeping for Pippa too. She had pushed the existence of the child from her mind, from her very life, because she was beyond bearing more rejection. Now she remembered the first time she had seen the little brown girl, years ago, walking with Lucien back of the basilica, one tiny hand enclosed in his. And the years between, until the last time—in church this summer—the dark unruly hair sticking out below a round gray-brimmed hat. Each time she had told herself the pain didn't exist, that the interest in the child was merely curiosity about a stranger. She hadn't looked for familiar features in Pippa—she hadn't! Then why the heartbreak now, why the draining sobbing that wouldn't be stilled, the eyes, swollen shut with tears, leaving a desperate emptiness more awful than the time in the mountains when she had heard the first cry of a child she had never been allowed to see?

She didn't fight the grief. She had never cried so quietly and it was like a healing. After a time she crawled onto the cot, and in the morning when she was wakened by the insistent knocking at the back door, she realized she had not locked up last night. She accepted the baguette that Pépi Hugo handed her without a word, standing speechless as he bowed politely and backed away, the puzzlement clear on his round face.

*   *   *

Pépi Hugo appeared at the back door of the château apartment late Tuesday afternoon ". . . bearing gifts of sweet rolls, tarts, and morsels of tempting information," Ygrec told Michelin later.

Although Ygrec denied doing anything to warrant repayment, Pépi insisted, going on to explain that M. Ygrec had held out a hand of friendship in an hour of need. Madame was forever grateful, Pépi was forever grateful, and no, he couldn't possibly stay. Well, perhaps just a small glass of wine would be welcome, as it had been a busy day. Jean-Louis was a great help, making the deliveries to the cafes and restaurants, but Mme. Hugo had insisted that Pépi himself deliver a fresh loaf to that poor Estelle Chamillion, as well as a few treats for her ailing mother. There hadn't been a sign of M. Valin Chamillion—naturally M. Ygrec had heard about the sad predicament of the man. He had problems, but then, didn't we all have problems, and drowning them in drink was not the best way. Still, one never knew why certain people turned to drink.

Take those poor Couronne sisters—now there was a sad situation; their aristocratic blood had been no advantage to them—a disadvantage if anything, as their father had been one for excesses, and the blood was bad. Lucien Anjou had been looking in on them because he had a kind heart, but now that Lucien was so distraught, he couldn't be expected to carry on normally, so Mme. Hugo had suggested that Pépi take the sisters some bread too, after he'd stopped at the Chamillions. Lucien was in a bad way, taking his grief and anger out on the soil—"Ashes to ashes, dust to dust," Pépi quoted with feeling. Yesterday the old corporal had dug up all the sod around the cottage and beneath the trees, after cutting down the old swing. Later he had gone off with his shovel and had turned over some of the garden patch at the back of the loge de garde—and today, would you believe it, he was digging Pippa's grave himself! Some of the neighbors thought it was not quite proper, but Pépi understood. Lucien did not hold too much with the church or burials ever since they had refused to bury his mother in consecrated ground, as it was said she had brought about her own death. Yet Lucien had sent Pippa to the convent school, so had not turned against God himself, just a few of His agents—this was only Pépi's opinion of course. There was no doubt the corporal was a man of many sides, but at least he didn't indulge in drink to soothe his heartaches.

Which brought Pépi back to the Couronne sisters and that strange old Mlle. Ghislaine. When she had finally answered the door this morning and accepted the bread, Pépi had been quite taken aback. Mind you, he hadn't seen her for some months, but she had been a common sight for years, shopping in the town once in a while, limping along in her old dark clothes with her head always covered, and quite often talking to herself. No one took notice anymore. But this morning she had appeared looking very odd indeed—very odd; and Pépi was suspicious she had been into the drink herself. Her face was sort of puffed up and she'd actually had her head uncovered—a sight she was, with a chopped white fringe sticking up across her forehead, the rest of her stringy hair in matted strands, hanging down like an old witch. She was dressed funny too, with a scruffy little fur cape on her shoulders. She hadn't said a word, not even thank you for the bread, and Pépi was afraid she was heading down the same path of temptation as that foolish Valin Chamillion. The sister, Amélie, must be feeling better though, Pépi added, as Dr. Desmaris, who was attending old Mme. Chamillion, had been heard to say so. The doctor hadn't been called to see Mlle. Amélie since the end of August, and Mlle. Ghislaine had not come in for more pain-killing pills for some time. Oh, well, the Lord worked in mysterious ways.

Pépi bid Ygrec adieu, and Ygrec was left with the thought that the Lord's ways were indeed mysterious, but it was about time that either he or the Lord got to work untangling some of the confusion of questions that had begun to surface.

Chapter Eighteen

The cottage at the end of the lane, so picturesque in its summer setting, took on the appearance of desolation once its natural decorations were torn away. Four days of stiff, biting winds had almost stripped the greenery from the stout vines that over the years had anchored themselves in the walls of the house and the aged wood of the window frames. Even the window boxes were left with barren sticklike stumps of what had been cheerful geraniums. Then the winds died, leaving a vacuum of stillness that soon filled with a yellow-gray fog that seemed to cling to everything, even the evergreens, distorting shapes and colors.

Lucien took little notice. It was a season like all seasons in his life, and he welcomed the fog because it turned the ceremony in the churchyard into a distant, impersonal happening. He had felt as if he were an outsider watching the silent townspeople tread like bare-headed ghosts through paths between the tombstones to listen to a stooping priest chant into another gaping hole in the ground.

Lucien had turned away before the burial service was completed and gone back to the cottage where he made up the fire in the stove. Warmth was beginning to be the one indulgence his advancing years appreciated. There had been a time when he could curl up in trenches or beneath pine branches or huddle in the dubious protection of a cave, and sleep, and awake refreshed, but no more.

There had been a time when few things had seemed important to him, he reminded himself, and vengeance, if he had ever uttered the word, had not been so much a matter of importance as a natural and basic part of his nature, like sleeping and eating. If it could be accomplished with little effort, so much the better. If it took planning, it was done accordingly, but in a near-automatic manner. To him, tutored by a father descended from starving men who had emptied the Bastille and ravaged the tombs of the St. Denis basilica, tossing the bones of royalty into the streets, vengeance was simply a right. It was a sensible method to wipe out injustice and cruelty. Sometimes there was nothing really personal involved. In wartime when the enemy invaded your country, you disposed of that enemy, one man at a time if necessary, using any method available. In peacetime if a madman brutalized the innocent, he was given assistance to end his miserable existence.

Lucien was sure that his friend, gendarme Ygrec, would point out that justice was meted out by the laws of the land, but there were many kinds of laws, and to Lucien, laws and rights were not the same thing. It had been four days now, and the gendarmes using their legal methods had done nothing. It was time for Lucien himself to begin.

The dim light was on in his bedroom and the door left open to warm the room. He sat in the semidarkness of the kitchen where he had been watching nightfall and thinking. He'd propped his feet on the open oven door and his big body was relaxed in his father's armchair, as relaxed as he'd been on Saturday night when he'd sat playing the game with Ygrec. He would now have to play other games with Ygrec, games of sifting and exchanging ideas and information. The old gendarme was deceiving, Lucien knew only too well. The outward skeletal frame hung with shabby clothes gave the impression of a man living out his days in peace, but the blue eyes smiling from beneath overhanging hoar brows never stopped probing. Yes, Ygrec was a good man to know, and with his help Lucien hoped to get vengeance.

The corporal was facing the closed door to Pippa's room. He had accepted Mme. Hugo's offer to pack all the girl's belongings and take them away, so now the room was bare except for the few pieces of old furniture. All worldly traces of Pippa were gone from his life, and that was good. His mind had cleared at last. The time of inactivity was at an end.

He wasn't certain where he would begin, but he would go on until he knew the truth—the awful truth. Tonight he would sit and think. Tomorrow he would visit his friend Ygrec.

He stood up, raised the circular top of the stove with the lifter, emptied the bucket of coke into the firebox, and was replacing the lid when he heard a new sound. He stopped to listen, then turned to the door.

Valin Chamillion seemed to be standing in the doorway in a shroud of fog. Lucien would have preferred to close the door in the and to his doorstep? Valin stumbled inside, smelling of licorice and Lucien was curious. What would bring anyone out on such a night and to his doorstep? Valin stumbled inside, smelling of liquorice and stale uncleanliness and Lucien shoved him onto a chair and closed the door quickly behind him.

There were no greetings. "I had to escape from the music," Valin mumbled, covering his ears with his hands. "Maman keeps it on night and day . . . loud . . . right through the ceiling into my room." Finally he lowered his hands, coughing a little. He had obviously not changed his clothing for days; the cuffs of his shirt were filthy, his sweater buttoned crookedly, and his shoes were untied.

Mon Dieu, Lucien thought, how did he ever find his way here in this state, but he said calmly, "You could use a hot drink, M. Chamillion," then reached over and pulled the kettle onto the glowing center of the stove.

"A drink? Oh, yes, monsieur, I will have a drink with you. That is what I have been needing . . . and to get away from the noise of the music; you don't know what it has been like . . . like hell . . ." His words came out in a jerky monotone.

"You have nothing to drink at home, monsieur?" Lucien watched his visitor closely. There was something odd about him, not just the dejected and disreputable appearance, but in the way he spoke—as if he was almost too tired to talk.

"At home? No, there is nothing left there."

"Then why didn't you go to the bistro?"

"I have no money."

"You must have money. You will have the commission for the sale of the Couronne land." And, Lucien decided, he must have had something to drink today to keep him from suffering the tremors. But what was ailing him? The answers to simple questions had to be dragged out. The familiar impatience began to build in Lucien. Why should he be bothered with this creature—why waste time with him? He spoke his thoughts at last. "Why have you come here to bother me with your tales of woe? I can be of no use to you. If you don't like the noise of music in your home, as you say, and if you have nothing to calm your nerves and feed your cravings, then go elsewhere. Go to Greece as you planned. You can drown your troubles with anisette there more easily than here."

The room was still in semidarkness, but the wooden chair in which Valin was slumped happened to be spotlighted in the weak shaft of light from Lucien's bedroom. Valin raised his head slightly, and the shadows deepened the gray lines around his jowls, and even the steel-rimmed glasses did not hide the pockets beneath his eyes. He looked like a street vagabond, with his tangled colorless hair and his neglected attire, but it was the stoop of his shoulders and the way his hands hung unclasped across his knees that produced the total effect of depression and near defeat, that and the weary monotone of his words.

Valin spoke at last. "Estelle has all the money."

"Why would your sister have all the money. Did you give it to her?"

"It is too complicated . . . but I have an idea. . . ."

"How did Estelle get the money?" Lucien insisted. "Explain, monsieur . . . one thing at a time . . . remember?"

Valin seemed to be thinking and trying to choose words. "I didn't believe she would . . . she could . . . I was sick, monsieur, I was very sick. M. Dubois brought the money . . . the check, to the house, because I was sick. I signed it. . . . I didn't know what I was doing, so I signed it. Then Estelle took it to the bank . . . the day before they buried . . . buried her, Gabrielle. . . ." He turned his head away from the light and took a shuddering breath. "Could I have a drink, M. Anjou?" He coughed again.

"I am making the coffee." Lucien was spooning coffee grains into the old pot, but he kept watching, listening carefully.

The agitation began almost immediately. Valin moved his hands, rubbing them together as if they were cold, and the trembling became obvious, so he rubbed them on his knees. "Not coffee, please, monsieur. . . ." He looked around desperately. "A little wine, perhaps?"

Lucien didn't reply and the desperation began to rise in Valin's words, then a kind of craftiness. "You ask why should I come here," Valin went on slowly. "You ask why should I bother you. When I had something to offer before, you gave me a drink . . . I was useful to you, wasn't I? But I am no longer of use, so you would turn me out . . . offer me coffee and turn me out. But that is not so, M. Anjou. I have an idea. . . ." He rubbed his dry lips with his fist. "Just a small glass of wine for now," he pleaded, holding out one hand like a beggar.

"I had no intention of turning you out, but what idea have you got that could interest me?"

"A way to get some money . . . for both of us. You would like some money too, wouldn't you? They say that you want to go back to the mountains now that . . ." Valin was now watching the old corporal's face. "You don't believe me . . . I can tell . . . but it's true. I wasn't too drunk that night, at least not like they said. It is easy to fool those who want to be fooled."

"Which night?" Lucien barked.

"The night . . . that Saturday, I think. . . ." A hoarseness came and went in his voice.

"Which Saturday? I will not be fooled . . . I will not be blackmailed for the price of a mouthful of wine!" The words cracked.

Valin began pleading with both hands. "It is not what you think. It was the night . . . no, it couldn't have been Saturday . . . that was last week. . . . It must have been Tuesday. It was the night I saw Gabrielle, when she was still alive, by the garage. You must remember the night . . . when my car was out of gas that afternoon, and I saw you later, after dark, near my car. . . . Maybe you saw him too."

Lucien suddenly moved. He grabbed Valin by the shoulders and pulled him to his feet as if he were a rag doll. "What did you see?"

"I can't think . . . I can't think," Valin stuttered. "You're hurting me. It was the Hugo boy . . . the one with the motorcycle . . . with Gabrielle."

Lucien swung Valin around and shoved him into the armchair this time. Then he threw open the cupboard beneath the sink and brought out a bottle. He jerked out the cork and shoving the bottle into the outstretched hands, stood back and watched the trembling man suck at it like a baby.

"That's enough for now," Lucien said firmly, pulling the drink away. "Now talk and talk sense."

Valin lay back and his face was lost in the darkness of the chair wings and his words came thickly. "It was that night, after the car was out of gas . . . so I went back to the garage later, and the young man there . . . the one with the hair . . ."

"Henri."

"Yes, Henri . . . he wouldn't give me my keys so I could go home. He made me leave, pushed me, said to walk home. What else could I do, so I walked a way, and then I got angry. I said why should anyone keep my keys from me . . . they were mine . . . so I went back. I was walking, you understand, and my head was clearer. I wasn't that stupid with the drink, and I could see . . . and I saw Gabrielle; just like I saw you later when I left, checking to find if my car was all right. That was good of you, Corporal. But before that, they were there back of the garage, Gabrielle and that Hugo boy with the beard. I wouldn't have known who he was . . . with the beard, because he never had one before, but I saw him near your house that day when I came . . . waiting for your granddaughter . . . and I remembered. He was driving around the town on his motorcycle too."

Lucien caught his breath and was going to cry out, What day . . . what day?, but he kept still, telling himself there would be time. It would confuse Chamillion to interrupt now.

"She was close to him, Gabrielle was," he went on in his jerky sentences, but there was emotion in his voice at last, ". . . standing close . . . just a boy, but she would turn away from me to a boy, just because he had money and was young. Well, I know where I can get some money now." His voice had dropped swiftly to a whisper and Lucien had to strain to hear.

Lucien handed the bottle back, and once more watched the wretched man tip it up and suck at it, then cradle it against his chest with both hands.

"Tonight when the music went on and on, I couldn't stand it . . . the music . . . 'La vie en rose' . . . and how she looked at me that afternoon. It was Saturday that afternoon, like last Saturday. . . ." He lifted the bottle and some of the wine ran down his chin, but he didn't bother wiping at it. "She put her clothes in the suitcase, and she sang . . . and she laughed . . . she laughed at me. She was my wife." He drank again, his chest heaving a little, the cough sounding raw.

Lucien waited for a few seconds, then began prompting in a quiet voice. "What else did you see? She was with Jean-Louis Hugo, and then what happened? How long did you wait?"

But Valin wasn't really listening; he went on with his own succession of thoughts. "Estelle has all my money and she says she will only give me two francs a week. But I thought of you . . . You can ask the Hugo boy's father for money, and then I won't tell the gendarmes. Pépi Hugo must have a lot of money." Now his voice took on a slyness. "You'll help me, won't you, Corporal?"

Lucien ignored the foolish proposition. "You waited, did you, until the boy went off on his motorcycle?"

"He didn't ride it. They were standing arguing . . . bargaining. She looked into her purse and held out her hand. But Henri, in the garage, he was working on something . . . pounding, so I couldn't hear, but I could tell . . . she wanted her money first. He started away, but she called him and he came back. She was selling herself . . . selling herself. I couldn't stay to watch. . . . I went away and was sick."

"Didn't you go up to her and demand she come home with you, like you did in the Khedive? She was your wife."

But Valin didn't reply. He nursed the bottle between his crossed arms, close to his chest, bending over in a fit of coughing, then rocking back and forth in the chair until it became a kind of rhythm and a few mumbled words were audible. "She was just asleep . . . I looked there . . . she was asleep. Don't be afraid . . . I won't hurt you . . . just asleep." The singsong voice went on, chanting like the priest in the fog.

"Where was she asleep?" The sharpness was back in Lucien's words, but at last he realized he was wasting his time as the mumbling continued until it became soft sobs. The head began to thump on a single spot on the back of the chair, the glasses sliding crookedly down the nose.

Lucien removed the glasses and placed them on the table. "It was as well you came to me, monsieur," he said softly. "The gendarmes would not understand the way I do, if you went to them, and as you say, the Hugo boy's father has money and wouldn't want any scandal. You are very tired and sick. You should lie down and sleep a little." Lucien's voice droned on as he lifted Valin to his feet and across the room and into the bedroom, where the light revealed starkly the ravaged appearance of the small man. "I will go out and get you something to drink. A little anisette, perhaps?"

"Yes, a little . . ." Valin coughed as he fell across the big bed. Then as Lucien pulled a blanket across the shaking shoulders and switched off the light, "Don't turn me out . . . I can't go there . . . she is not there . . . I can't go back."

"I know," Lucien agreed. Then he strode through the darkened kitchen to the door, donned his coat and beret, locked the door softly behind him, and disappeared into the enveloping fog.

* * *

"Come along, M. Chamillion. Wake up! It is I . . . your friend Corporal Anjou. Open your eyes! I have something for you to drink, to refresh you. Sit up . . . that's the way. We are going for a walk. I have found someplace for you to stay until you feel better, and someone to look after you.

"Drink it all . . . very good . . . now just a little more. It is almost daylight, but it is cold. You should have worn a coat. Still, it will be warm where we are going. Stand up now! You must keep awake until we finish our walk and then you can sleep again.

"Put your arm in here . . . it is an old sweater. I know it is too big but I will roll back the sleeves . . . like so. Now, the other arm. We don't want you catching pneumonia in your weakened state. You already have a bad cold.

"See out the window . . . another night is almost over, and we should not waste time. We wouldn't want the gendarmes to know where you are going. They might want to ask you more questions . . . and they wouldn't give you anything but water to drink."

This time Lucien did not bother to lock the cottage door behind him.

Chapter Nineteen

The fog began to lift in midmorning and by noon the cold air became clear and the sun broke through in snatches. Ygrec, anxious to get outside, dressed warmly in a scarf and heavy coat and had a protesting Michelin drop him off at the park adjacent to the burial grounds.

"I have to get a new lead for Mademoiselle Larme," he explained. "I refuse to have her chained . . . the clanking sound would offend her ears and mine as well, and Pépi Hugo told me that there is a shoemaker close to avenue Côte who will make her a strong leather one."

"Excuses, excuses!" Michelin replied. "Just because you can't stand the new femme de ménage. Well, don't blame me if you come down with the black plague, as Vanessa would say."

A large person, who called herself Mme. de Cosse had come yesterday afternoon. She was dour and plodding and Ygrec said she smelled like garlic and body odor, and she depressed him. She had done a good enough job of cleaning up the kitchen, but the cold supper she had prepared had been dry and tasteless and both men had been thankful that Pépi Hugo had brought them meat pies.

"Vanessa wouldn't have allowed such a person through the door," Ygrec grumbled.

"And Vanessa wouldn't have allowed you outside the door today. You coughed half the night."

"Pic, pic, pic!" Ygrec slammed the car door and stepped out onto the narrow sidewalk. He'd been given directions on how to find rue Lutétia, which was really where he was heading, but he turned in the direction of the Église and half considered looking for Pippa's grave. Then as he glimpsed the gravestones, so many crookedly neglected, he decided against it. It would be better to devote his energies to the living, and he turned away leaving the spires of the church behind him.

The first area he passed was typical of the old town. The charm of the narrow cobbled streets was shadowed by too many tall stone buildings on either side, with bedding hanging to air from grilled-window balconies, and bits of washing dangling damply from high-strung clotheslines that shut out what little sun appeared from time to time above the chimney stacks. The few people who passed, many Arabic in appearance, were hurrying and unsmiling. Finally he

turned a corner and looked down avenue Côte which was longer than
he had expected, and as he was already beginning to weary and get
a little short of breath, he decided to try a short cut, a back lane that
seemed to form the base of the triangle in the direction of rue Lutétia
and the intersection where the Côte Impériale garage was situated.
He slowed his pace. There was nothing to see but grimy high stone
walls and locked rear entrances, but soon he came to what was obviously the back lot of the garage where a few cars were parked on the
graveled lot. There was not a motorcycle in sight. He followed the
side driveway, then paused by the front to catch his breath and take
in the details of the place. It seemed typical of such car-servicing establishments in an out-of-the-way district, an office adjoining the garage, all in need of painting and tidying. It appeared deserted, and
not a car drove up to the single gas tank while he was there. He
headed across the intersection and down rue Lutétia.

The street was much as Pippa had described it, narrow and cobbled, with a few more shops other than those she had mentioned. He
kept to his tortoise pace and was relieved to see the gleaming display
window of the Pâtisserie Hugo.

Mme. Hugo was delighted, enchanted, overwhelmed to meet Pépi's
kind friend, the famous gendarme Ygrec. Her husband and Jean-Louis
were both out at the moment, finishing deliveries, but would be back
soon. Monsieur must come into the parlor and sit, and have a café
au lait. It was a chilly day and she had heard about Monsieur's chest
condition and he must rest and warm up. Indeed, M. le Blanc the
cordonnier would make a fine lead for M. Ygrec's dog, but he was
shut today. He always closed on Fridays. Would monsieur like a
mocha cake or a lemon cream tart—both fresh from the oven this
morning—perhaps one of each? Monsieur could certainly do with a
little more flesh on his bones.

Ygrec was overwhelmed too, not only by the effusive greeting, but
also by Madame's appearance. He had to remind himself that it was
only early afternoon, for she was dressed as if she were going to
spend a gala evening at the opera, back in the prewar era. Her firmly
corseted body was enclosed in royal purple, cut low, although little
of her healthy flesh was exposed, as her neck and generous bosom
were heavy with gold chains and crystal beads that matched her earrings. Her lips were pink, her cheeks pinker, and the heavy dark
twists of curls on the top of her head were held in place by rhine-
stone combs. He covered his astonishment with a smile of admiration,

and as she ushered him past the shelves laden with cakes and breads and into the back room, she mentioned that she felt one should always be well attired when meeting the public; it gave a shop an air of respectability. Ygrec agreed enthusiastically and followed her through the big warm kitchen and into the living quarters beyond.

He had hoped to be seated in what appeared to be a very comfortable old chair in the dining room, and where, as Pippa had mentioned, one could see the comings and goings along the street as well as the entrance to Anjou's Lane, but he was led through the room and into another.

The parlor was less a shock than Madame because he had mentally prepared himself for its décor, having observed the tastes of the decorator. As he surmised, it was a stuffy, spotless cubbyhole of a place oozing with tassels, lace, brassy gold, souvenirs, and carved furniture. He admired the photographs of the Hugos' two daughters, each smiling stiffly from encircling, puffy wedding veils, and he was tempted to examine closely the enlargement of Jean-Louis as a starched and serious choirboy, but resisted, and allowed himself to be seated on a backbreaking, slippery horsehair sofa.

At first she talked through the open dining-room door, pausing each time she passed the doorway to gesture and smile. Ygrec heard about Pépi's father, who had begun his career as an apprentice cook at the old château and had graduated to master chef in Paris, and of Pépi's sufferings while held prisoner of war by the Germans.

Finally there was a break in her recital and Ygrec, who had been waiting for such an opportunity, tactfully led to another subject. "I passed the churchyard on my way here but decided not to stop today. It has been a time of sadness for you . . . for all of us. I have been told that you have been of great support to the bereaved families, madame."

"Well, M. Ygrec, one must do what one can. I never have been a person to speak ill of the dead, but I'm afraid that Gabrielle Chamillion got her just reward and will not be missed . . . except for a time by her husband, I suppose, but the day will come when he'll realize he's better off . . . although of course it's hard to tell. I can't say he's any different now than he was before, drinking all the time, worrying that poor Estelle to death, and now he's staying out all night. I told her this morning, 'Valin's a grown man and if he wants to drink himself into the grave, it's up to him. He'll come home when he runs out of money, and no one will buy him a drink,' I said, 'just like he used to do.' He would be gone for whole weekends, M. Ygrec, before he got married. She wasn't much good herself, that Gabrielle, but she married more trouble when she married him!"

Madame didn't stop talking while she served him, and Ygrec patiently sipped politely at the rich coffee, from a silly cup with a butterfly handle that he was sure was going to slip from his fingers, and munched on iced cakes that were delicious but much too sweet.

"But at least Estelle has a little money now, and I must admit I can give myself some credit for helping her. She may appear not too bright at times, but I will say this for her, that once she makes up her mind she won't change it. It was the day before the funeral when M. Joddard's son-in-law so kindly delivered Valin's final check to the house. . . . Valin had been crying into his Pernod and wasn't fit to come downstairs, and I happened to drop in with some rolls and sweets for their invalid mother. Estelle took the check up to him and he signed it and told her to go to the bank and bring him the money. . . . He wasn't at all nice about it either; I could hear him, M. Ygrec, and he was very nasty. So as I was on my way home anyway, I went along to the bank with her and I said, 'Estelle, if you don't use your wits, you and your mother will end up without a roof over your head,' and I could tell she knew what I meant. She did exactly as I told her and cashed the check, but she put most of the money in a new account under her own name. Do you realize, monsieur, that poor woman had never had any money she could call her own, ever in her life before. She had always been beholden to her mother, or her brother. It's a sad thing. When I got home, I said to Pépi, 'Well there's a bit of money that brother of hers can't drink up!' and Pépi agreed it was a good thing."

Ygrec, wiping his long, awkward fingers on a bit of embroidered serviette, agreed, then once more led into another subject, that of the sad plight of Corporal Anjou.

Madame, ignoring Ygrec's protestations, refilled his cup and was off again, praising Lucien Anjou's courage in his period of grief. "He keeps busy outside, digging mostly . . . he even dug the child's grave." She patted at her eyes. "It's good he can keep occupied out of doors. He can hardly bear to go into the cottage, with Pippa gone. He had me pack everything she owned and get it right out of his sight, poor man. I still think it was some Algerian transient who killed her. They're everywhere, you know, and he may have tried to steal something from the cottage and was discovered by Pippa, so he killed her and dragged her off wrapped up in a rug . . . you've seen them carrying their rugs over their shoulders, I'm sure. He hid her body in the woods, not expecting it to be found so soon. Don't you think that sounds logical, monsieur?"

"There are many theories," Ygrec replied. "What does your husband think?"

"Well, he doesn't exactly agree with me, but he thinks it must have been a stranger. Who else would do such a thing to an innocent girl?"

"And your son?"

Madame had begun to gather up Ygrec's empty cup and plate. "Jean-Louis won't talk about it at all. He just leaves the room when we bring up the subject. It has affected him deeply . . . she was like a little sister to him, you realize, M. Ygrec."

Ygrec nodded. He was longing to ask more questions about Jean-Louis and about other small matters, but he was also beginning to long for his own chair back at the château, as his legs and back were aching from the cramped position he'd been sitting in. When the voices were heard in the kitchen, he had trouble hiding his relief, and he unwound his legs to stand up.

"Oh, they're back, monsieur. Pépi will be so pleased to see you." Then Madame called out, "Pépi . . . you'll never believe who has come for a visit!"

The bland fat face of the baker beamed as usual at the sight of Ygrec. He was devastated that monsieur had to leave so soon, but understood that Ygrec didn't like to leave his dog so long with a strange femme de ménage. They would all be glad when Mme. Michelin would be able to return home—what a dreadful shock she had suffered, and what a blessing she was feeling better. Of course they wouldn't hear of their good friend taking a taxi; they insisted that Jean-Louis drive him back. It certainly would be no trouble; it would be their pleasure.

Ygrec thanked Madame graciously, then followed Pépi out through the kitchen to the back lane where the delivery van was parked. It had HUGO ET FILS, PÂTISSERIE in freshly painted black lettering on its faded-gray-paneled sides. So, thought Ygrec, Jean-Louis has decided to "waste his talents" and trade his "artistic soul" for a loaf of bread and all that it implied. How very interesting.

Jean-Louis, who had been removing stacked trays from the rear of the van, turned, smiled, and held out his hand for the introduction.

He had acquired his mother's charming courtesy, and he was in workman's clothes like his father, but there the family resemblance ended. He was of medium height, very slim, his hair thick and dark, and his clean-shaven chin very white in contrast to his tanned cheeks and forehead, but he had not shaved off his long sideburns. He wore a dark turtle-neck sweater beneath his open shirt.

When thanks were once more exchanged, the young man helped Ygrec into the van. He drove carefully, glancing at the old man a few times, and answering his questions readily. Yes, he found St. Denis a little dull and confining sometimes, but his father and his mother wanted him to stay home, and some time he might go on with his education, although he wasn't sure what he really wanted to do—there was lots of time for that—he wouldn't be nineteen until December.

His motorcycle had been repaired as it only had a bent front fender. No, he hadn't had any accidents with it before. He was glad it hadn't been badly damaged as he was hoping to turn it in on a car before long.

Ygrec, perched precariously on the small lumpy seat beside the young man, watched the first drops of rain spit on the windshield, and listened, and more and more began to wonder what kind of a personality lay behind the politeness and the "right" answers, and what true expression was revealed in the eyes that were being so carefully trained on the road. Then they turned off the boulevard and onto the curved driveway leading to the château and Ygrec realized he was running out of time, so pushing tact and caution aside he changed his line of questioning. "Did you have anything to do with the death of Pippa, Jean-Louis?" he asked bluntly.

The muscular hands tightened only slightly on the steering wheel, as the van was brought to a smooth standstill adjacent to the building just past the front entrance. "I told them at the gendarmerie—" he began impatiently.

"Never mind what you told them . . . tell me . . . tell me!"

"No, monsieur, I did not." The voice was still controlled. The motor of the van was throbbing gently and the rain began pattering just as gently on the metal of the roof.

"Would you mind turning off the motor and talking to me for a few minutes?" Ygrec watched him reach over and twist the keys, then stare straight ahead. "Thank you. Now I shall try to be as brief as possible. You understand, I expect, that I had become very fond of Pippa in the short time I knew her, and also that I am an old detective with a consuming curiosity and a deep aversion to violence."

"Yes, monsieur."

"Do you resent these questions?"

"No, monsieur."

"You are being too polite, Jean-Louis."

For the first time Ygrec detected feeling in the reply, a kind of impatient exasperation. "I am not hiding anything about Pippa. I told the other gendarmes and I tell you . . . I have nothing to hide except that I saw her when I was supposed to keep away from her. I would watch for the times when her grandfather went out, and we would talk through the parlor window because it is at the far end of the house away from the lane and there are shrubs all around the back."

"Did you ever go inside?"

"No, I didn't. She came out once, that was all . . . and it wasn't for very long. She didn't want to hurt her grandfather. It upset her when she had to lie to him." The dark eyes moved and Ygrec thought he could see a flash of caution before the young man turned away to watch the moisture beading, then meandering down the streaked windshield. "Then Saturday night, when she knew he would be gone quite a while, as he was going to visit you, we went out for a walk, to talk, because she was still upset."

"What was she upset about?"

"About not being able to see me, mostly. She thought we could go away together, but I told her that was a foolish idea . . . and besides, I didn't have any money. She always did have romantic notions, wanting to live like the people in books she read."

"You were going to work for your father and save your money, I presume?"

"Yes."

"And what about Pippa going off to the Académie?"

"It wasn't a prison, and she would be home in the summer. That's what I told her."

"Did you indeed?"

His hands grasped the spokes of the steering wheel and his voice rose in impatience. "Yes, I did!"

"That is better," Ygrec commented softly. "The politeness gives way to some emotion. I have recently become very weary of so many angelic people wherever I turn. Everyone has noble thoughts and pure motives, and it's not natural, not normal. I myself want to get angry and lose my temper, being surrounded by so much innocence, for somewhere very close by there is someone doing a superb job of covering up guilt. Perhaps you could help me, Jean-Louis. I would like to know all about Pippa . . . her likes and dislikes, her family and friends, because in her background there may be a motive for her death."

The little rain shower had ceased and inside the van was silence and yeasty smells, but it also became close and confining, and when Ygrec began to cough, the sounds seemed very loud. Jean-Louis remained bent over the wheel, listening quietly.

Ygrec was tired now. He began to move restlessly. "It might be better to continue our talk later on," he decided. "The dampness disturbs my lungs and the subject of tragedy disturbs both of us. Would it be convenient with you to meet again this evening? I shall be alone and would welcome company." He reached for the door handle.

Jean-Louis sat up slowly. "If you wish, M. Ygrec . . . this evening after I have finished helping my father." His politeness returned. "Sit there and I'll go round to open the door for you."

But Ygrec waved him back. "I am not a cripple yet." He stepped out carefully onto the sidewalk beneath dripping evergreens. Then he leaned over before he closed the door. "I was sorry to hear about your motorcycle. Have you had it repaired yet?"

"Yes, monsieur."

"Good. Thank you for your ride and for your time. Au revoir."

Ygrec straightened and turned, a tousled, shabby old man, but tall and erect, his appearance completely disguising the fact that he was decidedly disturbed.

Chapter Twenty

It was late when Michelin returned. Lucien had stopped in for a few minutes, but Jean-Louis did not come. The fire was almost burned out and so was the old gendarme. He, as so often lately, dozed in the chair, shoes off, his feet resting on the stool. The dog, with her head on crossed paws, was stretched out across the long sofa, which was forbidden territory.

"Well, old man, this is a fine sight," Michelin observed as Ygrec opened his eyes sleepily. "A glass, an empty cognac bottle, and the two of you unconscious." He whistled sharply, "Down, Mademoiselle! Not even Vanessa allows you to sleep on her best velvet."

The dog raised herself slowly, eased onto the floor, and almost crept out of the room. The two men eyed each other.

"You have become a nag in your old age, garçon," Ygrec muttered. "The cognac bottle was practically empty to begin with, and I have had a hard day."

Michelin slumped down on the warm spot just vacated by the dog. "I haven't exactly been on a vacation either, but what have you been doing to make you so irritable?"

"I am not irritable . . . I'm preoccupied, and I'm too weary to go into the dull details of the whys and wherefores. I have been doing a lot of thinking, though. The corporal came in for a short time. He is not himself, which I suppose is not unusual under the circumstances, but he was uncomfortably restless."

"Did he want anything in particular?"

"I have no idea what he wanted. Neither of us mentioned Pippa. I took the opportunity this afternoon to visit Mme. Hugo, which was quite an experience, and Jean-Louis drove me home. The young man knows all the right answers, which troubles me, but when I asked the corporal about him, the reply was, 'He is his mother's son,' and when I asked for more information about the Chamillion woman and her husband, I got another evasive answer. Then the corporal decided he had to leave. He was like a stranger. It is all very frustrating. Did you have the opportunity to talk to Sergeant Corvette today? Is there anything new?"

"Nothing from St. Denis, and I wish you'd stop asking. If anything does develop, I'll tell you. As for me, I've got a headache and sore feet. We've lost our drug pusher, Tusette, and even I have to take to the streets following up useless leads."

"Lost him! I thought he was safely in cells."

"We couldn't hold him. . . . I thought I'd told you."

"Well, you didn't." Ygrec sounded annoyed. "But let me guess. The drugs found in his car turned out to be milk sugar."

"Corn flour."

"So. . . ." The old gendarme pursed his lips. "I should have guessed, and if you'd had your wits about you, so should you."

"You're the one with the second sight, not me," snapped Michelin.

Ygrec sat up and shook a long finger. "Hold that temper, garçon, and don't take your frustrations out on me. Use your brain . . . think! Tusette is a professional. If he had been making a routine delivery, he would have taken every precaution; first, not to be followed by the law or anyone else, for that matter, and, secondly, most assuredly not to be noticed. He would have taken great care not to be speeding on a highway, whatever the time of day or night when he was carrying narcotics. Therefore, one could presume that he knew he was not carrying narcotics . . . and one could also presume he must have been angry or frightened if he was rushing back to St. Denis at some ungodly hour in the morning. I cannot see anyone in his position longing for an encounter with the law, so I doubt if he was thinking clearly. It took Vanessa, didn't it . . . an innocent like Vanessa, to point the fact out, and you didn't listen. You never do, you know, garçon. What was it she said? Ah, yes, that normal people get a tired feeling at five o'clock in the morning."

"Touché, old man."

"Never mind the apologies . . . and if I were you, I'd stop wasting my time looking around here for Tusette. I expect he'll turn up in Marseilles sometime, if his body isn't fished out of the Seine first." Ygrec stood up, poking crossly at his rumpled old brown robe. "I'm really too tired to pretend to be tactful, so just one more question: What was Gabrielle Chamillion carrying in her purse when she was killed? I suppose she had a purse, or is that presuming too much?"

"I haven't the faintest idea. I keep reminding you that I don't work out of St. Denis. I just live here because my wife decided she didn't like the smell of the city."

"Well, stop reminding me because I know where you work. You can find out from Sergeant Corvette, can't you?"

"I expect so, but what excuse can I use?"

"By the saints, garçon, I don't know how you got promoted! Have you no initiative? You are developing into the dullest man I've ever met. Think up a good lie if you have to, as Vanessa would say."

"It seems to me she is being quoted just a little too often recently. Would you suggest that she become the detective and I stay home and try to learn to make coffee?"

Ygrec glared. "Excellent idea. You really are beyond human aid, and I'm going to bed. Why don't you sit here and think up a few good lies to tell yourself to explain your inexcusable stupidity? Oh, by the way, when you talk to Sergeant Corvette, check again on the coroner's report on Pippa Anjou's death."

"What specifically?"

"Everything . . . every little detail, that's what."

"You are particularly impatient tonight, old man." Michelin's sarcasm was showing.

"And you are particularly insensitive. Your mind is not on your work. I will be glad when Vanessa comes home."

"So will I."

"Have you told her so?"

"She knows it. I don't have to tell her. She'll be home when she's feeling better."

The two men had been standing facing each other, sparring with their words. Ygrec threw up his hands in a gesture of despair. "I don't think she's going to be 'feeling better,' as you put it, for some time to come. Now give that a little thought. As for me, I am going to apologize to Mademoiselle Larme for the way I allowed you to order her out of the room, and then I'm going to sleep." The old gendarme bowed formally and stiffly and walked away.

But Ygrec couldn't sleep. He lay in the darkness and thought of pleasant things; Vanessa's laughter, Piaf's music, Mme. Lachance's soufflé, but still the worries, large and small, insisted on surfacing. Vanessa and Paul, so stubborn, so set in their ways; Lucien Anjou and his brooding preoccupation this afternoon; Jean-Louis Hugo with his perfect manners and perfect answers. Why hadn't the young man come back tonight as he'd promised? Then Pippa—always Pippa. What strange combination of genes had produced her oddly dramatic personality? He could see her wide eyes, her expressive face as she exaggerated the bits of gossip—but how much was exaggeration? Who else had she mentioned besides the Hugos and the Couronne family? There was the mortician, M. Fouschie, Ygrec recalled, and a young man called Armand who was a relative of Mme. Céleste at the neighborhood bistro. It would cost nothing to at least talk with more of the girl's acquaintances; it was little enough to go on but was the only fresh idea he could think of. Tomorrow, if the weather was at all decent, he would see what he could do. Most certainly he would attempt another interview with young Jean-Louis.

Ygrec finally slept, although restlessly, and he awakened later than usual, so was still undressed when Pépi Hugo arrived at the back door. Ygrec was surprised, as Pépi had been coming each day with his little treats in the late afternoon when he could stop for a minute and visit. He was also surprised that the fat man's round face didn't light up as usual when the back door was opened.

"I have had to come early today, M. Ygrec," he apologized, "as I will be doing all the deliveries myself. Jean-Louis' motorcycle was stolen last night, even though it was locked, so he has gone searching for it. He is upset. Mlle. Estelle Chamillion is upset too . . . I have just come from there. Her brother has not been seen for two nights now and she's gone to talk to the gendarmes. I tried to tell her he would come home when he ran out of money for drink, but she says he didn't have any money to begin with and she has dreamed up all sorts of wild stories about him being dead because he knows too much. Before he left, they had a quarrel over money and he said he could get money from someone else because he knew who had killed Gabrielle. She always has been the hysterical kind." Pépi shrugged dolefully, handed over some croissants and meat pies, and departed.

I keep being caught unprepared, Ygrec told himself, also rather dolefully, and he sat down at the table, still in his nightwear, to eat a croissant with his tea. Afterward he played with his empty cup, looking at the different images in the soggy tea leaves as he twisted the cup at different angles, wondering if he, like the fortune tellers, could read something from the formations, but all he could see was Pépi's sad face because it was fresh in his mind. Then for some reason he thought of the silly little cup and the café au lait that Mme. Hugo had served him, and he could see her prim parlor where not a speck of dust was allowed to collect. He wondered where Jean-Louis and his sisters had been allowed to play as children—what kind of a child had Jean-Louis been?

He dressed absently, carelessly, putting on clothing that both Mme. Lachance and Vanessa would have instantly ordered him to take off to be laundered. He washed and shaved absently too, taking his time, not looking at himself, but seeing other faces in the steam as it rose to cloud the mirror in front of him. He paced the rooms in his sock feet, and the dog followed him for a time until she gave up and sneaked back on the velvet settee again. He tried to read a magazine, but closed it without remembering a word. He put on Piaf's record of "La vie en rose" then switched it off. He made tea again and left it until it was cold. He noticed the day outside was the same as the day before. He wondered if it would ever be noon, and if Michelin would have time to come home.

Ygrec had the back door open before Michelin had the car door closed, and Michelin didn't even get his coat unfastened before the talking began.

"I was impatient last night, garçon, and I admit it. I had so many things bubbling up in my mind that they clouded my thoughts. I have not used my common sense, not listened to my instinct, but I am myself once again today. Will you drive me to rue Lutétia . . . please?"

Michelin was taken aback. The old man had not said please in more years than could be remembered. "Right now? It's barely noon."

"Right now."

"Very well, but put on some shoes, and as Mme. de Cosse won't be here until one o'clock, we'd better take the dog along. Don't you think we should eat something first? My stomach is empty."

"I'll beg a tart from the Pâtisserie Hugo for you. Now while I'm lacing up these cursed boots, tell me what you found out from Sergeant Corvette. You did talk to him, didn't you?"

"You are wound up this morning. The Chamillion woman's purse contained one lipstick, one . . ."

"Don't be idiotic! How much money was she carrying and did she have any drugs of any kind?"

"No drugs . . . about twenty-three hundred francs."

"Did she now!" Ygrec, who had been perched on a kitchen chair bending over his boot, looked up with interest. "I wonder if she was about to buy something or had just been paid. How very interesting." He bent over once more, puffing a little, tugging impatiently at the laces. "Now what about Pippa . . . and never mind all the big words that the doctors are so fond of quoting."

"It is as I told you a week ago. She was either hit on the side of the head or fell on something as there was a contusion . . . a cut . . . a large swelling and a hairline fracture of the skull. She was probably knocked unconscious by the blow, or the fall, but it wouldn't have killed her. She was strangled afterwards. There were no signs of human blood or flesh on the birdbath in the Couronne gardens."

"So . . . it is even more imperative that I have another visit with Jean-Louis Hugo, and this time I will not be so polite. Pépi was here early this morning and said the motorcycle had been stolen. There's something very odd going on."

But Michelin wasn't listening. He had spied the dog on the settee again and was saying, "I apologize if this is going to offend you, Mademoiselle, but if you don't get off there this minute, I will take you down and hand you over to Sergeant Corvette, and he will put you into a cell next to Jean-Louis Hugo, who is being held for being in possession of cocaine."

Ygrec's shoelace snapped.

* * *

Ghislaine was trying to braid her hair. "Over and under and over . . ." she told herself in a singsong voice. She was standing in Amélie's bedroom with her back to the three mirrors. Her coif and the old clothes had been tossed onto the bed and she was wearing the black crêpe-de-chine dress with the long fitted sleeves and her own handmade brown leather shoes. Lucien had moved her few belongings from the "cell" bedroom when he'd prepared it for the sick man. Her feet felt nice in the shoes—light and free, almost dainty—and she had managed to tie the laces without too much difficulty.

She was having trouble with her hair though, as the strands kept slipping from her grasp. Finally she pulled at the plaits impatiently, pinning them on top of her head in a haphazard fashion, but smoothing the fringe across her forehead before she reached for the hat.

She couldn't remember when Amélie had bought the hat, but it was when they were young—she'd had it after they'd returned from the mountains at the end of the war. Amélie had been wearing it that Sunday when she'd stood in the door of the cell bedroom. "Please, Amélie," Ghislaine had begged, "I could pray better in church." But Amélie had gone on tying the gray tulle veil at the nape of her neck and smoothing the black satin brim. "And contaminate the basilica!" Amélie had nodded toward the bucket of water by the cot. "You will go on repeating the rosary as you wash down your room, and pray Our Lord will find it in His heart to cleanse you of your sins and forgive you, for I never will." The door had closed, the bolt slid into place, and Ghislaine, long past tears, had dropped to her knees, her cold bare feet exposed beneath the hem of her flannel nightdress.

It is quite a pretty hat, Ghislaine decided, as she turned and bent over to admire herself in the mirrors. The brim shaded her features. She'd removed the gray veil, replacing it with a pale blue one that had been wound around a turban in Amélie's hatbox in the trunk room, and she'd pinned a sprig of frayed silk gardenias to one side. As she pulled the veil firmly beneath her chin, it bent the brim down on either side and she was reminded of a sunbonnet she'd worn as a child, and she felt very gay and young.

She paused in the hallway at the top of the stairs to listen. M.

Chamillion was now locked behind the "cell" door. She hoped he'd said his rosary as she'd instructed. He was a very sinful man, telling those lies about people. She would be glad when Lucien took him away, but in the meantime it gave her something to do, keeping an eye on him and giving him his medicine, although she'd never liked even the smell of licorice.

It wasn't the kind of day that one would choose for a walk, as the clouds touched the tops of the evergreens and the still air was cold, but it was a good time for her first venture out in daylight. M. Chamillion had finally settled down and Lucien had gone to the market and to do a few errands, so he wouldn't be back until late. Lucien didn't know about her walks away from the confines of her own little garden; it was one of the secrets she had managed to keep from him. She was practicing for the day when she would walk grandly down the streets of St. Denis to the basilica, looking as elegant as the lady she was born to be. Her first excursions had been in the darkness when she knew she wouldn't be seen, but she'd kept stumbling over undergrowth, and afterward her foot and ankle had ached, so the walks had been short. Today she would go even farther than the rose arbor, perhaps even to the back of the château. She wondered if that nice old gendarme was still visiting at the château, and if his dog was all right. She'd really quite liked the dog, if it hadn't tried to dig up Amélie. She didn't believe what Lucien had said about Amélie not being in the garden. What else could one do with a body except bury it?

She was glad she had put on the little fur cape and she hugged it closer to her shoulders and wished she'd remembered to wear the gloves. One wasn't properly dressed without gloves and she must remember them for her first great entrance into the basilica. Wouldn't heads turn, seeing Mlle. Ghislaine Couronne, the last of the aristocrats, walking down the magnificent aisles, and wouldn't Lucien be proud! She would hold her head high, and not limp; that was what she was practicing now.

The shoes felt fine, and she placed her feet carefully on the narrow path, trying to avoid getting mud or damp leaves on the nice leather. She grasped the fur cape to her neck with one hand, and held up the skirt with the other, and managed to pass through the opening in the hedge without mishap. She took no notice of the unmoving bleakness of the gardens, nor did she reach into her mind for associations with the past, for she was happy planning for the future. She lifted her chin and smiled, and the path became wider and smooth, the formal flower beds neatly trimmed and bright with autumn blooms. Nothing disturbed her, until she approached the birdbath. It was on her left, and all around the undergrowth had been trampled, revealing the vine-twisted pedestal. She stopped, dropping her skirt, slowly curling both cold hands into the warmth of the cape. It was ugly now, that birdbath, the squashed grass around it dank, cold—colder at night— and it was no longer Couronne land.

She pushed the fur up over her mouth, whispering into the clutched mass, "I should have moved her . . . I should have, but how could I? And I didn't know . . . I thought it was still the woman . . . that horrid woman. I forgot . . . I forget . . . when you upset me, Amélie, I forget. . . ." Ghislaine was murmuring louder now. She'd turned off the path and was stumbling, thistles clawing at her skirts, the mush of accumulated compost soaking into her shoes, weighing heavily on the weak foot. The ankle slid inward, and she fell but quickly dug her fingers into the moss that crawled along the marble pedestal over the rim, and her tears were of anger. First she sat, brushing at the slimy leaves that stuck to her cuffs and the front of her cape, using the tip of fur to wipe at her cheeks, then she stood, catching her breath. She wasn't hurt—not even the ankle pained, but the elbow of the dress was torn and burrs stuck to her skirt.

"I never liked this dress anyway," she said aloud, then repeated the words defiantly, "I never liked this dress . . . black is for burials!" She straightened the hat, lifted her head haughtily as she'd seen Amélie do so often, picked up her skirt, jerking it furiously away from more grasping weeds, and stumbled back to the path. She had planned to walk as far as the château, and nothing would stop her, not even the confusions in her mind. "I won't think about it," she went on aloud. "It was the only way, and I'm not sorry, and I just won't think about it."

It was peaceful around the château; nothing moved except the one car. Ghislaine couldn't see who was driving, but the bareheaded, tall gendarme let his dog into the back seat, then got into the front himself. She was glad the dog was all right. It was really a friendly nice dog, but she hoped it never came back to the loge because if it did, this time she would really have to get rid of it.

Chapter Twenty-one

Ygrec was very surprised to find the Pâtisserie Hugo was closed at noon on a Saturday. He tried the street door to the shop, then while Michelin waited in the car, he went to the back, but the lane was deserted and the rear door locked. He stood at the corner, looking down the lane through the stripped trees at the Anjou cottage, but there was no sign of life there either, not even a wisp of smoke from the chimney to tease the pendulous skies above.

"I have an idea, while I'm in the neighborhood," Ygrec said to Michelin as he leaned through the open window of the car. "I'm going over the road to the mortuary. I have had a real curiosity about the mournful M. Fouschie, as Pippa used to call him. In the meantime, you can go and order a new lead for Mademoiselle from the cordonnier around the corner . . . you might as well have her fitted for a new collar too. When you are finished, I will meet you at the Bistro Céleste over there." He pointed to the sign across the street.

M. Fouschie's premises were set well back from the street, with a long, narrow, cobbled driveway running along the side of the grimy stone building to the entrance and a large locked garage at the end. Chipped printing that had been painted on the tightly curtained window of the door read: G. FOUSCHIE—ENTREPRENEUR DE POMPES FUNEBRES. Ygrec rang the bell and was answered by a hollow echo. He rang again and looked up to the second story, but the grilled upstairs windows reflected only gray silence. He turned away and retraced his steps to the street.

There were a few customers in the Bistro Céleste, but only one man near the front bar. He was bald and gaunt with angular cheekbones, a prominent pitted nose, and a flushed complexion. He wore an old-fashioned, high, starched collar with a black artist's tie above a disreputable fitted black coat that had velvet lapels. A long arm stretched across the clean bare table in front of him, reaching for a wine glass. When he noticed Ygrec, he lifted the glass and peered over it without changing his morose expression.

Ygrec wanted to laugh. The man was so typical, so straight out of fiction, that he couldn't be real. However, Ygrec approached the table without hesitation and said very politely, "M. Fouschie?" The man nodded, and Ygrec went on: "May I prevail on a few moments of your time? I am Gendarme Maurice Ygrec, now retired. I am doing a little private investigation into the death of Mme. Gabrielle Chamillion."

The mortician looked up, pushed a chair from beneath the table with one extended leg and a very large foot enclosed in a pointed black shoe, and called out in a singsong voice, "Céleste! The Riesling!" He then regarded Ygrec who was seating himself. "Ygrec, did you say? Never heard of you, but still, I seldom do know the names until I read them on the death certificates."

"I am visiting Inspector Michelin of the Special Branch who lives in the Château Couronne," Ygrec volunteered.

"Never heard of him either but I'll take you at your word. The château . . . well, well, what a coincidence. Men may come and men may go, but the Couronne name remains to haunt us all. Do you like Riesling, monsieur?"

The mortician had a far-reaching voice, almost a soprano, which Ygrec had not expected. Somehow the clichéd image of the man would have been complete had he mournfully clasped his hands and whispered, or at least spoken in hushed tones. Again Ygrec managed to contain his amusement and kept only a polite smile on his face. "Thank you, monsieur," he said, "but do let me buy the wine. It will be my privilege, as you are allowing me to take up your time."

"I agree, M. Ygrec . . . I agree. Now where is that Céleste? Do you like pâté de foie? I never touch it myself. Liver is liver, and after a lifetime of repairing the aftermaths of postmortems, one has had enough. But they say it is very good here . . . the pâté. Céleste has the touch . . . if you have a strong stomach."

"My stomach is the least of my worries, M. Fouschie."

"Good. You don't look the delicate type, although your skin is a poor color. Do you have circulation problems?" M. Fouschie didn't wait for a reply. He emptied his wine glass in one gulp, then held the glass aloft.

A few customers were wandering in and were seated, then a thin, tired-looking woman in unobtrusive dark blue appeared beside Ygrec.

"Some of your famous pâté, Céleste, and leave the bottle," M. Fouschie said absently. "My new friend here wants to know about one of my recent works of art, and I am going to need sustenance." He waved the woman away with surprisingly long white fingers, then went on to Ygrec. "Mme. Chamillion had firm skin . . . fine texture. It wouldn't have lasted, of course; it never does when it is neglected.

Still, she was quite a pleasure to work with . . . really only needed touching up on the face . . . it was very discolored, unfortunately. But she had fine facial bones and I must admit she looked well when I'd finished, almost alive. It was one of my prouder moments when her husband viewed her. 'She's just asleep,' I said to him, and he wept, and so did I. It was a touching scene. Mind you, we were both a little intoxicated."

The quiet Céleste placed the bottle of wine on the table, also a plate covered with tiny toast triangles smeared with pâté, and Ygrec was beginning to wonder if he really felt hungry after all, but he managed to say cheerfully, "It is gratifying to find someone who enjoys his profession, monsieur. but I'm afraid my interest in the woman is from the viewpoint of my own profession. . . . Why did she die violently?"

"I see your point, M. Ygrec." The mortician lifted the bottle and refilled his glass, ignoring Ygrec, who finally helped himself also, then picked up a morsel of toast. "But," the man went on, "I cannot see how I can help you, so I'm afraid you are wasting your time. Still, you are not wasting my time. I seldom have company. Most people pass by on the other side, so to speak, as if by ignoring me, they can also ignore the inevitable fact that one day I will be their closest companion."

Ygrec was trying to swallow the pâté but choked a little and raised his hand to cover his mouth. He finally washed the food down with a mouthful of wine and decided to try to change the subject. "This is excellent pâté. Do you come here often, monsieur?"

"Oh, I do . . . I do. It is my home away from home when I have no company next door, if you understand my meaning. I am a man alone. I once had a dear companion who shared my life, my all, and he often said, 'One dies alone'; so since his passing I have decided that in learning to live with loneliness, I am practicing for the inevitable myself." He separated his fingers, placing them against his bony forehead and closed his eyes, taking on a total picture of suffering.

I am getting nowhere, thought Ygrec, and he kept looking toward the door, hoping to see Michelin. The room was half filled with patrons now, and it was becoming less peaceful. A pale youth, also in unobtrusive blue, was helping Céleste with the serving. Ygrec decided to try again. "Did you also perform your artistry on the remains of Pippa Anjou?"

The eyes opened quickly and the hand reached out for the wine.

"I did not . . . did not, and the very thought pains me. I shall never understand Lucien Anjou . . . never! Our firm, since it was first opened by my great-uncle Gervais, has always handled the clientele of St. Denis, but the corporal called in an outsider. I can tell you, monsieur, I am hurt . . . hurt to the quick." Now the fingers were pressed against the breast pocket of the black coat. "We were skilled enough to preserve the remains of the aristocrats, and Great-Uncle Gervais himself performed a miracle on the last Conte de Couronne, so I am told, and believe me, monsieur, he had little to work with. Sometimes when I am in a nostalgic mood I go through the record books in my office. Uncle Gervais was fastidious about detail. He wrote down everything . . . the condition of the deceased, the chemicals and cosmetics used. I must admit to being lax in that direction myself."

"Perhaps the corporal wished to spare you the pain of seeing his granddaughter when she was . . . shall we say . . . not at her best? You must have known her quite well, living so close," Ygrec suggested.

"Of course I knew her. How could I help it, seeing her pass my domain each day going to school? She was always friendly, and spoke to me nicely . . . not like some . . . not like that Jean-Louis Hugo, who laughed behind my back. That was what made it so difficult for me to tell the gendarmes I had seen her with him that night. I did it to protect her reputation. Céleste's nephew Armand . . . the young man over there who is serving the beer . . . he was with me and we both agreed we had to report it. I knew Lucien Anjou's feelings about motorcycles. Lucien's son, Jacques, was killed in a motorcycle accident. Jacques was the girl's father you realize. He wasn't buried here, unfortunately. It was as well that Lucien . . ." M. Fouschie stopped in midsentence to gulp more wine and reach for the bottle again.

"You were saying?" prompted Ygrec.

"It was of no consequence. I get carried away sometimes . . . overemotional. It is one of my great weaknesses, my friend used to tell me, but one of my strengths as well. I have a tender heart, monsieur . . . too tender for my own good." The mortician's thoughts were coming in jerks and he wasn't looking at Ygrec, but rather over his shoulder at someone else. Suddenly he called once more, "Céleste, another of the same," then to Ygrec, "We don't want to run short . . . it will be a long afternoon."

It won't be for me, Ygrec told himself. Already he was getting tired, but he tried one last line of questioning. "It must have been an honor to serve the Couronne family. I have heard that a Mme. Fouschie was companion to the Couronne sisters when they were children. Would she be a relative?"

"Of course, of course. She was my aunt, Marie-Cécile. Now, *she* was a cross to bear! For a time her name was only whispered in our family, even though she was not a blood relative. But when I was a child and would have temper tantrums, they would shake their heads and say I was getting like Aunt Marie-Cécile, which was supposed to make me feel disgraced. But I liked her. I had no mother, you see, and she used to bring me presents, and she wore the most exotic perfume! I can smell it yet." He lifted his nose and sniffed daintily. "She had been a nun, but left the order, so you can imagine the disgrace back in those days . . . a nun stripped of her habit, and then marrying! It was unheard of. Fortunately, her husband . . . that would be my uncle Gaston . . . all the names in our family begin with "G" . . . he died suddenly, and the family didn't have to have anything more to do with her. It was after that she was taken on as companion for the little Mlle. Amélie. I wasn't born then, of course. I am of the age of Mlle. Ghislaine. I wasn't supposed to speak to them, nobody was, but sometimes my aunt would sneak me into the château when I was small, and later I visited her at the loge de garde. Amélie was the pretty one. The ravages of time took their toll on her. Aunt Marie-Cécile was very fond of Amélie . . . very fond . . . too fond." The mortician seemed to be drifting into the past, his face flushed with wine, and he was staring at nothing on the table top. Finally he added, "Ghislaine was always odd, even before she fell. I often wonder if she was meant to be . . . it seems wrong she was left."

Ygrec was becoming confused and the room was stuffy now, with many of the customers smoking. His chest was tightening and he knew he would have to get outside soon, even if it meant waiting on the sidewalk for Michelin. He wheezed a little, and tried to clear his throat and the distraction brought the mortician back to the present.

"I am enjoying your company, M. Ygrec," he commented almost cheerfully. "People don't talk to me, as I explained earlier, so I sit alone and drink too much wine. Now what was it you wanted to know about the unfortunate Gabrielle Chamillion? If it was about her addiction, I doubt if it had been going on for long, as her nasal passages were only slightly inflamed."

Ygrec was coughing and managed to suppress his astonishment by again covering his face with his hand.

"We all have our little crutches, monsieur," the mortician went on in a rather sober and philosophical manner. "If I had to live with M. Chamillion, I expect I would turn to something for relief, and cocaine is so easy . . . no needles if you sniff it. I will admit to you in confidence that, even after all these years in my profession, I have a dislike of needles. I almost have to close my eyes each time I inject the preservatives." He sniffed again, but this time with distaste.

Ygrec wanted to stay, to ask more questions, but he was now feeling as if his own nasal passages were plugging up, keeping the air from his lungs. He managed to push his chair back and stand, before the wheezing began to make him lightheaded, then he heard Michelin's voice and turned toward the door with a feeling of blessed relief.

"Come, old man . . . the air is fresh outside," Michelin said, supporting Ygrec with a strong arm.

"The wine . . . I have to pay for the wine. . . ." Ygrec gasped between coughs.

"I'll see to it when I have you safely in the car. I'm parked right by the curb," Michelin replied as he propelled Ygrec through the open door.

"Next time! You can pay for it next time, M. Ygrec!" The old gendarme heard the mortician's voice behind him. "But should we not meet again on this earth, do keep in mind that I, Gratien Fouschie, am at your service, and that my rates are reasonable."

* * *

That night, Ygrec was able to smile at the mortician's parting words. "I may be in bed, but it's not my deathbed yet," he said to Mademoiselle Larme, who didn't even raise her head from the foot of the bed. "Still," he went on aloud, "it appears as if my little outings are at an end for a time."

He was feeling much better, although he was still very tired. It had been a hurried trip from the bistro and Michelin had almost called in a doctor, but Ygrec had taken his medications and his inhaler had helped, and Mme. de Cosse had agreed to stay to serve Ygrec supper. Michelin had gone off after his usual warnings, and Ygrec slept the rest of the afternoon. Later he had taken the soup from Madame, which he forced down, to persuade her that all was well, and sent her on her way. He had slept once more and now it was nearly nine o'clock.

He hadn't expected Michelin to be so late again, but Mademoiselle was a good listener, so he was feeling quite cheerful. He sat propped up in bed, with the table light shining brightly beside him, and was surprised at how contented he was to merely lie back and think. It hadn't been a wasted day, in spite of the setback. He had learned a great deal. Now he could begin to put things in order.

Why, he asked himself, did everything seem to lead back to the Couronne dynasty? It was as the eccentric mortician had stated—the name remained to haunt the community. Ygrec began to pound at the pillows behind him, to twist and jerk at the blankets. Finally the dog looked up as if to say, 'Lie still!' and Ygrec grumbled aloud, "If you want to get back to sleep, you'd better move to the floor. You know I can't keep still while I'm thinking." The dog almost slid off the bed, stood looking up at Ygrec for a moment, then suddenly turned her head to listen to a sound that Ygrec could not hear and padded quickly out of the room.

It would be Michelin at last, Ygrec knew, so he lay back with his eyes closed and his hands folded over the untidy sheet, pretending to be asleep and certainly completely relaxed. He wasn't in the mood for another lecture on taking care of himself or on leaving investigations in the hands of officialdom.

At first Ygrec didn't know why he was recalling the shape of M. Fouschie's nose, and the man's reference to exotic perfume, but he supposed it was because he was smelling perfume himself, which was ridiculous because . . .

He felt her touch and opened his eyes the same instant.

"Dear old man," Vanessa said, brushing his rough cheek with her fingers, "have you been misbehaving again?"

Ygrec reached for her hand. "Go ahead," he said joyfully, "lecture me . . . be cross with me . . . but stay with me because this may be my last day on earth!"

She started to laugh and he joined her, then lifted her fingers to kiss them. "What miracle brought you?" he asked.

"I don't think even you would refer to him as a miracle. It was Paul. He called me this afternoon, just when I was needing an excuse to come home, and a friend of my father was driving to Paris, so here I am."

"If you weren't so stubborn, you wouldn't need an excuse to be where you belong, but I'm glad I could be of some use."

"Well, if you want to go on being useful, you are going to have to do what you're told. It's obvious you won't listen to Paul, so I'm going to call the doctor . . . and there's no use protesting that you're feeling better because, as you say, I'm stubborn. Now give me back my hand so I can at least take off this raincoat."

He looked at her with an angelic smile and replied nonchalantly, "Whatever you say, chérie. I wouldn't think of arguing with you tonight, as we can't have you getting upset, can we? Not in your 'delicate condition.'"

Vanessa didn't even look surprised. She just smiled back at him. "You have known all along, haven't you? And I don't think Paul even suspects."

"That's not surprising. I always was a better detective than he. Black plague indeed!"

"Then let's keep it our little secret, you and I, shall we? Just for the time being?"

"Do you think that's wise?"

"I have my reasons."

"Aren't you happy about it?"

"Oh yes . . . yes, I am. But I'm not sure about him. He was unattached for thirty years, and he still can't get used to me sometimes. But one thing at a time as you always say. Shall we begin by getting you on your feet first?"

"As you say, chérie."

Chapter Twenty-two

Ygrec "held court" in his bedroom for the next few days. Most of his visitors didn't stay long. Vanessa was his self-appointed "social secretary," she told him; she was also his guardian and his warden, he complained to her.

Lucien Anjou came first, quite early Sunday morning. He was disturbed that Ygrec was being confined to his bed, but was assured that it would only be a temporary arrangement. He had heard of the arrest of Jean-Louis Hugo and informed Ygrec that apparently the motorcycle had been discovered at the side of the tombs near the basilica early Saturday. An anonymous phone call had alerted Sergeant

Corvette, who had examined the vehicle, waited until Jean-Louis had turned up to claim it as his own, then had him held for possession of narcotics for the purpose of trafficking. The cocaine in a plastic bag wrapped in foil had been strapped beneath the seat of the machine with common adhesive tape. Lucien knew no more, or at least professed ignorance, except to say that Pépi was so upset that he had burned his croissants and was considering hiring an advocate.

Very convenient. that anonymous call, Ygrec thought, but he kept his thoughts and theories to himself, asking no questions. When Lucien left, the old gendarme sent a message with him to Pépi Hugo.

Shortly after noon, Ygrec had a surprise visitor. When Vanessa ushered the mortician into the bedroom, Ygrec peered over the sloping shoulders at her face, swallowing a smile. She was a picture of amused disbelief, even though she had been told about Ygrec's session at the bistro with the strange man.

"I trust you haven't come to measure me for a coffin just yet, M. Fouschie," Ygrec said immediately, to break the strain and give them all an excuse to smile.

"Indeed, no . . . oh, no indeed. I was truly alarmed yesterday, M. Ygrec. I became quite emotional with worry and spent a restless night, and although I met my friend Corporal Anjou this morning and he assured me you were feeling better, I had to see for myself. The corporal also briefed me on your wartime exploits. I feel a kinship to you . . . a true kinship!" He declined to be seated, preferring to stand by the window of the bedroom, his shoulders hunched beneath the black coat. He looked tired, the lines around his pronounced nose gray, his thin jowls dropping over the yellowed wing collar.

"Yes," the melancholy man went on, "it is gratifying to see you breathing properly, although your skin is a poor color. I passed Mme. Hugo on her way home from mass and she looked haggard . . . very haggard. I am sure you have heard about the Hugo boy, M. Ygrec. The sins of the mother shall be visited upon her children, as the wise saying goes. That boy was always sneaky and mean, always irresponsible, and his mother encouraged him. This is her reward. We reap what we sow!"

Ygrec listened attentively. Yesterday the mortician had seemingly been carried away by his own oration, yet had revealed a few interesting facts; today he might be even more informative. The old gendarme managed to keep to a tone of pleasant interest. "I expect that the Hugos are upset, but the evidence—the drugs—could have been planted to incriminate Jean-Louis. After all, the motorcycle had been stolen, yet it was found in a most convenient place."

"Then you have reason to believe they may not charge the Hugo boy? You know, of course, that a reliable source has now reported seeing him pushing his motorcycle out of the lane near the garage that fateful Tuesday when the Chamillion woman was killed."

Ygrec didn't know, but shrugged. "I have no reason to believe or disbelieve anything, and I am in no position to make judgments, for my information has been only gossip . . . hearsay. I am just pointing out that we should not jump to conclusions."

"Of course . . . of course. I simply thought that the Inspector had possibly uncovered more information, and as you are in his confidence . . ."

"Sergeant Corvette is conducting the investigation, monsieur, and I have no more access to facts than you. I only wish I could help, for I was fond of little Pippa Anjou. I have a nagging curiosity and would like to know more . . . much more. As there appears to be a connection in the deaths of the Chamillion woman and Pippa, I keep wondering if there could have been some thread that tied them together while they were living."

The mortician pressed his long immaculate fingers together at the tips and observed Ygrec soberly. "Indeed you are curious . . . yes, indeed. I have been wondering for many days now if someone would have the wisdom to turn over the rocks and reveal that nest of maggots. I said to myself yesterday, 'This Ygrec has a way of unearthing things,' that's what I said . . . 'but will it open old wounds?' I understand you are a friend of Lucien Anjou, M. Ygrec."

"I am."

"That being the case, if I were you I would leave the past to the historians, but of course I am not you, so I am wasting my words. That has always been another of my great weaknesses, monsieur. My friend, my dear friend used to say to me, 'Gratien, you waste your strength needlessly, trying to impart your wisdom to those who will turn from your advice.'" M. Fouschie now had his palms pressed together as if he were about to break into prayer. However his words were anything but pious. "That *petite rosse*, Gabrielle Chamillion, was Pippa Anjou's mother. She married Jacques Anjou when she was seventeen and left him shortly afterwards. She'd had a taste of freedom from the stifling patriarchal village of her birth in the French Pyrenees, and she wasn't about to let an infant keep her there."

This time Ygrec could not contain his astonishment. He stared at the mortician. "Did the corporal know?"

"She was a veritable Delilah, that one," Fouschie went on, obviously in his element as the center of Ygrec's attention. He separated his hands, using them to emphasize, to accentuate his explanation, which was as indirect as always. "She used men, especially weak men. Jacques Anjou got her out of the village . . . Valin Chamillion got her off the streets. She was trying to move up the ladder, but she was in too much of a hurry this time. She even tried to use me!" He laughed. It was the first time Ygrec had heard him laugh, and it was, not surprisingly, a sad sound. "We all have our little weaknesses, you will agree, but she misjudged mine." He laughed tightly once more. "Whether or not she went to Lucien Anjou, I have no way of knowing. I advised her against it, but as I mentioned, my advice is seldom heeded. People think I am a pitiful fool, an attribute I no longer try to discourage."

Ygrec had gained his emotional balance. "Would it be impolite of me to ask you how she tried to use you, M. Fouschie? I would be the fool if I tried to pretend that it was logical to think she was attempting to be installed as your mistress."

"Not at all, monsieur, not at all. Your honesty is refreshing. It was drugs . . . cocaine . . . what you wish. She was under the impression I might be interested in obtaining some drugs. She was a foolish woman. I met her . . . let me see now . . . it must have been about a month ago. She was peddling heroin at that time . . . risky business, and I told her so." The hands were imploring. "Heaven only knows where she got the idea I would be interested in such a dangerous substance."

"Why would she approach you at all? Was there not a danger you would report her to the gendarmes?"

"I have a reputation for minding my own business, M. Ygrec. Besides, why should I? She would only deny it. I saw none of her wares; also it is known that I have little use for the authorities in this place. In the past when I have been harassed, they turned their backs, and once when vandals broke into my offices I called the gendarmerie, but because nothing was stolen, they ignored my demands for justice. Now I sit back with sealed lips when they run around in circles. I sit back and laugh."

Ygrec sighed to himself. Once more he was allowing the conversation to veer off the subject. "How well did you know Gabrielle Chamillion?" he asked patiently.

"Not well . . . not at all well. But in spite of everything, she was entertaining. She was not dull. I cannot bear people who are dull."

"You say you met her first about a month ago. How often did you see her after that?"

"Three times . . . not counting the last fateful visit when I was able to perform my artistry on her earthly remains. I will admit to you that I encouraged her, for she aroused my interest. At first I pretended that I might be a potential buyer . . . for a friend, an unnamed friend. She was unhappy with her lot in the Maison Feu Follet, the ancestral home of the Chamillion misfits, and what could I do but sympathize. She was working at the time as a . . . shall we say, a waitress . . . in a place off boulevard des Anges toward Paris, Le Chat Rouge. It is a common place, M. Ygrec. I wouldn't recommend it. Dreadful food and worse service. Mind you, the day I was there they were in mourning; I was called to meet a client, the partner of the proprietor, who had been shot in the face. I really couldn't do much with the face, so I simply sealed the casket. One's talents can only be expected to stretch so far and no farther."

"I see that, monsieur." Ygrec was pressing his own hands together with impatience. "But if you did not know the woman well, why did she take you into her confidence, about her past and her supposed youthful marriage to Lucien Anjou's son?"

Fouschie held up one finger. "Do I detect a note of doubt in your voice? Well, M. Ygrec, I was doubtful about the story too, at first, but she convinced me! She had a certificate of marriage . . . Norbonne . . . she had been married in Norbonne. If you wished to check, I'm sure you could write to the registry there. As for her sudden intimacy with me, you may indeed ask." Both hands were flung outward and the mortician laughed once more, a less jarring sound this time as if he really found the situation amusing. "My youth? My charm? My masculine charisma? Or was I a father figure, as they are so fond of quoting these days since Freud became so quotable! Not at all . . . not at all. At our second meeting, which took place in my office, she was feeling very morose, and she boasted that she was related to the aristocracy . . . the Couronnes . . . for all the good it did her. I was intrigued and informed her that at one time I had known the family rather intimately. Need I say there was, after that,

an overwhelming interest in picking my brains. She wanted money
. . . money to go off and lead the good life, and she thought she
might demand money from the Couronne sisters. Although they appeared to be living in poverty, she thought they might be sitting on
buried treasure, almost literally . . . family heirlooms and so on. In
many ways Gabrielle Chamillion was naïve . . . a romantic. So I said
to her, one does not waste time trying to rob an empty crypt, and she
agreed, which was why she had not gone near Lucien Anjou, a poor
old corporal living on a pittance of a pension. She had absolutely no
interest in Pippa. The one time I mentioned the child, she looked at
me as if I must be demented to consider she might harbor any moth-
erly instincts. Gabrielle loved one person . . . herself."

"I think you came to know her rather well, monsieur," Ygrec said
thoughtfully. "However did she come to meet Lucien's son?"

"She was born in the same village in the Pyrenees as Jacques
Anjou. It was not well known, but it was known, that Jacques Anjou's mother was Ghislaine Couronne. The two sisters, the Couronne
sisters, had spent the war years there. The world is a small place, M.
Ygrec, and it is round. One cannot be pushed off the edge into obliv-
ion, and neither can one's past."

"So . . ." breathed Ygrec. "Lucien is married to Ghislaine
Couronne. . . ." It was as if Gratien Fouschie had transported him
into another world with the telling of the strange story, and now he
looked about the familiar bedroom with the modern blue papered
walls and white curtains; the hedge outside the windows, its tiny
leaves heavy with a seemingly unmoving gray drizzle; then back to
the ceiling above his head where elaborately carved cornices were the
one reminder that this room had been decorated for a Couronne.

Then Fouschie's voice brought him back from the momentary excursion into the past. "Not at all, monsieur . . . not at all. He was
married to the older sister, Amélie. She was rather beautiful when
she was young, but also very strange . . . possessive . . . calcu-
lating, even as a child, which in some way may account for such a
peculiar arrangement. Ghislaine had a kind of charm too, but she was
more like a vacant pixie, at least to my way of thinking. Small things
pleased her. She always adored Lucien, which could have been why
Amélie married him."

"Mon Dieu! How long have you known this, monsieur?"

"About Lucien and Amélie? Oh, for years, many years. I have
lived here all my life, even during the occupation. It was with great

relish that I devoted myself to pleasing the Boche. I accommodated them in many ways. I tended to the dead officers while hiding escaped refugees, mainly Jews, in the crypts of the basilica, then secreted them out of the area in coffins. I had a wit in those days." He smiled his sad smile once more. "They called me a collaborator, and I had to keep silence. Few knew the truth. Lucien knew, and he saved me. Toward the end of the war my countrymen were most unreasonable about collaborators . . . instant trial, instant guilt. But you were asking about Amélie Couronne, were you not? There was a time when Lucien took me into his confidence, a trust which until this moment I have kept. Also my cousin Guy was a priest and was able to be of some help arranging the annulment of the marriage . . . nonconsummation, of course. He is no longer with us . . . poor Guy."

"And the other relationship concerning Gabrielle Chamillion and Pippa? Exactly when did you learn about it?"

The mortician pondered seriously, pulling at his wide nostrils with his fingertips. "Let me think now . . . I believe it was during her second visit with me . . . Gabrielle's second visit. After we became acquainted at Le Chat Rouge, she came to my domain. She had walked out on her husband that night and I offered her a temporary haven out of the rain, which she accepted. The third and last time she came, she brought the marriage certificate, and she enlarged on the details of her life. We shared a little wine, and as she was already suffering the aftereffects of another kind of temporary stimulation—I would say she was on the cocaine by then—she was in a strange mood. We had a few things in common, other than a need to escape from a mundane existence. She wasn't fond of her husband, and neither was I. He had no soul." The mortician sniffed disdainfully. "He was also a snob."

"Can you recall the date of that third visit?"

"It was the night before she died."

"I see." Ygrec was indeed beginning to see. "You must feel a great loyalty to Corporal Anjou," he added softly.

Now Fouschie patted his lips with his expressive fingers. "Loyalty? Yes, one could say so."

"But for me, after only two encounters, you can but feel little more than a passing curiosity, so why have you honored me with your confidence?"

Gratien Fouschie did not attempt a reply. Instead he seemed to unfold himself from beneath the enveloping black coat, straightening his shoulders slowly. "I must take my leave. Mme. Michelin warned me not to tire you and you are looking quite gray."

Ygrec did not try to keep the man. "I thank you for coming." He stretched a hand across the bedclothes, touching the mortician's cool fingers.

"I may come again, should I be passing this way, but life is a fleeting thing and one often has the opportunity to pass by only once." He bowed, and again left Ygrec feeling slightly puzzled.

Later, when Ygrec related the visit to Michelin, they both had to smile at the doomsday attitude of the man, but that was before the Hugos arrived. Afterward even Michelin began to feel puzzled and a little concerned.

*   *   *

Mme. Hugo was attired in her magnificent best, as if to show the world that she was not affected by stress. Pépi appeared in his usual formally askew fashion, and his hand was trembling a little when he made his greetings. Both were subdued. Pépi sat throughout the visit mostly staring out the window at the distant lights that wavered in the darkness; Madame did the talking.

"As you say, M. Ygrec, an advocate demands a large payment before he will consider a case, and as today is the Sabbath, we will have to wait until tomorrow," Mme. Hugo said. Her perfectly coiffured dark head was held high, and the little jewels in her wide choker necklace sparkled in the light from the bedside lamp. She was seated near Ygrec's right, nearest the door, and she held her clasped fingers calmly in the lap of her black taffeta dress.

Ygrec lay back on his pillows, trying to follow Vanessa's directions to relax and not thrash around the bed. He hadn't needed the doctor to tell him he had a "tired heart"; he had been sitting up in a chair to eat his evening meal and had been content to return to the bed. But he had been impatient for this talk with the Hugos and was stimulated by the challenge. Could he get at even a part of the truth? Would they trust him to help them?

"Jean-Louis will need the counsel of a professional, madame, for I expect he will have to appear in court, but if you can be honest with me, we may be able to save everyone a great deal of time. Could you start at the beginning and tell me what you know about this whole business of your son, and, shall we say, his dangerously foolish indiscretions?"

Pépi looked at his wife, but she didn't appear to lose her poise and didn't take her eyes off the old gendarme's earnest face.

"It is well beyond the time of excuses and reasons and recriminations, Mme. Hugo," Ygrec prompted. "I'm sure you realize the drug charge may be indirectly linked to the death of Mme. Chamillion, as it has now been reported that a witness saw Jean-Louis in the vicinity of the garage about the time she was killed. I repeat, it is a time for honesty . . . the truth as you know it. Your son must have taken you into his confidence by now, if he didn't before."

"Yes, he has talked to me, monsieur," Madame said at last, then paused, trying to choose words. "I should have confronted him sooner, but I was trying to do what was best at the time. I found a small bag of white powder among his possessions, in the back of a bureau drawer. I wasn't snooping, monsieur, really I wasn't. He is inclined to be untidy and I was straightening the things in his drawers. I was sure what the bag was . . . After his troubles last spring, when he was spending so much time with that wild group of boys and he got into a little trouble over the hashish, I have always been afraid. I found it, the little plastic bag, wrapped in foil and pushed into an empty cigarette package. I knew then what he must be involved in . . . I knew he must have brought it home with him from the Riviera. He came Saturday. I found the bag on Monday. I was frightened, frightened for him . . . for all of us. I may have done a foolish thing, but I emptied out the white powder and replaced it with corn flour. It looked the same, and if he was found with corn flour what could anyone say? I wanted to talk to him about it, make him throw the bad stuff away himself, but I was afraid he would just pack up and leave home again, and get into worse trouble. That's what he did in the spring . . . he went away almost without warning because I tried to make him see sense."

Madame shifted a little in her chair and recrossed her plump black silk-encased legs. She avoided looking at Pépi, continuing as if he wasn't in the room. "Jean-Louis would never argue with me. Even as a little boy he never talked back. He was always polite and affectionate . . . and smiling. Even when he went ahead and did what was forbidden, and I had to correct him, he would smile sadly. It was hard to stay angry with him." She half smiled in recollection. "He would admit that he had been naughty, and then he would kiss me and hug me and tell me what a pretty mother I was and that he didn't deserve such a nice home. He wasn't often disobedient. His sisters complained that I was favoring him, but he was good. He never had temper tantrums like they did. The worst he ever did was to take money from his sister's little jewelry box in her bedroom, and that was to buy me a birthday present because he was too small to earn any money of his own. We didn't want him helping out in the bakery . . . he would get flour and icing on his good clothes . . . he looked so nice in his clothes."

For the first time her voice trembled a little, and for the second time her husband looked over at her, and Ygrec could see the moisture gleaming on the round forehead and beneath the sad dark eyes.

She seemed to sense Pépi's anxiety, for she glanced at him reassuringly, then turned back to Ygrec. "There was one other time that I suppose I should mention. Jean-Louis was forbidden to go near the mortuary. M. Fouschie, they say, is a harmless man, but I never liked him. It's a fact he made friends with the Boche during the occupation, no matter what excuse he gave. I wasn't here myself, but I heard, and it's a fact. Besides, he is a cheap man . . . always buys stale bread when he can, and haggles over the prices, although he must have money, never having a family to support . . . which no one expected of course. He is . . . he is not much of a man . . . so it is said . . . He is, he was . . ." Madame was fumbling for words.

"I understand," Ygrec nodded.

"Some of the older boys used to taunt him . . . laugh and make remarks behind his back. You know what boys can be, monsieur. They enjoyed it when he got angry. They would ring his doorbell and run away when he came . . . things like that. Pépi used to get cross with the boys, because he is always too kind about people. . . . Walk in the shoes of the other man, he used to say, and he told Jean-Louis to keep away. For me . . . well, I'm more practical, and I thought M. Fouschie was a bad influence on the children, asking for trouble, and most of my friends agreed with me. Still, Jean-Louis was forbidden to go near. But he did go there once, about four years ago it would be, he and Céleste's nephew, Armand. They broke a window downstairs in the mortuary. They wanted to see what a dead person looked like, they said afterwards, but the coffins were empty and so was the office; so they threw a few things around, spilled things, then they went upstairs because they knew that M. Fouschie was next door in the bistro. It was when M. Fouschie's friend was staying with him . . . a quiet man, he was, I must admit, older, mannerly when he came to the pâtisserie. He always bought fresh rolls and complimented Pépi on his cooking. He was seldom seen out except to shop once in a while. The boys said things to him . . . it was because they got frightened when they found him there. He had been ill. He died not long afterwards . . . two days afterwards, from a stroke, so it was said. Pépi paid for some of the damage to the place and so did Céleste. We do have a sense of honor, M. Ygrec, and Jean-Louis was sorry afterwards and went to confession and did penance. He was only fourteen years old. He was never in any trouble after that until last spring, and again it was because he was in the bad company of Armand and some other older boys."

Ygrec was pulling at the sheet and jerking at the lapels of the old dressing gown that covered his pajamas. He wanted to get up and pace around the room, to work off the unsettled feeling that was building inside him. He couldn't hurry Mme. Hugo; he didn't want to hurry her because she was painting more detail with her words than he'd ever imagined, but it was very hard to lie still. "You say, madame, that Jean-Louis went off this spring with his friends because you were displeased with him. What was the problem at that time?" he asked.

"I told him he was to stay away from Pippa Anjou. She was throwing herself at him . . . really she was, monsieur. Pépi could have been right at first, that she didn't know what she was doing because she hadn't grown beyond childhood in most ways, but her body had developed, and on the weekends she would go around wearing little but those skimpy blouses that were too tight and those silly long skirts she made for herself, and her grandfather was too blinded by his adoration of her to see what was going on. You should have watched her like I did, sidling up to Jean-Louis so close and looking up at him, telling him how handsome he was and talented, and things like that. So I promised him the motorcycle if he would keep away from the Anjou cottage, and he promised he would. But a few days after he got the machine he packed up a few things and hugged me and roared away. We had two postcards from him in four months, monsieur. I pretended I heard every week . . . only Pépi knew I hadn't." She lowered her head and Ygrec felt she had become carried away and had admitted something she had not intended. She covered her mouth with a hand and didn't look at anything.

"So that was why, when you found the little bag of white powder in his drawer, you kept the knowledge to yourself?" Ygrec asked thoughtfully. "Yet the bag that Sergeant Corvette found yesterday, hidden in the motorcycle, was cocaine mixed with another potent substance. There must be more to the story, madame. Did Jean-Louis sell anything to anyone?"

She nodded, then Pépi spoke up for the first time. "She was trying to protect him, monsieur. He is our son. She never thought of the consequences. She didn't even tell me, not until yesterday." The pudgy man sounded exhausted.

Madame took up the story again but added more quickly now, "I was wrong. I admit I was wrong, but I wanted to keep him out of trouble. If he was given the chance to grow up without getting into something serious, he would be fine. He's smart, M. Ygrec. He always did well at school."

Ygrec nodded sympathetically, then tried to get back on the subject again. "Have you any idea whom he contacted . . . how he found a buyer for the drugs? Has he told you about that?"

"Last night, monsieur, he finally talked to me last night. They let me see him at the gendarmerie, to ask about getting an advocate. He told me he went to the waiter in the Cafe Khedive. Last year some of his friends knew where to get hashish . . . it was from a waiter, who knew people who bought and sold it . . . and other kinds of drugs too. So the Saturday he arrived home he went to the cafe. He had Pippa with him, so he just talked to the waiter for a minute, then later he went back . . . the next day, the Sunday. He was told to meet a woman back of the basilica on Monday night, and he did. He had no idea the woman was Gabrielle Chamillion then, because he'd never seen her before. He sold her the bag of corn flour, although he didn't know it wasn't the real drug, and she paid him . . . twenty-two hundred francs. And that's all there was to it to begin with." Madame's voice was nearly a monotone now, and she kept smoothing her skirt with her hands and looking down at her shiny black shoes.

"I see," Ygrec said. "Why did he want the money, Mme. Hugo?"

The reply was soft. "He said it was to go away from St. Denis . . . not to be just a cook . . . that's what he wanted first. Then he saw Pippa again. She wanted to go with him. I suppose he wanted her to. He was going to use some of the money to buy a car. They were going to go off together, at least they had talked about it, and then he decided she was too young . . . it would be too much responsibility and I think he was afraid of what the corporal might do to him. Lucien would search them out wherever they went, so he decided to go alone, but he didn't know how to tell her. He tried to tell her earlier, but she wouldn't listen, so that night—the night she died— he'd arranged to meet her in the old Couronne gardens, but she didn't come, M. Ygrec. He was late, you see, because he'd had the motorcycle accident, and she wasn't there. He was afraid to go to the cottage in case Lucien would be home by then, and he wasn't feeling too well after the accident, so he decided to wait until Sunday. He was shocked . . . horrified, when he heard what had happened to her. We all were." Madame's voice finally broke and once more she turned away to cover her mouth with her hand.

Ygrec spoke to Pépi, who had stood up and moved to place a comforting hand on his wife's shoulder. "It sounds so simple, but there are witnesses to testify that Jean-Louis was seen on Tuesday night with Gabrielle Chamillion, that he was seen earlier on the fatal Saturday night with Pippa, and now the drugs have been found on the motorcycle. Either Jean-Louis is lying, or an attempt is being made to incriminate him. If that is the case, why?"

"We keep asking ourselves that, Monsieur," Pépi replied. "M. Fouschie is the main witness, and we think he is trying to get back at Jean-Louis for what happened that time four years ago."

"That is very possible." Ygrec pursed his lips. "What became of the money that your son received from Gabrielle, madame?"

She had dried her eyes but was still swallowing a choke in her voice. "I was going to finish explaining, monsieur. He didn't keep it . . . he couldn't keep it. Gabrielle tasted the powder and said it was no good . . . that he had been fooled by whoever he'd got it from in Dramont. Jean-Louis was upset, of course, but he gave the money back. He's not dishonest . . . young and foolish, but not dishonest." She began to cry softly once more.

"Perhaps we have talked enough for one night, Mme. Hugo. Wouldn't you rather go home and get some rest?" Ygrec tried to be reassuring.

She nodded her head. "There isn't anything more to say. That is all that happened."

Ygrec sighed. "Have you told this to anyone else?"

"No, monsieur."

"I expect you will explain it all to the advocate tomorrow?"

She raised her eyes, and the rouge on her cheeks stood out in isolated pink blotches on her tired face. "There's no need. Jean-Louis didn't do anything wrong. He didn't break any laws . . . I saw to that. They can only say that there were drugs found on his motorcycle, but anyone could have put the package there. Someone is trying to ruin his life, and I think it is that mortician. It is a nightmare . . . a nightmare." She was barely whispering.

Pépi spoke for the last time. "M. Ygrec is right, Marie-Thérèse. We have talked enough now. You need some rest." He placed his hand beneath her elbow and helped her to her feet.

They said good night briefly, and Ygrec could hear them murmuring to Vanessa in the hallway, then the door closed behind them.

Ygrec had had enough for one day as well. He was alseep when Vanessa came in with his hot milk, so she turned off the light, leaving him as he was, in his robe, his tousled gray head slumped down on the pillows, his chest laboring slightly, his thin face too pale.

Chapter Twenty-three

Monday morning the serious young doctor with the owlish glasses prodded and poked and listened to Ygrec's chest again, then ordered new medicine, more rest, and fewer visitors. He also suggested that Mme. Michelin rest more . . . after all she'd had that problem with cramps only last week, so Vanessa, although forewarned about the "smelly" Mme. de Cosse, decided not to discharge her until a replacement could be found. At noon the plodding woman showed up, admittedly reeking of garlic, but in a fresh, striped dress and a large, clean apron. She looked Vanessa up and down, announced that she would "see her duty and do it," and that Madame's child would be a girl. She also announced that she did not allow dogs in her kitchen. A nearly speechless Vanessa fled to the haven of Ygrec's bedroom, where the two comforted each other with much subdued laughter.

M. Fouschie paid another visit to the château while Ygrec was resting after lunch, but he didn't get past the front door. He left his doubtful wishes for the improved health of M. Ygrec and the continued health of Inspector and Mme. Michelin and "disappeared into the drizzle that had spawned him," Mme. de Cosse quoted. Again the amused Vanessa was almost speechless at the woman's sudden role of authority and her command of the language, as was Ygrec, who had felt her main method of communication was to grunt with disapproval.

Admittedly it was a nasty, drizzly day and even Mademoiselle

Larme balked at the suggestion that she needed a walk, so Vanessa did not insist, but for the third time, Mme. de Cosse took over. She ordered Vanessa to bed for an hour, donned a great dark oilskin coat, picked up the lead, and ordered the dog out the back door. "And Mademoiselle Larme actually went out into the rain with her tail wagging," Vanessa reported to Ygrec later, "so Madame is worth her price in entertainment if nothing else!"

It was a restful day for the old gendarme, and he would have been contented had he been able to push away his sense of unease. He longed for any news but heard nothing until late afternoon when Corporal Anjou arrived looking as preoccupied as Ygrec felt.

"You are fortunate to be confined indoors on such a day," were Lucien's first words after the usual greeting. He ran his fingers absently through his damp hair before crouching on the edge of a chair by the bed.

"Perhaps so, but I wonder, would you say the same for Jean-Louis?" was Ygrec's curious reply which made Lucien look over quickly. "I kept waking during the night and thinking about him. It is obvious someone arranged his arrest. Has he had an advocate appointed for him yet?"

"You must be feeling better, my friend. You are not wasting words. Yes, a Maître Dalmas has been hired, on the recommendation of Mme. Michelin, so Pépi said. He works with the firm of Maître Matieu who bought the Couronne property, I believe."

"That will cost poor Pépi a great deal. It is a pity. Pépi is a good man. He deserved better, wouldn't you agree?"

This time Lucien only stared at the floor between his damp boots. "He is a good man," he repeated slowly.

"We had a long talk last night," Ygrec went on. "Jean-Louis apparently opened his heart to his mother. It was a very curious story, Corporal. The boy had become involved in a little illegal trafficking, it seems, but had a change of heart and returned his ill-gotten gains . . . a considerable amount of money. Isn't it gratifying to know that honesty still prevails even among the younger generation?"

Lucien seemed to shrug but did not raise his head.

"However I am getting off the subject that I wanted to discuss with you. I have been hoping you would come today, as I have become acquainted with a M. Fouschie. I found him to be a very unusual man, an enigma. I believe that you have known him for many years. Would you say he is trustworthy?"

Now Lucien did sit up and it troubled Ygrec to see the lines of worry on the big man's face, as if an aging process was taking place before his very eyes. "Yes, I have known Gratien Fouschie since we were boys. Once I thought he was weak. I was mistaken."

"Then I take from your tone that behind his foppishness there is a strong personality?"

"You may."

Ygrec rubbed his head back and forth across his mussed pillows and glanced outside. "Dusk is falling again. The nights grow longer," he said thoughtfully. "So often we seem to end up talking in the dark, don't we? Are you not curious as to what M. Fouschie and I had to discuss?"

Lucien leaned forward again and supported his forearms on his knees. "I know you well enough now to realize you will tell only what you wish to tell. I cannot see what Gratien has to do with my problem, or yours for that matter, but if it will help to find out who . . . who hurt Pippa . . ."

"It might help; it cannot harm. I shall be as honest as possible with you, Corporal. Out of vengeance, would M. Fouschie have the means or the wit to plant drugs on Jean-Louis' motorcycle?"

"The means . . . possibly. He has the money to buy whatever he wants, and I expect he knows where drugs can be obtained, but that is no secret. At the Cafe Khedive one can obtain almost anything if one can pay for it. The wit . . . oh, yes, my friend, Gratien has the wit, but your presumption that he would risk so much for revenge, that is a different matter. He has always disliked Jean-Louis, but he wouldn't waste his energy on hate. He held no love for Céleste's nephew Armand either, but he has been doing what he could to straighten the boy out, with little success, I gather. Armand is weak and not too bright, but Gratien has always been fond of Céleste herself. She was a victim of the Boche during the war . . . Armand has been a victim of the peace and of the drug culture."

"I see . . . I see," Ygrec murmured. "So, if Fouschie says that he and Armand saw Jean-Louis Hugo with Mme. Chamillion the night she died, one could take them at their word? There would be no ulterior motive?

Lucien seemed to stiffen and straighten. "I didn't know . . . I thought it was only her husband who saw them together . . . Jean-Louis and Gabrielle!"

"Did M. Chamillion say that?"

"Isn't it what he told the gendarmes? I'm sure . . ." Lucien's words died as he stood, making move to leave.

"Perhaps he did. I have had so much on my mind, with the two tragedies, I tend to get a little confused. It is a pity that M. Chamillion has chosen this time to go off on a drunken holiday, if one can call it that. I would very much like to meet the man myself and talk with him. I have a theory that becomes more and more logical, but to prosecute, the gendarmes need facts not theories." Ygrec sighed and tapped himself on his temple. "Of course . . . of course . . . it was Pippa that M. Fouschie saw with Jean-Louis. We keep coming back to that young man, don't we, Corporal? I must take a little time to think, then I would like to talk to you again. Could you come back later this evening when I have been able to put my thoughts in order? It helps to talk to you and, by then, Inspector Michelin should be home and there may have been some new developments at the gendarmerie. If we are really lucky, they may have found the absent M. Chamillion . . . his sister is getting quite hysterical about him, and he has been reported officially missing." Then Ygrec changed the subject completely as he watched Lucien reach into his pocket for his beret. "You are very fond of your old beret, are you not, my friend?" He smiled wearily.

"We all have our little crutches. I seem to feel more in command of a situation when my head is covered. I expect it is a habit from my army days."

After Lucien had gone, the old gendarme lay back in the dusky stillness and thought, yes, we all have our habits . . . and one of mine has been attention to detail. I am sure that Jean-Louis Hugo was never mentioned in connection with M. Chamillion's testimony. Where was the pathetic little drunken agent? Did the corporal know more than he was admitting? These questions and others began to be placed in order in Ygrec's mind. What about Jean-Louis on the Tuesday night Gabrielle had died . . . not Monday, as mentioned by his mother, but Tuesday? When the possibility came to him, it was like a little pain for all the innocent ones who had suffered and would have to suffer more.

* * *

"Where is he?" Lucien demanded of Ghislaine.

She was in her usual position with her needlework, sitting by the fireplace, and she barely looked up. "Where he always is, Lucien. Where else would he be with the door locked?"

"There is no need to lock the door. . . . He's not a prisoner, and he's not well enough to go anywhere alone. Has he eaten anything?"

"I told you this morning, he won't eat. He coughs and mumbles silly things and he spilled his soup at noon. I have decided he is not a nice person, and I will be glad when he's gone."

"I am taking him away tomorrow. There is someone who wants to talk to him, but I will have to clean him up first."

It was as if she hadn't heard. "I think I am getting the sniffles. I hope I didn't catch his cold. He has a dreadful cold . . . it could even be pneumonia. I had pneumonia once and they said I was quite delirious and almost died. It can be very serious, pneumonia can." In spite of the words she seemed almost gay.

Was she sounding different? Lucien wondered. She seemed so calm. The nervous gestures, the fluttering hand reaching to cover her cheek, were no longer apparent. She had been well behaved for days, and he didn't trust her when she was being agreeable and cheerful. She looked no different. She wore the coif, the old sweaters, the same stained skirt, the woollen socks she kept on her feet when the boots were off. The table lamp was pulled close to her work, and she poked the needle into the fine mesh of the tapestry in a haphazard fashion, pulling it slowly out the other side. The design was becoming as muddled and undisciplined as her thoughts appeared to be, even more so in the last week. When she spoke of Valin Chamillion, she was inclined to use Amélie's voice, but with Lucien she was her own childish self.

"I took him in to please you," she went on, thrusting the needle into a spot that had been worked over and over, "but he will not wash and now the room smells. It's a horrid room and I hated it, but I always kept it clean. Even when I was ill, I scrubbed it every day; but when I take the bucket of water and the soap up to him, he either knocks it over or just stares at it."

Lucien was very tired. He had not been sleeping well at night, tossing and turning, and when he did sleep he had a recurring dream of pedaling a bicycle through sand, and he would wake exhausted. This afternoon he had tried to rest in the cottage, but his mind had churned like the wheel in his dreams. Would this continuing nightmare never end so he could rest once more? He wanted to sit for a moment now, yet an unease was building. Was Ghislaine keeping something from him again?

He started toward the hallway and the stairs. "Did he take his medicine?"

"Don't keep at me, Lucien. It's been hard on me . . . all this extra work and when you get cross at me, I get upset and I forget things."

"Did you give him the anisette, Ghislaine?" he repeated, more gently.

"I really don't like the smell of it," she replied evasively. "The whole upstairs smells very unpleasant. I'm glad I'm comfortable down here. I sleep quite well these nights. It's very cheerful being able to look over at the fire burning away. Have you decided to bring your own bed here when you come, Lucien? I expect you are used to your own bed. There's a fireplace in Amélie's room, although it hasn't been used for years. I think you will have to sweep out the chimney; Amélie said she thought it was blocked by an old bird's nest. Did you know that in Germany the storks build their nests in the chimneys all the time, and it's very bad luck to move them? I saw them once . . . the nests . . . the last time I went to get my foot fixed by that special doctor. He was German, but he was a very good doctor anyway, although of course that was before the war. Oh, I almost forgot, Lucien . . . Dr. Desmaris came today, but I heard the car coming up the driveway, and I peeked out the bedroom window, and then stayed very still where I was until he went away. He knocked at the back door as well as the front and I didn't think he would ever leave. What shall I do if he comes back again? It wouldn't do for him to find that Amélie wasn't here in her bed when she's supposed to be so ill."

Lucien, who had been only half listening, turned swiftly, and retraced his steps. "Which bedroom window? Where were you when the doctor came?"

"Up giving M. Chamillion his medicine. He didn't drink the medicine. It's still up in his room."

"Why wouldn't he drink the medicine, Ghislaine?" Lucien's mouth felt suddenly dry.

She had stopped her sewing, letting her hands fall onto her lap, and she looked up at him, biting her lower lip, then she dropped her head.

He turned back, the apprehension growing. She couldn't have, he said to himself, as he felt for the light switch, then hurried up the narrow staircase through the gloomy illumination. The bedroom door was locked, as she'd said. Perhaps he was exaggerating things in his own mind and nothing was wrong. He pulled the bolt back impatiently then felt inside for another light switch.

The grilled window met his eye first, then below it the black iron bedstead and the jumbled bedding. "M. Chamillion?" he whispered as he stepped inside.

A glass of cloudy liquid sat on the chest of drawers that stood against the left wall below a highly hung crucifix. The chest and the bed were the only pieces of furniture left in the room. Valin Chamillion lay half huddled in the opposite corner, a gray blanket twisted around his body, his trousered legs and sock feet outstretched on the bare floorboards. The bed pillow was beneath his head, which was turned to one side.

Lucien bent down and turned the face over. Above a growth of pale beard the skin was blue tinged, the closed eyes mummified like parchment. Lucien lifted the stiff shoulders, feeling gaunt bones beneath the filthy clothing. The chin rested stiffly on the chest, the rigid arms remained crossed beneath the blanket.

Lucien left him where he lay, switched off the light, and made his way slowly down the stairs.

Ghislaine had obviously rekindled the fire and was standing pouring herself a glass of wine. She lifted the bottle toward him. "I have always loved the color of Burgundy, haven't you? See how warm it is when it catches the light. Would you like some?"

"What have you done this time, Ghislaine?" he asked wearily.

"I have poured myself a second glass of wine . . . only the second, Lucien. Look you can see from the bottle . . . it is still almost full." She put the bottle on the table and tasted from her glass.

"He's dead, Ghislaine. He's been dead for some time."

"I know but don't worry about it. He wasn't a nice man . . . you said so yourself. . . . You said he was punishing himself, making his own hell on earth. I heard you telling him, and I thought about it and decided that was a fine thought of yours. I used to tell Amélie that you had very fine thoughts, and that she shouldn't worry about the child . . . that it wouldn't have the mind of a peasant. It was wrong of her to give the baby away, but when I tried to tell her, she got very angry and forbade me to mention it and, of course, by then it was too late." Ghislaine smiled vaguely, each feature of her pinched little face clearly outlined as she lifted the glass once more. "I always loved you, no matter what she said, Lucien."

He watched her. He had become quite fascinated. "Hell on earth," he muttered.

"I didn't hear what you said . . . it's this coif that covers my ears. I don't have to wear it, you know, but I'd gotten used to it and it keeps my head warm at night. That's what bothered Mme. Fouschie when she was a nun. I remember her saying that her head got very warm in the summer, but still, when we were young, Amélie decided I would become a nun. I suppose she thought if I married the church, I would stop wanting to be married to you. They wouldn't take me at the convent though, because I couldn't learn things." She giggled a little inanely. "But sometimes I could have learned more than they knew. I just pretended because I didn't like it in the convent."

Lucien had dropped onto a chair, his head lowered into his hands. When Ghislaine noticed, she stopped talking for a minute and stared. "Why are you so quiet, Lucien? Have you got a headache? I hope you haven't caught the cold too."

He looked at her at last. "What did you do to him, Ghislaine?"

"Don't you care that I love you? I know I'm old and not pretty but you're old too, and I don't mind at all. Even when things were so awful and I wanted to die, I couldn't let myself, because I loved you. Don't you care?"

"Yes, I care." He sounded drained. "But you must tell me what happened upstairs. You can't keep on doing these things, because I can't keep on covering up for you. One lie leads to another. First Amélie, then the dog . . . now this. What am I going to do?"

"You could always bury him with Amélie."

"Ghislaine . . . you are killing me too . . . with worry." There was almost a break in his voice, and he swallowed and looked around the room, as he did so often when he wanted to control himself, to bring reality into focus. At last his eyes settled on the bottle beside a second wine glass on the table. He nodded. "I think I will join you in a drink after all," he said softly, "and then we will sit down and you can tell me about it. I won't be cross."

"I knew you'd change your mind!" In her haste and excitement she tipped the bottle, slopping some of the wine down the edge of the glass, where it spread unevenly to overlap the other stains on the white cloth that had been on the table since the night she had thrown the chicken at him. Something seemed to jog her memory, and as she refilled her own glass, she said, "I'm glad the big dog is well . . . the dog that belongs to your friend, the gendarme. It hopped right into the car the other day with the gendarme, as lively as could be."

"Why don't you sit down here, Ghislaine, on this side of the fire, and I'll take the other chair there." He held the back of the chair for her, pushing it just a little closer to the warmth, then handed her the glass of wine. "Are you comfortable?"

She nodded and smiled, smoothing the rough skirt with her free hand, then crossed her sock feet over the hearth rug, as if she were dressed in lace and satin. The gesture touched him as it never had when she was purposely acting out the role of the child-lady.

When he had seated himself, leaning into the flames, warming the sides of the goblet with his big hands, he went on quietly. "Yes the dog is well, and my friend gendarme Ygrec is quite well too. When did you see them?"

"Oh, the other afternoon when I was on my walk. They were by the back of the château."

"You have been getting some exercise?"

She shrugged a little shyly and smiled again. "I was keeping it as a surprise for you, Lucien. I'm practicing walking like a lady, and I dress up nicely with a hat and everything, although that day I forgot my gloves, which was just as well, as I tripped and fell by the bird-bath. I didn't hurt myself, but if I had been wearing gloves they would have got all dirty. As it was, I muddied the dress and tore it, so when I got home I just threw it into the fire here. I never liked the dress anyway; it was Amélie's black silk. Black is not a becoming color for me. Mme. Fouschie used to say . . ."

"I'm glad you didn't hurt yourself," he interrupted gently, "and it's good you are getting out into the fresh air, and you aren't afraid of people and being seen. I expect if anyone should ask you about Amélie, you would be able to pretend she is well."

"Oh, I don't have to pretend because, you see, I'm certain that Amélie really is fine. She is in heaven with the saints, because she prayed a lot that Our Lord would forgive her sins. That is the trouble though . . . when I die I don't want to go to hell, but I would rather not go to heaven and see Amélie again. Do you think hell is a very dreadful place, Lucien?" She sighed, tipped her glass, and leaned back into the shadowy confines of the chair. "Pippa is in heaven too because she was pure. All children are pure. I do hope Amélie isn't mean to her up there. I cried when I knew Pippa was dead. I don't really know why I cried but I couldn't stop. When I saw her by the birdbath that night, I didn't know it was her or I would have sat right down there in the wet grass and cried and probably caught a bad cold. But I just saw the dark hair and the pink skirt, so I thought it was the woman in the pink dress who came here to see me and wanted me to give her my money. She was not a nice person, Lucien . . . the woman in the pink dress, I mean. You saw her the day she came to ask about selling the land. She came back again, and I didn't tell you because you told me not to talk to anyone who came. She was wearing such pretty shoes that I wanted to see her close up . . . but she was a very common person who told lies, and I was sorry I'd given all Amélie's pills to the dog, otherwise I would have asked the woman in for tea and fed the pills to her." Ghislaine was quite out of breath after the long explanation. She took a little time, then finished the wine in two gulps.

Lucien was astonishing himself at his control, although he now realized his hands had been contracting, almost crushing the glass he was nursing. He had not even taken one sip and now he thought of setting the wine down, but he waited, not daring to make a movement that might break into Ghislaine's train of thoughts. Let her go on, he had cautioned himself when she had mentioned the birdbath and Pippa—don't interrupt—don't! Later he would berate himself for not having the wisdom and patience to sit with her long ago, to show her gentleness and kindness—yes, and love. Now he willed himself to relax his hands, to ease back into his chair away from the light, hiding the anxiety that might have been visible in his expression, his eyes. The wine was having an effect on her, of course. Her words came slower, with small hesitations, the odd blur; still the words came and he listened to every syllable, every inflection. It was a Ghislaine he had never heard since her one natural, happy period in that other world in the mountains.

She was gesturing now, the angles of the cut crystal of her glass picking up then shooting out little lights as it moved in an arch. "She told me her name that last time . . . Gabrielle . . . like the angel Gabriel, you know . . . but she was not an angel . . . not at all. She said she was Pippa's mother . . . wasn't that ridiculous? . . . and that the money from the land was half hers . . . half Pippa's. She said she had decided to tell Pippa and that she would take her from you, so I said that was a good idea because you didn't have money for the girl's school anyway. The oddest thing, of course, was she

thought we were married, Lucien . . . you and I . . . and when I get
frightened sometimes, I laugh; so I just laughed and laughed, and she
thought I was laughing at her. She got very angry." Ghislaine giggled
a little now, thinking of it. "Her eyes were all funny . . . very large. I
really don't think she was right in the head, Lucien, the way she went
on, but I was only a little bit frightened because I knew she was telling lies. I told her so too. . . . I said she'd made it all up because I
wasn't married to anyone. It was then she said terrible things about
me . . . about how I looked and that she'd talked to M. Fouschie,
the mortician, and he'd said that you and I were married. Wasn't that
silly? M. Fouschie wouldn't know anything, not even about you and
Amélie, because his aunt died a long time before you and Amélie
went to Paris. That's one time I remember because I was still at the
convent, but the Germans were coming, so they sent me home and
when I got here the house was empty because you had gone with
Amélie. I think I cried that time too. But nobody knew about you
and Amélie, did they? Are you listening, Lucien?"

"Nobody knew, Ghislaine. Everyone was trying to get out of
Paris, so things were rushed. Nobody asked questions in those days."
It was as if he were talking to himself, the words coming absently.
"We weren't even young, but we all acted like children. War brings
its own kind of madness."

She stirred restlessly, dropping her goblet to the carpet, shifting
her legs. "I don't want to talk any more, Lucien, and I don't want
you to talk. I'm sleepy. It's been a difficult day . . . what with M.
Chamillion being so . . . difficult . . . and everything." She yawned.

He knew it had been a mistake to think aloud, to recall the past.
He leaned across, proffering her his own glass of wine. "The woman
in pink, the one called Gabrielle . . . did she tell you her other
name, Ghislaine?" When she ignored him he placed the glass on the
raised hearth and went on speaking in soothing tones. "Did she say
her name was Gabrielle Chamillion?"

"Oh, yes, and I expect she was. She's dead now, isn't she? That's
why M. Chamillion was upset, I suppose . . . but now they're both
together . . . in hell. I'm quite sure she never prayed and I know he
didn't, although I tried to get him to say his rosary. I even gave him
my precious rosary chain to use, but he broke it and threw it at me.
It was the only present you ever gave me, Lucien. I treasured it
so. I never told Amélie where I got it; I just said I stole it and she
believed me, otherwise she'd have broken it too. It's in the pewter

mug up there on the mantelpiece. You'll fix it for me, won't you, Lucien?"

"I'll fix it tomorrow when the light is better."

"That's nice." She yawned again, raising her hand to cover her mouth, leaning back to curl against the wing of the chair. "Not that I say prayers any more . . . you see, with that M. Chamillion and his wife in hell with our papa, and Amélie in heaven, there is simply nowhere for me to go when the time comes. I wish I could stay right here like this with you forever. Of course, Lucien, if you and I died together, at the very same instant, you could look after me wherever we went." The thought seemed to please her. She lifted her head to peer out at him, a white little face with large eyes in an oval of black like the leather-masked faces on old dolls. "Could we do that . . . please, Lucien?"

"If you wish."

"Do you promise?"

"I promise." He found he was almost enjoying the playing of her games, and he didn't have to force sincerity into his words. "And now that the afterlife is settled, we must decide about the earthly remains of M. Chamillion. It might be wise to place him in a ditch somewhere. Everyone seems to think he has gone off looking for drink, so would not be surprised if he died of it, but first I must know how he deid. What happened this afternoon, Ghislaine? Will you tell me what happened upstairs?"

He knew she was trying to be helpful but that she was indeed very tired. The words were spaced with tiny hesitations and her voice was as soft as a child at prayers. "I had to keep him quiet because of the doctor. I put a pillow on his face and sat on it."

"On the bed?" He was testing her because he didn't quite trust her.

"Oh, no Lucien . . . don't be foolish . . . how could I do that? He was on the floor in the corner. I think he was very sick; he couldn't even hang on to the cup of soup at noon, and you know how he was . . . afraid of things that he kept seeing in the room when they weren't there at all . . . and hearing music. That's why he was making a fuss earlier. He ordered me to turn off the music even though I didn't have any music on. He was hiding there in the corner with the blanket twisted around him when I took up the anisette like you told me to. Then I heard the doctor's car and I was afraid he would make another fuss. I just took the pillow off the bed and put it on his face and sat on it. He didn't move hardly at all, just a bit at first. By the time Dr. Desmaris was gone he wasn't breathing. I didn't mean any harm . . . he was very sick anyway. I put the pillow under his head afterwards so he would be comfortable. When I was wicked, Amélie took away my pillow and I could hardly sleep it was so uncomfortable. I use two pillows on my cot now."

"I see." Lucien was able to see it all.

"I am very tired. May I go to sleep, please?"

"Of course. Tomorrow when you are rested, will you tell me about the night you saw the person in the pink dress by the birdbath?"

"Oh, yes."

"But just one small thing tonight. Did you see anyone else near the birdbath that time? A man, perhaps?"

"I'm too tired." There was a beginning of petulance.

"I know, ma chérie, I know, and you have been very patient."

He thought her eyes opened a little. "You called me chérie . . . did you really call me that?"

"Yes, chérie. Was it a young man?"

"Yes."

He had waited this long; he could wait longer. There was no hurry any more. Jean-Louis was already in custody.

He covered Ghislaine with the quilt from the cot, as he had done the night Amélie had died. He had felt a choking emotion for her that night. Tonight it had become even stronger. Was it something more than pity? God help me, he prayed as he mounted the narrow staircase, a sense of urgency beginning to build in him. I've got to protect her . . . she's all I have left.

Chapter Twenty-four

Ygrec's feelings of urgency also grew with the coming of night, so much so that he felt he could not remain in the confines of his bedroom. He considered getting dressed, but decided not to be too ambitious too quickly and settled for an attempt at brushing his hair, and a change of dressing gowns. For Christmas last year, Vanessa had given him an elegant robe which he had never worn. Now he looped the braided cord as carefully as he could around his thin waist and stood in front of the long mirror to eye himself critically, straightening the satin lapels over soft plush. The dark wine color wasn't bad, he decided; it distracted from the sallow tone of his skin. He felt far from the necessity of M. Fouschie's services at the moment, but he also felt a bit uncomfortable and overdressed.

"Now, garçon, don't say a word. Just this once, no lectures or reminders of doctor's orders," he said to Michelin as he walked erectly into the warm salon and settled himself comfortably in his favorite chair.

"Don't talk to me, old man," a surprised Michelin replied. "Vanessa is the one to convince. I must admit you're looking better and quite handsome, I might add, if I'm allowed."

Ygrec ignored the compliment. "Where is she?"

"Having a rest with Mademoiselle, as usual. She still tires easily. She's anemic, she says."

"Is she indeed!" Ygrec gave him a searching look, but went on blandly, "Well, it's a good time for us to have a little talk. I have seen you hardly at all these last few days."

Michelin laughed. "What nonsense . . . I spent a long time having coffee with you not more than an hour ago."

"Perhaps, but I heard you on the phone just now. What did Sergeant Corvette have to say?"

"I was about to go in and tell you. Jean-Louis Hugo has been released from custody. They couldn't hold him on the evidence they had . . . anyone could have planted the drugs on his motorcycle, during the night, when it was out of his possession, as Maître Dalmas pointed out. It was a foolish attempt on the part of some person to have him arrested, and they can't track down the rumor that he was seen with Gabrielle Chamillion that Tuesday night she died."

"I thought as much, so now we wait again," Ygrec said thoughtfully. "No matter what wild tales he supposedly told his mother, they would both deny everything officially."

"You don't sound pleased, old man."

"I have an admiration for Pépi Hugo, but more than that I cannot say. I repeat, we must wait for developments, and while we do, we may as well have a game of trictrac."

"And no doubt, a small cognac."

"If you insist, garçon. It has been known since early time that . . ."

". . . that cognac is good for tired hearts," Michelin finished, as he arranged the backgammon board between them and pulled up a chair. "You keep repeating yourself, old man, a sure sign of senility

. . . and don't say, 'pic, pic, pic,' or I shall refuse to get the cognac."

"Oh, pour the drinks, and let's get on with the game." Ygrec smoothed the lapels of his robe with pale fingers. "This is kind of a celebration tonight, I think. It may be our last game for a time, because as you know, I have heard from Mme. Lachance that she is home in Moulins, so as soon as I am able to travel, I will be going back to the village." He smiled a little sadly, then went on placing his white discs in place on the board as he talked. "I know what you are about to say, so don't say it. I am loved here . . . I am welcome here always . . . but it would not do, not at the moment. You and Vanessa must live your own lives in privacy. You must be allowed to love alone, and quarrel alone, and learn to face problems together . . . but alone. Later perhaps, I will come back and be prepared to stay longer, but not now. I am too inclined to take sides, to give advice, to want to interfere when I see you both making foolish mistakes. Right now, as a matter of fact, I am tempted to pick up these dice and throw them at you because you are so blind, and I can't even tell you why. So instead I shall shake them like this"—he shook the little felt-lined box and the dice rattled dully—"and throw them on the board. Violà! Double sixes! Perhaps this shall be a successful evening after all."

Michelin watched while Ygrec moved his discs on the board, then shook the dice himself. "Voilà, yourself . . . you are not as smart as you think. I have double sixes as well . . . and to reply to your nasty remark about my stupidity, have you told Vanessa of your intentions to return to Moulins?"

"What's that got to do with anything?"

"I wouldn't know myself, but I would guess she will be very unhappy if you take Mademoiselle Larme away right now, and we don't want to upset her when she is in a 'delicate condition,' do we?"

Ygrec sat back. "You know!"

"Give me credit for a little common sense. And what a ridiculous phrase to use . . . 'delicate condition' indeed! It sounds like my old grandmother who actually did tell me that babies sprouted from special pine cones in the woods."

"Well, don't they?" Ygrec started laughing and Michelin joined him.

"She's a little uneasy," Michelin went on more seriously. "She's had some problems, and the shock of finding Pippa didn't help, so we don't talk about things very often, not yet. That's why she says she's anemic, you understand?"

"I understand."

Vanessa was the first to interrupt the game. She was surprisingly placid when she saw Ygrec was out of bed and remarked only that "someone" had good taste in colors for him, but it was obvious now that he wasn't the "satiny" type, although he was looking quite handsome. Ygrec felt that she had never looked more beautiful and yet she was wearing only an unadorned black quilted robe and her hair was tied back carelessly. She sat in her happiest position in front of the fire at Michelin's feet with the dog's head near her crossed legs, and she watched the men playing, smiling from time to time as Ygrec added to his winning scores.

The second interruption was a phone call for Michelin, and Ygrec listened impatiently to the one-sided conversation.

"I hate to admit it, but you were right, old man," Michelin enlarged, on his return to his chair. "The body of Raoul Tusette has been found in an alley near the left bank. I suppose a knife in the back was his reward for paying a ridiculous sum of money for a bag of corn flour, as I am now convinced is what happened. We'll never be certain what he was trying to do the night he was picked up here, but our informers say he was out to get vengeance on the person who set him up, once the panic over Gabrielle's death died down. He may not be a great loss to the world, but Mme. Hugo's efforts to protect her son have had far-reaching effects."

"I wonder about that . . . I wonder," Ygrec muttered. "In a way it's a great pity. Now there is no one to connect Jean-Louis with Gabrielle . . . there's only that bag of corn flour, and it can't talk. In his unnecessary attempt to clear himself of a false charge of possession of narcotics, the young man admitted his connection with drugs. I wonder if that was the purpose of the plant on his motorbike all along. But I keep getting carried away . . . you mentioned the Cafe Khedive on the phone . . . what was that all about?"

"They are questioning the waiter from the cafe, as well as the proprietor. Our agents have known for a long time the place is notorious, but they kept still, hoping for better leads. Now we can't wait any longer. They'll call back if they can get either of those *cochons* to talk."

"Drugs are your department. I'm still very concerned about other matters. I wonder where the corporal is. He said he might come back tonight."

The two men went back to their game, and eventually Vanessa

went to bed to read. Ygrec kept glancing at the french doors at the end of the room, thinking of the night that Lucien had appeared, carrying the dog, but tonight he saw nothing but drizzling darkness outside, nor did either doorbell ring. About ten o'clock Michelin suggested that the old man go to bed, but Ygrec shook his head and sat back, his hands on the arms of the chair, staring, unseeing, at the game in front of him. After a time he picked up his discs and proceeded to place them in two neat little piles like gambling chips. "I'm gambling with my friend, Corporal Anjou," was all he said, and held up his glass for more cognac.

"I'll keep you company then," offered Michelin, standing to reach for the bottle. "I will probably have to go out later, and there's no use disturbing Vanessa."

The expected phone call came as Michelin was sitting down.

Once more Ygrec listened, holding his rotund glass high between both hands, rolling the amber liquor back and forth gently, breathing the aroma, finally sipping, then staring into the depths of the glass, remembering the color of Pippa's eyes.

"The waiter at the Khedive has named Jean-Louis. The boy brought in a sample of high-grade cocaine cut with mescaline for testing, the Saturday night he arrived home. The next day, Sunday, he was told he would be contacted by a woman."

"This is getting ridiculous!" Ygrec savored his drink again.

"Ridiculous?"

"Jean-Louis . . . in and out . . . in and out of the gendarmerie. It's like a comedy, realizing, of course, that comedy and tragedy are totally dependent on one another. I suppose that Sergeant Corvette has gone to arrest him again. Poor Pépi."

"They can't find him. He's not at home and neither is his motorcycle. They are setting up roadblocks."

Ygrec frowned. "So . . . this is unexpected! How I wish I could talk to Mme. Hugo, although no doubt she would feign indisposition."

"Why Madame?"

"Because she was not truthful with me . . . or with her husband. Pépi is not a good liar, as I'm sure she must know."

"Well, you can't see her, so go to bed or you'll be sick tomorrow. I have to interrogate the Khedive suspects again, and I may be late, so don't try waiting up for me." Michelin turned, then turned back quickly, alerted by a rattling at the french doors.

"It's the corporal," exclaimed Ygrec. "He's come after all. Quickly, garçon, let him in."

Lucien didn't apologize for dripping on the carpet, nor for the late hour. "I have been to the gendarmerie," he said, as he allowed Michelin to lead him to the fire. He crouched on the edge of the chair, appearing out of place with his big wet boots, soaking pant legs, and old army greatcoat that gave off an acrid smell of wetness.

"You know then that they are searching for Jean-Louis?" Ygrec asked.

"Yes." Lucien rolled his beret between his hands. "He was selling drugs . . . They know that now, and he did meet Gabrielle Chamillion . . . that's what they say at the gendarmerie. I got the feeling they think he may have killed the woman, but Pippa . . . they said they had nothing more about Pippa, and I know . . . I know . . ." He seemed to shiver. "I thought they would find out before . . . today when they had him there . . . before they let him go. I thought he would get mixed up with his lies and they would make him tell."

"Tell what, my friend? What do you know? Did you plant the drugs on his motorcycle?"

Michelin, who was about to leave the room, was stopped by the sharpness of Ygrec's words. He leaned against the darkened doorway, remaining as quiet and as unobtrusive as possible.

The corporal turned his face away, his jaw tight. "And if I had, would you really expect me to say so? Where would I get drugs? Do I look like a rich man? Do you think I would stoop to peddle drugs?" There was a weary anger in the words.

"I apologize, Lucien." Ygrec used the Christian name for the first time, and purposely. "It was unfair of me to take advantage of a friendship. But may I ask another question, a fair one, that to me has a bearing on the case? Would Pippa arrange for a rendezvous in the Couronne gardens? Would she go there alone at night to meet anyone?"

The reply came instantly. "Never! She was half afraid of this whole area, even in the daytime, and nothing would have brought her here alone at night. She exaggerated old tales, and believed the Couronne land was cursed . . . haunted."

Ygrec nodded. "Did you ever try to discourage these fears she held?"

"No."

"Why not? You are a sensible man. You don't believe such nonsense."

"I wanted her to keep away from the place."

"Why?"

Again Lucien looked away. "Does it matter any more?"

"Perhaps not. Only you would know." Ygrec sighed. "But it could matter, and sometimes one lie leads to another, one cover-up to another, with heartbreaking consequences." He raised a hand to massage the back of his neck. "I shall give you an example. Mme. Hugo, in trying to protect her son, from exactly what, we yet don't know . . . but still, she tells me that Pippa had arranged to meet Jean-Louis in the Couronne gardens the night she was killed. They were going to run away together, presumably, but Jean-Louis was having second thoughts about the plan, and he also had an accident with his motorbike. We know that the rendezvous story is a lie, do we not? Therefore we doubt the rest of the tale."

Lucien had stopped twisting his beret. There seemed to be a slight steam rising from the side of the wet coat that faced the fire; otherwise there was no movement anywhere.

"Very well," Ygrec went on. "Now for lie number two. Madame told me she'd found what she believed to be drugs in Jean-Louis' bureau drawer, two days after he arrived home. She destroyed the drugs, substituting a harmless substance. I feel that Madame has a strong character, but surely even she would have shown signs of more stress had everything she related been true. Think! If your only son was involved in the trafficking of hard drugs, would you have carried on cheerfully with life? Then comes a drug-related death. If you had the slightest suspicion that your son might be responsible, could you have kept from confronting him? One can cover up so much, but there must come a time when smiles become forced like cracks in the face, when lines and pockets begin to form from loss of sleep. How did Madame appear to you during that crucial period? Ask yourself. The woman who served me café au lait and cakes was not putting on an act of cheerfulness!"

The old gendarme's voice had risen, but now it dropped. "I have done all I can in an unofficial capacity. Now I am tired. I suggest that someone in authority question Mme. Hugo about the movements of her son since this whole disastrous chain of events began. I don't believe for one minute that it was Madame who 'found' drugs and made a substitution. Due to other evidence, the authorities are con-

vinced that someone did a switch, but it wasn't Mme. Hugo! Why?"
Ygrec's glance took in Michelin in the shadowy corner as well as the
pale-faced corporal. "Jean-Louis knows his mother; he knows her
obsessive curiosity, her prying ways. Would he have left cocaine in a
drawer in that small, immaculate house? The idea is ludicrous!"

Michelin spoke up at last. "If Mme. Hugo didn't make the ex-
change, who did? If Jean-Louis wanted to put it in safekeeping for a
day or so, and didn't dare hide it at home, where . . . ?" He
stopped, looking over at Lucien who sat bent over staring at his
hands. "Pippa?" The name was whispered, then repeated. "Pippa!"

"She loved him, in her own childish way. She would want to protect him, even from himself. Think back . . . she was ill . . . with
worry." Ygrec was also looking at Lucien, reading the big man's silence as pain.

"Would you also agree, then," Michelin went on, "that Jean-
Louis was responsible for the death of Gabrielle?"

Ygrec raised his eyebrows and shoulders in one movement. "One
has to make so many presumptions, and as with Pippa there is no
proof . . . but it is only reasonable to suspect the boy. Gabrielle is
sent to purchase cocaine. The meeting with Jean-Louis certainly
could have taken place on the Monday, as Mme. Hugo said, but
there must have been another meeting on Tuesday. Gabrielle's contact, without a doubt, was Tusette. Now, he is a professional. He
must have realized almost immediately that he had not received
value for his money, and I can see him furiously tossing the little bag
of corn flour into the glove compartment of his car. Then what
would he do? He would be afraid, as well as angry, especially if he
had a hierarchy to which he himself was accountable. He would
begin by sending Gabrielle back to confront Jean-Louis . . . to demand a refund, or equivalent value in drugs, on pain of dire results. It
would be up to her to arrange the meeting with Jean-Louis. When
they meet, there would be harsh words, to say the least . . . and
threats? Of course. She is found with a large amount of money in her
purse. The garage is near the bistro, and it is not that late at night;
the young attendant is still working. Jean-Louis realizes he could be
seen by someone, by anyone. Can't you imagine that in his panic,
fearing he could be accused of killing for gain, his being illogical
enough to stuff the money into her purse to cover himself? 'Who . . .
me?' he could say. 'I know nothing about drugs or money. Search
me! Why should I harm her? I have no motive.'"

"What about her husband? It could have been her husband." It was Lucien who spoke, his voice sounding hollow, almost hoarse.

"Yes, it is possible, but from what I have been told about the little man, it does not seem probable. I may be wrong. If the truth were known, I would prefer to be wrong, but, again, does it matter, for we are talking only of theories. Hopefully when her husband and Jean-Louis are found and interrogated, we will learn the truth."

"They will release that boy again," Lucien muttered slowly. "They have that important advocate with his big words."

"I am going to the gendarmerie," Michelin said quickly. "If you wish to come with me, Corporal, I will be pleased to drive you." He strode out to pick up his coat from the hallway, and Lucien, after a mute nod to Ygrec, followed.

The door closed leaving the smell of musty wool and an uncertain echo.

Chapter Twenty-five

Lucien sat on a bench in the dank hallway of the gendarmerie, staring at the trails of mud on the worn floor, taking little notice of the black boots that carried the mud. He was now a familiar figure to the local gendarmes, so they in turn paid little heed to the big bent man wearing an old-fashioned greatcoat and worrying a worn beret between his stained hands. Inspector Michelin had gone into Sergeant Corvette's office, and Lucien was wondering which way to turn. He knew he was wasting valuable time sitting here, but he was almost lightheaded with fatigue. He longed for his bed, yet felt uneasy about Ghislaine. Had he remembered everything at the loge de garde?

He looked up at last, nodding absently to an older gendarme who had just entered from the outside. "Bonsoir, Corporal," the officer said, pausing to remove his fogged-up eyeglasses, wiping them on the sleeve of his uniform. Suddenly Lucien almost cried out. Instead, he mumbled something, then dropped his head, in case the thumping alarm in his throat was visible on his face. Mon Dieu—the glasses—Valin Chamillion's glasses! Time and time again he had seen them, where they had been forgotten that night last week, shoved back on the kitchen table with old newspapers and dirty dishes that had accumulated since Pippa had gone. As he'd finally cleared the dishes last night, he had lectured himself for leaving the glasses there so long, but the stupid little man had been too irrational and blinded by the drink that Lucien had continuously fed him to keep him quiet, to see anything anyway, so the glasses had never been missed. Now they belonged with the body; they would have to be fetched tonight.

The cobbled streets were slippery, and the thick unmoving mist that had replaced the drizzle, transformed the street lighting into eerie oases and, like desert mirages, created deceiving distances. The more he tried to hurry, the longer the streets became, until he began to doubt himself and his own reasoning, wondering if in his fatigue and confusion, he had taken a wrong turn back at the gendarmerie. At last he saw the familiar neon sign of the Côte Impériale garage; it wasn't far to rue Lutétia now. He increased his pace, almost willing his tired muscles to move, but in his anxiety to get across the intersection, he misjudged the oncoming diffused glare of a car until it was almost upon him, and he had to step back quickly. He avoided the vehicle but not its swishing splatter of gutter water. He was left standing dripping and breathless. The anger, the fury that instantly steamed to the surface of his mind was directed at a faceless motorist, but in reality it was an outburst of all the accumulated emotions he had kept so well concealed for so long. It grew until he felt blinded by it, even more so than the fumbling hopeless creature who had once wept for his glasses; and now Lucien himself found that he was crying. He let the tears come as he stumbled on, down the familiar narrow street, past the silent bistro, the shuttered mortuary, the darkened pâtisserie, until he reached his lane.

For the first time since Pippa died, he dreaded entering the cottage. It was as if she were there inside, and he didn't want her to see his tears for fear she would be upset and worried. "Are you hurting, Gran'papa? Why are you crying?" He sank down on the step of the little piazza where so often he had found her waiting for him. "The table is laid, Gran'papa. Will you push me on the swing before supper?" It was where he remembered her best that last day, looking so serious, hemming the new pink skirt that earlier had brought a tiny smile to her worried little face. "I shouldn't have left her . . . I shouldn't have punished her . . . I shouldn't have been so unfeeling. . . ." The guilt welled up now, replacing the earlier anguish. He raised his damp face and empty hands, trying to scream out at the horrible, heavy, suffocating silence, but the hurt was too overpowering for sounds.

Then something penetrated the silence, and Lucien stiffened, alert, hands still in the supplicating position. It came again—a kind of muffled scraping—then once more.

He lowered his arms slowly as he stood. This time there was a different sound, almost a thud. Lucien was back in the mountain trails, treading like an animal, each foot carefully raised, then lowered on the spongy undergrowth, pausing when he reached the far corner of the cottage. Until the death of his mother, a neat pathway had led from the lane to the seldom-used front door. Afterward the door had been boarded over, the little parlor ignored, but sometimes on sunny days, Pippa would open the shuttered window to the fresh air. Lucien had discovered her there more than once, addressing the vacant horsehair sofa, where a mythical audience applauded her dramatics, her poetry.

The shutters were now open, the window wide on hinges that Lucien had oiled in the spring. The movements inside were soft but audible, and he saw pencils of light circle and disappear. He stepped closer to the window sill, which was about level with his shoulders. He peered, then moved back. The mist hung, clinging to the shrubbery, and in the eerie shading created by the streetlight at the end of the lane, the tree trunks appeared artificially outlined, like dimensional drawings.

Odd light beams jerked, held, moved again. The intruder seemed to be searching the one room. As far as Lucien could tell, no attempt had been made to open the door that led to the rest of the cottage. Lucien waited, oblivious to time, discomfort, fatigue. At last he heard a faint scraping and the skinny beam tunneled through the open window before the light blanked out. Lucien pressed closer to the tree. His eyes, now fully accustomed to the dark, could make out the movements as a form lengthened over the window ledge, legs appeared, dangled, and finally doubled to a thud as feet met the mushy ground. There was complete silence for a long second until an arm reached up and the window gradually began to close.

"Don't bother closing it, Jean-Louis. It will be easier for me to reach it from the inside," Lucien said in a clear voice.

There was instant movement, a quick shuffling, a snapping of branches, then Lucien held the struggling man by his thick hair, quickly pulling the head back—and back. Fists flailed at Lucien's chest.

"Enough!" The big corporal's single word was like a curse, as his free hand lashed against a cheek, whipping the black head one way,

while his other hand snapped the head back again. "Now, walk . . .
very carefully. We shall continue this encounter inside, where you
can see my face and know how tempted I am to crack your neck."
The grip was moved to the collar of the jacket.

By the time they reached the back door, the shoulders beneath the
jacket had wilted, and Lucien was able to pull the key from his
pocket and turn the lock with little effort. Jean-Louis, half stumbling,
half dragged over the kitchen floor, hit the wooden armchair in a
heap. Almost the same instant, the overhead light flashed on.

He had on a dark, ribbed-necked sweater beneath a zippered blue
leather jacket. His chin was darkly tinged with beard growth, his
thick hair disheveled. He raised his head slowly, then to Lucien's
utter astonishment, appeared to be managing a smile, disarming, almost shy. "It looks like you caught me, Corporal Anjou. What can I
say?" The smile brightened. "I expect the truth is the best defense. I
thought I could hide out in the room in there . . . nobody goes into
that room, especially not you. Then when I got inside, I decided it
wouldn't be such a good idea. I didn't think it was fair to get you
mixed up in my troubles"—he shrugged and sighed a little—"even
though I haven't done anything wrong. I really am sorry, Corporal."
He touched the cheek where welts were appearing in rosy streaks,
then pulled at his jacket, straightening it.

He's sorry! thought Lucien, wanting to scream the word and laugh
bitterly at the same time, but as so often lately, he kept his silence,
telling himself, as he did with Ghislaine, Don't interrupt . . . keep
him talking . . . it will come!

Jean-Louis was looking at Lucien again, the lips still tipped in the
smile, the eyes unblinking. "You know I wouldn't break into your
house like a common burglar to steal, monsieur . . . you know me
better than that . . . and what have you here that I could possibly
want? What I need is to have someone tell the truth for a change.
You know they tried to frame me." The laugh was soft and mirthless.
"I admit it was a stupid idea . . . to come here. I knew the minute I
got inside . . . but I've been in that jail twice already, each time for
no reason at all. That Sergeant Corvette is paranoid . . . absolutely
paranoid. He runs around the gendarmerie like a headless chicken,
shouting orders . . . canceling orders . . . well, monsieur, you must
have seen him yourself."

Lucien had been standing, half leaning on the door, his hands
hanging at his sides. As Jean-Louis went on, Lucien began to feel

chilled—first his shoulders, then his chest, his thighs, his knees. He looked at his hands—no, they weren't trembling. His mind was trying to handle two overlapping voices; first, Jean-Louis', then his own, each one demanding priority. It's the coat, Lucien told himself. It's wet—it's heavy—it's unnecessary. Take it off! "Headless chicken . . . seen him yourself." The printed-on smile remained on the false face. Couldn't Pippa have seen the deceit? How could she have been so blind! Blind! The glasses— There they were on the table. I must remember the glasses.

The heavy dark blue coat dropped to the floor. He moved to the table, leaning against it as if for support, his hands behind his back as if he were leaning on them.

"By tomorrow," the persuasive young voice went on, "they will realize they can't charge me with anything."

The eyeglasses were in Lucien's hand, then in the back pocket of his pants.

"I have an expensive advocate . . . the best in Paris . . . and Mama explained everything to that old gendarme who is the good friend of Inspector Michelin. I have committed no crime, and I can prove it. By tomorrow . . ."

At last the big deep armchair was supporting Lucien's uncertain knees, and his fingers felt comforted as they grasped the familiar frayed arms. It was time to interrupt—to stop this excursion into the fanciful world of lies that was being created. "Where did you hide your motorcycle?"

"What? . . . oh, that. I knew they'd think I'd gone off on it. That's the first thing those idiots would look for. I expect they've got roadblocks set up all the way to Marseilles. Good luck to them, sitting out there with bleary eyes." The laugh was tight again.

"Where is it?"

"You're a friend, so there's no harm telling you. You really are our oldest and most faithful friend, aren't you? Papa thinks you're as important as de Gaulle ever was, did you know that, Corporal? I was brought up on stories of your adventures in the war, and your bravery. While other little boys heard stories about kings and dragons, I was kept entertained by true stories about you." Jean-Louis stopped, sensing a stiffening of the hands in the opposite chair. "Of course . . . the motorcycle . . . it's hidden in those lilac bushes at the back of the cottage . . . just below your bedroom window. Isn't that a—"

"Enough!" This time the word was an obscenity. "If you were searching in my parlor for your cocaine, Jean-Louis, you waited too long. You should have come back right after you killed her, while I was too demented with shock to think clearly. You persuaded your doting mama to clear out Pippa's room, didn't you? And you helped her carry the boxes away. She told me . . . stricken with grief, as you were, you offered to do a kindness. Such a devoted neighbor you became . . . and such a devoted son!" Lucien's fists were doubling, pounding slowly, rhythmically on the arms of the chair, as an accompaniment to the measured words. "Jean-Louis, you never in your rotten useless life offered to carry so much as a loaf of bread for your mother. She swallowed your lies, and I swallowed hers . . . until I began to use my reason. You wanted to search her belongings for your filthy drugs."

"You're demented . . . your own grief has twisted your mind. I was devoted to Pippa . . . I was . . . and I hurt for you, really I do, Corporal. I know how you feel. You're old, and—"

Lucien stood quickly, and in one stride had both hands on Jean-Louis' shoulders, towering down over him. "Don't you ever belittle me! Oh, yes, I am old"—his voice rose—"and strong, and I am not the law. I have my own law. I have no fear of reprisal for brutality. I can smash your face until you will never be able to manipulate anyone with that practiced smile again. I can beat the truth from you without a twinge of conscience or regret, or pity. But, I know the truth!" He was raising Jean-Louis' shoulders higher and higher, until without warning, he slammed him back, and the chair with its occupant went crashing toward the stove.

"You're out of your mind . . . you know that, don't you . . . you are." The words came in gasps as Jean-Louis covered his head with his arms and backed farther away along the floor, with doubled knees and kicking legs, finally coming to a halt against the wall.

Lucien paid no attention. "I found your vile hoard, so lovingly wrapped and tucked into the empty cigarette package. Would you like to know where Pippa in her innocence hid it?"

"She burned it . . . she said she burned it. . . ."

The words were out at last . . . the first admission of guilt. It was like a shot of alcohol to Lucien's system, but he kept his voice controlled. "She put it in a pocket of an old sweater that had been hanging on the back of that door for years." He indicated the closed door to the salon where a faded workman's jacket hung from another nail.

"It was a sweater that was never used . . . but the saints were with me, and it was worn in an emergency, and then I knew. I didn't plant all the drugs on your mototcycle, Jean-Louis. I kept some . . . I thought you might want it sometime."

The arms were lowered slowly, and the exposed forehead, now very white against the new beard below, appeared. "You did it!" The smile was replaced by a look of disbelief, a near-tearful anger at the injustice. "I thought you were my friend. I should have known . . . they said it was a bungler, an amateur."

Again Lucien paid no heed, pounding ahead with his own words. He stood straight, calmer now, almost thoughtful. "Since the beginning I have been faced with a problem in my mind. Now I am face to face with it . . . you. What shall I do with you, Jean-Louis Hugo? Should I hand you over to the fumbling gendarmerie? I don't think so. In spite of everything, I have an admiration for Sergeant Corvette, and that high-priced advocate, as you correctly called him, could make a fool out of everybody again, as there is a singular lack of evidence, of witnesses. You saw to that, didn't you? The foolish Chamillion woman, who you thought was trying to trick you, saying that you sold her worthless flour . . . until, of course, Pippa in her honesty told you the truth. Imagine that innocent one wanting to protect you! And then Pippa herself. Did you strike her before you got to the Couronne gardens, or did it happen there?"

Jean-Louis moved, as if to speak, but Lucien raised a hand. "No more . . . no more lies. You were seen . . . seen there in the gardens, standing over her. What happened beforehand is the only detail I can't get straight in my mind because I dare not think about it too often. It is so easy for me to kill . . . I was taught to kill with one hand. Whatever the truth, I have no doubt that you have rationalized it all in your own mind. Has it ever kept you awake at nights . . . has it?"

The young man had pushed himself up into a half-sitting position, as close to the wall as he could manage. When he spoke, it seemed as if he had regained a little of his composure, because, as Lucien instantly recognized, the wheedling smoothness, the false charm, were back in his attitude, his expression. The lies were not lies because he really believed them to be the truth. "It was an accident, M. Anjou . . . Corporal . . . you must see it was an accident. I wouldn't hurt her. I've always looked after her. Remember the time she fell from her bicycle and you weren't home. She hit her head that time too. I

never left her. I carried her home and when I couldn't find you, I
went for help to Mama. It was the same this time. She could be very
clinging, you know, and I just pushed her away a little and she fell
. . . against the motorbike. I couldn't believe she was dead. I tried to
wake her up. I called her . . . I begged her to wake up." Jean-Louis'
expression was quite blank, even his eyes, as if he was not seeing
Lucien or anyone. The more he spoke, the more sincere his words.
He nodded a little once, agreeing with himself.

"So afterwards, you strangled her with the scarf to make it appear
identical with the other death . . . the Chamillion woman. You were
afraid your motives might be misjudged. It was so possible that M.
Chamillion had killed his wife, wasn't it? Why the demented man
would want to kill Pippa too, didn't enter your mind then because
you were frightened, you couldn't think clearly. It was a mistake but
understandable."

The smile almost surfaced again. "You understand, monsieur! I
knew if we could talk quietly together, that you would understand.
That other woman . . . she was unimportant . . . just a tart. She
made me angry. She wouldn't listen. She wanted the money back.
She said I was a liar and she knew my kind . . . as if she could! Just
a tart, she was . . . and saying I wasn't even much of a man. She
offered herself to me, you know . . . as if I would dirty my hands on
her!" For the first time there was a smoldering tone. Anger was there
too—and some uncertainty, thought Lucien, watching carefully—even
a false bravado.

Lucien was back in his chair again, quiet, unemotional. "Did you
believe that Pippa had burned your drugs?" Lucien knew the answer
—it was the reason for the search of the cottage tonight, but he
wanted to hear more.

"No." Jean-Louis straightened his back against the wall and drew
up his knees. He was wearing new-looking shoes with built-up soles,
Lucien noticed. He bent over absently to rub at the scuffmarks on
the stubby toes. The rubbing became more intense as he talked, the
petulance, as sometimes with Ghislaine, showing in a preoccupation
with a physical flaw to cover up a childish nervousness.

"What made you think she lied?"

"She couldn't lie to me. It always showed in her face. When I told
her I knew she lied, she didn't try to deny it. But that was later. She
said it was hidden where no one went, where no one would know
. . . but she wouldn't give it to me, even though I promised to take

her away so she wouldn't have to go off to that school alone. She kept lecturing me . . . like a mama. I had one mama . . . that was enough and I told her so, and she cried but she still wouldn't give it to me. I never saw her so stubborn. I'd put all my summer money into that . . . it was a business deal, Corporal . . . purely a business deal, like buying and selling shoes." He was still polishing at the toe of his shoe with his wrist. He added, without looking up, "I wouldn't have taken her away, Corporal. I wouldn't have done anything that dishonest."

"I'm sure you wouldn't." The remark was purposely reassuring. "But, Jean-Louis, my problem is still unsolved. What shall we do with you? I am going to have to think about it. However innocent your motives, I find your presence here in my home . . . Pippa's home . . . contaminating. I don't want to do anything I might regret later, so I need time. I am very tired. When I am tired, I always postpone any action. I think I do have a place for you to stay the night . . . or what is left of it. The room is bare . . . only the essentials, really, but there is a bed and blankets, and possibly some hot soup. Yes, I think the place should do for tonight. Stand up, Jean-Louis. You and I are going for a walk."

Chapter Twenty-six

"Ghislaine . . . Ghislaine, try to wake up and listen to me. Where did you put that old sweater of mine?"

"Sweater . . ." The question had been whispered; the reply was mumbled.

"The one M. Chamillion was wearing the night I brought him here."

"It must be in the cell room."

"It's not. I tidied the room earlier when I took him away. There's nothing there except the blankets covering the Hugo boy."

"Is the boy asleep?"

"Yes. He'll sleep until morning. But I need the sweater. Did you put it away somewhere, Ghislaine?"

Lucien had wakened her after he'd taken Jean-Louis through the front door and settled him in the little bedroom so recently vacated by another. Ghislaine's lack of interest in the latest occupant upstairs was not surprising, as she was still stunned by sleep. She had ac-

cepted Lucien's waking of her as simply another of his nightly comings and goings. When he had bent over her in her cot in the kitchen,
touching her cheek lightly, she had opened her eyes slowly, saying as
always, "Is that you, Lucien?"

Now she half sat up, covering a yawn, then pressing her fingers to
her cheek in the old uncertain manner. He had added some small
logs to the fireplace embers, and the flames were licking in uneven
spurts, producing an erratic light in the otherwise darkened room.
Ghislaine, in her coif, and grasping the bedclothing to her neck, was
an indefinite blur.

"It's quite cold," she said. "Is that why you want the sweater . . .
because you are cold? It's really not a good sweater at all . . . frayed
at the front. If I were you, I should throw it out and buy a new one.
We have plenty of money now."

The chattering had begun—she was becoming more alert. He
waited quietly, looming above her, not needing to see her face, listening to the inflections in her voice.

"I remember now, Lucien," she went on. "I put it in Amélie's
room. I was going to burn it with those dresses of Amélie's I didn't
like." She peered up at him. "Why do you need it? You're wearing
your thick jacket."

"I don't want to wear it. There's something in the pocket I want."

"Do you mean that little packet of white powder? I looked in the
pockets . . . I always look in pockets, because sometimes I find
things. Once I found four francs and another time . . ."

"What did you do with it?" He tried to conceal his apprehension.
"Did you throw it out?"

"Oh, no. I thought it might be a headache powder, and I often get
headaches. Have you got a headache now, Lucien? I wouldn't be surprised. You haven't had a good rest for such a long time, what with
burying M. Chamillion, and then finding that Hugo boy in your cottage trying to steal things. Won't he try to steal things here, Lucien? I
hope you don't intend to keep him here very long. If the gendarmes
didn't always ask so many questions, you could take him there."

"He won't be here long, and the door is locked. Now about that
white powder . . . Can you remember what you did with it? I want
to get rid of it because it's not just for headaches. It's a dangerous
drug, very strong, even stronger than Amélie's pain pills."

The fire had caught and the light was brighter. She was sitting on
the edge of the bed tugging at a quilt. He reached down, lifting off

the top coverlet to wrap around her shoulders, and he felt a wave of protective sadness as he touched the tiny bones of her shoulders beneath the ugly gray nightdress. "I know you are sleepy, and I'm sorry to waken you, but these things I'm doing are important. I'm trying to protect you . . . both of us."

"I know, so we can stay together here, and wherever we go after that too. I'll try to remember. Is it poison?"

"Not when a little bit is used properly, but only doctors are supposed to have it."

She hugged the coverlet closer, staring past him into the flames. "I'm thinking . . . I've been thinking," she began earnestly.

"Yes."

"I've been thinking that you should go to see Dr. Desmaris and tell him that Amélie is better, but she still needs pain pills sometimes. Then he won't wonder about things and come here again."

"I've been considering that too, Ghislaine. I plan to go tomorrow. Now, about the little packet . . . ?"

"I might have put it in the pewter mug on the mantelpiece up there, with my rosary beads that got broken." She paused, pressing at her cheek again. "Lucien, did you put M. Chamillion with Amélie?"

"No." He was reaching above the hearth for the mug, and he hesitated for a second, then went on searching. "It's not here, Ghislaine. The beads are here, but that is all."

"Oh . . . well, then I shall have to think about it more when I'm not so confused. Tomorrow, in the morning, I'm sure I'll remember." She crawled back on top of the cot, burrowing beneath the pile of blankets, like a baby, comforted by the bundling. "You should sleep too."

"Very well, we'll talk in the morning. I shall sit here for a little while and rest. Then I have a small errand to complete before daylight and after that I can have some sleep."

"That boy upstairs . . . he hurt Pippa, didn't he?"

"Yes, but there is no proof."

"Does he know Amélie's not here?"

"No. I explained before, but I expect you were not quite listening. I brought him in the front way." Lucien had added a large log to the fire and was settling himself as comfortably as he could in the chaise longue. His fatigue was more than physical; there was a weariness of spirit unlike anything he could remember. He stretched out his legs, adjusted his jacket, put his head back, and allowed himself the luxury of closing his eyes for a moment.

When next he opened his eyes, Ghislaine, dressed in the old disreputable garb, was rattling the stove lids, and streaks of a weak daylight were sifting between the slats of the shutters.

He wanted to jerk to his feet, but the awful fatigue was still with him, compounded by a stiffness in his limbs that was half paralyzing. The first panicky thought that surfaced was overlapped by another more serious problem . . . then another, and another, until he began to feel battered. It took all his self-control to set them aside and tell himself, "I can do nothing now; the night is gone and I cannot bring it back, so I shall go on."

Ghislaine, bending over a pot, looked as gray as the light of the new day, but she sounded cheerful. "I have the soup you didn't eat last night . . . once the stove heats up. I quite like soup for breakfast."

He sat up slowly, then stood, removing his wrinkled jacket before taking over the lighting of the stove. It seemed he had spent the past few weeks doing little else than keeping fires burning, and somehow he felt a significance in the act. Right now he wished for hot water—a wash in good hot water, and a shave, but all in good time, he tried to reassure himself. He checked his watch; it was not quite the half hour past six.

"That boy, the Hugo boy . . . is he still upstairs? I have heard no sound."

"He's still there." Lucien paused to light a cigarette, then with the same match, lit the kindling, and inhaled the bitterness of the smoke, before adding coke and replacing the stove lids. Yes, he decided, there was a kind of symbolism in the act, and a bitterness. "I will take him some soup and bread later."

"What will you do with him, Lucien? I don't want him here. If he hurt Pippa, he might hurt me too . . . and steal things."

"He will harm nothing in this house, Ghislaine. Soon I will tend to him . . . take him away. Try to pretend he isn't here." He wanted to say more, but he knew she could not understand the complexities of a young man who had created a world of lies for himself, a world without conscience, where the only wrongs were those he felt had been directed toward himself. Ghislaine's make-believe world was not too different in some ways, but there had always been that eager innocence about her that set her apart. In her own way, she had the capacity to love others and to protect her loves as best she could. She had borne his child once, and the tearing of the child from her had left a void so deep it had twisted her already unstable little mind. Late as his gestures might be, he found he was being pulled toward her, for he was all she had left, and his pity was being transformed into a kind of need, even a strange love.

At that moment Lucien admitted to himself exactly what he was doing, what had been in his mind since his discovery of Jean-Louis in the cottage. He, Lucien Anjou, was about to join Ghislaine Couronne in her world, because there was no other way.

"Remember what I asked you last night, Ghislaine, about the small packet of white powder you found in the sweater pocket? Can you think of where you put it? It's very dangerous if it's used improperly. There's enough to kill a man. I will have to destroy it."

"I'll think about it, Lucien, but first I need some hot tea. Do you want to take hot tea up to the boy too?"

"Yes."

"Then I'll make enough for all of us. The stove is heating quickly . . . you build an excellent fire, Lucien. Soon the kettle will boil."

They stood with their backs to each other, he, with the cigarette dangling from his lips, bending over to stir up the fireplace coals, she getting down soup plates and cups from the open cupboard.

"I must go outside for more logs and coke," he said.

"Yes, you do that. Did you say the white powder was poison?"

"If enough is used."

"Then I'll try to remember where I put it. Did the boy say why he hurt Pippa?"

"He tells a lot of lies, but I think it was because of the white powder. He had more of it . . . a great deal more. It could have made a living hell for a lot of people if he had sold it. People get to need it, the way M. Chamillion needed his drink. Pippa wanted to stop him from selling it."

"Then he is not a nice young man, is he, Lucien?"

"No, he's not."

She waited until the doors closed behind Lucien, then she pushed two of the three cups to one side of the table. "Lucien and I shall have hot chocolate for breakfast. It's much more nourishing. The boy can have tea, as he's not a nice person . . . and don't argue with me, Amélie." She spoke aloud in a very firm tone.

*   *   *

They played their game for the last time that evening. The setting was unchanged, although Lucien was more rested and Ghislaine less confused. He had slept on Amélie's bed most of the day, then refreshed himself with a wash in steaming water in the kitchen basin, holding the hot cloth to his face, trying to soak out the throbbing behind his temples that had plagued him even in sleep.

"The boy hasn't eaten a thing all day, Lucien. He didn't even drink his tea this morning," she commented innocently, as he dried his face.

"How do you know?"

"I peeked in on him while you were sleeping. I locked the door afterwards, so don't be cross with me."

"He's dead, Ghislaine."

"I know. I touched him. It doesn't bother me so much to touch dead things any more, but I'll feel better when he's gone. I didn't put the white powder in his tea, Lucien . . . really I didn't. I thought about it . . . very seriously, but I decided you wouldn't want me to waste it on him. We might need it, you and I, in case one of us goes first. I couldn't even enjoy heaven without you, Lucien."

"I understand. It was a wise thought. Where have you put it for safekeeping?"

"I've wrapped it in a tiny piece of cloth, and I'm almost finished sewing it onto the back of the tapestry. It makes a bump on the back, but nobody will think to look on the back anyway. The picture on the front is going to be very breathtaking. Have you noticed . . . it's of the ancient basilica."

"I've noticed."

"What did you do to the boy? I promise I won't be cross . . . or tell."

"In the Maquis, one learns to destroy evil, quickly and silently, with a hand."

"Where will you put him? With M. Chamillion?"

"This time I think he will have to be put with Amélie."

"Where is Amélie? I was going to plant some nasturtiums on the asparagus bed in the spring, but if she's not there, I won't bother."

"Would you like a glass of wine, Ghislaine? I found another excellent bottle of Burgundy in the cupboard."

"Thank you, that would be very nice. You really are a very thoughtful person, Lucien. I used to tell Amélie . . ."

"Ghislaine, it would make me very happy if you didn't mention Amélie any more. Could you do that to please me?"

"I will try, Lucien . . . I will truly try. What would you like to talk about now? Shall we think about the springtime and plan our garden?"

They finished off the wine with their light meal, then Lucien went out into the night on his last errand. He left her in the chair beside the bright fire and the lumpy tapestry. He walked doggedly back to his cottage, breathing the cold still air into his lungs, hoping the freshness would renew his strength, and still the ache in his head—and his heart. He would have to climb the tree again; it was the only safe way. After the gendarme Ygrec and his dog returned to Moulins, the garden might provide a more lasting tomb, but not until then. Ghislaine had been right—the dog was a danger.

He unlocked the door of his cottage, walked unseeing through the dark, deadly empty kitchen to his bedroom, where he took the flashlight from his bureau and flicked it on. He made his way up the steep ladder stairway to the attic, rolled up his father's other poaching net, and tucked it beneath his arm. His mountaineer's piton hammer and a handful of piton spikes were dropped into his big pocket. He left the way he had come, locking the cottage door out of habit.

He was sweating when he reached the loge de garde, although his breath formed little puffs that hung in the air. The new moon provided just enough light, and he looked up, murmuring an unbidden prayer. The ladder and the coil of rope lay where he had left them, in the frosted overgrowth along the side of the house. He propped the ladder against the tallest of the pines that hugged the great naked oak, and with the heavy rope looped over one shoulder, he climbed the ladder, soon disappearing into the uplifting foliage. The branch he chose was lower than Amélie's branch, but just as sturdy. He dropped one end of the rope over the branch near its base, then tying and knotting it to the other free end of the rope, gradually began unrolling the coil as he descended from bough to bough, but pausing every few feet to pound a piton firmly into the tree trunk, testing each before moving down to hammer in the next.

Back on the ground, he left the knotted ends of the rope dangling and went back to the house. He let himself quickly into the front hall, stepped silently up the stairs, then descended slowly with his burden. If Ghislaine heard him, she made no acknowledgment.

Jean-Louis was at least twice the weight of Amélie, but Lucien could only trust that his pulley system would work once more. He dropped the body to his feet, wrapping it in the net, rolling it over and over, then unknotting the rope ends, he quickly formed a hangman's knot and placed it around the legs of the stiffened form, tightening it in place. The loose end he tied around his own waist, and he mounted the ladder once more. When he reached the lowest firm branch that would hold his weight, he sat, with his legs akimbo, bracing himself firmly, and he began to pull. It was a painstaking process, but eventually the net-entangled body reached the thick foliage and gradually disappeared from sight. Lucien looped the rope on his prepared piton spike, climbed, pulled, looped again, but the task was telling on his strength. His arms and shoulders began to rebel against the strain until at last the rope slipped through his hands before he could anchor it, tearing the flesh from his palms. There was a splintering of branches but a lower piton held. Lucien leaned forward against the tree trunk, closing his eyes against the pain and tasting the saltiness of his sweat.

Amélie had been slung much higher, away from any possible discovery, but he knew now he no longer had the strength to hoist Jean-Louis to the same height. It was impossible to be certain in the darkness, but surely the spreading limbs of evergreen needles were thick enough now to provide a temporary hiding place for the body. It would have to do; he barely had enough power in his arm to anchor the net where it was. He wiped at his damp face with a sleeve, then knotted the rope carefully on the spike, and untying the remainder from his waist, he fastened it firmly around the branch as he'd been taught to do when he had helped his father hang the swing. He would check carefully tomorrow when it was daylight. For now, it would hold. He descended slowly, painfully, the hurt in his hands a counterirritant to greater hurts that he doubted would ever heal.

* * *

"Oh, poor Lucien . . . your poor hands. I'll bathe them for you and then put on clean cloths like I did for your friend Gendarme Ygrec. I'm a very good nurse; Amélie always said so. M. Ygrec's hand got better, you told me, and so will yours. He said he would bring my serviette back, but I told him not to bother. I didn't want him around here with his dog . . . and those eyes of his that smile right through a person's thoughts. Did you say he was going home soon, Lucien?"

Chapter Twenty-seven

The more that Ygrec's physical condition improved, the sadder he became, and once again progress in the investigation came to a standstill. Nothing of note happened until the following weekend, and even then the only unusual development was the wedding and its aftermath. Later, Ygrec would explain that the solution to the St. Denis tragedies had obviously never been fated to be understood by mere mortals—to be catalogued properly in a file then tucked away —to be forgotten by all but the bereaved, or by old gendarmes who had time to reminisce. It was a lesson in humility.

Jean-Louis Hugo had disappeared—"temporarily," Sergeant Corvette kept reassuring those who cared. Mme. Hugo was "resting," and the younger daughter had come with her colicky baby from Rouen to help out in the pâtisserie. Pépi carried on somehow, although Mme. de Cosse stated that his "croissants were suffering." Lucien Anjou seemed past suffering or caring about anything. He had become one of the "walking wounded," M. Gratien Fouschie was heard to say in the bistro, and no one could disagree.

M. Fouschie was becoming a habitual caller at the château, in spite of Mme. de Cosse's rude disapproval, which was plain for all to see, but Ygrec found the man amusing in a morbid kind of way. He came midmornings, because, as he explained without apology or excuse, "I'm usually too impaired after my liquid luncheons in the bistro to carry on a stimulating dialogue." His visits were short, and he never would accept anything to drink, but he did bring Ygrec an excellent bottle of Montrachet 1961, from his own wine cellar. "Say the word . . . simply say the word, M. Ygrec, if you find it pleasing to your palate," the mortician elaborated, "and I shall keep you supplied and provide you with more to cheer your dull days when you return to Moulins. I was a connoisseur in my prime years, but now precious wines are wasted on me. My taste buds have deteriorated in direct proportion to my disgusting consumption of Céleste's Riesling, and by her clientele. 'Ye who are about to die, I pity you,' I say as I raise my glass to the beer-quaffing peasants in the bistro and mock their discomfort. Then I drink their health. I am like the eye of doom. The more sensitive rush off to live a little before it is too late. The majority turn their backs and slink away into their burrows. Lucien Anjou used to raise his glass too, and we would smile at each other, but I am disturbed about him recently. I always felt he was one of the élite when it came to facing life . . . and death. Le Loup Noir was a man to be honored, never mocked. Now he's practically living over there in the loge de garde. Observe . . . yes, observe how the mighty have fallen . . . and it pains me. He even took Mlle. Ghislaine Couronne shopping yesterday; he borrowed my wheezing deux chevaux for the occasion. Ghislaine looked like she'd been resurrected from my great-aunt Georgette's attic, poor demented creature. It is all very interesting . . . most interesting."

"He talks in riddles," Michelin remarked when Ygrec repeated the conversation. "I'm wondering if now he's trying to feed you information, rather than pick your brain."

"For what purpose? He never mentions Pippa or the Chamillions any more, or even Jean-Louis. Corporal Anjou is a mutual friend, but his daily comings and goings are of no great concern. I haven't seen the corporal since the night Jean-Louis disappeared, but grief wears many cloaks. Here, in the château, we are bound to remind him of Pippa. At first he couldn't accept the finality of her death; now he probably can't bear the anger, so pushes the fact away by ignoring it."

Thursday morning M. Fouschie did not arrive, and at noon, Ygrec sleepily enjoying a return of the bright autumn sunshine, wondered aloud what had happened. Mme. de Cosse provided the reason. "No doubt he's as happy as a vulture hovering over a fresh carcass, although how fresh the carcass of M. Valin Chamillion must be after all this time, I shudder to think." Ygrec was instantly alert, but Mme. de Cosse could add nothing to her brief statement except to say she had heard the man had been dead for some days. Madame's daughter worked for Sergeant Corvette's wife.

Ygrec was alone except for the dog. Vanessa had gone to the city to shop, and Michelin would not be home until evening. Ygrec tried to rest on his bed after lunch but gave up after a short time, went to the telephone in Michelin's bedroom, and called the mortuary.

Indeed, the mortal remains of M. Chamillion were now resting in a tightly sealed casket in the "outer chamber," M. Fouschie announced, his voice sounding shrill, the words slightly blurred. A preservative would have been a waste of expensive chemicals as there was little to preserve after the ravages of time, and a morning under the coroner's scalpel, had done with him. Fouschie had gone on, warming to his subject without prodding, volunteering that the sister,

Mlle. Estelle Chamillion, no doubt following her nose, had discovered the body crumpled in a corner of the dilapidated conservatory that adjoined the house, while searching for a broom to shoo a lovelorn cat off the premises, as the animal had been disturbing "maman's" rest. Mlle. Estelle was now under the doctor's care. At this rate, the whining dowager, maman, would outlive them all and would have to "pick up her bed and walk," with no one to wait on her. Wouldn't that be an amusing twist of fate? "She looked down on me as an untouchable in years past, the dowager did." The chuckle at the end of the phone indicated a note of satisfaction.

When had the unfortunate man died? Had there been foul play? Ygrec could almost see the mortician's long fingers being placed against his forehead, in a gesture of deep concentration. It was hard to say . . . indeed it was hard to say . . . deciding the exact time body and soul had drifted apart. Even the coroner could make only an educated guess. The consensus was a few days ago, perhaps four. There was degenerative brain damage, extensive liver damage, indications of a recent severe bronchial infection, as well as other various medical signs of a misused body, none of which alone would be responsible, but the combination obviously had been fatal because the man was dead . . . extremely dead. The death certificate read, chronic alcohol poisoning. "I shall be at your doorstep tomorrow morning bearing complete details and another bottle of wine," had been Fouschie's parting words.

When Ygrec put down the receiver, he didn't know whether to laugh or to mourn—not for a man whom he'd never met, but for the last hopeful lead in the search for truth.

The old gendarme went back to his room and to the packing of his suitcase, which he had promised himself to complete before evening. Michelin would be off duty for the weekend and had agreed to drive him to Moulins Saturday morning. If he got some of his things out of the way today, tomorrow wouldn't be so difficult; he could pretend he wasn't going anywhere. Vanessa, he knew, wouldn't help him at all. She wouldn't even discuss his leaving.

He was refolding a sweater for the third time, the empty valise lying on the cedar chest at the foot of his bed, when she arrived home.

She peeked around the corner, ignoring the obvious. "Oh, good, you are going to get changed for the evening. Well, just put that old sweater back in the drawer . . . I have a new one for you." She had been holding her hands behind her back. Now she twirled around in her stocking feet, holding up a soft blue cardigan. "Surprise! It's cashmere. Blue is definitely your best color. I've had a fabulous afternoon! I bought myself a wild new dress . . . like a Polynesian nightgown, but very expensive and chic. I showed it to Jules Matieu and he absolutely hated it . . . said it did nothing for my figure. Then I told him about my expanding waistline and why, and he nearly went into a decline, practically crying that I had ruined my life and his layout for the spring styles. It took two vodkas to revive him. The studio was in an uproar anyway, so my announcement really finished things off. Jules closed early then took me for a drink. . . . I ordered Vichy water which definitely put him into a depression. Such lovely gossip! Roget . . . that's the brother who is the engineer . . . well, Roget's wife has run off to Majorca or somewhere with a poet who is quite mad. She is quite mad too, of course . . . keeps trying to 'expand her horizons' with drugs and things. I thought she had her talons into Damon . . . Damon's the advocate who bought the Couronne gardens, but now he's decided he doesn't want the property and has put it up for sale again. I'd love to buy it and build a house there, but Paul wouldn't approve at all."

Ygrec became almost breathless just listening to her. Before he had a chance to say anything, she kissed him warmly on the cheek and ordered him to try on the sweater while she poured "a little something to brighten you up before Paul gets home. You look a little subdued."

Rather than argue, Ygrec closed the suitcase and did as he was told. Friday, Michelin phoned that he was sorry but his days off had been postponed until the first of the week as his work had piled up. Vanessa decided to have the second bottle of M. Fouschie's superb wine for supper to celebrate "nothing in particular." The empty suitcase remained on the bench in the bedroom until, while Ygrec was out walking, Mme. de Cosse put it back on the top shelf of the wardrobe. The evening was pleasant, although Ygrec was very quiet. He said he'd run out of words and went to bed early, dreading the coming of Monday.

Saturday when the news of the wedding broke, even the mortician admitted he was practically at a loss for words, although he managed to come up with a few almost original quotations. He arrived shortly after ten o'clock in the morning, looking even more thrown together than usual, and there were shaving nicks on his jutting chin. He volunteered that he had "indulged in a bottle of my own magnificent Médoc 1952, to wash down my breakfast croissant, which was unutterably stale. Perhaps I was hasty in judging myself after all, my revered M. Ygrec. I have discovered my taste buds are not completely anaesthetized. It was a brilliant wine . . . brilliant! God knows I needed something to cushion the shock!"

For the rest of the short visit, which took place in the sunny end of the salon and under the intermittent glare of Mme. de Cosse, who insisted on dusting the furniture with concentrated devotion, Ygrec was addressed in "revered" terms. Vanessa left by the back door to walk the dog, shaking her head with disbelief. Only then did Gratien Fouschie elaborate on the wedding.

"Thou shalt not uncover the nakedness of thy brother's wife, although in this case the nakedness would hardly apply, would it? I wonder if the prophets gave any thought to 'thy sister's ex-husband?' On the other hand, 'You without sin shall cast the first stone.'" He rolled his eyes and shrugged. "I don't hold with bothering about sins of the flesh anyway, but I can assure you, my revered friend, that it is the most astonishing development to have taken place since my uncle Gaston married the defrocked nun, bless her sinful heart. When Lucien married Amélie Couronne he was well into his thirties, and one would presume he knew what he was doing. Did I ever mention that Amélie was quite, quite beautiful to behold . . . inclined toward lesbianism, I could have told him, but in those days one did not utter the word. But this! I am almost without words . . . without words!" He took on the familiar pose of suffering, with his fingers pressed to his lowered forehead.

Ygrec reached to the table for the nearest decanter and was instantly able to persuade the mortician to join him in a glass of sherry —not Ygrec's favorite drink, nor, obviously Fouschie's, who made a wry face, emptied the glass, and went on talking.

The wedding had taken place at eight o'clock that morning in the smallest private chapel of the basilica. "No warning . . . not even banns. I wonder how Lucien managed to circumvent tradition . . . although I shouldn't wonder. He has always found a way . . . always."

"But that was a matter of only a few hours ago, M. Fouschie. How did you come to hear the news so soon?" Ygrec asked.

"Quite simple . . . I was a witness . . . myself and Mme. Céleste. At the crack of dawn, I was summoned from my bed by the telephone. I took for granted that Amélie had died. . . . I've had a casket reserved for her for some years now. I was speechless when Lucien told me what he wanted. Little wonder that when it was over I ransacked my wine cellar." He sniffed deeply. "A little more of that ghastly sherry, if you please, my honorable friend. It is a drink only fit for aboriginal females in their dotage, but desperate times call for desperate measures."

Ygrec poured. They lifted their glasses. "I wish I could think of a suitable toast for such an occasion," Ygrec said thoughtfully. "At least it is a pleasant morning . . . the best for many days. Perhaps it is a happy omen."

"Happy? Happy? Already today is a disaster, but wait until tomorrow. They are going to church tomorrow! I heard him promise her he would take her to early mass . .   'Mme. and M. Lucien Anjou,' walking down the aisle of the basilica! St. Denis will never recover."

"Why do you think it is such a disaster, monsieur? Two lonely old people could . . ."

"Disaster?" The mortician stood then, rather unsteadily, raising his small empty glass. "Disaster? It's the funniest thing I've heard in years . . . and years . . . and years." He started to laugh, his odd deep gasps filling the room. *"Au revoir, monsieur . . . á demain.* I shall now go to my abode and dust off my esteemed uncle Gervais' silk hat for church tomorrow."

Mme. de Cosse, dust rag in hand, glowered tight-lipped from the hallway. Ygrec stood up, watching the departing apparition in disreputable black, and he fingered his new sweater, wondering if he should wear it tomorrow. The incense and close air in the chucrh would choke him, he knew, but he would try to persuade Vanessa to take him where he could stand outside to watch the parade at the end of the service.

Chapter Twenty-eight

There was a smell of snow in the air, that new October Sunday, although a shy sun kept the day bright until noon. But in the shaded areas, the hoarfrost of dawn remained, and the parade of faithful and unfaithful to the basilica were warmly dressed.

Vanessa, as curious as Ygrec to see the "bridal couple," had been only too pleased to drive him to the church in time to watch the departure of the congregation at the end of the early service. They left the car parked in front of the firmly shuttered Cafe Khedive and stood to one side of the enclosure to the great doors. Ygrec, wearing his heavy coat and muffler, but bareheaded in spite of Vanessa's warnings, held her furred arm in his own and watched for familiar faces.

Mme. Hugo, her defiant head and wide shoulders adorned with mouton-trimmed black, was supported by the faithful Pépi in his starched white collar, stringy tie and Sabbath overcoat. Drab-blue Céleste was alone. Uncle Gervais' silk topper did nothing to detract from M. Gratien Fouschie's unkempt appearance, although Vanessa felt the hat gave him an air of delightful debauchery, as it was a little too small and was perched on the mortician's large bald head at a precarious angle. At last when M. Lucien Anjou and his bride descended the wide steps, arm in arm, Vanessa let out a little gasp, and even Ygrec could hardly suppress his astonishment. Lucien, erect and dignified in his old blue army greatcoat, towered above a tiny figure resplendent in an outfit suitable for a summer garden party at the turn of the century. Her face was hidden beneath the wide brim of a silky pink hat, the crown circled with masses of lilac veiling entangled with small clumps of flowers. She was wearing an elbow-length brown cape of some kind of fur which later Gratien Fouschie described as reminding him of "my cousin Genice's pet rabbit when it suffered the ringworm." The white dress beneath the cape seemed to have an eyelet neck-hugging high collar, laced with blue ribbon, long very full sleeves, also eyelet-trimmed at the wrists, and a long, gathered skirt finished with two layers of wide flounces. Her white-gloved hand clutched Lucien's arm as he guided her slowly down the steps, past murmuring onlookers who vainly tried to mask their stares, through the gateway, and at last, Ghislaine limping markedly, over the road to a vintage deux chevaux parked near Vanessa's Mercedes.

"I feel like crying . . . it's so sad, and yet so beautiful," whispered Vanessa.

"I wish I'd had the chance to say good-by and wish them well," Ygrec replied, then looked over to see M. Fouschie approaching, bowing and lowering the hat in a grand gesture.

"Mme. Michelin . . . my revered M. Ygrec . . . bonjour. You were wise not to attend the farce, although Lucien Anjou has not completely lost his sense of humor . . . and timing. He and his child-bride arrived late and sat at the back, and now half the populace of St. Denis will spend the next week suffering from stiff necks from trying to peer over their shoulders and follow the faltering old priest at the same time. Only Céleste and I had the wisdom to choose a back pew, and as I have long forgotten all forms of service except that prescribed for the burial of the dead, I simply sat enjoying the discomfort of others, and contemplating. Why it is that so many believe that calloused knees and an aching back can facilitate the purification of one's questionable soul is quite beyond me! But I digress. I trust I am not keeping you from other pressing business, Mme. Michelin"—he bowed once more in Vanessa's direction, then looked straight at Ygrec almost seriously—"but I feel that M. Ygrec might be interested in the subject of my holy contemplations."

Vanessa murmured something resembling "Not at all" and tried to keep from laughing, but Ygrec felt a strange twist in the mortician's attitude and listened carefully.

"Until today, I had given little thought to the reaction of Amélie Couronne to this sudden happy ending to an otherwise Gothic horror story, but as I gazed in fascination at the incredible outfit that adorned the younger sister, Ghislaine, my temporarily sober and evil mind began to fill with suspicion and apprehension. I have now decided that, after an extended and hopefully alcoholic noon repast which Céleste is preparing for me, I shall go the loge de garde to pay my respects and to save my friend Corporal Anjou the trouble of returning my noble deux chevaux. Would you like me to pay your respects also, M. Ygrec?"

"That would be kind of you, M. Fouschie, and as I am returning to my home in Moulins tomorrow morning, would you say adieu as well." Ygrec hesitated, raising a hand to straighten his muffler and rub the back of his neck against his collar. "Perhaps, monsieur, if you could spare the time, you could stop in at the château on your way. I have just remembered that I have a serviette belonging to Mlle. . . . excuse me . . . Mme. Ghislaine, one which she kindly lent me when I injured my hand in her garden a while back. I would be obliged if you would return it."

"*À votre service,* monsieur." The tall hat was once more flourished, and he turned quickly and hurried away.

Vanessa's observant eyes had been moving from the one man to the other. "What was that all about?" she asked. "It sounded as if you were talking in code. The politeness was overwhelming!" Then she pulled at Ygrec's arm. "But come along before you catch another chill. You can explain in the car."

"There's nothing to explain, chérie."

"Of course not . . . nothing at all! I'm beginning to know you almost as well as Paul." Suddenly she stopped talking, to raise her face and stick out her tongue. "Snow, Maurice . . . I felt a snowflake on my nose . . . and there's another landing on your hair! Wouldn't it be simply perfect if we had a snowstorm?"

"Chérie, it's only October. Those few flakes are melting the minute they touch anything . . . look for yourself."

But Vanessa wasn't looking. She stood, her bright hair tossed back, her eyes tightly closed. "I'm wishing," she said mysteriously. "I'm casting a spell. I'm willing that the snow will keep falling and falling and keep you here until Christmas . . . perhaps even spring."

Ygrec started to laugh.

"Shhh," she whispered. "Don't interrupt until my spell is finished. Besides, I know you're secretly wishing the same thing, so just close your eyes too, and help me concentrate."

He kept smiling but his eyes were wide open. He wasn't thinking of weather at all; he was mulling over the mortician's words.

At first, as Ygrec had pointed out, the fat, damp snowflakes melted the minute they touched the earth, but by the time he had wakened from his afternoon rest, the world outside his window was being transformed into a Christmas-card scene. It may slow up traffic tomorrow, he thought rather bleakly, but it won't hold it up. His large suitcase was already packed and stood in the hallway. In the morning he would stuff his nightclothes into the small valise and be on his way. Even Mademoiselle Larme was feeling the tension and had been dogging Vanessa's heels all day.

When M. Fouschie arrived shortly before three o'clock, brushing the heavy wet snow from his shoulders and bald head, he did not waste time with obvious talk of the weather except to say the driving might be slippery, but, as he was enjoying the "edifying effects" of a joyous wake provided for him privately by Mme. Céleste, driving was the least of his worries. "Rest assured, my revered monsieur," he went on in a surprisingly hushed tone, "I shall convey your messages and the serviette to the occupants of the loge. The wake, incidentally, was not the result of this morning's celebrations, but rather the disappearance of Céleste's nephew, Armand. I preferred to consider it a cause for rejoicing and by the time we had finished off the repast with a rather dull, but adequate bottle of champagne, I persuaded her to share my opinion, particularly as Armand emptied her cash-box as a farewell gesture. Ah, youth . . . youth! The world would be poorer without the excitement they provide . . . and the reasons for drinking to their departures."

"Possibly, M. Fouschie, but I can't help feeling sorry for Pépi Hugo. Did you notice his face this morning? He looked ten years older."

"Little do they know it, but the Hugos are better off without that mildewed seed. Do pardon the cliché, but he was born with a forked tongue, just as Armand was born with a weak will, as well as a weak stomach. I tried . . . heaven knows I tried for Céleste's sake to provide gainful employment for Armand in my art, but even a whiff of embalming fluid would make him lose his breakfast. Ah, well, he will be picked up in some hole in Paris once Céleste's money runs out. But we waste time, monsieur, and tomorrow will soon be yesterday. We must talk, you and I." He had remained standing just inside the doorway, his wet shoes forming rings on the carpet. Once he peered into the quiet salon but made no indication that he wished to stay.

"Won't you come in and sit down, then, M. Fouschie? The Inspector is on duty, and Mme. Michelin is resting."

"I feel too unnerved to sit . . . I must walk, I must collect my thoughts. In other circumstances I would suggest you take a stroll with me, but this snow is hateful stuff . . . hateful. It is nature's way of playing tricks on us. Indeed it is nature saying, 'Look, all is pure, all is white"; but beneath there is the same decay. Also I keep losing my balance, giving people the impression I cannot hold my wine." He almost smiled. "But don't be fooled by my jocularity, monsieur. I am greatly troubled." He stroked his angular, damp head, pressed his fingers on his forehead, and looked altogether miserable.

Ygrec spoke softly. "Is it because you feel that Mlle. Amélie Couronne could be dead?"

Fouschie moved his hand, blinked his eyes, and stared at Ygrec. His reply was spoken in a stage whisper. "Those were my very thoughts. Of course she's dead, but her casket lies empty in my storage room."

Ygrec nodded. "I also began to think this morning. From what I have learned of the personalities of the sisters, I could only surmise that Mlle. Ghislaine was dominated by the elder sister. Therefore if Mlle. Ghislaine felt free to, shall we say, cast off her pauper's garb and to marry after all these years, the domination had somehow been removed."

"Exactly . . . exactly! And I know even better than you. For years, ever since Lucien's retirement from the army and return to his father's cottage here in St. Denis, he did not set foot near the loge de garde, and when he brought the little Pippa here, he saw to it that she wouldn't go near either. Then this spring when Amélie became ill, he began to help a bit with the outside work . . . but still, I doubt if he gained admittance, or wished to. Suddenly he's almost living there, now he's married Ghislaine. Amélie, even on her deathbed, would not have allowed it. She had Ghislaine in fear of her own thoughts, her own voice. Amélie must be dead, but why the secrecy? And where have they put her?" Fouschie wasn't dramatizing now; he was deadly earnest, a side of his character Ygrec had never seen.

"I see," Ygrec pointed out gently, "but what do you wish to do? Ghislaine is a lonely old lady, and Lucien is our friend. Does one knock on their door, remark on the inclement weather, wish them a long life and happiness, then request that they produce the body of someone we can only presume is dead? I cannot feel that our interference would do anything but harm. Can this situation be connected to the recent crimes? It is ludicrous to feel that either of them had anything to do with Pippa's death. In his grief, Lucien may have acted unwisely in other matters, but who are we to say?"

"Once more you read my mind, my revered M. Ygrec. I am torn with indecision . . . torn!"

There was a long moment of thoughtful silence, until Ygrec spoke again in a conspiratorial hush. "It has come to me that I feel like a little stroll in the clean air, and, unlike you, I have always found new snow quite delightful. If I dress warmly, a short walk should not be harmful to my tender lungs."

"And I could drive you back in my ancient vehicle. Somehow, this conversation has had a sobering effect on me, and my legs feel disgustingly steady."

Ygrec took his heavy coat from the hall closet, donned it, wrapped the long scarf around his neck, tucked it quickly inside his sweater, and fastened the coat. Then he paused, reached up to the closet shelf, and produced his old gendarme's kepi. "If I wear a hat," he whispered, "Vanessa won't be so cross when she discovers I'm gone. It's a blessing the dog is with her behind closed doors. I really don't feel up to chasing around after an excited animal today."

They closed the door very gently and didn't utter a word until they were out on the virgin-white sidewalk, and approaching the parking lot, when Fouschie suggested, "It's a little heavy walking in this wet snow. I'll keep ahead and you follow in my footsteps. It may be a case of the blind leading the blind, but I don't want you collapsing at my feet. Amélie Couronne's casket is much too small to fit you, even if I doubled up your legs."

Ygrec chuckled. "I admit the visibility is not all one could desire. Already you are beginning to look as if you are sprouting a white wig."

"M. Ygrec, this is not an amusing situation," Fouschie chided. "It is a deadly serious pilgrimage . . . deadly! I am suddenly desperately in need of a little alcoholic sustenance and am beginning to wonder what we are doing."

"We are going to wish our friends long life and happiness," Ygrec replied, "and I haven't had so much fun in years. I feel like a little boy playing truant from his classes, and I have a long-overdue sense of well-being. I keep wondering if some of my bodily afflictions have not been aggravated by simple boredom."

Suddenly Fouschie brought himself to a halt, and Ygrec nearly tripped into him. "We are both suffering from delayed senility!" the mortician announced. "What about the serviette? We've forgotten it."

"Ah, why worry?" Ygrec shrugged. "There's always tomorrow. I doubt very much that the corporal and his new wife will be going anywhere."

"Quite right, quite right." Fouschie shrugged too and proceeded on his way. By now the two had almost traversed the parking lot and were approaching the old gardens. Ygrec couldn't help noticing that the scene had become one of rare beauty. There was no wind and the crystalline flakes floated, then collapsed onto each other, weighing down branches and producing the effect of a landscape of continuous white bumps and curves. The air felt remarkably balmy.

"It will turn to rain before evening and be washed away by morning," Fouschie predicted, looking back at Ygrec and noticing the trail of soggy footprints left in their wake.

Ygrec agreed silently, then the two figures disappeared through the white mounded arch that had been the old rose arbor; one stooped black-frocked man brushing impatiently at snowy shoulders and bony head, the other erect and allowing the flakes to settle on the brim of a faded blue kepi and add to the lightly flecked effect of his tweed coat.

* * *

"He can't have gone far, and he's taken his hat and muffler," Vanessa explained to an incredulous Michelin, trying to hide her own anxiety. "I heard him talking to M. Fouschie, and I thought they'd gone into the salon, but when I got up they were nowhere to be seen."

"He's really out of his mind. He'll break a leg as well as catching pneumonia on a day like this. I know he doesn't want to go back to Moulins, but he's carrying things just too far!" Michelin stood in the doorway of the kitchen, his uniform covered by a long waterproof coat, his cap in his hand.

"Paul, I'm certain he's gone to the loge de garde to say adieu to Corporal Anjou . . . that's what they were talking about after mass this morning. If you go now, you can head him off in case he decides to drive back with M. Fouschie. Take my car . . . it's got better tires."

"It will be quicker for me to walk, Vanessa. The cars are sliding all over the roads. If that drunken old Fouschie does get his wreck started, they'll end up in a ditch for certain. Come to think of it, I did see a trail of mushy footprints through the snow in the parking lot."

"Do you want to take Mademoiselle Larme? She'd love a run. She hasn't been out today."

"Hardly! I may have to carry the old man back, and I don't need an excited dog to add to my problems."

"I suppose." Vanessa sounded resigned. "But, look . . . the snow seems to be letting up. It was just a short freak storm. I'm sure Maurice will be all right, as long as he doesn't start back in that old car."

* * *

By the time Michelin reached the gate opening in the lilac hedge, he was breathless, worried, and angry. When he stepped through, within sight of the little house, he was astounded. The background to the scene reminded him of a child's picture-book drawing of an icing-trimmed gingerbread house, surrounded by whipped-cream-topped trees, but there the fairy tale ceased. As Vanessa had pointed out, the snow was diminishing. A heavily hung sky above the trees seemed to be lifting, to allow a faint rose filtering of late afternoon light, which added a touch of unreality to the setting, but the characters were all familiar.

Ygrec, his old kepi pushed back on his untidy hair, was staring up at a huge evergreen tree, the branches so weighed down with wet snow that they were bent almost at right angles to the trunk of the tree. M. Fouschie stood to one side, his angular profile also lifted high, the sifted snow on his shoulders forming white epaulettes on the black coat. Two more figures watched from the lean-to shed at the back of the house: Lucien Anjou, tall, grizzled, dressed in workman's blue, and Ghislaine Couronne, in little-girl white with ribbons and flounces. Michelin could not read their faces, but while he watched, Lucien lifted an arm to wrap protectively around the small woman, and she turned to hide her face on his chest.

Michelin had observed the tableau in one quick glance, then he too raised his eyes to the great pine tree. Something was hanging between the upper branches, something that appeared to be elongated and twisted in faded netting. As he took a step forward, Ygrec turned, and the mortician lowered his head. Both old men were pale-faced.

"Bonjour, garçon," Ygrec said. "Voilà!"

"Bonjour, Inspector," said Fouschie. "There's a second one up higher."

Michelin acknowledged the greetings with a curt nod and moved away, closer to the foot of the tree.

The mortician stepped back, then as his foot crunched on something in the snowy mush underfoot, he glanced down. An object gleamed momentarily. Glasses? The thoughts raced through his mind and he frowned. Yes, steel-rimmed spectacles—the kind that Valin Chamillion had worn! Last week he'd wondered, as he'd sealed the casket; now he felt apprehensive. He was about to bend down when he stopped himself and glanced around. Ygrec was watching him curiously, but the Inspector was completely preoccupied with the grisly hanging object in the tree. Gratien Fouschie stared back at Ygrec for a long second, then without a flicker of expression, he moved his foot again, this time slowly but firmly, pressing the evidence deeply into the mud.

"Whose . . . ?" mouthed Ygrec.

"Leave the dead to their tombs," Fouschie murmured, barely moving his lips. "We have unearthed too much already. Where the undeserving go, even the blind can feel the flames."

Ygrec's only response was a mute nod.

Michelin's voice brought them back to reality. "It would take a strong man to perform such a conjuring trick up in that tree." It was a statement that went without denial. The three men turned and started slowly toward the two wooden figures propped by the door of the gingerbread house.

Then the old gendarme stopped, raising a hand. "Let me go alone. He must have had good reason. He is still my friend."

Epilogue

My dear Mme. Lachance:

As I hurried when last I wrote, I neglected to ask you to do me one more kindness. Will you please mail me my rubber overshoes, which, I believe, are in the back corner of my wardrobe in the bedroom upstairs. Vanessa insists that I remain indoors on rainy days in case I might get my feet wet, and Inspector Michelin is being overprotective as ever and refuses to let me drive anywhere with my new friend, M. Gratien Fouschie, because he feels the car is very old and unsafe.

M. Fouschie and I have taken on the responsibility of seeing to the well-being of Mme. Ghislaine Anjou, during this difficult period while her husband, whom I mentioned to you in my last letter, is confined in cells awaiting his trial. She has already been moved into the Anjou cottage to be nearer the shops and kind neighbors. She spends most of her days working on a tapestry, and I must admit, my good Mme. Lachance, that I wish you were close enough to give her some instruction in needlework, as the stitching she has done so far leaves much to be desired. Still, it keeps her occupied and she won't let it out of her sight. I am afraid she is a little peculiar.

I keep well, as does Vanessa. She is looking at houses to buy and hopes to find something suitable soon. There was a rumor that the whole of the Couronne property would be listed for sale after Mme. Ghislaine (Couronne) Anjou moved away, and the Inspector actually considered buying a section of it and building a house but decided that the district holds unhappy associations. It was just as well that he and Vanessa did not set their heart on the property because we now hear that there is some problem with a will and that the land will go to the church.

Mademoiselle Larme sends her affectionate regards, as do I, and we look forward to seeing you in the spring.

Ygrec